Dragons, Magic, and Me
Volume 1 The Box

Vic Broquard

# Dragons, Magic, and Me
# Volume 1
# The Box

## Vic Broquard

Dragons, Magic, and Me Volume 1 The Box
First Edition
Copyrighted © 2015 by Vic Broquard
ISBN: 978-1-941415-79-5

This is a work of fiction. All characters, organizations, and events portrayed in this novel are products of the author's imagination and are used fictiously.

Published by:
http://www.Broquard-ebooks.com
Broquard eBooks
103 Timberlane
East Peoria, IL 61611
author@Broquard-eBooks.com

Artwork by Crooked Willow Studios.

For Morgan and L. Ron Hubbard

# Table of Contents

# Chapter 1—Curiosity

"Felix, we have to join the search for the Duke's missing son," Diana, my twenty-one year old twin sister, exclaimed, waving a poster in front of my face, as if I hadn't seen it already. I had—dozens of them—plastered on storefronts of Byron Falls. Her blue eyes focused on mine, drilling her intention into me for us to join the search. I accepted the offered poster and scanned it, hoping to discover more information than was on the copy I'd read an hour ago. There wasn't.

"I agree, Diana. We should help with the search. After all, the Duke's kid is only twelve. Besides, we have an opportunity to put our magic training to good use. What's the point of our spells if we never use them to help others?" I didn't expect an answer. Diana and I were mages-in-training, more or less, working under the tutelage of Mage Locklard, but I admit we were fanatical about magic. I'm convinced that's what started this whole thing.

"Okay, where do we start? Posters say he was last seen down on Bakers Street."

"Right, we'll start there, but I suppose many others have already been there asking questions. Still, I don't know where else to begin. Who would want to kidnap a kid anyway?" She briskly walked down the street, our feet raising small dust clouds from the summer-dried dirt street. "And why did the Duke wait four days before posting the Wanted Posters all over Byron Falls?"

Dodging our way around carts, wagons, other townsfolk on foot, and children playing in the streets, I replied, "The most likely reason is for ransom. You know, kidnap the Duke's kid, and ask for a pile of gold ducats in exchange for his safe return. Excepting now, I don't think that's what's going on here."

"Why do you say that, Felix?"

Someone tossed a chamber pot's contents out a second story window of the clapboard building we passed, but we both mostly dodged out of the way. Without breaking our strides, Diana barked, "Clean," and the unmentionable liquid, which had landed on her blue cotton dress, vanished. I had to cast four Clean spells on my brown cotton pants.

With the odor on my leg gone, I answered, "Look, it's been four days. That's a very long time to hold a kid hostage. Heck, you have to feed them and restrain them. If it was kidnap for ransom, I would've expected the Duke to have received the ransom demand maybe even the very day his son went missing."

"Makes sense," Diana replied, biting her lip, her forehead lined. "So we're forced to look at other motives then. But what? Revenge? Surely, the Duke has made enemies."

I had to agree with her. True, he probably had enemies, though I wasn't privy to such knowledge. He's run Byron Falls for twenty-five years, so there's a good chance one out of the twenty thousand-some inhabitants hated the Duke. If that person was behind it, I'd not give a hoot for the kid's survival chances. Revenge could be a nasty business. I guess I hadn't answered Diana for too long, because she tugged at my shirt sleeve and jarred me with, "Well, what, Felix? Revenge? Or something else?"

She could be insistent.

I finally answered, "I think revenge is out. Look, if we had a beef with the Duke, we'd be more likely to go after him directly, not some kid of his. Heck, he has five children."

"Well, if it's not kidnapping for ransom, then what is it?" Diana asked perplexed.

I'd seen that look on her face before—a cross between a glare and a frown.

She spat out, "You don't suppose some sexual pervert took him, do you?"

I sighed. Diana was bright. That was the very idea I came up when I first read one of those posters; however, she just worked this out twice as fast as I had. "That would explain the snatching of the kid with no ransom note. If so, finding the pervert will be tough—probably has the kid tied up in some building. Pick one. There are only several thousand of them in Byron Falls proper, ignoring the nearby farms to the south."

Seeing that I validated her suggestion, Diana added, "Or the pervert could have come from the Dark Forest to the north, from Boling Hills to the east, or from The Fields to the south. It's been four days, so the perp could also be eighty miles away from here. Pick a direction. But I had another idea. What if the kid just took off to go play in, say, Sage Creek, as we used to do when we were kids? Maybe he went swimming and met with an accident—you know, drowned or was hurt."

"Undoubtedly, the Duke's men have already searched all the likely locations his son frequented. I certainly would have. Still, I suppose we should do that just in case they missed something." I smelled freshly made bread, a sure sign we had reached Bakers Street and its dozen shops. Sweet childhood memories came to mind. Mom always bought us a fresh loaf and a honey pot.

Suddenly, we came upon a crowd and abruptly halted.

"Looks like the Duke and his men are here and a whole lot of others," Diana whispered, as we both looked at the dense crowd of people ahead of us. "Glad we aren't here to buy bread."

I chuckled at her tease. "Are all these people trying to find his kid too? The posters did offer a gold ducat reward."

We tried pushing our way into the milling throng in hopes of finding out what was going on or at least hearing what the Duke was saying. That worked for a few seconds until we ran into the immovable walls: the Hagan brother and sister, dragons—gold dragons to be precise.

"Drago, Carla, fancy meeting you here," I began politely enough. The two were currently in their morphed human forms. My philosophy: one should always be polite to dragons—unequivocally. Although I'd never seen the Hagans in their dragon forms, others in our magic class had and told us that both were around ninety feet from nose to tail, giants, probably weighing close to half a ton—immovable objects, even in their human forms.

Dragons. Yes, our world has many dragons—just not many in one locale, and if you want to remain alive, there are three critical details you must know about dragons.

One, dragons can morph at will between their true dragon form and that of a human. Yes, they can look like us, mostly. Carla and Drago Hagan are gold dragons. Hence, their human forms tend to have a yellowish hue, while a black dragon's human form tends to have a slight blackish tinge to it and a red dragon's human form tends to have reddish tint about it. The hues are subtle, but not easily mistaken. However, when in their human form, their eyes always give them away—coal black.

Number Two, dragons are at the top of the food chain. So don't pick a fight with a dragon; there are less painful ways of committing suicide.

Number Three, while you might be able to pacify a dragon with gems or gold, the best way to befriend a dragon is with magic. All dragons dearly love magic. It's said you can win a dragon's heart by teaching him or her to cast a spell they don't know or by giving them a magical object such as a ring.

Wait. If you want to stay alive and in one piece, then make that four critical details. Some dragons tolerate humans, while others don't. Four, stay away from Red, Black, Green, and White dragons, for they loathe people. Gold dragons tolerate us and sometimes befriend humans, but most others are neutral and avoid us.

The Gold dragon Drago acknowledged our presence. "Ah, it's the Pelingham twins. Mage Locklard asked us to join the hunt for the Duke's son. You here for that too?" His booming bass voice rose above the crowd's noise, and he topped my six-foot frame by an inch.

Diana answered for us. "Hello Carla, Drago." Carla

4

stood just under six feet, a good four inches taller than Diana did. "Yes, we are. Have you found any clues yet? We've only gotten started. We're too far back to hear what the Duke is saying."

Both dragons had light blonde hair, contrasting with our dark brown hair. Considering all four of us had long ago learned beginning spells, with Diana and Carla one couldn't tell too much else about their appearance for certain, because they often made use of the Alter Self spell.

The golden hued Carla replied, "Not much. We're just starting—Mage Locklard's orders. We did hear the Duke a few minutes ago. He said nothing that isn't in the posters."

Drago grumbled, "Felix, we can understand someone kidnaping a human child and ransoming him or her, but the Duke hasn't received any note. That's why he's out here trying to scare up clues. Admittedly, Carla and I don't know much at all about you humans and your motives. Mind if we tag along with you and your sister? Otherwise, I don't see how we can be of any help whatsoever, and we don't want to upset Mage Locklard."

"Sure Drago," I answered. "Diana and I also agree. This can't be a kidnaping for ransom. We don't think it is a revenge thing either. If it were, someone should've found the kid's dead body by now."

Carla's face twisted and frowned. "What could it be? Do human children get lost or something? Baby dragons have an innate sense of where their home is located, so they never get lost while learning to fly."

I answered, "Well, little children can get lost, but in this case, his son's twelve years old and likely knows every inch of the town, much like others his age. Besides, he'll be of age in two more years. So no, I think we can rule out his wandering off and getting lost. We're now thinking he fell victim to a sexual predator or went off somewhere, such as the creek, and got hurt."

Diana added, "What's terrible is that if we only knew him, we could cast See Through Another's Eyes and find out where he's at."

"Ah, that would be a good use of that spell," Carla admitted, adding, "but neither Drago nor I know that spell yet. According to the Duke, no mage knows his son well enough to cast these kinds of spells. At least that's what we heard today."

Diana then suggested, "Okay, let's split up. Carla and I will check around town and see what we can dig up on predators and such, while you and Drago check out the places he and his friends often visit just outside the town. Maybe he drowned in the creek or something. We can meet up at the Boar's Head around suppertime."

I liked her idea. It covered more ground, though I felt uneasy with a dragon following me around. "Sure. Let's see if we can find the kid. Come on, Drago. The posters mentioned his usual haunts. Let's check them out."

As Drago and I headed eastward from Bakers Street, he said, "Hey, thanks for letting us tag along. Honestly, we know very little about the behavior of you humans."

"That's okay, Drago. Besides, Diana and I know almost nothing about you dragons. So we're even there. Say, would a dragon possibly snatch a twelve-year-old boy?"

Drago chuckled deeply, a sound far lower than one would expect from a six foot human. "Hardly. Humans taste bad, though I suppose if a dragon was starving and there wasn't anything else around, he or she might eat one. Also, I heard once a dragon kidnaped a child and ransomed him, but the Duke has ruled out kidnaping for ransom, saying it's been too long without any ransom demand."

"Okay. Had to ask. Here's the creek. Let's see if we can find the boy."

Drago and I began hiking along the creek and soon came to the "pond," a deep pool where children often went swimming. Today was no exception. Six were splashing and having fun. I spotted two adults sitting on a log, watching over the children, a wise action since the disappearance of the Duke's son.

6

We walked on downstream. Next, I asked Drago to change into his dragon form and fly along the creek looking for the boy's body, while I hiked along on the ground looking for any signs. Three miles later, we headed back up the stream. I was hot, sweaty, and tired. We'd found nothing at all. When we reached the pond, I stripped down and took a dip, figuring I'd get cleaned up the easy way.

Finally walking up the bank to where I left my clothes and constantly muttering, "Dry Self," I noticed the two adults were still here. Four other children had joined the original six. One of the women spoke up, "Looking for the Duke's missing boy?"

"Er, well, yes we are," I replied.

Drago just nodded.

She looked at her companion, twisting her face before replying sardonically, "Figures. Our children go missing and *no* one does anything, but when it becomes the *Duke's* kid, half Byron Falls is out looking for him."

I was looking at all the others in the pond, but hearing this, my head snapped around to stare at the woman. "Excuse me, but are you telling me that other children have gone missing too?" Automatically, I slipped into thread-pulling mode, for this was news to me. How many children? When? Time of day? Last seen locations? Pressing questions bounced around my mind faster than I could have spoken them. Drago saw my startled expression and paid closer attention to the woman.

"Yes, I lost my middle son a month ago. Nine have vanished since spring, but no one has done anything about it, not until the Duke's kid goes missing. Says a lot about our ruler," she barked acidly.

I would be bitter too, if it had happened to my son. "Excuse me, ma'am. The first I heard of any missing children was today when I saw the posters. If I had known about the other nine, I would have responded back then. Please, tell me what you know about the others. Are they all boys? When did they go missing?"

A few minutes later, I was convinced the problem

was now ten times larger, and I had many more facts to digest.

Drago bellowed, "Ma'am, we'll find those who have done this to the children and see that whatever they did to the kids happens to them. Whatever bad they've caused must come back upon them."

She perked up and spat out, "Right. Live by the sword; die by the sword."

Drago added, "Live by the spell; die by the spell. We'll see they get what's coming to them. Of course, we dragons never kidnap our children."

She shot back, "And if they murdered my son, please see that they die very painfully and slowly!"

"I give you my word," Drago declared solemnly.

I had visions of Drago pulling off the perp's arms and legs, one appendage at a time, while searing the socket with his fiery breath to prevent blood loss. I'd learned more about dragons in the past few hours than I'd learned all my life.

Walking back into town, Drago opened up. "Harming children is about the worst thing a dragon can do to another dragon, worse than harming him or her. You see, a dragon female is only fertile once every ten years. Therefore, our offspring are precious to us. That's a good thing for many reasons. Look, we often live for five hundred years. Heck, if we proliferated as you humans do, I'd have five hundred kids before I died. Now that would upset the balance of nature." He bellow-laughed.

I smiled, for I couldn't disagree with him, realizing if Drago so desired, he could perhaps father fifty children before old age took him, assuming he found a willing mate.

We met our sisters at the Boars' Head. From experience, I knew Carla and Drago considered these meals merely a very light snack. They took off once a week to dine on antelope. As Diana and I ate our supper, I outlined what we'd learned.

"It's much worse. Counting the Duke's kid, ten boys around his age have been abducted since early spring. All were last seen on Bakers Street. Some went there to

8

purchase bread for their mothers. They claim the Duke hasn't done a thing to find these missing children, at least not until now."

Drago butted in, "Nine of the boys came from the poorer families living at the southern edge of Byron Falls. I'll wager they goofed up when they kidnaped the Duke's son. Now they've brought real heat down on themselves. There must be a hundred of us looking for the boy."

Carla spoke up, "I'll bet they'll just kill the boys. That way, they can avoid being discovered. We should find dead bodies soon, don't you think? Get rid of incriminating evidence."

Although appreciating the efforts Carla and Drago were expending on behalf of us humans, as far as I was concerned, these conclusions didn't fit. "No, I think the boys are still alive and will remain so." Suddenly, all three gave me their full attention. "You see, they've abducted ten boys thus far. We can rule out a sexual predator, too. No matter how lustful you might be, ten boys in just three months are far too many. Besides, we've found no dead bodies. Therefore, they remain alive, which means they must be fed, clothed, and housed. Conclusion: someone has a great need for ten young boys, and that powerful purpose hasn't been fulfilled yet or we'd start finding corpses around the area."

Diana duplicated my conclusions and added, "Felix, I think you're right. Someone or someone's have been abducting young boys for the last three months. I agree with you—abducting ten can only mean they are serving some key purpose. I'm sure whatever it is, it's still ongoing, but what can a twelve-year-old boy possibly provide that an older boy couldn't? Anyone have any ideas what they could possibly be using the boys for?"

Blank stares answered her.

I sighed and volunteered, "As I see it, there's only one way we're going to make any real progress."

"Out with it," Diana declared.

"Go undercover and get kidnaped. Look," I explained my bright idea, "we can use a Morph Me spell, turning me into a twelve-year-old boy, and then dress me in rags. I can wander around Bakers Street and get myself abducted. Meanwhile, you can monitor me with your Watch Through Another's Eyes and Hear Through Another's Ears spells. Together, we can apprehend those who are responsible and rescue the boys."

"Felix, that could be very dangerous."

"I know, Diana, but they won't be expecting to kidnap a beginning mage. We all know enough spells to handle them." I attempted to put her mind at ease. It worked.

"True. We know enough spells that could kill, but you be careful. Drago, Carla, we three best keep close watch on him. I don't want any harm to come to my brother."

# Chapter 2—Into Action

Magic is activated or powered by intention and a clearly stated Cause. No—exotic things, such as toad tongues, sprigs of garlic, or bat's wings, have anything to do with the casting of magical spells and neither do fancy wands, though there are some enchanted wands, but those cost a fortune. Mage Locklard had drilled into our noggins that a spell is defined by a properly stated Cause and powered by the caster's intention. I know both are true, since nothing at all happened until I got the initial case clearly stated. Only then did my first magic spell detonate, a Clean spell.

Intention supplies the power behind the spell. Mage Locklard teased us mercilessly when we were learning to cast our Magic Missile spell. He used to taunt us with, "Are you sure this is going to work? Don't be silly, Felix. Do you really expect a missile to shoot from your finger? Get real, lad." The first time he said this to me, my spell failed. Yes, he slammed us apprentices hard at first, but he got each of us over our feelings of inadequacy, and our intentions became strong, the motivating force behind spells. I can honestly state from my own experiences, the more powerful the spell, the greater the caster's intention must be to activate the spell.

The next morning, the four of us gathered in our small house. Concentrating, I marshaled my intention and barked with total conviction, "Morph Me into myself when I was twelve years old." Of the four of us, only I had this spell down pat, though Diana had managed to cast it once.

Carla and Drago continually failed with this spell, due in part to the fact that they constantly morphed between their true dragon form and their human form, and couldn't imagine any other form. Mage Locklard theorized they lacked the conviction necessary. "Conviction drives intention," he explained to us many times. "No conviction, no intention. If you aren't convinced this will work, your intention will sputter, and the spell will fail to detonate."

Magic flashed. My body felt strange. Suddenly, everything in the room grew in size, and I felt weak, as though I hadn't eaten for days. I looked down at my arms and legs, and began laughing. My body was exactly as it had been when I was twelve, skinny and short. Of course, my shirt and pants no longer fit, humorously so.

"Okay Felix," Diana took charge, "we have to get you looking like one of the boys from the slums."

A half hour later, my pants had more patches on them than anyone could count and was just as dirty as my threadbare shirt. Stained moccasins, similar to those worn by most everyone in Byron Falls, covered my feet. In short, I looked the part. With two coppers in my pocket, I headed off to Bakers Street. At first, I felt very uncomfortable, expecting everyone on the street to stare at me. However, the opposite happened; they ignored me. Reaching the bread makers' section of town, I relaxed. Diana milled around outside one baker's shop. Carla perched on a distant roof where she could see the entire length of the street. *Now to get myself abducted.*

I walked up and down the street. Hours slipped by, but I didn't starve. Occasionally, I slipped into a baker's shop and bought a copper's worth of bread, eating it slowly while walking the street. Near suppertime, Diana called out, "You there, young boy. Want to earn a copper?"

I looked around. Seeing no other boys beside me, I stayed in character. "Yes ma'am."

"Here, carry this bag of bread for me." Diana handed me a large sack filled with loaves of bread.

Dutifully, I followed behind her all the way back to our home.

I was tired and hungry. "This getting abducted is hard work," I exclaimed, while she hastily set about fixing some supper.

After three incredibly boring days, I still wasn't abducted. By now, I did see some of the Duke's guards occasionally patrolling Bakers Street. Perhaps, they were spooking the abductors. The next day, after purchasing a bit of bread, I walked south beyond the row of baker's shops, entering foul smelling tanning section of town just north of the slums. I found an out of the way log to sit on and proceeded to eat the bread, while watching a few workmen pass by.

From behind me, I hear a word barked, "Paralyze." Suddenly, I couldn't move a muscle! That's not entirely true. My body's involuntary muscles still worked. My heart pumped and my lungs worked, but I couldn't move. I was frozen to that log. I felt arms pulling me backwards, and I reactively fought to keep from falling, but my limbs wouldn't budge. I admit that was a wild few seconds— trying desperately to keep from falling, but not a muscle in my body responding. My heart couldn't race, breathing stayed normal, and I couldn't gasp. Panic didn't result in an adrenaline flow. My captor didn't let me hit the ground. Rather, he put me on a rug and then covered my small body up. He lifted me over his shoulder, hidden from view. From the periodic downward pressure on my chest, I knew he was walking. Yes, this kidnapper was very good at his craft. Those ten boys had no chance at all. Wrapped in the rug, I had no idea where he was taking me.

Sounds were faint and muffled. Soon, I gave up trying to figure out where we were going, depending on Diana, Carla, and Drago to be following and monitoring me. After several minutes, I began to detest this Paralyzation spell I was under. My nose itched fiercely from the carpet dust, but I couldn't move a twitch.

My abductor had a deep voice. "Got another one for you."

I felt my body being laid on the ground or floor. I was helpless as he unrolled the carpet with my body rolling along like a piece of candy. Worse, once I stopped, I couldn't move my head to see where I was at or my captors, but I could hear another voice chanting a spell. This meant both men must be mages! Just as I began to panic, his spell detonated, and I caught the words, "Moronic Mind."

Hey, this spell is the bane of all magic users

everywhere. My IQ suddenly dropped far below average; I felt incredibly stupid and gullible. Morons don't cast spells. In fact, Mage Locklard explained only those with an exceptionally high intelligence could ever cast the topmost power spells. Those of average intelligence just might possibly be able to learn to cast the ungraded useful spells, such as Clean and Mend, but they had no chance to learn even beginning Grade 1 spells.

Hands removed my ragged shirt and pants. Then, I heard another spell detonate. Although I heard the words, "Morph Him into a Young Man," thanks to the previous spell, I had no idea what that meant. My body instantly grew into roughly what it had been before I cast my own Morph Me spell, but now, I was still paralyzed and had no idea what was happening. My mind was a confusion of perceptions that made no sense—small, now much larger. It was probably a good thing I still couldn't move, since I probably would have said, "Whee, look at me growing up," or something equally stupid.

The man with the deep voice then said, "Cancel." I wanted to ask him cancel what, but couldn't. Suddenly, I could move again and very nearly collapsed onto the floor. His strong arm latched onto me, preventing my slump. He was probably expecting such a reaction.

Involuntarily, I looked up at his face. He had such pretty, coal black eyes, and his skin had a black hue to it. In my stupidity, I managed to say, "Pretty."

Then, the other man demanded my attention. His hands twisted my head around to face him. He wore robes.

At once, I said, "Bath time now?" I had no idea just how stupid I sounded. Embarrassing.

"I am Archmage Titus. My assistant Mage Max. Do you know what a mage is?" he asked.

"Ooh," I replied, my eyes opened wide. After a long pause, I hazarded, "Spells?"

"Yes, we cast spells. Now then, what is your name?"

"Er, can you talk slower please?"

"What. Is. Your. Name?"

After a long pause, I finally figured out the answer

and proudly replied, "Felix."

"Good, Felix. You are a fine lad. You so want to help us. Don't you?"

"Help you? Sure. Help you. Yes, help you. Am I being helpful now? I'm a fine lad. What's a lad? Is it good to be a lad? I think I was small."

"Yes, it's good you want to help us. You're being very helpful now. You'll always be very helpful to us, won't you, Felix?"

"Yes, Felix be helpful. Always. Good Felix."

"Right. Now look at these." He held several gemstones in his hands. "These are what we're searching for."

"Pretty stones."

"Yes, but these are small ones. We're looking for large ones, like these," he explained, indicating those in his right hand which were at least an inch across or more. "You will help us by digging for the pretty stones."

"Oh, yes. Felix helps dig. Here?" I asked, getting down and scraping the dirt at my feet. I was in a mine of some kind, but now that I could move again, that information eluded me.

"No, Felix. Come with us. We'll show you where to dig. We have a pick and shovel for you to use. Ten other lads are helping us, too. You'll fit right in, but it's lunch time. I bet you are hungry. Right Felix?"

"Hungry? Yes, Felix hungry."

"Max here sees that you lads get three good meals each day. Follow me."

We walked deeper into the mine. Soon, we entered a side chamber where crude beds lined the walls. An oak plank table sat in the center of the room, surrounded by log stump chairs. Ten other men were eating their lunch as we walked in. Max handed me a new shirt and pants, but I definitely needed his assistance getting into the clothes.

That done, Archmage Titus explained, "Now here is your place. See, nothing but the finest food for you lads."

Ten heads nodded in total agreement.

I looked at the gruel before me and nodded too.

Actually, the food probably wasn't fit for a pig, but my reasoning powers were now almost non-existent. I ate it rapidly.

After eating, the ten headed back to work, while Max led me along after them. He gave me a pick and a shovel. In simple terms, I was to dig out the rock face. Any pretty stones we found were to be placed in one bucket. We shoveled the resulting talus into one of several wheelbarrows, which Max emptied periodically. He also kept the many lanterns going, which provided us with plenty of light to see what we were doing.

Thus, I began to "help" them by digging for gemstones. "Oh, I found one. I think so," I exclaimed, brushing the debris off the red ruby.

"Oh let's see," another lad gleefully insisted, as he and the others stopped working and came to look at my pretty red stone.

Max had to intervene. "Well done, Felix. Okay, lads, back to the digging. We must find many more before supper." In fact, Max was needed, for if left to our own initiative, we'd ogle over every gemstone that one of us found, getting very little done.

By suppertime, I too had added a handful of pretty gemstones to the wooden bucket. Archmage Titus joined us and examined its contents.

"Excellent work, lads," he said. "You've helped us very much today. Just look at all the pretty stones you have found. Very well done, all of you. Now go wash up and get some supper. Thank you." Eleven dirty faces beamed back at him, reflecting the praise we were given for our work.

All I wanted to do was to help the two men by digging for more of the pretty stones. Nothing else mattered. If it had only been me here, I would have gone on digging for gemstones until I died. Titus and Max certainly had a profitable scheme going here.

I think a week passed. However, I could no longer count to seven to keep track of the days. As long as they kept praising me for my help, all I wanted to do was dig for more pretty stones. Alas, my memory of my state while I was a "moron" isn't so good.

# Chapter 3—Rescue

"Okay lads," Archmage Titus began his daily pep talk to us eleven *boys*. "Today, we truly do need many more gemstones, the pretty stones. So lads, I'm counting on you to do your best today. Find many stones."

Stupidly, we grinned and nodded that we would. Eagerly, we walked swiftly down the mine tunnel to the working rock face. That's when the confusion began.

***

"It's confirmed, Drago," Diana declared with a deep sigh. "They are under the influence of the Moronic Mind spell." The three met at Mage Locklard's home.

Unknown to me in my current state, the three had carefully monitored my abduction and subsequent situation.

Carla added, "According to Mage Locklard, this spell can't be canceled or dispelled, even if we knew how to dispel magic."

Drago's deep voice bellowed, "Well, that's a fine mess. How do we cure them? Eleven will need the cure."

"Says here, we'll need a magical potion," Carla answered, reading from her precious spell book.

Diana suggested, "All right, let's get to work. We have to brew eleven cures before we rescue them. Lord knows how they will react if we rescue them while they are under the spell's influence."

"Probably like very little children," Carla theorized. "What materials are we going to need? Anyone brewed such a potion before? We haven't."

Thankfully, after hearing the three and finding out why they wanted to brew such a large batch, Mage Locklard stepped forward. "I keep a small supply on hand for use when I teach the spell. However, I don't have enough for all eleven. Since it is the Duke's son, I'll lend you a hand brewing the potion. We dare not risk a goof."

Diana glared at him. That he implied he'd risk a

goof if the Duke's son weren't involved irked her, but the implication was completely missed by Drago and Carla.

Between the gathering of the ingredients and the careful brewing of the large batch of potion, seven days passed. Nevertheless, I later learned Diana checked on me several times during the day using See Through Another's Eyes spell. In addition, Mage Locklard worked with the three to teach them how to Dispel a Magic Spell. Yes, when I found this out later on, I was highly envious of them over this new spell.

The undoing of the Morph spell is simply that of casting an effective Dispel Magic. I say simply, but it isn't quite as easy as it sounds. You must take the level of the caster of the Morph spell into account, compared to that of the level of the caster of the Dispel Magic spell. If that ratio is one to one, then the caster has a fifty percent chance of success per each casting. As the ratio goes upward, the chance of success is lowered by five percent at each increment. Thus, even a top-level archmage can have his spell canceled by a Dispel Magic being cast by a low level adept; the chance of success never is lower than five percent. The reverse is also true. An adept's spell can be dispelled by an archmage, whose chance is never greater than ninety-five percent.

Thus, since the Archmage likely cast the Morph spell on us eleven, they figured that in all likelihood several attempts would be needed. While the Morph spell might be canceled on the first attempt, certainly it would be canceled by the twentieth attempt. Multiply that by eleven and you can see the problem the rescuers faced. No way could they get the Morph spells canceled quickly. In addition, the potion cure would take several days to work its magic.

Thus, Drago formulated their battle plan. If I had been in my right mind, I would have felt for Diana. She had to depend upon two dragons to help rescue me and the other boys.

"Look," Drago explained, "we know this Max fellow is likely a Black dragon. If so, he spews out a very caustic cone of acid. If you are hit with it, expect it to eat through your clothing in seconds. I've seen their acid dissolve antelope flesh clear down to the bone in less than a couple of minutes. So if you get any on you, drop everything and get the acid washed off somehow and fast.

"Leave Max to me. Carla, you and Diana get to the eleven and lead them to safety, but watch out for that Archmage fellow." He didn't exactly spell out how they were to deal with such an incredibly powerful magic user.

The mine's entrance was located outside of town, very carefully hidden among tall boulders and pine trees. A talus pile indicated a mine was nearby, but as the three approached, each felt fear.

"It's getting stronger. We should just run away from here," whispered Carla, unable to pin down the true source of her growing fright. Diana didn't say anything, but her legs and arms were shaking visibly, eyes darting rapidly about.

Drago glared, fighting the revulsion, and grasped what was happening. "It's an Antipathy spell. Let's see if we can dispel it."

All three focused, concentrated their intention, and spoke the command words. Magic flashed and the fear and repulsion vanished. One of the three spells worked, though they didn't know whose had canceled the spell over the opening. Diana smiled, "Teamwork."

Drago headed inside first, followed by Carla. Diana brought up the rear. For several minutes, the trio walked silently down the dark tunnel illuminated only from the outside. None dared cast a Light spell, which would surely announce their presence.

"This is private property," bellowed Max, stopping all three just after they entered the large, square, staging area forty feet across with three stone columns supporting the ceiling and illuminated by ten oil lamps.

"Surrender now and it will go better for you. We know what's going on down here and that you have kidnaped eleven young boys," Drago barked.

"The hell I will. Die, dragon!" Max transformed into

20

his Black dragon form. A great geyser cone of acid spewed from his mouth. Anticipating this, Drago remained far back in the chamber, allowing himself plenty of room to dodge out of the way of the cone of acid, before transforming into his Gold dragon form.

Meanwhile, with their precious potions in a leather backpack, Diana and Carla slowly moved off to the far right corner of the chamber. However, Diana and Carla were not so lucky. A bit of Max's acid splattered on their arms and on Diana's face, resulting in instant burning. Both emptied their canteens over the acid, and wisely continued running further down the tunnel, leaving the chamber to the two male dragons. Soon, the tunnel opened into another chamber. Eleven "men" were hard at work mining for gemstones on the far wall. Off to their left, they saw the "kitchen" and "dining room." Off to their right, Archmage Titus stood close to a side tunnel. He was watching over the workers, as Diana and Carla rushed into the chamber.

Titus reacted, rapidly casting a spell. It triggered seconds after they entered the chamber. Diana suddenly became immobile, frozen to the spot with a Hold Human spell. In hindsight, that was the Archmage's undoing. In his haste, he saw what appeared to be two human females running into the chamber. Had they both been that, the rescue would have ended with their joining the eleven boys digging for gemstones.

I just turned around and said, "Whee. Can I play, too?" Worse, I didn't even recognize my sister or Carla, at least not right away. Perhaps that was because of the acid burns on her face and their arms.

When asked why she did what she did hours later, Carla explained, "Well, he's an Archmage. What's my puny beginning spells going to do to him? Nada." Carla chose not to use any of her native dragon breath attacks, because in the confined space of the chamber, she couldn't shoot a bolt of electricity at Titus nor could she breathe out her cone of searing flames. Thus, she merely continued to run toward the man, colliding with him, and knocking him to the ground.

"Hey, you knocked Titus over. Get off him. He's our friend. We're helping him," I declared, annoyed she'd done that. "What are you doing?" As all eleven of us workers paused to see what the two women were doing, the sounds of cracking bones broke the otherwise stillness of the chamber.

In the next instant, two things happened. We had no idea how badly Archmage Titus was injured, but it must have been significant since his In Case Of or Contingency spell activated. His body vanished from the chamber. We'd read about this terrific spell. The caster specifies which circumstances are to trigger the tandem spell. For example, if I am badly wounded, teleport me home, or perhaps, if I'm stunned, teleport me to safety. The uses are as varied as the casters. As best we could tell, Carla's physical attack on him triggered his spell and he vanished. The second he disappeared, his Hold Human spell on Diana ended, and she stumbled forward, but managed to keep from falling or damaging the potions.

"Hey you. Bring Titus back," I yelled at Carla.

"Yeah, bring him back here," another yelled.

Soon the chamber echoed with similar cries.

Apparently, we alarmed Diana because the next thing I knew, I slumped to the ground as I fell asleep. She'd cast a Sleep spell on us, and all eleven of us workers dozed off.

"Go see if Drago needs any help, while I get the curing potions in them," Diana suggested.

As Carla dusted herself off and headed back the way she'd come, Drago's booming bass voice echoed, "No need. A Black is no match for a Gold. I beat the crap out of him, and he hightailed it out of here. We've a slight problem. In the fight, we collapsed the entrance tunnel. Carla, you were burned by his acid! Oh dear, Diana, you, too. Your face!" The left side of Diana's face and her left hand were red and crinkled from the acid. Likewise, Carla's human-appearing face was similarly disfigured, along with her entire left arm.

22

Bravely, Diana said, "I hope it isn't too bad. At least, it's stopped throbbing. Come on. We've got eleven Morph spells to dispel, and I've got to get this potion down their throats."

"Okay, we'll do the dispels, and you take care of the potions," Drago took charge again.

An hour and another Sleep spell later, the ten boys were resting peacefully, their bodies back to their original forms and with the potion to cure the Moronic Mind spell in their systems. After Diana got me to drink the potion, I insisted on staying awake, though I was still fighting being "stupid."

Drago continue to lead in my absence. "Okay, now let's search the place and see if there is another way out of here. If not, we're trapped and going to have to dig our way out."

Carla suggested, "But couldn't we Shadow Walk our way out?" By that, she meant the unique ability all dragons have to somehow step through the shadows from one place to another. In some ways, I'm told it is similar to a teleport spell, except teleports are instantaneous and a Shadow Walk takes time to move from place to place. Actually, the usual usage of their special skill is to travel between known worlds. If a dragon is familiar with a world, it can Shadow Walk from the world it's on to another familiar world—a fine bit of magic!

"Yes," Drago admitted. "That's how Max departed. I suppose we could have the boys sit on our backs and we could take them with us. But how demeaning, Carla. I'm not a horse, so we best find another way out of here."

Carla chuckled.

Our two dragon friends headed off to search, while Diana sat down beside me.

"What happened? Face looks bad," I struggled hard to make myself sound intelligent.

"Acid. Black dragon spewed it on us. How bad is it? Can you tell?" A tear trickled down Diana's cheek.

In spite of still being heavily under the influence of the Moronic Mind spell, I sensed her fear and grief, her loss. Neither of us had any illusions about being pretty, attractive, or handsome in my case. We weren't homely, though Diana wasn't going to win any beauty contests. I knew what she wanted: a husband and a family, along with magic of course. As I gazed on the raw, acid-eaten left side of her face, Diana saw what I saw. Without a mirror, she did the next best thing, using the See Through Another's Eyes spell. By the time I realized what she was doing, it was too late.

She broke down, sobbing, "Now I am so ugly no one will marry me."

I didn't know what else to do. If I'm honest with you, even if I wasn't still mostly under the influence of the Moronic Mind spell, I still wouldn't know what to do. I put my arms around her, pulled her up tight to me, and held her. I had a silly urge to say it'll be all right, but wisely, I kept my mouth shut. How could it ever be all right? I must have done the right thing for her, since she quickly stopped crying and pulled away from me. "We best find a way out of this mine, Felix."

"Titus goes that way," I tried very hard to say it intelligently. I'd seen him coming and going from the right passage from this main chamber.

"You stay put. You need to sleep and recover from the spell," she insisted, but I followed behind her anyway.

Time enough for sleep once we rescued everyone. At the end of the tunnel, we found a crude, wooden, spiral stairway.

"Hey, Titus could be up there," I struggled to say coherently, doing my best to warn her. He was an incredibly powerful mage, and we were just raw beginners. If we came upon him without the support of our dragon friends, we'd be toast. I couldn't actually say this at the time, but I had mental images of Diana and me being served up on a breakfast platter. Maybe it was just the effects of the potion swirling in my veins.

Diana turned to face me. "I've sent them a Message that we found this stairway. They are on their way, so we have backup in case we run into Titus." Diana, good old

Diana, she must have sensed what I meant by my short sentence and acted accordingly. Soon, Drago and Carla joined us.

"Not sure it will support us all at the same time," Drago's voice boomed up from below. "You two go first. Yell if you run into trouble."

Diana and I climbed an estimated two floors before the stairs ended at a crudely made door. She listened. Slowly and carefully, Diana opened it. I held my breath, expecting all manner of incredibly nasty traps to go off. I think Diana did, too, but nothing at all happened. We moved into the room and called for the dragons to join us.

We found ourselves in a spacious living room, filled with two couches, two sofa chairs, an eight-foot long oaken table with eight chairs, and a small writing table and chair in one corner. For a minute, we both just stood there dumbfounded. My moronic mind just couldn't make any sense of what I was seeing. How did we get from a mine tunnel into someone's living room? I collapsed onto the couch, as the potion finally put my body to sleep, which it needed.

***

Some twelve hours later, I awoke. Though not back to normal, at least I didn't feel like a complete moron and could think somewhat. I smelled fried chicken and my stomach growled.

"Ah, Diana, he's awake," Drago's deep voice bellowed.

I found my old clothes lying next to me on this strange couch. Diana had gone home and brought them back for me. After dressing, I ate some fried chicken, while the others brought me up to date.

Drago explained, "We returned the children to their parents. Actually, the kids knew where to go; we didn't, except for the Duke's son. He's given us each a hundred gold ducats. There's no sign of the Archmage. He's flown the coop, as you humans say. I think we might know why. After you eat, we want to show you something."

Diana broke in, "Yes, this is weird. This house isn't

supposed to be here—at least no one can recall having built it. As far as we can tell, the neighbors said it just appeared one night. Now come. We want to show you around this place, before we take you outside."

"How many bedrooms does this home have?" I asked, feeling that perhaps the potion wasn't working. So far, she'd shown me a dozen bedrooms, each nicely furnished. The kitchen was large, as was the dining room. Its table could seat at least twelve people.

Drago bellowed, "Felix, we measured the inside dimensions. It is two hundred feet by two hundred-fifty. Now come outside. This you have to see for yourself." He dragged me outside.

I turned around and faced the door. I gaped, stared, and rubbed my eyes! I was facing a box perhaps ten feet on a side, complete with a door I'd just exited. "I think the potion didn't work," I mumbled.

"No, it's working, Felix," Diana declared. "It's this box that's weird. It just appeared here four months ago. The neighbors claimed Archmage Titus lived here, but he was a recluse. The box is larger on the inside than on the outside."

"Extra dimensional magic spell," Drago said as though he was familiar with that very high-level spell, which I knew he wasn't. "Mage Locklard told us about it."

"I don't get it. So Titus enchanted a box to be his house?" I attempted to make some vague sort of sense out of the mind-scrambling observations.

"That was Mage Locklard's conclusion," Diana put in, "but that's doesn't align with what we've seen inside the box or house or whatever you call this enchanted thing."

"What do you mean?" I muttered, wondering how this could get any more confusing. Was I ever wrong.

"Come on. We've been waiting for you to recover," Drago said very diplomatically, causing me to wonder even more. I followed them back inside. We sat on one of the comfortable couches in the living room.

Drago nodded to Diana, who explained. "Okay, Felix. While you were asleep and after we got the children

26

returned to their homes, another spell detonated here inside this room. Afterward, we told Mage Locklard about it, and he said we had seen some kind of Programmed Image. Anyway, it delivered a message to us."

"Talk about weird. Out of nowhere, this face appeared and spoke to us. Drago, let me know if I duplicate it properly. It said, 'Mage Titus has abandoned the Box and the Mission. The Box needs new magic users to train in all levels of spells from the Helpful Spells through those of ultimate power. If you wish to become powerful mages, press the Activate button on the wall.'"

"She's said it about right," Drago added. "This thing—it's called the Box. We've no idea how it can train anyone. It's just a box house sort of thing. Still, we're curious. Anyway, we've waited for you to recover some before we did anything."

I responded, "You're kidding me, right? This Box thing wants to train us?"

Diana smiled, "Yes, that's what the thing said. Mage Locklard only knows up to a few Grade 6 spells. What do we have to lose? If it doesn't work, we're still Mage Locklard's students."

"Right," put in Drago. "This is intriguing magic, if I ever saw any, and Archmage Titus has fled the scene, probably because Carla nearly killed him. So we can take his place. What do you say, Felix? Shall we try it? It certainly can't hurt. Grade 9 spells are calling to us!"

"Well," I rubbed my chin and then forehead. Too many things just didn't add up. "I suppose it won't hurt for us to press that Activate button. If it's a programmed illusionary sequence, we can listen to what it has to say and then make our decision."

Was that greed I saw in Drago's eyes as he pressed the red Activate button? Either greed or an insatiable desire to possess more magic. As soon as he pressed it, the magic activated. We saw what appeared to be an older mage with a foot-long white beard, long white hair, and piercing blue eyes, dressed in a white robe standing before us. I found it just a tad unnerving. For sure, this was a very high-grade spell.

"Welcome mages and mages-to-be. I, the Box, am very glad you're on board. I look forward to teaching you all the spells you desire, through those of the ultimate power, Grade 9. I will present you with your next batch of spells to learn and a binder in which to keep these pages pristine. Please make use of the three Casting Rooms to avoid damaging the interior of the Box. I sense there are four of you at this time. Four copies of the first batch of spells will appear at the conclusion of this message. While you are practicing these new spells, the Box will take you to the next situation for you to rectify. Once you've handled it, the next batch of spells will appear, and so on until you have mastered all of the spells you desire. Food and water are provided, compliments of the Endless Water Jug and the Everlasting Food Bowl. Appropriate apparel will be provided upon all arrivals. May you achieve the mastery of magic that you desire."

The illusion vanished, and four packages of book pages appeared, along with a binder to hold them. Three holes were punched along one edge, matching three rings in the binders. None of us had ever seen binders such as these, but we eagerly leafed through the pages. The first page held more directions. Each was to address the Box, providing it their name and the spells they already knew how to cast. After that, spell pages for these known spells would also appear, so that each mage's binder was complete.

After I looked over the instructions and glanced at the other pages, I felt a faint vibration in my legs. "Do you feel it? Something is vibrating. Besides, what did it mean by situation for us to rectify? What situation? Handle it how?"

"I've no idea what it meant, but I feel it too," Diana commented. "I'll check outside. Maybe some of the townsfolk are doing something nearby."

She left the living room. Shortly, she yelled, "Hey! Something's going on. The door is locked and barred! We can't get out."

I ran to join her, and the Hagans were right behind me. Sure enough, a metal bar had slid across the door, locking it in place. Further, a message in bright red letters was painted on the bar: Do not open while in transit. All four of us stared at the bar and writing.

"Well, crap," I said. "We're trapped in here for now, so I guess we might as well go practice and fully explore this box. Where are those casting rooms anyway?"

One by one, we did as instructed and soon had even more pages for our new spell binders, the ones we already knew. Looking over what we were given, I saw several very interesting spells for me to learn, including Charm Human, which I thought would be a most useful spell in tight situations. Gentle Fall would also be a very good spell to know—anything to avoid getting hurt.

We spent what we believed was five days mastering these new Grade 1 spells. A few higher-grade spells were among this first batch, including the spell that had trapped Diana, Hold Human. Yes, during this time, we four were elated and highly motivated to learn these new spells.

By the sixth day, we were bored. We'd mastered this batch of spells and had taken to examining our living quarters, beginning with the kitchen and bathroom. From the onset, Diana had served up our meals, which the rest of us now saw was little more than pulling on a lever. Out came a bowl of this blue-green, porridge-like substance. It tasted acceptable, but after five days of it three times a day, we complained.

Drago declared, "When we stop, we should lay in some decent food, don't you think? Maybe we can put an antelope or two in an unused bedroom."

Carla seconded it.

"I'll see what we can buy. At least, we have a hundred gold ducats now," Diana suggested.

Next, we took a bath, but only after we figured out how to work the controls. We had never seen the tub and fixtures, let alone the sit-down, white porcelain chamber pot affair, which emptied when its only lever was pressed down—convenient, but foreign to us all. During this time,

Drago and I carefully examined the women's healed faces and hands. Both were permanently scarred with reddish, rough skin—anything but attractive. Neither said much about it to us at this point. Besides, even they were curious about our new "home," where strange was a gross understatement.

# Chapter 4—The Red Light District

The low humming sound stopped. We felt a slight jar, but not enough to do more than rattle my teacup on the table, though I could see small waves on the tea's surface for a moment. "Hey, something's up," I called out to the very bored others.

From the living room, Drago declared, "I think we're somewhere now. The bar on the door has moved back and is hidden. It's about time. I'm getting very hungry. We need an antelope a week, you know."

Diana spoke up, "First thing, I'm going to pay a visit to Bakers Street and lay in some fresh bread. Then, I'm going to drop by our place and get more clothes. I'll see what I can find for food supplies."

As we headed out the door, a sign we hadn't noticed before appeared. It read: Press here when you've handled the situation.

"What situation?" Drago grumbled. "Not until I've feasted on an antelope!"

We stepped outside and froze in place, mouths open, gaping, eyes staring around and upwards. A roaring noise drew our shocked attention skyward where a sleek, long, silver bird-like machine rose up into the sky, while steadily increasing in speed until it vanished from sight, only to be replaced by another. We weren't in Byron Falls anymore. Heck, we weren't even on our own world. I saw two moons in the sky. Our world only has one. We just stared in total disbelief.

Our box had turned into a brick building, matching the others along the block, each of which was of single-story construction. However, the Box now had a sign over its door that said: Health Inspectors.

We stood on a narrow white strip, raised a few inches above the main portion of the street, also whitish, but strange moving vehicles with people inside them traveled along the road. These vehicles made noises, but their sounds were dwarfed by the roar from the silver birds, landing or taking off from somewhere not too distant.

More importantly, we saw people walking along this narrow white strip. Some men wore grey tweed pants with a matching jacket and colorful, thin strips of material hanging from around their necks. Others wore some kind of uniform that was both greyish and sterile looking. The very few women we saw wore expensive dresses akin to those worn on formal occasions by some village noblewomen or they too wore the greyish uniforms.

The air held no trace of pine, woods, or fields. Whatever the odors—kind of an oily smell, mixed with a pungent, breath-stifling smell—we didn't find them pleasant. Hastily, we stepped back inside the Box's doors, where we were greeted with our familiar living room. However, we noticed now there was some clothing hanging on racks—apparel matching that worn by the men and women on the street—apparel that hadn't been there before we stepped outside. I concluded somehow the Box had fabricated or duplicated the clothing being worn by the local men and women here, but that the Box needed a few minutes to observe and fabricate. Without a word, we four picked out something we liked and changed.

Now looking like the locals, we again stepped outside our door. This time, no one paid much attention to us. Further, whatever the language being spoken, we seemed to be able to understand it. Later on, I realized the Box was providing us an extension to our basic spell Understand Language. Likewise, we could read the signs over the various doors of the brick buildings adjacent to our box. The first one read: Unarmed Escorts.

We noted the greyish uniformed men and women observed these signs and entered the establishments. Only a few dressed as we were actually entered these buildings, while they did enter other nearby buildings, one of which appeared to sell food items, as witnessed by the sacks being carried out from it. One other detail was obvious.

This world also had dragons. We saw two Black dragons and a Red dragon flying, but they kept well away from the location where the silver flying birds were making all the noise.

Upon spotting the flying dragons, Drago declared, "Have to eat. We'll be back in a while. Come on, Carla. Let's find dinner."

The two morphed into their dragon forms and took flight. For the first time, Diana and I saw the actual forms of our Gold dragon friends. Impressive. Each was about ninety feet from nose to tail and glistened in the sunlight. Power, grace, and beauty—that's how Diana described our dragon companions. I could only agree.

A bit later, having walked around the immediate block, Diana and I found ourselves back before our Box. She said, "You know, Felix, maybe we're supposed to be Health Inspectors. We should see what kind of store this Unarmed Escorts is. They must provide burly fighters if they are unarmed. You'd think they'd at least carry swords. How can they protect anyone if they are unarmed?"

"I don't know. These sound foreign to me. Pedestal Escorts? What can that possibly be? Well, we're near the Unarmed Escorts doors. Let's pay them a visit. I think you might be on to something. Pretend to be Health Inspectors. Come on."

Together, we entered the building's main entrance. Nothing could have prepared us for what we were about to see!

"Hello and welcome to the Unarmed Escorts of the Red Light District. I'm Lexi, your host. I'm sure we have just the unarmed woman or man of your dreams here. Every one of us is a beauty queen. We're proud of our people, who are simply the best escorts money can buy. Whether it is for an hour or a day, you may be assured of the most beautiful man or woman on your arm, providing for all your needs."

I'm afraid I stared at Lexi. True, she was one gorgeous looking young woman about our own age with knee-length wavy blonde hair and light blue eyes. Her face was angular, and her lips, full. Lexi was incredibly shapely with a full bosom, yes, a beauty queen. However, she appeared to have no arms. She wore a light blue dress that had a bit of flair below her shapely waist, but a dress that was certainly far too short, barely covering her knees. I'd never seen such shoes. They matched her dress but had tiny heels, which I later learned were five inches tall. Lexi could easily don and take off these shoes by herself, which I soon saw was a necessity, since she used her toes as Diana and I did our fingers.

Diana was also gaping, but Lexi then said sympathetically, "Whatever happened to your face and hand? It must have hurt really badly."

"I had a run in with a Black dragon, but we succeeded and rescued eleven boys," Diana answered, but quickly changed the subject, which I knew was very sensitive for her. That she'd even said this much about her disfigurement made me proud of her. "We're Health Inspectors. We need to check on everyone here."

Unfazed, Lexi bubbled, "Oh all right. We're not busy now, but by evening, we'll be swamped with customers. As you can see, I really do have arms and hands, only they're dead. They are folded and secured across my back so they don't get in the way or cause troubles. They can, you know, cause problems. If you break a bone, you can't even feel it. We're all very healthy, but I guess you'll need to see that for yourselves. Follow me. I'll take you to our courtyard display area, where everyone gathers so customers can pick their beautiful companion. Then, you can check on us all."

Lexi led us through a curtained doorway that opened onto a formal garden of sorts. Flowers and vines grew along the back walls, adding a unique ambience to the space.

She explained, "Our beautiful women will be lining up on your left, while our beautiful men will line up on your right, just as they do when a customer comes. I'll also summon our manager, Peter. I'm sure you'll want to talk with him. Back in a moment."

34

Lexi walked slowly across the courtyard, her hips swaying seductively. I swallowed hard. Although her long hair partially covered her back, I now saw her dead arms. Her forearms were horizontal to the ground and tied securely to her back beneath her dress.

When we were alone, Diana teased me, "Keep your thing in your pants." She added, "Gosh, Lexi is the prettiest woman I've ever seen. I wonder what terrible accident she had. I bet it must have been painful."

"Honestly, she's still extremely pretty, and she must be sharp, too, to be the host for this establishment, but what exactly do these people do? Escorts?"

Diana giggled. "Wrong meaning, big boy. Prostitutes. Well, they must accompany men, but I suspect they also provide sexual favors. Oh Felix, your face just got red."

I gave a silly sounding giggle. "Sorry. I missed that completely. I was so struck by how beautiful Lexi is that I missed it entirely. I think you're right. What have we stumbled into this time and where are we? I have more questions than answers."

As women began walking slowly into the room from both the left and right sides, Diana whispered, "Oh my god!"

I blinked and rubbed my eyes, believing I must be dreaming. Dozens and dozens of incredibly beautiful young women, dressed similar to Lexi and wearing these strange tall-heeled shoes, sashayed into the courtyard; every one of them apparently had dead arms. They smiled at Diana and me, while watching us closely. I gaped and lost count. Then, from another side door, Lexi and a man wearing a suit entered and came up to us.

Lexi smiled seductively and explained, "Diana, those on your right are actually men. Though they might not look like it, I assure you they most certainly are. Felix, all these on your left are women. And this is Peter Hamish who owns these four businesses."

Peter was thin and several inches taller than me. He alone had rather short hair and a countenance suggesting he was very annoyed, bordering on angry, with us. "How dare you make an unannounced visit? I run a law-abiding, clean establishment here. Every one of my women and men are in perfect health, verified weekly by our doctor. So what's the meaning of this? On whose authority are you here?"

Lexi's smile soured. I sensed she felt Peter was insulting us. There are times when you have to make a snap judgment call and then live with what you've done. This was one of those times. I had no idea what our Box meant by "handle the situation." Heck, I didn't know what the situation actually was here. However, I knew enough to know I needed to find out, and not because I was surrounded by a group of incredibly beautiful, young women, but because they had no alive arms. What was going on here? Was someone intentionally harming them? While I could imagine some young woman having a terrible accident maiming her for life, I couldn't grasp several dozen together at one spot and all quite pretty. So I acted and cast my spell, barking, "Charm Human Peter."

I felt magical energies activating. Peter's face and demeanor changed immediately. Now a pleasing smile appeared. "Esteemed guests, how may we be of service to you?"

Lexi's mouth opened, but she made no sound. Diana smiled. I continued to take action. "Ah, Peter, you have a fine establishment here, but Diana and I do need to have a thorough look around and checkup of your people. You know, the usual health reasons. I'm certain we'll find nothing amiss. By chance, is Lexi here available to show us around and introduce us to your people? We hate to bother such a busy man as yourself."

Still smiling, Peter replied, "Oh course. Lexi, you give them a tour. Answer any questions they might have." Then, he winked at her, adding, "And if they wish some company this evening, why, you make sure they have their choice—on the house. Now, if you will excuse me, I do have business to handle." He bowed politely and marched off.

"Wow. Whatever did you do to Peter? He was livid

when I told him the Health Inspectors were here. I thought he was going to yell at you or something. After whatever you did to him, he's acting as if you're the king or something."

Again, I made a split second decision. I told Lexi the truth. "Magic. I cast a magic spell on him, charming him. I could see he was bristling for a fight or argument, and I didn't want that. This way, everything is much more amicable. No need for trouble."

"You mean *real* magic?" she asked, her eyes opening wide.

I didn't know what she meant, so I replied, "Is there any other kind?"

Lexi giggled. "Sure. Lots of them do sleight of hand tricks—you know, the hand is faster than the eye. But this was *real* magic? Wow."

I decided to start finding out answers. "So Lexi, these are women," I said indicating with my hand all the women to our left. Then, I frowned. Turning to my right, I said, "I'm sorry, but these look like women too, not men. Have you made some mistake here?"

Lexi giggled and nodded to them. A pair of what I thought looked like gorgeous women came over to us. "I'm Ben. This is Henry. And yes, we're both men. You can pull our dresses up and check for yourselves. Many often do, because we really do look like women."

Their voices were deep. I decided to trust them. Besides, I'd be too embarrassed to pull up their dresses. They too were "unarmed," that is, they appeared to have dead arms, as did Lexi and the many women.

Diana spoke up, "So are you fellows available to escort women? Do you get many clients?"

Ben chuckled. "Duh, hardly. Just ask Lexi here. It's rare that we're asked out."

Henry interjected, "Mostly because the customers are men from the nearby spaceport. Few men are interested in us. Honestly, we both prefer to escort women."

I sensed a deep, profound sadness in Henry's voice,

though Diana would be a better judge of such things. Wisely, I turned the conversation in a different direction. "Say, I can't help noticing the men and women here have lost the use of their arms."

Diana interrupted me, "I'm so sorry that everyone has met with such awful accidents. Do you have someone here to assist you? I can't imagine how helpless you must be."

To our amazement, Lexi, Ben, and Henry all laughed. She explained, "We surely aren't helpless—not as you and so many others must think. We do most everything for ourselves, though it sometimes takes us longer to do it. Ben, Henry, why don't you head back to your place? I'll give them the tour and bring them by to see your apartment soon." Both men nodded to her and left, as did the many women.

Finally alone with us, Lexi spoke more freely. "As we get started, there's one detail I have to make certain you understand. Whatever you do, don't spend the entire night here. That's the only rule. Now then, you both sound like foreigners. You must not know about us, so I should explain."

I sighed. "Yes, we're strangers. What is this world and city called?"

Lexi lowered one eyebrow, while raising the other, rather quizzically. "Halcion-3 and this is Briton, where the aliens built their spaceport, but that was fifty years ago. You must be foreigners not to know that."

"We are indeed. And what are those flying silver birds making that awful racket?" I asked.

"Spaceships. The aliens come and go in them, flying them to other worlds, or so they say. We just take their word for that, but they do pay well for our company of an evening. I talked to one man about that some years ago. He said they often spend a whole year in space before making landfall. So when they finally get their feet on solid ground, they want some companionship. I can't imagine being isolated and alone for an entire year. Can you? Anyway, I can see why they want us so badly."

"Yes, Lexi," I answered. "So what tragic accident happened to you? How did Peter ever find so many beautiful women and men who have had such horrid accidents?"

If Lexi had hands, she would have fidgeted with her dress. Instead, she twisted her torso this way and that, as she explained, "I don't know. Five years ago, I was living in my village of Esterbrook, and then I woke up here, just as I am, arms quite numb, dead they say." She frowned. "I found my hair was much longer, and I was quite pretty, too."

Suddenly, her eyes glazed over. Lexi whispered, "I am a very beautiful woman. I must please both men and women. I must satisfy their sexual needs as only I can. I am not physically limited. I can do everything for myself. I use my feet as naturally as others use their hands. I must always obey Peter."

Just as quickly, her eyes sparkled again. "Oh, where was I? Come. I'm showing you around. Tonight, you can meet everyone from our groups." She led them into the small, personal apartments of the Unarmed Escorts, none of which had any doors, only dangling beads. "Each of us has our own apartment, but often, we help each other with our hair."

Some of the apartments were empty, while two or three women were together in other apartments, brushing out someone's hair. Uniformly, the women smiled at us two Health Inspectors, asking us to choose them for an exciting evening.

All I could do was swallow. I squelched a rising anger to exterminate whoever was harming these beautiful women, and then I wondered how the men could end up looking like the women.

As we left them heading for the next group, I asked Lexi, "Say, do men on your world often look like you women? And are all women so incredibly pretty?"

Lexi laughed. "Oh no. Certainly not. I've no idea why these men look like us."

Meanwhile, Diana asked one of the unarmed

39

women named Tiffany, "So are you being well treated? How did you come to be an escort? Did you choose this profession?"

"Oh, we're treated like the beauty queens we are—really we are." Then, her face frowned. "Wicked! I don't know how it happened. I just woke up as I am, but that was five years ago." Her face brightened up, "It's a wonderful profession. I love it."

Lexi said, "Well, there you've seen them all. We should head back now."

Diana asked, "Do any of these men and women know how they got like they are now? How their limbs died?" Lexi frowned and shook her head no.

We passed another door. "Say, what's in there?" I asked, growing curious about how all these people could have been so mutilated.

Lexi responded, "Oh, we're not allowed in there. I think that's where the doctor lives and does his work when one of us gets sick."

I decided it was time to get more information and ignored her protests. Unlike the other doors, this one had a knob, which I incorrectly presumed Lexi couldn't operate. I opened it and headed inside. A strange, pungent odor assaulted my nose.

"But we shouldn't be in here," Lexi protested, refusing to enter the door that Diana held open for her.

Just then, I ran into an immovable object. A deep voice barked, "Lexi is right. You aren't allowed in here. This Dr. Howard's personal office. I'm Adler, the bouncer for the escort service."

As I looked up at the towering man, I saw those coal black, inhuman eyes and knew I was facing a dragon. From the hue of his skin, I also knew he was a Black dragon. Further, in that moment, I remembered a Black dragon had mutilated Diana's face and left hand with its caustic acid breath. Hence, I back-pedaled rapidly.

"Excuse us. We were just looking over the escort service. Sorry for intruding."

Diana, shaking like a leaf in an autumn wind,

backed out, nearly knocking Lexi over. Her fear was well founded.

As we followed Lexi, I said, "It's okay, Diana. The Black dragon isn't coming after us."

"Sorry, Felix. I saw it and couldn't help myself."

"Is that how your face got injured?" Lexi asked timidly, her voice full of sympathy.

"Yes. Has he harmed any of you?" Diana asked.

"Oh no. Not at all. He helps us sometimes. Well, I should take a bath and clean up for tonight. Will I see you around six tonight?" she asked.

I detected both a timid and a hopeful sound to her voice. She was a very likeable young woman. "Yes, we'll clean up, get some supper, and be back to visit with everyone."

She smiled. Oh, that smile could melt anyone!

As we left through the front door, Diana whispered, "You need a cold bath." I laughed.

The Hagans weren't back yet, so we did just that, cleaned up, and then handled supper. Around five, the two returned. Hastily, we outlined what we had seen and learned, and that we were going back to observe around six.

"You be careful," Drago said calmly. "We saw a number of Black and Red dragons around this world, but none of our breed. We need to sleep after our large meal."

We agreed and headed next door around six o'clock to see the escort service in action.

*** 

While we were being given our tour by Lexi, Dr. Howard, Peter, and Adler met in the Prep Room, one which Adler kept us from seeing. "Damn it! Peter's been the victim of a magical spell!" Adler barked, before focusing and casting his own spell. "There. I've dispelled whatever they cast upon you."

"Damn, damn, damn. Now what are you going to do?" Peter exclaimed, touching his body in various places to ensure himself that he was all there and unharmed.

Dr. Howard said, "We need to eliminate them.

They're not from our world. Besides, I couldn't open their front door. That building of theirs—it just appeared. I swear it wasn't there yesterday."

"I'll try to gain entry later on," Adler commented, "but why eliminate them when we can put them to good use? We need to make two replacements for those who were bought by the aliens last week. No need to kidnap a pair. They've landed in our laps."

Dr. Howard chuckled. "Yes, Adler, I like that attitude of yours. No, Peter. We're not killing anyone. We'll merely add them to our escorts. Since they're so curious about us, we'll give them the total package." All three roared with laughter at the intended pun.

Peter fiddled with his jacket, not liking any of this. These people were Health Inspectors and apparently magic users. So much could go so very wrong. Adler saw him wavering and barked, "Don't worry, Peter. If they date one of the escorts, we'll see they stay the night. If they won't date, you'll see their drinks are spiked. Either way, Dr. Howard will be busy tonight."

Peter continued to fidget, but nodded his agreement. Long ago, he'd lost total control of his profitable escort service. That's not to say it wasn't profitable now. On the contrary. Under Adler and Dr. Howard's guidance, his income quadrupled. Still, what they were doing to the women and men didn't sit well with him, but he knew he couldn't fight a Black dragon nor could he go up against Dr. Howard. If he did, he might end up like the men in his service.

***

"Honestly, Diana, I've never seen so many beautiful women before," I whispered to her as we entered the courtyard behind the Unarmed Escort building and to which the four buildings connected. All the women and men we'd seen earlier were present and dressed up. A number of alien men in their strange grey uniforms were chatting with the women, accompanied by some local men in suits.

"Actually, I've never seen anyone as beautiful as

these women are," I added. "The duchess comes the closest."

"I agree, but she's not half as pretty as these women are. I swear they must be scouring the whole world to find the prettiest women and then doing this to them," Diana whispered back, clearly not sure exactly what was done to them to produce the different types of escorts with their numb or dead arms.

An alien was chatting with Peter, so I moved closer so I could overhear. "Yes, any of these fine women and men are for sale. One hundred credits per person, but you must take their helper along with them. Yes, that's one of their guards and helpers there; Adler is his name."

"So for a hundred, we can take them off to our own worlds with us?" he asked, seeking clarification that he understood Peter correctly.

"Yes, but their helper and guard man must go with them."

"Could this helper meet with an accident when we reach our home world? Honestly, I've got an entire staff that can look after her needs, which must be nearly everything."

Peter shrugged his shoulders indifferently.

The alien smiled and said, "Then, perhaps we have a deal. I would like to take six back with us."

Peter's eyes brightened. "You could take a male and female of each. They breed true. You could have as many as you desire." The alien had a strange reaction, looking sharply at Peter. The two ambled off, whispering about the proposed deal.

I couldn't believe what I was hearing, but unfortunately, the pair moved out of hearing range, and Lexi came up to me to chat. Before we could talk, I heard a loud voice exclaim, "Damn it. You'll come with me anyway. I don't give a crap that I've not paid for more than a chat." All eyes turned to the alien, who chose to pull on Carli's dress, since she didn't have any arms to grab, ripping it slightly.

Again, without thinking, I reacted. These were

wonderful women who deserved all the kindness anyone could give them, considering how terrible their physical state must be. At least, that was how I saw them at this moment. I focused and barked, "Sleep him!" Right there in front of all the escorts, the argumentative, drunken alien slumped to the floor, snoring loudly. I walked over to Carli and said, "Are you hurt?"

"No, he was drunk and refusing to pay. He's ripped my dress. Now I'll have to go change and probably miss being chosen tonight."

"Here, let me. Mend Dress," I barked. Again, magical energies flashed, and her torn dress was instantly as good as new. In fact, no one could tell it had been ripped. Many eyes saw what I'd done. More importantly, Adler, the Black dragon, hastily joined us, picking up the alien with one hand and carrying him out of the courtyard. He was strong, but then he was a dragon.

When he returned, he politely said, "Thank you for handling Carli for me. Rather a rowdy bunch tonight."

I wasn't sure if he was sincere or not, but at least he was civil, a good starting point I hoped.

Diana whispered, "Felix, do you suppose Adler is testing us to see how much magic we know?"

My sister was dead on. I'd not even considered that and felt foolish, but when another rough up occurred, I again intervened, this time rescuing Tiffany. Honestly, my heart went out to these people. Later, Diana used some magic to assist another woman who ran into a bit of trouble with an unruly customer. When she acted, I kept an eye on Adler. He merely watched as Diana handled the man, putting him to sleep and assisting the woman with her torn dress. Only then did he walk over to cart the man outside.

If nothing else, I decided we were making a good impression on all the escorts, showing them we were on their side. I naively thought this would go a long way with Peter. Trouble was, I still had no idea just what the Box thought we were supposed to "handle" here. What were we to remedy? I took Diana aside and asked her if she had any ideas. "Are we supposed to close down this escort business?"

Diana laughed. "Felix, don't be silly. Every town has its red light district. There's no escaping that. You fellows just can't keep it in your pants. Still, we've found no evidence of disease, kidnaping, or mistreatment of the women. They are eating well and seem healthy to me, certainly not abused that I can see. I just don't get it."

"What about men purchasing the women and taking them off world?" I relayed what I'd overheard earlier.

She bit her lip. "Now that isn't good. I wonder if the women have any choice. If they don't, then perhaps that's what we're supposed to halt. On the other hand, if they have a choice, then that can't be it. Who are we to interfere with another's life choices like that? I wish that Box would be more specific in what it wants done. Besides, Felix, how did it know there was trouble here that needed handling? This is another world entirely. And how do we get home? I'm beginning to think we made a serious mistake with this Box."

"Come on. Let's get something to drink. I think we're going around in circles." I thought it was a nice touch—serving ale at this establishment. Of course, we'd already seen a couple of men drink too much and pay for their foolishness. I brought us each a mug of their dark ale. Sipping it, she and I discussed other options, which seemed limited just now. As far as we could see, there weren't any crimes being perpetrated. Perhaps morally what they were doing was questionable, but they were providing a service for these men apparently cooped up for long periods in their silver ships.

Neither Diana nor I realized our ale had been drugged. Quietly, each of us doped off. Later, Lexi said it looked as if we just dozed off for a bit. She said Adler carried us out of the main room, but she couldn't see where he'd taken us.

What then happened to us can only be viewed by Diana and me as magic, dark magic the likes of which we'd never seen or heard of, and yet here on this world, it was perfectly explainable and even understood by many, as we later found out. We owe a good deal to Carli, the woman I helped earlier in the evening, for she saw us dropping off to sleep, figured we had been drugged, and saw Adler carrying us away. Quietly, she slipped off, following him, staying in the shadows. After the dragon carried me inside Dr. Howard's personal office and headed back for Diana, she slipped inside and hid, her curiosity roused. Minutes later, she saw Adler entering, carrying Diana, lying her body down next to mine.

"Dr. Howard, both are here and ready for your magic," Adler barked. He turned and left.

Dr. Howard's goatee and moustache gave him a distinctive look, a man not to be trifled with or perhaps a man who meant business. According to Carli, he carried each of us into a room that had no windows, laying us side by side on a bed. He placed a sonic-visio machine on our heads—we don't know what else to call it. A sound recording played in our ears, while many short videos or movies, as these people called the moving pictures, somehow played into our minds via our eyes and ears. Diana and I considered it as merely some unknown form of magic.

Carli then watched him go down into the basement, returning with a strange cylinder with yellow and black stripes on it along with some kind of warning, which she was unable to read. She watched him set it up in our bedroom and open a valve. She could hear a hissing sound, and Dr. Howard hastily left the room and building! Carli stole into our room, saw the gas escaping, saw the machines on our heads, and decided to leave, too. She was certain something bad was happening to us, but she didn't know what. Even if she had known what they were doing, it was now too late for us.

# Chapter 5—Welcome to the Unarmed World

I awoke with someone's words echoing through my mind and moving images of unarmed people going about daily activities. For a minute, I just listened to the words. "I am very beautiful. I must please both men and women. I must satisfy their sexual needs as only I can. I am not physically limited. I can do everything for myself. I use my feet as naturally as others use their hands. I must always obey Peter."

*Why should I always obey Peter?* That made no sense to me, and I finally came fully awake from what others told me had been a coma. I muttered, "Why should I ever obey Peter?"

"Oh, you are awake at last, Felix." I recognized that voice—Lexi. She said, "We didn't know you wanted to be like us. I'm so glad you are, Felix. Now you are very beautiful too."

I was lying on a bed. Diana was right beside me. Sitting on the edge by me was Lexi and Tiffany, while Ben and Carli sat on the other edge beside Diana. I was naked and so was Diana. I used my arms to sit up, but nothing happened. Looking down, I should have screamed, shrieked, cried out in terror, or something similar. *But I'm not physically limited. I can do everything for myself.* Such thoughts swept through my mind. Awkwardly, I sat up. My arms were numb, though dead was a better description. I could no longer move them or my fingers in the slightest. They looked skinny and a dull grey, and I could see why Lexi called them dead arms. However, I also had large breasts, just as everyone else had, and my hair must have grown significantly, as it fell to my hips. I did gasp, before I looked over at Diana, who was also struggling to sit up.

"Diana, you look gorgeous! Your burn scars are

completely gone," I exclaimed, before I saw we were both facing a mirror so we could see ourselves.

"Felix, you look like me, a woman. Oh no! Our arms are dead, too. Oh, I guess that's all right, since I use my feet as naturally as others use their hands." She had a silly look on her face. "Why did I say that? Felix, we're helpless. What's happened to us?"

Tiffany giggled and said, "Wicked, but we're not helpless. We use our feet. You'll soon see. You should get dressed. We always help each other with this."

Carli added, "I know what happened. I saw it, but I don't understand it."

Ben spoke up, "Diana, you look fabulous! I do hope you'll allow me to help you get familiar with how we do everything."

"I want to scream, I think," I exclaimed, confused still.

Diana wailed, "I'm terrified and helpless, but maybe not. It's so confusing. Well, Ben, my ugly, burned face is gone, and so is my plainness. I do look very attractive. My left cheek matches my right cheek, and my crooked ears are straight. That's something, but I'm helpless, Ben, quite helpless, but then I'm not physically limited, am I?"

Ben replied cheerily, "No, we're not limited, Diana. You're very beautiful now. We just do things differently, as all the images in our minds shows us. You'll see. We should get you dressed."

Finally, I did scream, more out of annoyance than terror, though I'd be lying if I said there wasn't any fear in me. Rather what seemed so simple and easy in the images in my mind turned out to be awkwardly difficult in practice. One way of looking at it is that my feet and toes just didn't know what to do. A frustrating half hour passed before Lexi and Tiffany had me dressed.

Diana had just as rough a time of it as I had, though Ben and Carli did their best to make her feel at ease. Lexi's comment said it all, "I think you just have to give yourself time to get used to doing things this way and practice. I remember I had a lot of trouble at first too."

I did feel better with my "foreign" body covered by a dress similar to the one Lexi wore. About the only partially successful motion I did make was using a brush in my foot, helping Tiffany brush out Lexi's golden blonde hair and then in turn helping Lexi brush out Tiffany's raven hair. Both women's hair touched their knees, while my wavy brown hair now touched my lower back. In turn, they did mine, but I promised to get a haircut soon. By then, Diana and I were terribly thirsty and famished. Lexi and Ben anticipated this and led us to their kitchen, where lunch was waiting for us, compliments of several giggling young women whom we'd met on our tour.

Again, Diana and I tried to follow the images in our minds of other young women and men using their feet to dine, but frustrations set in again. We were going to need loads of practice. That much was clear. Finally, the mental conditioning broke down. I screamed, which shattered what little remained of Diana's conditioning, and she screamed along with me. The yelling didn't last long before we got it out of our systems for the moment. However, it shook up Lexi, Eve, Carli, and Ben.

Lexi asked, "Didn't you want to be like us?"

"No way!" I exclaimed. "They put something in our drink and did this to us while we were unconscious."

"Wow, you two look very different," the deep bass voice of Drago broke in on our conversation. The raven-haired beauty called Tiffany led the Hagans into the kitchen, but Tiffany was curious and stuck around, soon joined by several others. "Can you tell us what happened? We have been checking on you for the last five days, Felix, but until now, you weren't responding. Peter said you were in a coma. We believed him."

I answered, "Damned if I know what happened, Drago. We were in the courtyard with everyone, sipping some ale I think. Next thing I know for sure is waking up naked in a bed a short while ago. Wait, Carli, didn't you say you saw what happened to us?"

The young woman with curly black tresses said, "Yes, I was curious and followed Dr. Howard. But didn't you and Diana want to become like us? Peter said you did."

"Hell no, we didn't want to become like this! Diana didn't either. If I can't cast magic spells now, I swear I'll kill them brutally." I had to back off and let my anger subside a little. If I couldn't use magic, I sure as heck wouldn't be able to harm them, not now, not as Diana and I were.

Drago grunted, but then said, "But Felix, magic isn't in your arms, at least Mage Locklard never said anything about that. It's Cause powered by the caster's Intention. That's what he always told us."

Carla added, "Felix, Diana, you should try to cast some spells and see if you still can. I sure hope it works."

I was near a panic. If I'd lost my ability to cast spells with the loss of my arms and hands, how could I live? Magic was everything to me. Diana too. I took several calming breaths and focused on my dirty plate. "Clean Plate," I commanded. Yes, I had an audience. Lexi, Carli, Ben, Eve, Tiffany, Kelly, and Angela watched me closely.

I've never been as happy as I was when magical energies flashed, and my plate became spotless. "Hurray!" Lexi called out.

"It works!" Carli added. Several others cheered as well and then again when Diana's Clean spell detonated.

"That's encouraging. I'm going to try harder spells," I declared. Yes, relief was evident on my face. Diana heaved a huge sigh, as I cast Morph Me spell, my most powerful spell, a Grade 4 spell. Everyone gasped. Now I appeared just as I looked before all this happened. I was even wearing the same suit.

"So you are back to normal?" asked a confused Lexi.

I canceled the spell, reverting to my new form and dress. "No, Lexi. A powerful spell allows me to change my physical form, but it only lasts a day or so and can be canceled by other mages. Still, I'm able to cast it. Diana, if we can't figure out how to get by using our feet and toes like these people do, I can morph us back into our old forms every day."

Diana grinned. "Felix, that's an incredible relief. It's

damned scary being like this—as they are—but I think we'll get used to it in time. Right Ben?"

Ben jumped in, "Right beautiful. Give yourself time. Heck, it took me weeks before I was able mostly to do things for myself. I think everyone needed some weeks to get used to all the new ways of doing everything. Felix, you and I—we have to be positive. There's no going back, so we have to be positive now. We all do. We just focus on how to do things now."

Knowing I hadn't lost my magic skills, I asked, "All right. Carli, please tell us what all you saw. We need to know what happened to us."

Carli smiled and began telling us what she'd seen. I'd never met someone like her before. She had an eidetic memory. Thus, her recall was amazing. However, once she finished, the beauty queen asked, "So Diana, you didn't want to be like us, an Unarmed Escort? You didn't either, Felix?"

Diana sighed. Although she wanted her burned face to vanish, she didn't want it this way. "No, Carli. I wasn't pretty before the run in with the Black dragon, and my face was an awful mess after that, but even so, I'd never want to be as your group is just to look beautiful and not have everyone cringe when they see me. However, with all these moving images in my mind, I can see given time and practice, I can get as able doing things as you all are, but this isn't something I'd wish on my enemies."

"I—I thought so," Carli's voice faltered. Then, her long suppressed emotional dam gave way. Tears streamed down her cheeks. "I didn't want to be like this either. They took me in the night while I was sleeping. I woke up here like this. Everyone else seemed so well adjusted that I pretended to be so too."

Carli's confession shattered the other's blocks. Lexi began sobbing, blurting out her own similar story. However, the grief and emotion that Ben displayed was even greater, for he felt as if he'd lost his own sex and identity, even though his male organ still functioned properly. Hearing all the crying, others in the Unarmed

Escort group quietly came to see what was happening. After more whispers, their own mental blocks yielded, and they released their years of suppressed loss and grief.

Amid this, Peter walked in, initially to verify his two newest escorts had awakened and were adapting well. "What's going on here?" he cried out, seeing all his Unarmed Escorts jammed into the kitchen and dining room, along with the other two Health Inspectors.

I didn't hesitate. He focused and barked, "Charm Human Peter." Magic flashed and the owner was once again totally under Felix's influence. "How dare you do this to us?"

"But I didn't do it, not to you and not to any of these escorts. Dr. Howard and Adler are the ones," Peter protested.

Diana leaned into me, calming me down. I asked, "All right then Peter. What's your role in all this? How can you sell these people as sex slaves?"

"Hey, years ago, I had a respectable escort service here, all legal, and everything. Then one day, that Black dragon Adler and Dr. Howard showed up. 'You do as we tell you, Peter. If you don't'—Adler spewed acid on my chair, and it fumed and dissolved. 'Do as we say, and you'll make a tidy profit.' Honestly, I didn't have any choice. They did it all. They told me every one of the women and men they added to our escort service volunteered to join— that each wanted to be like this. None has ever said they didn't, and everyone seemed to adapt and do well. Lexi, you have done so well that I made you the hostess."

I suspected he was telling the truth. Hell, if I didn't have the Hagans with me, I'd be terrified of Adler too. As I said, dragons are at the top of the food chain. If I believed him, then I needed to consider what my next question should be.

However, Lexi responded to his plea. "No, Peter. I kept hearing that calming voice in my head, kept seeing all those incredible movies of others doing incredible things, so I assumed I was the odd woman out, that I was somehow different. As you can see, we all were taken against our will and turned into these forms."

All Peter could do, as he looked from tear-streaked face to face, was say, "I'm sorry. I didn't know, not really."

I took control again, "So Peter, why were they doing this? Are they perverts, sadists, or something?"

"I don't know exactly. Dr. Howard isn't a medical doctor, but a psychiatrist. He likes to experiment on people, that much is clear, behavioral modification I think he calls it. Adler wants to sell the escorts to aliens, though I've no idea why. I've kept all the profits I've received. Maybe I can recompense everyone somehow," Peter pleaded.

Again, I strongly suspected he was telling me the truth as he saw it. He was still under my Charm spell. At least the sobbing had more or less stopped.

I insisted, "All right, we need to find these yellow and black stripped cylinders that Carli said did this to us. Come on, everyone, to Dr. Howard's office and his basement."

Peter wavered, "But what about Adler? If he's there, we'll be killed. Even so, Dr. Howard has a gun. He can kill us all."

"I'm going anyway," Diana declared firmly. "If Adler kills me, maybe that's a blessing."

"Oh Miss Diana, don't say that!" exclaimed Ben, aghast. "You are a most beautiful woman, possessor of great magic still."

"Obviously, not great enough to prevent him from doing this to me. Come on. I want to find out what he did to us and how. Maybe his magic can be undone, reversed, or something."

Good old Diana, my thoughts exactly. Find out. Learn. Lexi and I led the way. Yes, I still needed her, because I wasn't very familiar with the layout of their buildings.

"You can't come in here!" barked a surprised Dr. Howard. We were a large group marching into his main office building, where his diabolical work had been done.

"Charm Human Dr. Howard!" barked Diana. "Now

we'll get some answers." She was mad. Her grief, I sincerely hoped, was behind her. She'd beaten me to him. "Show us those yellow and black striped cylinders. What's in them? Where did you get them? What does that gas do?"

I could tell he was fighting against Diana's spell, but couldn't totally refuse her, and was barely able to say, "Basement." He headed there, and we followed. I think I speak for many. We were most curious to learn what had happened to our bodies.

A dozen of the yellow and black striped cylinders lay stacked neatly in one corner of the basement. As I neared them, I saw four labels. I focused and cast a quick spell that allowed me to read this foreign writing. Unarmed, Pedestal, Hopper, Waddle. There was only one cylinder each for the latter three and nine in the Unarmed stack. At least, the more horrific mutilations were obviously limited in number. I rationalized what I was seeing.

"So Dr. Howard, how do these work? What do they do? Where did you get them?" Diana commanded.

His face contorted. He obviously didn't want to reveal anything, but the spell compelled him to cooperate with Diana. "Genetic mutations. These biological genetic agents cause a mutation in a person's DNA and a subsequent rebuilding phase of the entire body's structure. Takes five days or so."

"So where is the reverse spell?" Diana asked what she and I most wanted to know. "How do we undo what you've done to us?"

Dr. Howard gave her a strange look, as though she was under a Moronic Mind spell. That was my opinion of his look. "It's a genetic mutation to your genes. Can't be undone or reversed."

I admit that at this point I did feel as if I was an idiot. He was saying words, which my translation spell handled, but the words held no meaning for me. Genetic? Genes? Mutation? The auburn-haired Eve spoke up. "He means this isn't a magic spell as yours are. This stuff makes permanent changes to our bodies' structure. I should know, since I was planning to major in genetics just before I was abducted and altered. Think of it as permanent magic, Felix."

The letdown I felt must have been visible on my face—Diana's too, for Eve looked at us and then said, "Make him tell us where he got this terrible stuff and why? What's the point of doing this to us?"

Diana didn't react right away. I think she was as shocked as I was to hear this straight up and un-softened. "Yes. You heard her. Where did you get this awful stuff and what's the point?"

He rattled off some name that was meaningless to Diana and me, but Eve seemed to recognize it. Dr. Howard said, "For my part, I have been perfecting my behavior modification methods. Until you two came along, my theories were working out very well. All of these escorts— women and men—completely accepted their new situation without the slightest protest. Admirably so in most cases, though I admit it took several weeks before each got the hang of using their feet and toes. Why did you have to screw up my research?"

Diana wasn't through with him. "So what has Adler got to do with this?"

"He's my enforcer and, well, he's a dragon. I have to pretty much do what he wants too," Dr. Howard admitted. "He'll be back soon, and I'll have him dispose of you two," he growled angrily.

Diana wasn't through with him. She persisted, "What's he want you to do with these escorts?"

Dr. Howard glared at her, but had to answer. "He wants me to keep on selling them to the aliens who visit this world."

"Why?"

"Damned if I know or care. He always sends along another dragon with the escorts to act as their helpers."

Drago groaned. "Now I know for sure what Adler's doing, Felix. This isn't good. He's expanding the number of worlds Black dragons know about and can travel to using our Shadow Walk. Me, I know of six worlds, but it seems the Blacks and Reds are expanding the worlds they know about and inhabit. Worse, the aliens who come here have these flying silver birds. Who knows what else they've invented. Now the Blacks and Reds could well get their hands on such things and upset the balance of power among all dragon-kind. Not good, Felix, not good at all."

Carla added, "You see, we think of what Dr. Howard did to you and these other escorts as being a magical effect. Dragons, like some humans, are intensely interested in learning as much magic as possible and in having many magical items. We love all things magical. Adler may well try to obtain one of the alien silver flying machines simply because to us it is magical. Who knows what manner of new 'magical' things these aliens have on their worlds? But now the Blacks and Reds are there and are very likely acquiring some, which is not good for the balance of power among us dragons."

"Well, we can't do anything about that right now," I pointed out. "But I'd like to see how he almost made me think I wanted to be an escort when I woke up. How is it I have all these images in my mind? I keep hearing a voice too, but I don't believe what it's saying."

Since Dr. Howard was under her Charm spell, Diana spoke up, "You heard him. Show us how you made us want to be escorts when we woke up."

"No, you'll steal my secrets," he protested.

"I know where he has the machines," Carli explained.

I nodded and she led the way, with Dr. Howard protesting all the way. We saw two machines. One Carli explained was a simple playback recorder. Using a toe and over Dr. Howard's continual protests, she pressed a button. We all heard him saying, "I am very beautiful. I must please both men and women. I must satisfy their sexual needs as only I can. I am not physically limited. I can do everything for myself. I use my feet as naturally as others use their hands. I must always obey Peter."

"That's what's in my head!" exclaimed Lexi.

"Mine too," Carli added.

"Me too," Ben said. Soon dozens of others agreed. These words were in their minds, quite strongly when they first awoke as an Unarmed Escort, though they had diminished in intensity over time.

The other machine played a very lengthy series of what Carli called movies taken of other unarmed women going about daily activities and such. Every one of us recognized these as the moving images we saw in our minds. Dr. Howard explained, "You see, I wanted everyone to have the very best chance of surviving this and doing well in life."

"No," I barked back, "you wanted to ensure we'd all go along with your scheme willingly and easily, without any protests."

Dr. Howard squirmed, "Well, that too."

"All right, one more question, Dr. Howard," Diana said firmly so he'd have to answer it. "Why turn men into looking like beautiful women?"

"Just an experiment to prove my behavior modifications actually works. Until now, they worked just fine on the men here. Ben, Henry—you men didn't even protest, but accepted your new escort roles. It should have worked on you two, but I must have goofed up something in the process."

Ben cried out, "What the heck did you think we'd do? We woke up to find ourselves looking like women and completely helpless. You had better believe I kept my mouth shut. I was scared out of my mind! We should turn you into one of us and see how you like it."

For the first time, I saw Dr. Howard flinch, visibly shaken by that suggestion. I said, "Drago, tie him up for now, while we figure out what we're going to do here to straighten out this mess."

"My pleasure." Drago set to work, while I led the others and Peter back to the courtyard.

# Chapter 6—Handling the Unarmed

Once we arrived in the courtyard, Peter, who had been silent all through the questioning of Dr. Howard, spoke up. "Felix, those alien cylinders—they should be properly destroyed. We could call in government officials. They'll ask their alien friends how to do it safely."

That was the best idea yet. I had no idea how to destroy them safely, though I knew there was a very high-level spell that would have been perfect for it, except I was a long way from knowing that spell. Hence, allowing others who knew how to handle such dangerous cylinders seemed the ideal way to proceed. I said, "All right, Peter. That's a good idea. Please call them in right now." Peter nodded to me and left to do so. Still, I had an uneasy feeling.

Diana felt so too, whispering to me, "Felix, I sort of sense someone is watching us, an invisible person."

Diana solidified my own thoughts. That was it. Someone was invisible and watching us—my uneasy feeling. I relayed a warning to Drago and Carla.

At this point, the other escorts came into the courtyard, entering from the opposite side to where we were located. All seventeen of them made their slow way into the courtyard, curious to see what was going on. Hopper Sam was already with us, standing beside his Unarmed girlfriend, Sofia. Quite by accident, several of these slow moving women bumped into the hidden Adler. The Black dragon let out a bellowing roar, and three things happened nearly simultaneously.

Adler in his dragon form became visible standing before the seventeen, several of whom had bumped into him and fallen over. First, Adler cast a spell, but from this distance, I couldn't hear any of the words. Suddenly, my already large breasts swelled up even larger, until they were as large as my head and completely popped out of my dress top. Startled, I saw the same thing happening to us all. Second, Adler let out a belch of his acid breath, which

58

landed upon and completely soaked seventeen escorts, who suddenly began screaming in excruciating pain. Third, Adler's wings began flapping, great gusts knocking half of us off our feet.

I staggered. I tried to flail my non-existent arms to keep from falling over. Didn't work. I hit the ground hard, but even lying on the bricks, I shot my Magical Missile at the fleeing Adler, and it hit him. I doubt he felt more than a pinprick though.

Drago fumed. He looked at the seventeen whose flesh was being dissolved by Adler's acid. I think he knew he could do nothing for them, and he changed into his dragon form, swooping upwards after Adler. Seconds behind him, Carla also changed and headed off in pursuit. By now, all of us were knocked off our feet from the three gusts and awkwardly struggled back up.

For a minute, a stunned silence reigned. A putrid odor filled the air, but mercifully, the seventeen had already died, though the acid would continue to dissolve their bodies for some time. My chest felt like some massive weight was about to pull me over, but I ignored it and focused. "Wind," I chanted.

Grasping what I was doing, Diana joined me, adding her Wind spell to mine. Together, we blew the noxious odor up and out of the courtyard.

"Lexi, get everyone back inside the Unarmed building," I called out. My request ended her stunned state, and I heard her issuing orders to follow her inside. By the time that Diana and I entered bringing up the rear, all the others were now crying, yelling, or talking wildly. Shock and dismay were common.

Lexi sobbed, "Why? Why did he kill them?" She asked what was on everyone's mind.

Heck if I knew the answer, but she and the others were desperate to have a reason why, so I said, "Adler was magically invisible, spying on us, probably trying to see what we were going to do next. They bumped into him, ending his invisibility spell. He probably just got infuriated with them and retaliated. Black dragons hate us humans, which is why I think he was behind doing all this mutation stuff to us all."

"Why do they hate us so?" Carli asked. "We don't hate dragons, do we?"

*How do I answer that one?* "Well, I think dragons are much like people. Gold dragons like humans. Drago and Carla are friends of ours, back on our own world, wherever that is. He said Black dragons hate humans, and so do Red and Green dragons. I've no idea why they do, but I believe Drago."

"Dear God! What happened here?" exclaimed Peter. He'd just walked back in from the courtyard. "What happened to your breasts?"

"Adler's work. He outright murdered seventeen people," I explained. "He did something to us, but I don't know what. Drago and Carla went after him. What did you find out?" I asked, hoping to get his attention off the horrors in the courtyard and off our mammary glands.

"Oh, they are on their way. Sending in bio containment units. Be here in an hour or so. You should all go to your rooms and wait until I have more news," Peter said with a bit more confidence in his voice. I sensed he felt he was finally doing the "right" thing. He added, "I'll figure up your past wages and have them for you later on." That brought smiles to many faces. Hopper Sam asked if he could stay with his girlfriend since all the other Hopper escorts were dead. Peter agreed.

Diana whispered, "Felix, we should use our Clothes Alteration spell to adjust everyone's dresses. We can't go around with our monsters hanging out as they are now."

I agreed. We followed the others as they made their way to their apartments within the Unarmed Escorts building. First stop was Lexi's room, where Diana and I cast our useful beginning spell on our dresses and then Lexi's dresses, much to her relief. Then, we visited each of the others, altering theirs to fit as well. Carli's comment was dead on, "This is a good use for magic!"

When we finished up, Lexi found us and said, "They're here—all sorts of men. Peter wants to see you in the courtyard. Oh, and something happened to Dr. Howard too."

When we arrived, we saw several men collecting the remains of the seventeen women and men murdered by Adler. In addition, we saw three men who wore some kind of thick suits with helmets, though they carried the latter under one arm. The other arm pulled a cart loaded with some of the cylinders.

"Ah, here you are," Peter said cheerily. "What luck. They said the cylinders used to contain some form of biogenetic agent, but now they only contain compressed air. They are harmless, so I don't understand any of this anymore. Still, I'm disbanding everyone in my escort service. I've divided the profits, and each survivor gets their share. You two are the last ones. Would you like some financial recompense for what they did to you?"

Diana chuckled. "No, I just want my arms back, Peter. Have they found Adler?"

"No, he's vanished. Drago and Carla lost him; at least that's what they're telling the officials now. Oh, here they come," Peter explained, backing away from us, as the Hagans, now in their human forms, walked up to us.

"Lost him, damn it, Felix," Drago growled, very disappointed.

Carla added, "We think he cast an Invisibility spell or a Teleport spell. We've searched high and low for him, but had to give it up, because a dozen Black dragons swooped down on us. We beat a hasty retreat. Is Peter closing down the escort service?"

He answered, "You heard right. Just dividing the profits now. Many are leaving, heading to their hometowns now." Peter discussed additional details with us for another half hour before we were able to depart.

Just as we were leaving, two other men carried a stretcher with Dr. Howard on it. As they passed through the courtyard, they paused before Peter. One explained to Peter, "We'll take him to Albert Hospital for a thorough checkup."

We stared at what remained of Dr. Howard. His

arms ended at his elbows and his legs ended at his knees, and he had Waddle pads on his thighs. The man added, "His tongue is missing, so he can't talk. Does anyone know what happened to him?"

"No, we left him tied up for you," Drago answered. We looked at each other, but I knew none of us had the ability to have so changed the mad doctor. Drago added, "I think he's got the justice he deserves."

Peter chuckled, and the men continued carrying Dr. Howard away. The man looked terrified, but was only able to make gurgling noises.

At last, it was time for us to leave too. Walking through the Unarmed Escort building, we found nearly all the apartments were empty. Of the two dozen who were here, only two women remained, and they were slowly filling up a pair of carts with their belongings. They thanked us and said they were heading to their hometown when the bus arrived and would be living together. I presumed a bus was some form of transportation. Finally, we four reached the street and stepped up to the door of our Box. The Hagans held onto Diana and my new money pouches, each filled with what Peter claimed was a thousand gold dollars.

"Well, I think we've handled it, unless the Box wants us to try to find Adler," Drago declared as we entered our Box.

Once inside, Drago pressed the Handled button beside the door. The bar slid across again, blocking the door, keeping us from opening it. I felt a slight motion beneath my feet and said, "I think we've been successful and are moving again. Come on. Let's see if it gives out more magical spell book pages."

As we entered our large living room, we four stopped and stared. There sitting on our couches were a number of the Unarmed escorts. Lexi tossed her hair to one side and rose. "Hello. We're here to learn magic. We've all discussed this and have decided we want to learn to cast spells as you to do, so we're your apprentices, if that's the right word for it. Peter has given us some funds, so we can pay our own way. Besides, we need to stick together so we can help each other with some things that are hard to do by ourselves. We've each brought our few things in our carts."

I recognized all of them: Lexi, Carli, Ben, Eve, Tiffany, Kelly, Angela, and Vanna. I rather felt like a freak myself, but experienced relief seeing that I wasn't alone, that Ben was here. Still, none of us expected this to happen. Looking back, yes, I can see how it happened.

I swallowed, "Oh my. Er, guys, this isn't going to be quite what you expected. I think we're being transported to some other world. I have no idea if you can ever get back to the world we just left, your world."

Tiffany replied shyly but forcefully, "Wicked! But we really don't have anything there to go back to or any desire to go back. There's nothing there now but horrid memories. Besides, none of us can face seeing our families, not looking as we do. Being able to cast spells as you do is far more important. With them, we can help others in need, just as you four helped us."

Ben chuckled, "Well, we're in luck, gang. If we're moving, they can't toss us out. See, I told you this was a good idea. Besides, now I can help the beautiful Miss Diana. Look, Felix, you and Miss Diana are going to need a lot of practice. If nothing else, we can help you with that."

Diana looked at me with a curious expression. Drago and Carla merely looked bored. "Well, all right then, I supposed Diana and I can help you eight learn to cast spells, but first, we need to see if this Box will accept you as students."

I spent a few minutes explaining what little we knew about the Box and its operations. Then, all headed to the main console wall. Using my toe, I pressed the Activate button and said, "Box, we have eight more students. Drago, Carla, Diana, and I have handled the situation, so we need our new spell pages. Okay, gang. Let's see if the programmed illusion works right."

Suddenly, a fuzzy image of an old man appeared. "Your pages are coming now. One by one, have the new students state their name and receive their binder and initial Useful Spell pages." The illusion halted.

I nodded to Lexi, who proudly stood before the wall and the image, and said, "I'm called Lexi, sir."

One after the other, each stated their name. Once done, our pages began appearing, followed by eight binders and then eight sets of pages for them. With ten of us lacking arms to grab the materials, Drago and Carla did it for us.

When they retrieved Lexi's set, she said, "Put it on my shoulder." She then used her head to apply pressure to the binder, forcing it tight against her shoulder, and then carried it over to the dining room table.

"Look," exclaimed Carli, "the Alter spell is in here. We'll be able to alter our own clothes now, once we learn the spell, that is."

I spoke up, "First, we should get everyone a room, settled in, and some supper going. I'm hungry. We'll deal with magic tomorrow."

Again, Lexi took charge, "Felix, I'd like to sleep with you. We have found having several of us sleeping together makes it much easier to get some things done. If you don't mind, that is, Tiffany and I will sleep with you, while Ben and Carli sleep with Diana. Eve, Kelly, Angela, and Vanna can sleep together, if you have a room they can use. This way, we can all more easily get things done that we must. Trust us. We know."

I laughed. "Lexi, I trust you. You eight have years of experience being unarmed and we don't. All right. Let's get everyone settled in. We can use the spare room next to ours, Diana."

Raven-haired Tiffany and golden blonde Lexi pushed their carts into my room, while the black haired Carli and the brown haired Ben pushed theirs into Diana's room. Vanna had auburn hair. Kelly's was blonde, as was Eve's. Angela's hair was flaming red. The four took the room to the right of mine.

After helping them stow their dresses and heels, Diana and I led them on a grand tour of the Box, finally meeting the Hagans in the kitchen.

Drago said seriously, "Felix, we need to talk about this. Carla and I don't want to be the arms and hands for all ten of you."

Before I could reply, Lexi did. "You don't have to, Drago. We eight are all accustomed to doing everything ourselves. We're independent, excepting Felix and Diana, who will need lots of practice with everything. You'll see."

"Well, I don't know how you can be independent, but for now, I'll take your word for it. Felix, we'll help you and Diana some, until you work it out."

Carli chose this moment to speak up. "Say, since that man said the cylinders were harmless, containing only compressed air, can someone tell me how we were genetically modified? How did our bodies get so altered if the cylinders they used didn't contain the bio agent thing?"

"Good point, Carli," I declared. "So much has happened so fast that I've not had time to ponder the situation. Look, are you sure Dr. Howard didn't inject us with anything else?"

"Quite sure, Felix. Honestly, once the gas began coming out of the cylinder beside your bed, he acted plenty scared and got out of there fast. I didn't see him return until the next day."

"Okay, Carli," I replied, deep in thought.

She added, "So how did he change our bodies?"

"Perhaps," I said slowly, "he just said those big words to make us all believe that was what he did, that it was permanent, and that this couldn't be undone."

"Hum," Drago muttered, "could be spells then. If Dr. Howard didn't actually do this to you ten, then maybe Adler did it. After all, he is a Black dragon, and all dragons know some magical spells."

"True," I replied, "but what spells could possibly have done all this to us? Remember, these people have been this way for years."

Lexi looked at the others, and they quickly decided she'd been this way the longest of the small group. "Five and a half years," she said. "But I think some of the others have been there even longer. Do spells last forever?"

Diana answered her. "Lexi, some spells are permanent, but most can be dispelled. Many spells last for a finite duration, though as the mage becomes more skilled, their spell durations are longer, or so we were told. We know a simple beginning spell, Alter Self, which lasts for a day or so, but it can't be used to make such huge alterations in our bodies, just minor things."

I added, "A Morph Other spell could have been used, but, and this is a big but, they would have to know or have seen someone who is identical to you now. The spell copies the physical appearance of another. Each one of you looks quite different, so I don't think that's the spell he used. Besides, it's likely it couldn't have lasted five years without being renewed periodically."

Drago muttered, "Could be some form of a Wish spell, Felix."

Suddenly finding a reasonable explanation, I said, "You're right! Could well be. Normally, that most powerful spell isn't used frequently, because each casting of it ages the mage one year. Ten castings and the mage's body is ten years older. Heck, there must have been fifty of you—maybe more since some were sold to the aliens. The caster must have aged over fifty years. A human couldn't have done that much."

Drago chuckled, "No, but a dragon could. We live half a millennia. Fifty years isn't all that much time for us."

"Can that spell be undone or reversed?" Carli asked.

I answered with a sigh that told all. "No. It's permanent, unless the caster states otherwise. What bothers me are these giant breasts that suddenly appeared."

"That's never happened before," Carli pointed out.

Diana added, "I presume Adler cast some spell on us."

"Maybe it can be dispelled," I suggested. "Let's try, Diana. We've nothing to lose."

"Wait!" Lexi exclaimed, startling me. "Wait." She sighed. "There's something else you don't know about me."

66

Everyone looked at this incredibly beautiful, golden haired, young woman. "If all this was done by a magic spell and if you can dispel and undo it, then we'll revert back to the way we were before they cast the spell on us."

Not getting what she was worried about, I replied, "Well, yes. It works that way. If the spell can be affected by a Dispel Magic spell, then when it is successfully cast, it undoes whatever the original spell did to you. Mind you, not all spells can be undone by this spell, but quite a few can." I finally deduced what she meant, that something else was in play. "So what is it that we don't know about you that will interfere?"

She slumped visibly, sitting down hard on the couch. Lexi said, "Before this happened to me, I was ugly. Even my breasts were abnormally small. I was eighteen and my school's ugliest girl. After I woke up and saw myself in a mirror—well, just look at me. I look like a beauty queen, well at least until they grew so huge today. If you dispel the magic, I'll go back to looking truly ugly again." Lexi looked crushed.

"Oh my God, Lexi," Carli exclaimed, "I never knew that. Don't worry. I was my school's ugliest girl. I hoped to bury myself in the study of genetics so I could avoid most all people. When I awoke and saw myself, I just couldn't believe I was seeing me."

"Me too," squeaked Vanna. One by one, the others admitted similar situations. The obvious conclusion hit me. Dr. Howard only kidnaped ugly or homely young girls. Turning them into beauty queens only helped ensure they would more readily accept their new circumstances. Vanna added, "I'm not so sure I want to be returned to what I used to look like. It was awful—really, it was. What about the rest of you?"

Lexi answered for the eight. "Felix, I'm not sure any of us are ready to face looking like we used to look. We're all incredibly pretty now. Besides, we're able to do everything using our unique ways. What about you, Diana? Your face was so disfigured, but now you look just fabulous. Besides, all I ever wanted was to find a nice man, get married, and raise a family."

"Me too," Carli admitted, "but I knew no one would ever want to marry me. I wanted to have children, but I knew they'd inherit from me. I swore I'd not pass on my ugliness to my children. So I went into genetics instead."

Diana sighed. "It was embarrassing and humiliating when I saw people cringing at my burned face. Felix, just look how incredibly beautiful I am now. I can feel just what all eight of them are feeling right. Going back to looking terrible is a huge price to pay. I know I need to pay it, but they are able to do so much on their own that maybe they are right. We just need to practice lots more."

"Okay. I understand. Really, I do. I'm only going to try to dispel what Adler did to us today with these huge breasts. Later, we'll worry about the rest."

That said, I decided to cast it on myself first, not because I was being selfish, but so the others could see that nothing else was undone by the spell. I sincerely hoped this would work.

I focused and cast my spell. I felt magical energies flowing. Lexi's exclamation told all. "Felix! It worked! Yours are back to where they used to be."

I found it hard to tell. The dress no longer fit my reduced bosom. After Diana cast her Alteration spell, everyone could see that only Adler's latest modification to our bodies had been undone. I still looked every inch a woman, except in my panties, of course.

Emboldened by this success, the others allowed Diana and me to cast the spell on them. An hour later, all ten of us were back to the way we had been this morning. In addition, all dresses were altered to fit.

All this time, Drago and Carla sat on sofas watching us and listening to our conversations and fears. When we finally decided to turn in for the night and tackle learning magical spells in the morning, Drago and his sister had a private talk in her room.

Drago stated, "Look. We both know having them around as they are now is a liability. I'm sure they mean well, but without hands, how are they really going to be able to do much of anything? Certainly, not quickly as magic spells demand."

"I agree, Drago. Dodging spells is vital, but I doubt they can do much of that. On the other hand, Drago dear, you have to understand their position. I can't imagine what their lives were like when they were as ugly and homely as they claim to have been. If you or I were really that bad looking, why, we'd never be able to get a mate when the time comes. At least, this way, they look so gorgeous that shouldn't be a problem."

"Hum. I suppose you have a point. Still, I do wish they had their arms and hands. That would go a very long way to making this work out. We're obviously going to other worlds in this Box. It's also obvious there's incredible danger involved too. You and I were very nearly done in by all those Black dragons today. It's a miracle we weren't drenched in acid."

"We dodged well, brother. Yes, I agree. I do wish they had their arms and hands. I guess we'll just have to see what happens." With that, Drago headed off to his own bedroom. No one saw magical energies flashing an hour later.

# Chapter 7—Learning Magic

I awoke amid a sea of golden, brown, and raven hair. We three had the best night of sleep in a long time, especially Lexi and Tiffany. However, this morning, I had my arms and hands back, rather startling me.

"Wow!" exclaimed Lexi, as we carefully disentangled our hair.

"Wicked! Now this is interesting indeed," the alto voice of Tiffany added. "The only thing that has changed is that Felix has arms again. Fascinating. By the way, I haven't slept so good since I was kidnaped and brought to the escort place years ago."

"Me too," Lexi added. "Okay Felix, when do we get to start learning magic?"

"Impatient are we?" I teased her, pulling both women up close to me and giving each a passionate kiss.

I remembered what Tiffany had said about their world and marriage. "It's perfectly acceptable for a woman to have more than one husband and for a man to have more than one wife. The absolute rules are that they must spend equal quality time with each spouse and they must all have equal financial support. You can get arrested for playing favorites."

"This is *so* wicked! Did the spell just wear off?" asked observant Tiffany. "Or did you dispel the magic?"

"Tiffany, I didn't do anything. I don't think it just wore off. Something like this doesn't work that way. After all, you've been as you are for years. I think something else is at work here."

She countered, "Could it be this magical Box we're in?"

I hadn't thought of the Box in this context, but she'd made an astute point. It obviously was highly enchanted. She added, "Perhaps the Box knows you are its main helper and so it fixed you up partially so you don't have to spend weeks learning how we do things."

"You might be right, Tiffany," I validated her insight.

Just then, Diana excitedly called out, "Felix! My arms and hands are back. Nothing else is changed according to Ben here."

As everyone gathered in the kitchen and dining room, Drago agreed with Tiffany's conclusion, "The Box wants us four to be able to fulfil our missions, so it repaired the damage. That's what it looks like to me."

Vanna interrupted Diana, who had already begun to make breakfast for everyone. "Diana, let me help. I'm a good cook. I was a chef in training before I was abducted."

"Sure thing, Vanna, but aren't you going to need a whole lot of assistance?" Diana asked, but soon regretted it.

"Hardly. Just carrying things from in here to the table. Now that would be helpful, but I can manage if you don't want to do that," Vanna countered.

After dining on the best breakfast we four had had in a long time and after many accolades to Vanna, we headed to the casting rooms. I smiled, seeing eight leaning heads holding their spell books tightly against their shoulders. Whatever else was about to happen, I was convinced we had an enthusiastic bunch.

Drago and Carla had already insisted the eight were Diana and my responsibility, so I took charge and became their magic teacher. Within days, I discovered an aspect of myself I hadn't known existed. I loved being a magic teacher and found I was a natural at it, but that's getting ahead.

"All right everyone. Listen up. Here's the essential theory behind the casting of all spells. First, comes Cause. You must clearly state the precise action or thing you're attempting to bring into being. With these beginning Helpful spells, Cause is usually one or two words. However, as the spells become more difficult, the Cause stating becomes far more complex. Goof up the Cause, the statement of what you're attempting, and the spell fails. Second, comes your Intention. It's your intention that actually provides the energy or driving force or motivation that powers your spell, your Cause. As we mages say, it's Cause driven by your Intention that makes magic possible."

"So, it's time for our first spell, Clean. Diana has just conjured a small pile of dirt in front of each of you. Read the description of the spell. Then let's practice it. Remember, focus your intention. Clear your mind of all thoughts except the Cause you want to have occur. Then Intend for it to happen. Even the slightest doubt will cause the spell to fizzle."

Thus, I began to work with the eight, while Diana assisted me. Drago and Carla looked over their new spells and began working on their casting. While I wanted to look mine over and learn them, I needed to help the eight who had helped Diana and me.

I was rewarded some ten minutes later by an excited Carli, who began jumping up and down, "It worked! It worked! Dirt's gone! Yippee!"

I and everyone else congratulated her on her first successful spell activation. Shortly after that, the others got their Clean spells to fire. The ice was broken, as we say around Byron Falls in the wintertime.

After lunch, Diana and I were able to take time to work on our own new spells. The eight were doing well on their own for now. She and I added long desired spells to our arsenal, namely a Ball of Fire and a Bolt of Lightning. With these, she and I felt more confident facing dragons. Had we known these when Adler murdered the others and took flight to escape, we could have blasted him with these two power spells. True, dragons have some spell immunity, but cast enough times, one or more will get through his immunity and harm him. We could also now Hold a Human Still. Don't get me wrong. We still couldn't call ourselves mages. No, we needed to learn one key spell, the spell that defined that label: the Teleport spell. We both knew we were a long way from there.

However, I'm not complaining in the slightest. Our spell books now contained over forty Grade 1 spells, two dozen Grade 2 spells, and now four Grade 3 spells, along with our single Morph Self spell of Grade 4.

Drago's comment summed up our experiences thus far. "Look Felix. This is working out as promised. We go in, clean up a mess, and receive payment of many new spells. If we can keep this up, why, soon, Carla and I will know far more spells than any other dragon!"

That first evening as I sat on the edge of my bed with Lexi and Tiffany sitting on either side of me, I truly appreciated these incredible women. Lexi's angular face was perfectly formed. Tiffany's face was less angular towards her jaw, but her black bushy eyebrows accentuated her dark eyes, making her appear even more enticing. Lexi's forte lay in organizing things, bringing order to a confusion, controlling others, and, surprisingly, math. She could do large calculations in her head.

On the other hand, Tiffany's skills lay down an altogether different path. She had an intuition that exceeded mine. She had a knack for being able to detect a person's motives right away. Further, she was a master of geometry, which assisted her with quite a number of spells that affected areas. Her voice was a mellow alto, adding to her charm.

I suggested, "Now that I've my arms back, I was thinking of cutting my hair short like I used to have it—down to my shoulders."

"Don't you dare cut it!" Lexi declared. "We love it long. Looks good on you too. If you cut it, we'll sleep with others," she teased me.

"Wicked, Lexi. You tell him. Besides," Tiffany softened her tone, "with boobs as big as ours, you won't look a bit like a man."

I gave up that idea. As long as I had them, I was in a sort of limbo land, but that didn't matter to the women. I put my arms around them, pulling their bodies close to mine. "Great day all around. You both did very well." I gave each a passionate kiss.

During the week of training, I learned Ben was a master of computer machines, whatever those were, and he was something of a science whiz, particularly in the areas of just how things worked, whether it was a spaceship, computer, or a human body. In addition to her eidetic memory, Carli was knowledgeable in biology and genetics, two foreign areas to me. Well, so were Ben's, if I am honest with you.

I learned Eve knew much about chemistry and how to make exciting explosions, as she called them. I called them bombs. Kelly had taken lessons in flying the silver birds—the spaceships as she called them. Moreover, she was rather knowledgeable about alien worlds. Of course, we four were aliens as far as she was concerned. I guess I should be more specific. She knew about the alien worlds from those who visited her world via their silver birds. Angela was keenly interested in all things water or aquatic. She was always the first person to cast the next spell that involved water in any way. Besides being an incredible chef, Vanna was into all things dealing with fire. I've never seen anyone so eager and quick to learn a fire-based spell, as did Vanna.

As the week ended, I realized the addition of these eight apprentices filled in major gaps in our overall knowledge and experiences. Honestly, having seen a bit of their world, I can say we Byron Falls people are in the dark and that these eight provided illumination we'd otherwise not have. Even Drago admitted this to me. "They could well prove useful, Felix. Perhaps, they aren't as helpless as I first thought."

The next day, Tiffany complained, "What's with this? Only one spell in Grade 1. How many are there in the grade?"

"Forty some," Diana answered.

"Wicked! So why do we only have one? We want more, lots more," she said with a teasing, evil grin.

I replied as best I could. "Well, we think it works this way. The Box takes us to some location where there's a situation that needs to be handled. After we handle it, the Box hands us another batch of spell pages for us to learn. While we're learning them, the Box takes us to the next

74

location and situation."

"Can't we just go to some magic store and buy all the missing pages?" asked Lexi. "We have money or gold."

"While there are supposedly some magic stores, I have no idea where they are. Besides, we're not on my world any longer. Even so, the stores will be selling magical items, like enchanted swords, clothing, and other useful items, not spell pages."

"So how were you learning them? I mean before you got into the Box?" she continued to probe.

"Well, we four were apprentices to Mage Locklard. He was teaching us our spells."

"Can't we just go back to him and learn them faster?"

"Except we're not on our world anymore. We've no idea how to get back there."

"Well that's a find how do you do," Lexi said, a gorgeous pout on her face.

As if in answer to her protests, we felt the slight jar of the Box setting down. We had arrived at the next destination. Drago and I rushed to check on the door bar. "Ah ha," Drago declared. The bar that prevented accidental opening of the door while the Box was in transit was gone, revealing the notice to press the Handled button when we had handled this new situation.

# Chapter 8—A Cold Day in Hell

We waited a few minutes to see if new kinds of clothing would appear, but none did. Meanwhile, I cast my Morph spell so I looked my usual self instead of a busty beauty queen. Dressed in our leather trail clothing and moccasins, Drago, Carla, Diana, and I poked our heads outside.

Whoa! Six men had swords pointed towards us. One young woman wearing a leather top, shorts, and moccasins stood behind them, threatening us with a knife.

*Might as well attempt to be friendly.* I could always shut the door, but then we'd never be able to leave here until we "handled" the situation. "Hello. I'm Felix. My sister, Diana. Our friends, Drago and Carla. Where are we? Who are you folks? Oh, we mean you no harm."

I know that sounded lame, but these were fighters, likely skilled from their stances. This place was more like it. I felt as if I was home again, though I soon saw this wasn't my world of Byron Falls either.

They wore cotton shirts and loose fitting khaki pants, but all six were burly men, strong, robust, and in need of a shave and bath. I'm sure Diana would have pointed that out if she had the chance. Over my shoulder, trying to sound peaceful, she called out, "Hello there."

While the six men grunted, the lone woman spoke up. "Mages?" We nodded. She declared, "See, told you. Mages come to help us. I, Molly Brooks. We go now. Kill Duke. Kill Magus. You see," she added glaring at the six men.

One man grumbled, "Well, all right then, Molly. But how do we know they can cast spells? Granted, magic got this house here, but can they fight?"

Molly shrugged her shoulders. Her medium brown hair barely reached her shoulders, and it looked as though she'd trimmed it with her knife. Her face was round with soul-penetrating, greenish eyes. Her countenance suggested she was deadly serious, and I wondered if she ever smiled. She was tall and thin, though she looked as tough as the leather she wore. In contrast to the six men, she'd obviously recently bathed.

I fired off, "I'm sorry. We mages just arrived here. Where is here? What's going on? Why do you need us to fight? Who are we to fight? We aren't omniscient."

"Big words," Molly said. "You talk," she poked one of the men with her knife.

"Rainbow's End. That's what everyone calls our world here, but we're at the western edge of it, near Brackenmoor Swamp. More precisely, this here is Gleason Slums on the far edge of Beckworth, the largest city west of the capital, Imperial. If you're new here, I'm not sure this is goin' ta do you much good, except this is the slums, the garbage pit of Beckworth. Name's Edgar, by the way."

"Thanks Edgar," I replied with a smile. *I'm sure glad I Morphed Me into what I used to look like, instead of looking like some beauty queen about now.* My face felt a little hot too.

"Anyway, if you can fight, we could use you. Seems they took Molly's father and brother away. Arrested. Sedition. Hell, we call it Rightful Protesting. The Count's gone too far this time. Well, you'll soon see."

"So the Count runs this city?" I asked, trying to follow Edgar's thinking.

"Count Earl Beckworth. Countess Kayleigh is his wife and noblewoman. She's a bitter tongue. They live behind the walls of Beckworth Castle in the heart of the city."

"So Edgar, we have to storm a castle?" I asked, sizing up the situation. "Full of armed soldiers."

Edgar shuffled his feet a bit, looking down at them, as if they needed his attention. So did several other men. He raised his head, his eyes meeting mine. "Well, yes and no. Count has armed guards and soldiers, but this time of day, most are off rounding up other protestors, but he doesn't need them, not when he's got Mage Dietmar there with him. Don't need soldiers, not with him around. Never a nastier fellow, but you'll soon see. Anyway, we're about to head to the castle and see if we can find out what the Count did with her father and brother."

Drago butted in. "Felix, you and Diana go with them and check things out. Carla and I have to—well, you know what we have to take care of."

"Right. Go ahead. We'll scout around. We won't take any action until you join us," I advised. "Lead on, Edgar."

Looking around, the Box now appeared to be a rundown orange adobe building. We were standing in the rubble of what had once been a brown adobe structure. Six-inch lines on the ground outlined its former walls. Well, he did say this was the slums of Beckworth.

"Follow us. Stay alert for Count Earl's soldiers," Edgar advised. We stepped out onto the street made from bright yellow cobblestones.

Molly suggested, "Stop at dad's place. Maybe Jodi's seen them." Edgar grunted.

Quietly, the nine of us joined others on the street, heading east and south. The various colors of the homes struck me at once. Every shade of a rainbow could be found in the adobe bricks. We passed a red home, a brown building, a yellow house, an orange home, a blue warehouse, and even a green structure. I found I liked the colorful diversity.

Within a few blocks though, the people, clothing, and attitudes changed —remarkably so. Grubby, patched clothing gave way to well-made apparel. Gone were the covert stares at us as we passed by, replaced with pleasant smiles and the occasional head nods. Then, we saw the first of many noblewomen.

She wore a billowing blue dress, puffed out with layers of petticoats, but she moved very slowly, seeming to float along the street, albeit at barely a quarter of our pace. Molly spoke up, "Noblewoman."

"What happened to her arms?" Diana asked the obvious question. From her dress top, we could see she had shoulders and could see the upper portion of her arms.

"Bound behind her back," Molly hissed.

"Noblewomen bound. Always. Servants tie arms to their corsets. Never undone, except when bathing. Seldom happens. Servants are always with them. But leave when husbands come home. Tall heels. Tiny steps. They float along. Have to float. Boots tied together."

"Wait, Molly," Diana protested. "Are you saying all noblewomen of Beckworth are bound like this? Helpless women?"

"Noblewomen helpless. Not Molly. I refused. Big trouble," she replied.

Edgar grumbled, "She's right. Everywhere in our world, the wealthier women are all bound. They wear billowing gowns and float or glide along, but their helpers are always with them. Provides steady work for the poorer women of Rainbow's End. Lord knows how much my sister really needs the work and pay—she's being the hands of the Miller's Wife. Good job."

"Just how many noblewomen are there here in Beckworth?" asked Diana, as we spotted three more of these women moving slowly, but elegantly towards us. Now we saw each had a young servant girl following patiently behind them. Their faces looked cheerful enough as we passed them, and they smiled at us, particularly at Molly.

Molly grumbled, "Supposed to be me. I escaped. Half the women."

Edgar added, "Molly's short with the words, but yeh, half the women of the city are noblewomen. Anyone who has money wants their wife and daughters to become noblewomen. It's an instant status symbol. Everyone then knows you have money. Molly's dad is one of them wealthier men. Has a gem cutting business. So old Henry's wife is a noblewoman, as is his daughters."

"Not me. Escaped," Molly butted in bluntly.

"Er, right. Her sister Jodi—she's married to Lyle, who is a gem cutter," Edgar explained. He went on, "Them's that can afford it, begin binding and training their daughters to be noblewomen when they turn ten years old. Jodi and Molly here were bound when they were ten."

"This is criminal," I blurted out.

Diana was more diplomatic. "So Molly, how did you escape your bondage?"

"Didn't til I was sixteen. Ran off. They untied me to bathe me," she said, spitting on the ground.

Edgar chuckled, "And they've been after her ever since, trying to convince her to get rebound and be the noblewoman she was born to be. Me, I say how can anyone be born to be a noblewoman? Just foolishness. But if I was rich, then I'd probably have a noblewoman wife too. Hell, it's the best advertisement you can get—having a noblewoman as your wife tells everyone you're someone important, someone who is rich."

Diana persisted, "Didn't your dad send someone after you when you escaped?"

"I cut throat. Knife. Good tracker. Good hunter," Molly said, guardedly, but with some pride.

Edgar laughed. "She's right about that. Molly here's one great tracker and hunter. Be a stupid waste to bind her up and make her into a noblewoman. Hell, once they bind the woman, there's no way she can get herself free. She's dependent upon her servant girls for everything."

Another man laughed, adding, "But they are damned sexy looking—the noblewomen. Like gorgeous dolls, floating along the streets. I'll take one if I can ever make my fortune."

"Fat chance o' that," another chided him, slapping him on his back.

"We can wish, can't we?" he countered, and they both laughed.

Diana didn't drop the topic. "So this noblewoman thing is widely practiced?" I began to see where she was heading with this. Perhaps, this practice was just what we were supposed to "handle" here.

Edgar laughed. "In every town, hamlet, and city of our world, or so I've heard."

Hearing that, I had doubts this was our purpose. How could we possibly alter the practice if it was everywhere in this world?

80

Soon, we entered the wealthier section of Beckworth. Here the buildings were well maintained, though every color of the rainbow was represented within a city block. Men were well dressed, and every other woman wore one of the fancy ball gowns, which flared out a yard or more around her feet. Wagons kept to once side of the cobblestone street. One carried coal, one carried ore, and one carried a load of timber. Another wagon was loaded with pumpkins, while another had sacks of milled flour. Beckworth appeared thriving. Then we both smelled freshly baked bread and soon walked down Bakers Street, which brought memories of home to us both.

Molly and the six men with their swords kept the seedier side of Beckworth at bay. Pickpockets stayed well clear of us and also avoided the noblewomen, which I found surprising, since they'd be helpless prey.

Edgar noticed me and commented, "It's a death sentence if you harm or rob a noblewoman."

"So why are some of you protesting Count Earl's rule?" I ventured.

"You'll see soon enough. We're heading to the castle walls there," he pointed out. In the distance, I spotted the barbicans along the top of the walls. Colorful. They were bright red, while the walls were a rich blue. Soon, we approached the West Gate, one of the four main entrances to the castle complex proper, which occupied at least the equivalent of twenty city blocks square, positively huge.

As we approached the Cobalt blue walls that rose up some fifteen feet, we all stopped and gasped, especially Diana and me. Skeletons of men lined the walls, five on each side of the gatehouse. Each one was wired together and hung from a red barbican stone high overhead, silent guards to Castle Beckworth.

"Some of the freedom fighters," Edgar whispered, glancing around and looking for the Count's soldiers or guards. "His Mage Dietmar's work. Added a new one since we were last here."

Molly stopped. Since Diana and I were at her side, we did as well. Frankly, I was shocked by the sight.

"That's—that's dad!" she gushed. Edgar and the others stopped and pivoted to look at her.

How could she possibly know this one was her father's skeleton? The ten looked the same to me, bleached white bones. I could see tiny wires holding the many bones together as if the dead were still alive.

Molly sensed the men's disbelief. "Remember? Dad had a bad limp in his right leg. Broke it when a kid. Look at that new one. Right leg bones. See? Break healed all twisted. That's dad all right."

"Damn! You're right," Edgar cursed. "This isn't right—leaving the dead on display like this. Hell, he was a nobleman. We all deserve to be buried nice and proper."

"Why are they hanging there?" I asked.

"Strike fear in the minds of those who would protest against Count Earl's edicts," Edgar spat out.

"But how did they get his bones so clean?" asked Diana. "Didn't you say he went missing only yesterday?"

"That mage of his," Edgar cursed. "He's behind this and plenty more too."

Molly whispered, "Get him down. Bury properly."

"As soon as we do that, Molly, you know as well as we do, the Count will send out all his guards. We'll have to be fast about it," Edgar said, working out a plan as he spoke.

One of his men had a large sack, so I stuck my neck out, "Look, the wire that's holding him up is really thin. I know a spell that can cut it. Catch the bones in your sack, and let's run like hell away from here."

Edgar broke into a broad smile. "Son, I like you already. Tom, get your sack in position. I'll go distract the guards at the gatehouse. You mages do your thing."

"Meet at Jodi's place," Molly suggested. "Family plot nearby."

When Tom had the sack positioned, I focused and cast my spell, Slice. The skeleton dropped like a rock, bones clattering somewhat into the sack. Many hands stuffed those that didn't in there anyway. Just as we finished, one gate guard noticed us and sounded the alarm.

Edgar knocked the man in the back of his head with the pummel of his sword, but other guards responded. Hastily, we dashed down the street, following Molly's lead.

As several other guards came running out of the gate, Diana turned, focused, and barked, "Sleep Guards." Six men slumped to the ground, causing the remaining guards to stumble into them. During the confusion, the sleeping guards awoke, but we gained valuable time, ducking out of sight along a side street.

Molly had a knack for eluding pursuit. A half hour later and many side streets traversed, we stood outside Brooks' Gems, a single story orange adobe building, next to the bright red building, home of Jodi and Lyle, who had taken over the family business, since obviously Jodi wouldn't be able to cut gems, not as a noblewoman. On the other side of the store was her father's place—Molly's childhood home, a bright green adobe home. We ducked into the red building, where we ran into the noblewoman Jodi, Molly's sister.

Jodi and Molly's faces looked very similar, angular chin, high set brows, and wide blue eyes. While neither was a beauty queen as our friends were, neither was unattractive either. Jodi stood several inches taller than Molly, which we later learned was solely due to the tall heels she wore. Jodi's brown hair draped thickly down her back and out onto the flare of her green gown, giving her the appearance of a summer flower that had opened wide. What was striking was that we could see only her shoulders and upper arms; the remainder of them were tied across her upper back, lower arms parallel to the ground. She had a young servant girl who followed her wherever she went.

"Well, isn't this an interesting day. Molly returns," Jodi's barb greeted us, as we dashed inside the green home. "Have you finally come to your senses? Ready to become the noblewoman dad always intended? And who are these people?" She meant Diana and me, for Edgar handed me the sack of bones as we entered. He and his men left to do further scouting.

83

"My sister, Jodi. Her husband Lyle runs dad's business. Jodi, these mages come help us. Diana and Felix. Count Earl and his mage killed dad. Bleached his bones. Hung'em up on the castle walls!" Molly said more than she was used to saying at one time.

"Well, what did he expect would happen?" Jodi retorted. "He just kept hounding Count Earl, so I'm not surprised the Count finally had enough of him. So, are you ready to stop running around acting like some tomboy and take your place as a noblewoman? Lyle's promised to provide you your share of the profits. He has to, you know, since dad's now gone."

Jodi showed no signs of grief or even surprise that her father was dead. Further, the way her arms were bound reminded me of all the Unarmed women back in the Box. She turned her gaze to Diana and me. "My Diana, you are gorgeous. Are you sure you aren't a noblewoman yourself? You certainly should be. Honestly, just say the word and I'll have Anna here get you both properly dressed. It's positively disgraceful to have someone as beautiful as you are go running around in those smelly leather clothes. Maybe you can talk some sense into Molly here. Lord knows, I've tried. Did she tell you she has one ornery streak in her? When dad honored us both and dressed us up as noblewomen when we were ten, Molly here constantly complained and drove mother to her wit's end. Then, when she was thirteen and getting a bath—her arms were free while bathing—biggest mistake ever—she bolted and ran away. You can't imagine the awful scandal and disgrace that brought to mom and dad! It caused mom to die so young."

"Did not!" Molly barked. "Miscarriage. Bled to death. Stop exaggerating. We bury dad. Properly. Beside mom."

"Well, I suppose that's the only right and proper thing to do. I'll have Lyle dig a grave beside mom's in the family plot tonight. Honestly, Molly, when are you going to stop acting like some silly tomboy and become the noblewoman you were born to be?"

"I'll bury him now," Molly barked. "You can watch. At least, you can do that much."

"Don't be sarcastic, Molly. Of course, I can do that. I'll say the prayers too." Looking at us, she added, "Don't let Molly fool you. We noblewomen do many things. I help Lyle keep the company's books, you see, and I maintain our household, keep everything running smoothly. She's just a rebel. Don't let her fool you. We noblewomen are the most important women in the world. Come on. Let's walk to the family plot."

She rose carefully and began moving slowly towards the front door, her servant woman quietly following behind her. Jodi paused before Molly, "Say, have you heard anything about our brother? Sam's missing. He went after dad. I told him not to bother, but you know Sam. Almost as bull-headed as you are, Molly."

"No. I'll find out about Sam. Once dad's buried," Molly stated, forming more words than usual, which I took as a sign that her brother meant something to her.

Not far from their three homes, one entire town block was fenced off, forming a local burial plot for many who lived in this section of the town. Later on, we saw other burial plots located around the town. Diana and I couldn't help but lend a hand, proving to Jodi that we were mages-in-training. We cast our Dig spells, making short work out of what could have been a laborious task. Molly buried him, wires and all. Lacking any casket, she dropped the bag with his bones into the hole we dug. "Rest now, dad," she said softly, holding back tears.

Jodi, on the other hand, launched into a lengthy chant, "We are gathered here today to pay our last respects to our dear father as he joins our mother." She drolled on for five minutes, but mostly I tuned her out. Her voice lacked any real sincerity, any real emotion, quite the opposite of Molly. When she finished, Diana and I again cast our Dig spells, quietly covering up his remains. Only then did I notice a small stone not far from the new hole. "Janice Brooks" was carved on it, presumably their mother, though out of respect for Molly, neither of us mentioned it.

Solemnly, we headed back to the green home, no one saying a word. Once inside, Jodi again insisted Molly come to her senses. "Mages, you're welcome to stay here with us as well. I'll have Anna make up the guest bedrooms for you. I know Lyle will want to thank you for what you've done. It's only right and proper that he does so."

Just then, a loud knocking interrupted Jodi. Before she could order Anna to answer it, Molly rose and opened it. Edgar stood there grim-faced. I didn't need ESP to know he had some bad news to share. "What?" Molly said in her usual terse manner.

"Sam. The Count and Mage Dietmar got to him. Turned him into another pony-man. We heard he's going up for auction in an hour," Edgar explained.

Jodi barked, "What a fool! Now Sam's gone and done it. He never did do anything right, not like dad, who at least got himself killed."

Molly ignored her sister. "We buy him. Lead the way," she declared.

"Wait," Jodi insisted. "Anna, fetch my money pouch. Molly, if you insist on doing this, let me assist with some funds. You know how auctions can go, though I expect only farmers will be bidding for Sam now."

Molly nodded to Jodi, but said nothing, accepting the money pouch from Anna. Quietly, we slipped out of the green adobe home into the streets of Beckworth once more. Again, I felt at home. In the distance, we heard hammer upon anvil. The air was filled with odors of baking bread, of drying meats, and of horses. We'd just begun walking when we had to pull aside. A dozen horses came galloping past us, the Count's soldiers. They were returning and had a young man tied up on one of the horses. His face was set, but he had a scar over his forehead. I recognized a fighter at once.

"Damn! They caught one of the freedom fighters, Scar Face," Edgar explained. "Ill day indeed. What's the world coming to?"

With the commotion gone, I asked, "What's

happened to Sam? What's a pony-man?" I really wanted to know what was going on. I wasn't prepared for this perversion.

Edgar cursed and then said, "Mage Dietmar's contribution to Count Earl's justice. He cuts out their tongues, blinds them, and removes their arms. They wear only an open loincloth and defecate where they stand as a pony would. A leather harness is attached to their bodies, and they spend the rest of their lives being human ponies or oxen, pulling buggies or plows."

One of his men added, "Farmers like the pony-men, because they're cheaper than buying plow horses or buggy ponies. Many noblewomen buy the pony-men to pull them around town in their buggies, because it's a whole lot faster than they can walk. Sam's in a real mess now. Jodi's right. He would be better off dead, just as his father is."

"Why? Why is the Count doing this?" I asked, shocked a man could do such things to fellow men.

"Puts the fear of the Count in us all. Hell, son," Edgar declared, "hardly anyone now speaks out against the Count. If we do, we end up like Henry, a specter on the castle walls, or a pony-man like his son, Sam. Ain't nothing worse. Jodi's right. Sam would be far better off dead than a pony-man. Look, there's one now."

Diana and I turned to see a small, black buggy big enough to hold the noblewoman and her servant woman. Where the horse should have been, we saw an armless man, naked except for a flopping brown loincloth and a brown leather harness strapped around his torso. Empty eye sockets gave him a strange appearance. His feet were encased in some kind of boot that looked like a horse's hoof! Further, as he neared us, we could hear the clip-clop of iron horseshoes upon the orange cobblestones. Such must have been nailed to the bottom of the strange boots. They were sealed around his feet and rose part way up his calves. We could see no way they could be removed. A horse's bridle was attached to his head with an iron bit in the man's mouth. The noblewoman's servant held the reins, directing the pony-man, who obviously couldn't see where he was going.

"Good lord!" Diana exclaimed, as we halted to watch them pass by.

Edgar cursed again and added, "Buyer's biggest challenge is preventing the pony-men from killing themselves. They pretty much handled that one by blinding them."

Ten minutes later, we entered a town block that was mostly open. A stage rose prominently in the center. Here, the pony-men and others would be marched, put on display, and then auctioned off. We spotted signs announcing another sale today, and already a number of men and a few noblewomen had gathered. We joined them. I began to suspect we needed to "handle" the making of these pony-men.

We didn't have long to wait. Within a half hour, some fifty men and a few noblewomen with their servants gathered around the central platform, whose base rose six feet above eye level, allowing everyone an excellent view of the merchandise. A well-dressed man in a black outfit climbed up the stairs from the rear and stood prominently before the crowd.

"Noblewomen, men, welcome to the Count's Pony-man Auction. We have six fine, virile specimens for you today, but I'm told tomorrow we'll hold a very special auction at noon. None other than the famous rebel Scar Face will be auctioned off! Yes, Count Earl's men captured him today. So expect a very exciting auction tomorrow." He paused to allow the crowd to cheer this unexpected news.

"All right. Here we have our first pony-man for today." A young man held the reins of the terrified young man, who couldn't even see the steps he had to climb. I heard the lad whispering directions to the pony-man. My heart went out to the victim. If nothing else, I swore I'd put an end to this butchery of men. The man wasn't Sam, and I listened to the bidding. One noblewoman began the bidding at the minimum asking price, some ten gold. Several farmers soon out bid them, and I sensed the noblewomen were after a bargain-priced pony-man.

Molly's brother was the last to be auctioned off. She gasped when she saw him. Terror dripped off Sam like water, his face twisted and contorted in absolute fear. His empty eye sockets told all, but like all these pony-men, his tongue was cut off so he couldn't speak, and his arms had been removed at his shoulders. He wore the typical leather harness and had a bridle fastened to his head. The young boy led him to center stage and then marched him around for the buyers to see. He wore the same strange boots with real horseshoes nailed to the round soles. From his stomping, they must be heavy too.

Diana sensed the swelling emotions within Molly and nudged me. I glanced at her, and she nodded towards Molly. I took her hint. "Twenty-five," I began the bidding for Molly, who looked up at me, mouthing a "thank you." When I later bid thirty, the other noblewomen bowed out and many left, making their slow glide down the streets. I bought Sam for thirty-three gold.

"For another twenty gold," the auctioneer said to me as I began counting out the unfamiliar coins, "I'll throw in a buggy, suitable for any noblewoman and her servant. Obviously, sir, you aren't a farmer."

"Oh, is it that obvious?" I teased the pleasant man. I glanced at Molly and agreed, "But could someone show us how to harness the pony-man to the buggy? Is it done the same way we would a horse?"

It was, but we allowed the young lad to show us. He added, "Remember, the pony-man can't see or speak, so you have to give him good directions."

I tipped the lad a silver coin. "Thanks for being so kind to them." He smiled and ran off. With Sam hooked to the buggy, Molly took the reins and walked beside him, as we headed away from the auction center.

"Sam, it's me. Molly. Jodi and I bought you. I'll convince Jodi to keep you with her. It's the best we can do for you now." He made strange noises, but without a tongue and with the bit in his mouth, he wasn't remotely understandable. I doubt if he'd ever be understandable again.

I could see Edgar's wisdom; he'd be better off dead than living a life like this. I began to see what Count Earl was doing with these pony-men. Put the fear of such into the minds of ordinary men and no one would dare cross him or his orders!

Sensing my frustrations, Edgar said, "Last head count put the number of these pony-men in and around Beckworth at one thousand sixty-six, but there's likely been many more added since last month's totals were posted. Scar Face was the last of the major rebel players. I think it's time to head for the Rainbow Hills. Maybe Molly will come with us now."

Later, we pulled up beside the green adobe home of Jodi. Molly brought Jodi out to see their brother, returning Jodi's money pouch to Anna. Gliding out of her home, Jodi saw her brother. For an instant, her face showed surprise, but then she said, "Well big brother, you've certainly gone and done it now. I do hope you appreciate what I've done for you. I had Molly buy you at the auction. You'll be my buggy pony-man from now on. I'll speak to Lyle when he comes home. I think we can fix you up a stable with the horses out back, but we'll see. Since you can't see or speak and are completely helpless, you'll just have to do as I ask from now on. Anna will see you have food, though I'm not sure how you can even eat, but I'm sure we'll find out. Agatha has a pony-man to pull her buggy around town. I'll ask her how she keeps him. Meanwhile, Molly will lead you to the hitching rail and tie you up there. After supper, I'll have you take me to visit Agatha so we can find out how to keep you, Sam. Oh yes, dad's dead. Molly and I buried him properly."

Late afternoon, Lyle joined us. He was a tall, thin man with a nervous twitch in his left hand. However, whenever he was working on a gemstone, the twitch vanished. "Well," he said after Jodi explained all that had happened, "I suppose you can keep Sam as your buggy pony-man. You do need to have steady transport, dearest, but let's do keep him in the stables with the other horses.

We can't have him inside our home. Not practical at all. He now belongs in the stables. After all, he brought all this on himself. He should have been content to cut gems like the rest of us."

He went on, "Mages, thank you for being of such great assistance to my Jodi today. Please, stay with us for supper. I'm sure Anna already has the guest rooms prepared. I'd be affronted if you didn't stay the night with us. Molly too. This has to have been an awful day for you too, just as it has for my dearest Jodi here."

While I didn't like his covert voice, Molly did need us, and we agreed to stay the night. I sent a Message to Lexi, outlining briefly what we'd seen and learned today.

# Chapter 9—Treachery

I know. I should have been more careful. I shouldn't have trusted the covert Jodi and Lyle, but that's hindsight. We were polite, and felt we needed to support Molly, who had to face the loss of her father and brother this day. Anna gracefully fed Jodi, who chatted constantly throughout dinner, though most of her barbs were directed towards Molly, trying to convince her to become a noblewoman as she was supposed to have become ages ago.

When supper finished, Jodi and Anna departed, taking a buggy ride to her friend Agatha's home, putting Sam to work for the first time pulling them. Neither Molly nor we cared to watch that spectacle and chose instead to turn in early. Besides, all that food and drink had made me sleepy. Looking back on it now, I should have known we'd been drugged. Thus, we again made a bad error in judgment, one that would cost us dearly.

\*\*\*

"You've done well, Jodi, Lyle," Count Earl declared, handing him a heavy pouch of coins. "Our world would be so peaceful if everyone did their civic duties. Don't worry. I'll have Molly back with you as the perfect noblewoman tomorrow."

He was quite pudgy, though no one dared call him fat. Neither handsome nor ugly, he was average except in temperament. His mind, ruthless. His command over his lands, absolute. Much had come about after he'd accepted Mage Dietmar into his fold. Now that had worked out perfectly for both men.

Countess Kayleigh, four years younger than the Count, sat on her throne looking every inch a proper Countess. She added, "Only this time, instruct your servants never to untie her arms when they bathe her. We don't want her running off again. Dereliction of duties, I always say. We noblewomen have quite the image to uphold. I'm sure Jodi will see to it that Molly is quickly re-

92

educated, though it's much easier on a woman to be trained when she's ten than when she's an adult. Still, Molly's brought all this on her own head. I'm just so pleased we can finally turn her into a proper noblewoman. Might I ask how her brother is working out in his new supporting role as your buggy pony-man?" Her voice was cold, but her eyes were stern and inquisitive.

Jodi answered, "Excellent, Your Majesty. I took him for a drive to visit a friend of mine earlier this evening. Just perfect."

"Excellent, excellent, Jodi," Countess Kayleigh replied. "I'm so glad. I always say to Earl here, why don't we make them into useful pony-men instead of killing them? Men should be useful, especially those rebels who've cause Earl so much trouble. Don't you think so?" She looked straight at Lyle.

"Of course, Your Majesty," he replied politely. "Besides, their upkeep isn't any more costly than a horse, perhaps even cheaper. They require so little now."

"Indeed," she declared. "See Earl. You should instruct Mage Dietmar to make more pony-men and far fewer skeletons to hang on the walls."

Count Earl chuckled. "Yes dear. Yes. Now then, Lyle, you best head home. By now, my men will have removed the unconscious trio from your home. They'll be returned to you as proper noblewomen and pony-man tomorrow."

"Thank you, Count. While I could have perhaps handled the recalcitrant Molly, once she was drugged, I cringe at dealing with actual mages. I leave that to your mage," Lyle declared, bowing before backing up, while Jodi gracefully twirled around and began her slow, flowing walk out of the throne room. Once they exited the Manor House and headed down the main street to the gatehouse, they spotted a wagon rolling into the castle. Beneath blankets, Molly, Diana, and I lay in a drugged stupor.

"Carry them down to Mage Dietmar," Count Earl ordered, after lifting the blanket and looking briefly at the trio, convinced these two mages were the ones who had cut down Henry Brooks' skeleton from the castle wall earlier today. He followed his men as they carried the three bodies down into what had once been the dungeons, but now was the home and laboratory of Mage Dietmar.

"Ah more work, eh Count?" the cold, inhuman voice of Mage Dietmar greeted the small group descending the stairs to his chambers.

"Yes, my good mage. Molly here is simply to be turned into a noblewoman. Just have your assistants properly dress her. Now these two are the mages that stole your skeleton from the castle walls earlier today. Careful, they are mages, I'm told," Count Earl explained, handing Mage Dietmar a bag of gems.

"What do you want done with them?" Dietmar asked.

"Turn her into a proper noblewoman too, but without any chance she could use her magic skills against us. Him, do as you see fit," Count Earl replied. "I'll send someone to walk them back to the Brooks' place tomorrow morning." With that, he put all further thoughts of the two mages and the recalcitrant Molly out of his mind. Problems handled.

"Missa," the mage barked. His servant woman scampered to his side. "This one here, Molly, get her dressed as a proper noblewoman. I'll work on the other two shortly." He picked up Molly and carried her into the next chamber, laying her body down on a worktable for Missa, and then returned to the two mages.

Missa stripped Molly, depositing her clothes and few personal possessions in a side room, where she'd piled countless others' possessions. With a naked Molly, she then set to work dressing her properly. As she worked, she heard the mage muttering to himself in the next room, as he often did. He's a strange one, she thought.

"Now then, best be careful. Known mages. Best check for magic spells on them and magical protections. I hate surprises." Minutes later, he muttered, "Well, these can't be powerful mages. She doesn't have any magical possessions at all, but he's a different story. He's radiating magic. I best dispel whatever he's got on him." He focused and began casting his spells to dispel magic. After casting it five times, Mage Dietmar was finally convinced he'd undone all the man's protections.

"What have we here? A woman masquerading as a man?" Hastily, the mage stripped me of my clothes. "Well, now this is incredibly interesting! He's a man but looks like a woman. I've never seen a human quite like this before! Best check further." Some ten minutes later, he was satisfied there wasn't anything else going on with the human specimen. He chuckled. "I know what I'll do for you. Just the thing you must hate totally." Again, he chuckled and set to work, carrying Diana's body into his workroom.

He laid her on a narrow table and cast Paralyze on her drugged body, a Grade 4 spell. Next, he brought in his satchel of healing potions. Finally, he brought in his two vats in which he'd collected the caustic slime from his breath weapon. Dietmar was a Green dragon, whose breath weapon was almost as bad as a Black dragon's acid. His slime ate through human flesh in just a few minutes. He'd carefully collected vats of it and now put it to good use.

First, he had Missa come and strip Diana. Together, they tied her arms out to either side. After putting a pair of pans on the floor on either side of her shoulders, Dietmar began his work. Using a paintbrush, he began spreading his slime around her upper shoulders. Instantly, Diana was awakened from her drugged sleep!

Pain shot through her shoulders, but she couldn't move a muscle! She stared up into the eyes of Mage Dietmar. Recognition came instantly. Green dragon.

"Ah, eyes open at last. Yes, I'm removing your arms, mage. I can't have you getting free of the noblewoman's outfit and casting spells again. I'm afraid your casting days are over now. It's much like roasting a pig, I'm told. I simply baste around and around your arm like so and my slime eats right through your flesh down to the bone. Only takes a minute or so. Now for the hard part, severing the connection to your shoulder socket."

He gave a sharp pull, which was followed by a strange popping-like sound. The pain crescendoed, but with the popping sound, most of the pain simply vanished. From the corner of her right eye, she saw what remained of her arm dangling from a rawhide cord. Pop. Shooting pain and then relief. Her left arm vanished from its socket.

"Now then, don't move. I'll cancel the Paralyzation spell so you can drink these healing potions. If you don't drink it, the slime will dissolve more of your shoulders. If you try anything, I'll remove your tongue as I do with the pony-men." He canceled his spell and poured a healing potion into her mouth. Diana gulped it down frantically, before letting out a blood-curling scream.

"Excellent lungs. Now then, you'll be weak for a time, so I'll carry you into the other room where my assistant will get you properly dressed. Meanwhile, sleep will do wonders for you. Sleep," he barked, and Diana fell asleep instantly. He knew she'd likely waken as Missa struggled to get her dolled up in a proper noblewoman's outfit, but he planned to Sleep her again, once Missa had finished her.

He returned and carried my body into his workroom, laying my naked form on the same bench Diana had been on minutes before. Next, he dropped her arms into a vat of his slime and cleaned up the area slightly, before casting Paralyze on me. I awoke to incredible pain shooting through my right upper arm at the shoulder. I watched helplessly as the Green dragon worked on me just as he'd done with Diana minutes before. He explained as he worked, just as he'd done with Diana.

As he slipped my remaining arm out of its socket replete with massive pain, he said, "Well, now you can't cast spells any longer. I'm turning you into a noblewoman like the other two. Now you won't be able to appear as a man any longer." He laughed snidely, before canceling the Paralyzation spell and pouring the healing potion into my mouth.

I noticed it took four potions to heal the shoulders fully. Turning my head, I could see the pinkish skin covering the empty sockets. At least that horrid pain was gone, and I still had my eyes and tongue. I wasn't about to show him Diana and I could still cast spells, for he'd surely remove both of them if he knew we could. Like most people, he believed armless people were completely helpless, unable to do anything for themselves. Well, for these noblewomen, that would be mostly true, as we'd seen during the day.

He carried me into another dungeon room, where I saw Diana lying on a bed sound asleep. She now wore a nice green gown, quite similar to all the other noblewomen we'd seen today. It flared out some five feet around her. I could see her arms were gone too, but Molly's arms were still there. I said a small thank you prayer for that. While Diana and I could find a way to manage with our spells, Molly would be devastated if she lost her arms, though until we could find someone to get her out of the outfit, her arms were useless.

"This is Missa. She'll get you properly dressed as a noblewoman. Then, I'll help you get some much needed sleep," the dragon explained and hastily left the room.

I was too weak to protest any and let Missa do what she needed to do. The corset wasn't bad, merely designed to hold arms motionless behind one's back, lower arms horizontal. I didn't have any, but the corset also held up our warm stockings. I lost count of the petticoats she put on me. Soon, I too wore a fancy, billowing green ball gown. However, what bothered me most were the boots. They had tall wedge heels on them and reached halfway up my calves.

Once she laced them tightly, there wasn't any way for me to undo them. I noticed two rings on the inside of the ankles. She then fastened a corded rope between them, allowing me just enough freedom of motion to put one foot directly in front of the other. We hadn't seen this aspect today. No wonder they moved so slowly. They could only take minuscule steps. I groaned, but just then, the dragon appeared. Even though I knew he was casting Sleep on me, I didn't bother resisting. I was too exhausted to care. My last thought before drifting into slumber-land was that Jodi and Lyle must have turned us in to the Count.

While we slept, Mage Dietmar must have carried us up out of the dungeon. When we woke up, we found ourselves lying on top of couches. The smells of breakfast roused us, as Missa sat a large tray on the table. I concluded we were in one of the Countess's waiting rooms.

"Ah morning, noblewomen," Missa said politely. "I've a nourishing breakfast for you. Mage Dietmar says you need to eat well to regain your strength. After you eat, someone will walk with you back to your homes. Please sit up now."

Oh how I wanted to yell out, "How? We've no arms!" But I knew better. This world was filled with noblewomen who obviously could sit up and were just as helpless as we were, only I also knew we'd not get any relief if we could somehow get out of these gowns and boots. Instead, I lunged my way up, and then wiggled to sit on the edge of the couch.

"Oh no!" Molly cried out, finally realizing what had happened to her. She looked at us, noticed our empty shoulders, and cursed wildly. "I'll murder my sister for this!"

I knew I had to calm her down, but I saw it took everything Diana had to keep herself from breaking down.

"She and Lyle probably had little choice, Molly. After all, the Count had your dad killed and brother turned into a pony-man. Blame the Count and that Green dragon of his, who is masquerading as a mage. They are the guilty ones. Their days are numbered now!"

"I'll slit his throat just as soon as I get my arms free," Molly declared passionately, wiggling and struggling futilely against the bondage. From what little I'd seen, there wasn't any way for the strongest of men to bust their way out of this constraint. She'd have to have a servant or helper undo her arms, and I knew that wasn't going to happen anytime soon, not if Jodi had any say in it.

As we sat there, Missa fed us. I have to say she handled us perfectly. While one was chewing, she put another bite into the next one's mouth. We ate seamlessly, which I rather marveled over. When we'd finished, the Countess Kayleigh entered, dismissing Missa.

"Well, Molly Brooks, it seems you finally look like a proper noblewoman. You're to stay with your sister, Jodi, for the time being. Your two ex-mages too. I've left instructions for your new assistants to push all three of you hard, so you can quickly become models of noblewomen. Now off you go. James will escort you home, though as you know, it's a high crime to bother a noblewoman on the street. Still, Earl promised your sister an armed escort home, so James will do so. Just don't ask him for any assistance. In addition, Count Earl has declared today to be a holiday. The rogue Scar Face is going to be auctioned off as the newest pony-man. Now that promises to be a fine sale indeed. I wonder how high the bidding will go for him. The auction is at ten, if you're interested in watching. Now off you go. James will be waiting for you at the door."

She turned around and gracefully glided out of the door. I attempted to stand up and darn near fell over, flailing my non-existent arms wildly to keep my balance. Molly fared little better.

She cursed, "Damn it! Now I remember how awful this is. Our boots are tied together. Can only take tiny steps. Suppose to be gliding along. God, I hated this when I was ten and I hate it now!" I knew she must feel strongly about this because she'd again used a long sentence. "Take small steps. I'll lead. Getting up's a bitch if you fall. Maybe I'll kill my sister too!" she barked.

This time, I said nothing. It took all my concentration to keep upright and actually move forward a little. "God, we'll never make it all the way to Jodi's place," Diana wailed, after finally making the doorway out of this waiting room! I echoed her sentiments.

Actually, it took us until ten to reach the auction square, about halfway between the castle and Jodi's place. A large crowd had gathered today. Whoever this Scar Face fighter was, he was evidently very famous. As before, a half dozen newly created pony-men were being auctioned off. I had a hunch they'd do him last, and I was right. By now, my feet were throbbing. Two hours of taking tiny steps had done me in. Molly and Diana could barely stand up, and we had no choice but to take a long break and watch the festivities.

I thought about casting a Message spell to the Hagans, but they were off feeding, a necessary action since the Box couldn't produce enough human food to feed a dragon. Time enough for the dragons later, once we were stabilized or accustomed to our situation. I could Message Lexi, Tiffany, and the others, but they'd be exposed to harm unless they could somehow be dressed up as we were. In that case, they'd be nearly helpless too. *No, grin and bear it. Get to Jodi's place for now.* If nothing else, we would be far closer to the slums where the Box was located.

"Well, isn't this a pleasant surprise!" Jodi's voice broke in on my reverie. She and Lyle, along with hundreds of others, had come to watch this auction. "Molly, you do look so good now. You'll have men fawning over you. And your mages. Wow! You look fabulous, don't they, Lyle dear." He nodded appreciatively.

She continued, "I had no idea Felix was a woman. Both you and Diana make Molly and me look like ugly ducklings, right Lyle dear?" He nodded again.

"Please sister. We have to sit down!" Molly begged. "Our feet are killing us. We've been walking for two hours."

"Well, that comes from neglecting being a noblewoman for the last umpteenth years, Molly. Still, we brought the carriage," Jodi explained. "We came prepared to buy you your own pony-man and buggy, Molly, so you can get around town more easily. Lyle dear, we probably should get Felix and Diana each a pony-man and buggy too. After all, they'll not be able to cast any more spells. Dears, you can stay in our guest rooms, can't they Lyle?" She didn't wait for his response, but we heard him bidding on the next pony-man.

Jodi rattled on, "Once you get used to being a noblewoman, I'm sure you both will have many suitors. With your stellar looks, why, you're sure to attract the best of men, and that'll fully compensate you for your lack of being mages. Besides, women shouldn't be mages anyway. Our place is running our homes and raising our children. We've already hired a servant girl for you, Molly. We'll hire two more for you, Diana, Felix. Meanwhile, Anna and Clara can handled all four of us, at least for today. Oh, I do so hope Lyle can get us three new pony-men and buggies. The buggies aren't that expensive, and they are so darn convenient. I don't know why I never bothered to get one until now. Silly me."

Molly's ire rose the more her sister chatted. At last, she could take it no longer and burst out, "Jodi, how could you drug us and turn us in to the Count?"

Instantly, Jodi's face became deadly serious. She lowered her voice to a whisper. "We had to do that! After dad's actions got him killed and Sam's got him turned into a pony-man, we had little choice but to show him our loyalty. Now not another word. You know as well as I do that you have to be a noblewoman. It's wonderful the Count spared your friends and is allowing them to become gorgeous noblewomen too. Be thankful for what you have, Molly. If it wasn't for us, you too might be a pony-man or pony-woman. I wonder if they have pony-women. Lyle dear, do they?"

"Do they what?" he asked. "We've a pony-man for Molly now. We'll pick up a buggy when we pay for him."

"Have pony-women?"

"I don't think so. I've never heard of anything like that. Pony-men are able to work hard and more than earn their keep. Jenkins, who farms the forty just east of town, swears by his herd of pony-men. I'm not sure what a pony-woman would be able to do to earn her keep, my love."

"Quite true. Women haven't the strength you men do. Oh how exciting. Look, here comes Scar Face himself!" Jodi declared, though she need not have. His stumbling arrival on stage was accompanied by a fanfare.

The auctioneer's voice rose. "And now we have the country's most notorious criminal ever, Scar Face, who is ready to work hard for you as your pony-man. Don't worry. Without arms, a tongue, and eyes, his fighting days are over. He'll be as docile as a puppy, but like all new pony-men, right now he's in a bit of a shock. The bidding will start at a hundred for this legendary pony-man."

Again, I could sense the waves of terror radiating from the man being led in circles around the platform, unsure where he was putting a foot. I felt a wave of pity for him. No one should ever be subjected to this kind of humiliation and unending torture. I swore I'd put an end to this whole pony-man aberration or die trying, though at the moment, the how eluded me completely. I was almost as helpless as Scar Face was.

I was as amazed as everyone else was when Scar Face sold for one thousand six hundred gold, a heady price indeed. Someone just make a gargantuan profit, Count Earl I suspected.

As the crowd broke up, Lyle returned with Molly's new pony-man hooked up to her new buggy. Lyle explained, "Molly, you can drive your pony-man using vocal commands. Turn left, right, stop, go, and so on. If your servant comes along, she can drive him using the reins. No noblewoman would ever dare stoop to such a low level as controlling the pony-man with reins like a common servant girl. He should be able to pull you and another. So why don't you take Felix with you and drive your new pony-man home?"

"What's his name, Lyle?" Molly asked.

"No one knows. Just call him pony. I've already explained to him that if he obeys and does a good job pulling you, he'll want for nothing. Good food, warm stable, that sort of thing."

Molly saw she had little choice. Lyle was insisting she do this. We both moved slowly to the buggy. Then, I saw our first problem. Hobbled as we were, neither of us could get up the one step into the buggy. Lyle anticipated this and quickly came over, lifting Molly up and then me.

The reins were tied to the rail in front of us. Just as well, since neither of us could use them now. After Lyle lifted Jodi into their carriage, he did the same with Diana. Molly whispered, "We'll try to follow them. Okay Pony. Start going forward."

The poor man leaned into the ground, his iron hooves slipping on the cobblestones, but at the last instant, the buggy began moving. Molly found driving the buggy using voice commands a harrowing experience, but that was nothing compared to the fear radiating from Pony. Again, I swore to put an end to this kind of brutality and soon!

Once back at their green home, Lyle stabled the new pony-man next to Jodi's. Then, he lifted Molly and me into their carriage. "Since today is a holiday and since your new friends are going to be staying with us, Molly, Jodi and I thought that we'd take then for a ride around Beckworth and the countryside. It's rather pretty."

As we rode along, I noticed the houses continued in the rainbow colors we'd seen: red, orange, brown, yellow, green, blue, and black. When we reached the eastern edge of the city and slipped out of the city's limits, Lyle pulled over at Scenic Overlook, or so the sign read.

"Oh my goodness!" Diana exclaimed.

"Wow, incredible!" I added my enthusiasm to the mix. Rolling hills lay before us, but each soil layer was a different color, with every color in a rainbow present— breathtaking. I'd never seen anything like this before. Now, I understood why the homes were so colorful. One merely collected dirt of the color you desired and made them into adobe bricks.

Lyle proudly explained, "Rainbow's End. That's what this land is called. Out there due east, that way, some two hundred miles is our capital city of Imperial. There are all kinds of mines out there, to say nothing of farms." We gazed for some time. The rest of Lyle's tour paled compared to this majestic view.

As he continued our tour, I sensed how badly my sister wanted to scream, to attempt to cast a Morph Self spell, to do anything to get out of our awful situation. Honestly, I did too, but we wisely dared not try anything just yet. Neither she nor I had bargained for becoming mutilated in order to learn magic spells. A glance at her face told me she was doing the same thing I was doing: suppressing the whole experience, but I knew we couldn't do this for long.

We arrived back at their home near suppertime, where we were introduced to Molly's new servant girl, Clara, barely fourteen. Evidently, Clara had some experience dealing with noblewomen, because she knew what to do. Before long, we were seated for supper. Clara sat between Diana and me, while Anna sat between the two sisters. I felt silly having to be fed like this, but I had no real choice at the moment.

After a delicious supper, Lyle said, "Okay. So that we don't overwork our two servants, let's get the women ready for bed and into bed now. It does take some time. Molly, to make it easier for Anna and Clara to manage, we're putting you three up in the same room for tonight. Anna, let me know when Jodi is ready for me."

With that, he rose and left the room. Precariously, we rose and followed the servant girls. They put us up in the guest room that Molly had slept in last night. However, the wide beds had been moved elsewhere, replaced by very narrow beds, piled with pillows. Three of them lined one wall.

Molly flushed. "Do me first." When Anna and Clara began to undress her, she explained further. "This is going to be strange for you, I think. I forgot about one nasty detail: how they make us sleep. We're supposed to be demonstrating we're ready for sex with our husbands at any time. You'll see what I mean. This is the part I hated the most! God, I never thought I'd ever be stuck like this again."

I had no idea what she was talking about, but if Molly hated it, I presumed Diana and I would detest it too. They stripped Molly, leaving only her corset. Now we could see how they bound her arms. Both were horizontal across

104

her back, held immobile, and tied to the corset as well. All she could do was slightly wiggle her fingers, nothing more. As they helped her use a chamber pot, I looked away, feeling embarrassed once more. That done, they had her sit down on the bottom edge of the very narrow bed. Heck, the bed was barely three feet wide, if that. They leaned her back and onto pillows.

What came next shocked us. Each girl took one of Molly's legs and pulled it up and back, tucking it behind Molly's head, crossing her ankles there. Quickly, Anna slipped a cloth band around Molly's ankles, tying her ankles together securely. Without panties on, her privates were incredibly pronounced. Now I understood the open invite for sex with her husband. Molly too was embarrassed. "It hurts some, but in time you'll get used to it. Anna, they might not be flexible enough to get their legs behind their heads."

Anna smiled, "Don't fret. We know." Next, they prepared Diana for bed. Anna and Clara gasped at her empty arm sockets and ogled over her large bosom. Again, all they left on her body was the corset, which actually now served no purpose for us, though it held up our warm hose during the day. I think the two girls expected Diana not to be as limber as Molly was. After positioning her on the bed properly, they each took one leg and began raising it up and back, ultimately intending to cross them at her ankles and tucked behind her head as they had Molly. However, Diana wasn't so limber, and she cried out when they had her legs about a foot from the back of her head. At this point, they tied a cloth rope to each ankle and secured the other end to the front two head posts of the bed, forcing her legs to be stretched as much as possible.

Anna praised her, "There you go, Diana. You're nearly there. I think in a few days you'll be able to assume the proper bedtime position that all noblewomen do. We hear husbands swear sex is so much better this way. At least that's what we have been told." They then arranged her knee length brown hair across her front.

Both girls now came over to do me. My face

crimsoned, but I could do nothing about it, unless I chose to violate our guest status and cast spells on these young girls. I was loathed to do that and chose to endure the humiliation. "Oh my! Look, she's a he!" declared Anna.

"Maybe not," Clara added. "Her breasts are to die for and her hair is just fabulous." I decided to keep my mouth shut. Within a few minutes, they had me lying back on the narrow bed. Now I saw why it was so narrow. Bound up as Molly was, she couldn't move. No need for a wider bed at all. My flexibility left everything to be desired. They tied my ankles to the front posts, but they were a very long way from being crossed behind my head. After draping my long hair over my front, the two girls left.

As she departed, Anna said, "Lyle will inspect you shortly to make sure we've done our job properly. Diana, Felix, he did say he was ordered to get all three of you properly trained as noblewomen as soon as possible. So he'll probably come by and tighten up the ropes during the night until they are crossed at the ankles and behind your heads all proper like."

Okay, I moaned and groaned.

"I told you I hated this part the most," Molly whispered. "We can't move at all. I spent three years like this before I was able to escape. Damn. There isn't likely going to be any way to escape now. They'll probably never untie my arms, and you two don't even have them anymore. I'm so terribly sorry I've brought such an awful misfortune to you, when all you wanted to do was help me. I'm sorry, Diana, Felix. I really am."

Molly had just said more than she usually did at one time, and I knew this was affecting her too. "It's okay, Molly. We'll get out of this. Contrary to Mage Dietmar, we don't need our arms to cast our spells. It's their fault, not yours. Even your sister and Lyle aren't to blame. If they hadn't drugged us as the Count ordered, they'd be dead or worse by now, so it's not your fault in the slightest. God, my legs are aching."

Molly giggled. "You'll eventually get numb and used to it. We were always told that sex was supposed to be very good, but I escaped long before I could find out. Even if it was, that doesn't make up for being trussed up like this all night."

As uncomfortable as we were, we tried to doze. Perhaps an hour passed before Lyle entered the room, holding a dim lantern. "My god, you're a man, Felix. I thought they were crazy when they said you were. Well, still, I've got orders to get you three rapidly up to noblewoman standards or the Count will turn me into a pony-man too."

"Ouch!" I cried out as he tightened the ropes on my legs, drawing them up closer to my head. A bit later, Diana cried out too.

"Diana. Hang in there. I think I'll be able to get yours properly positioned in an hour or so."

"Well, let me make some inquiries tomorrow. Certainly, you three have to remain properly bound. It would be the greatest sacrilege ever to sleep unbound as normal peasant folks do. You'd dishonor everyone if you did that. Honestly, you two outsiders can't imagine the disgrace Molly has brought on the Brooks family these past ten years. Jodi has had to bear it, as has had her brother and father. Look. In our world, there's no higher honor or position for a woman than that of a noblewoman. We hold them in the highest regard." He repeated himself, "So you have no idea how much dishonor the Brooks family has had to endure these past ten years that Molly's been gallivanting around."

He turned to Molly. "Every time someone saw you, they'd report it to Jodi, Sam, or Henry, embarrassing them yet again. I'm very pleased that has come to an end, that you're now sleeping properly too. As soon as you regain control of your walking, I'll see they untie your legs. Now you can bring honor back to what's left of the Brooks." He turned and left.

Just as I was about to fall asleep, he returned, tightening the ropes again, until I nearly screamed. Hours later, he came by again, but this time, he was successful. My legs had gone numb, and he was able to tie them behind my head. I felt miserable and asked Diana to cast her Sleep spell on me, which she did, thankfully.

Pain! The next morning after the girls untied our legs, I couldn't move them from behind my head. When Anna and Clara each took a leg and did so, pain shot through my legs and up my spine. Diana fared not much better than I did. Even Molly cried out when her legs were straightened out again.

"Don't worry. In a few weeks, be no pain," Molly felt obligated to explain to us. "I was ten, when they bound me. Got used to it in a few weeks. We three got into nighttime position. So Lyle not in trouble with the Count."

The girls were efficient. After helping us to the chamber pot, they quickly got each of us dressed. However, I could barely stand. My legs almost refused to work. Anna suspected as much and kept an arm around me as she ushered me into the dining room. She and Carla kept an arm around Diana and Molly too, so I didn't feel so bad after that.

While we were eating—being fed is more like it—Lyle explained, "Molly, since your dad's passing, you're now entitled to a share in the profits from his company. Jodi does help me out some, but honestly, there's very little a noblewoman can do to help the company. So just so you know, I'll be giving you your share once each month. Jodi assures me it will be enough for you to live nicely on as befitting an unmarried noblewoman."

"Thanks," Molly forced herself to say. I knew that being very dependent was the last thing she wanted. However, she would need the financial support.

Once fed, Lyle headed off to work, while Jodi began making plans for us all to visit her dressmakers. "You can't keep wearing the same dress every day. Meanwhile, you three simply must practice your walking. Lyle told me he got you all into the proper nighttime position, so that's fabulous. Now you simply must learn to walk without having to be hobbled. While I'm helping Lyle with the week's receipts, you three go for a long walk around town. Be back around lunchtime. We'll see about dresses this afternoon. Plus, Lyle will let us know when there are more pony-men available so you two can have your own buggy transport. Now get going, Molly."

Carefully, we three rose, got our balance, and headed out of the door, held open by Anna. Once on the street, Molly again apologized, "Sorry about this. I'll make it up to you. She's right. If you don't learn to walk, the Count will harm you more. Come on. Let's walk. Easy does it. Don't fall down. Can't get up without help."

"Say, can you lead us back to our Box? The place where we first met you?" I asked. "We have some friends there who might be able to help us."

"Sure. It's a long walk. Go slowly."

"Is there any other way?" I couldn't help teasing her. I wanted to scream, to release all my suppressed grief, shock, and terror, but dared not yet.

She flushed. "No. Sorry. I get free. I get knife. I fight back."

Diana sighed and spoke up, "Well, I'm sure going to kill that Green dragon mage of his!"

"Huh?" Molly asked, turning her head slightly, while trying not to tumble.

"His mage. Mage Dietmar. Didn't you know? It's not human. It's a Green dragon, probably got here from the Brackenmoor Swamp, if what Drago tells us is true, namely that Greens love swamps."

"No way! You're kidding. Right? The Count has a Green dragon working for him?" Molly asked almost stumbling. Only wild wobbling allowed her to keep her balance.

"Yes. His skin has a greenish tint to it. His eyes—inhuman black orbs—dead giveaway," Diana explained.

"Well, damn! Now things make more sense. No wonder no one could get to the Count. Scar Face was resistance leader. For years, they've been trying to make the Count accountable. Explains so much," Molly exclaimed. "Well, now we're doomed, aren't we?"

"I suppose so until we kill that dragon," I interrupted the two. "This is pathetically slow walking.

Vic Broquard

We've only gone a couple of blocks and my feet are killing me already."

Molly giggled. "You'll toughen up. When I was ten, I spent a month getting used to walking. Lyle's under pressure to make us adapt fast. We best stop talking. Nearly fell there. You too. If you fall, it's almost impossible to get up."

# Chapter 10—Righting Wrongs

"This is ridiculous. We leave you two alone for one day and look at the trouble you get into!" bellowed a very annoyed Drago. We three took a couple of hours to walk the less than two miles to where the Box had landed, and I thought my feet might fall off before we finally reached it. The Hagans had returned with full stomachs only to find Diana and I had been missing since late yesterday, which alarmed our apprentices.

"Drago," I attempted to sooth the dragon, "we're alive. I think we've figured out what simply must be handled. But first, this is our friend, Molly Brooks." I began the lengthy introductions. And yes, Molly was shocked to see all the unarmed, but gorgeous young women and Ben.

As soon as I finished introducing everyone, Lexi spoke up. "Felix, the Box has fabricated dresses for us all, just like the outfits you three are wearing. Of course, we'll need some help getting into them, but then we can help you do what must be done, whatever that is."

"You look wicked, Molly," Tiffany added. "But aren't you rather helpless in that outfit?"

Molly replied, "Very. I hate it. They got me back into it. No way to get free. They'll never let me out of it again. Not after I escaped once."

I interrupted the women. "We best hold a conference and bring everyone up to date. Then, we have to figure out how to handle this mess. Honestly, what Diana and I've seen is horrific." I didn't mention the panic I felt or the embarrassed horror in my sister's eyes.

Just then, someone pounded or knocked on the door. Instinctively, I tried to get up to answer it and darn near fell over. Carla stepped in and opened the door. A male voice said, "We saw Molly go in here. We need to speak to her."

I recognized him; he was one of Edgar's men. So did

Molly, who rose and walked slowly across the living room. Carefully, I followed her curious about what was happening. Upon seeing her, he said, "Molly, so sorry about them getting to you. We tried to rescue you, but failed. Edgar got captured. We thought you should know."

"Damn. When?" Molly asked, reverting to her usual short sentences.

"About an hour ago. We didn't know they had already let you out."

"We have to rescue him."

"We can't. They're too strong. We'll all just get captured and turned into pony-men. I left Harold watching the auction platform. He has a bow. If they do that to Edgar and try to auction him, Harold will put him out of his misery."

"Damn. Okay. No one can live like that. Stay here. I'm talking with mages." Molly turned and headed back to where she'd been sitting on one of the couches beside me. She didn't have to repeat anything. We overheard the exchange.

Hastily, I related all that had happened, what we'd seen and experienced. While that took valuable time, I knew it was vital for everyone to know just what the actual situation was. Otherwise, any plan was doomed to fail, and because of the Green dragon, any such failure could well be catastrophic.

When I finished, Drago barked, "I say, let's fly over to that castle and end that Green's reign of horrors."

Lexi spoke up before anyone else could reply. "Drago, that won't work well. The Green will be alerted to your coming. Besides, in your dragon forms, you won't be able to get down into the areas where he's at. I've a better idea. Look, the Box has fabricated some noblewoman outfits. We're all coming along."

I started to protest, but Lexi cut me off. "We can't deal with a dragon, but we can take care of the Count's guards, giving you four time to handle the Green Dragon. First, though, we'll get rid of those awful heels you're forced to wear. With ordinary moccasins, we can walk almost normally, except for all the petticoats. Then we walk to the castle, and no one will know we're up to anything at all. Just a group of noblewomen out for a stroll. We can take them by surprise. I think surprise is important when attacking a vicious dragon, don't you think so, Drago?"

"Well, yes, of course, always, but the guards," Drago protested, unsure just what to say.

Lexi countered swiftly. "Look, if we can't sleep them, then we women have other ways of distracting the men. We'll keep the Count's men out of the fight, one way or another."

"Wicked," exclaimed Tiffany. "Love it."

"Get me out of this," Molly pleaded. "I fight too. Not like this. Helpless."

"We need you to guide us there, Molly," I replied. "If they see you wearing normal clothing, they'll know something is up, so we need you looking like a noblewoman. If we only knew the Create an Illusion spell, then she could wear her leather fighter's garb, but others would see her dressed as a noblewoman."

"Nice idea," Carla broke in, "but none of us knows that spell. Molly, as much as you want to fight and need to fight back, we need you to get us into the castle and to the stairs leading to the dragon's den. Yours will be a critical role, if we're to have any chance at this."

"But I fight too. Edgar's there," Molly continued to struggle to get her thoughts into words.

"Then, let's hurry this up some," I declared. "Diana, you and I best temporarily morph into a version of ourselves with arms so we can help them get dressed."

God, I hoped our spells would work. Diana still looked terrified, but her appearance changed radically after her spell fired. For a time, steel determination replaced her frightened countenance. I relaxed a little, saying a silent thank you to Mage Locklard for having taught us that spell long before we were ready to tackle the many other Grade 4 spells.

When Lexi finished dressing and stood before Molly

asking for her okay, Molly declared, "Not work."

Biting her lip a little, Lexi said, "Without the heels, the dress drags the ground too much."

"No heel clicks. No gliding," Molly added.

"So anyone seeing us would know we're not quite proper noblewomen?" Tiffany asked, as I finished buttoning her top.

"Yes. Raise suspicions."

Lexi sighed, "Okay then, we have to wear the boots and be hobbled too."

I realized what she and the others were giving up to help us. Just by dressing as noblewomen, they were going from independence to total dependence. That they were willing to do this made an indelible impression on me and on Diana, Drago, and Carla.

Thirteen of us soon headed out of the Box. Reluctantly, Diana and I canceled our Morph Self spells. I felt vulnerable and helpless once more. Glancing at Diana, I saw her bite her lip hard. However, the eight apprentices didn't say a word about how terrible they found walking to be. Once we hit Main Street and saw other noblewomen about, everyone realized we'd made the right decision. Further, when the others saw their first pony-man pulling a noblewoman in her buggy, their resolved solidified. Mage Dietmar had to go!

Lexi again amazed me. In spite of the difficulty everyone had keeping their balance and walking, she chatted with Molly nearly continuously, keeping Molly's mind occupied, as well as filling everyone else in on just what this phenomenon of the noblewoman was all about. It also helped pass the time it took to reach the castle walls, nearly three hours! The expected gasps accompanied the skeletons hanging on the walls to either side of the gatehouse.

We walked on into the castle grounds completely unchallenged. However, as we reached the Manor House, one guard stopped us, but Tiffany acted, casting Sleep. Drago caught the man as he slumped to the ground, resting him gently aside, while the rest of us entered. To the left, doors opened to the Royal Throne, where the Count and Countess were likely holding court. Ahead, stairs headed down towards what had once been the dungeons. We'd already passed the barracks housing all Count Earl's guards; they'd have to enter these same doors.

After Drago joined us, closing the double doors, I had an idea. "Slide the locking bar into place, Drago, so the guards can't get in this way. Okay, here's where we split up. The Green dragon's den is down there," I nodded with my head. "You stay here and guard our backs. The Count is likely behind those doors."

"Wicked!" Tiffany exclaimed, getting into this whole plot. "Count on us."

Descending in these outfits and heels was simply scary, but I reminded Diana we could cast Gentle Fall if necessary. Still, we were so slow that the Hagans went on ahead of us. In a way, it was wise that they did, for dressed as we were, neither Diana nor I could dodge much of anything, certainly not a slime spray from the Green's mouth.

Drago already had cautioned us against using our balls of fire in such a confined space, so Diana and I were ready to fire off our bolts of electricity or lightning, just as soon as we could see the fiend. I've said it before; it's worth repeating. Dragons are at the top of the food chain on any world they reside. This one was no exception.

We were going after a Green dragon. Drago had roughly described what its dragon form might look like, a ninety-foot long, snake-like body, greenish of course, with small appendages and wings on its back. According to Drago, Greens are poor flyers, preferring to hover or slither along in their favorite habitats, swamps. Diana and I had only seen him in his human form.

We had descended a little over halfway down when the battle joined. Drago and Carla took Dietmar by surprise, but he reacted as expected, morphing into his dragon form and firing off a cone of his vile, flesh-dissolving slime at the two Gold dragons, which simply had no room on the stairs to morph into their true forms. Both dodged, but Carla's head took a solid hit of slime. Her screams sounded the alarm throughout the castle. I rounded the bend, saw the situation, and began firing off Clean spells as fast as I could. A minute later, Diana fired off a Create Water spell, drenching Carla, removing the last of the slime.

However, Drago did shoot one bolt of lightning, wounding the dragon. Carla made her own choice. With the slime eating into her head accompanied by great pain, she chose first to fire her bolt of lightning at Dietmar. One shot was all she could muster, for after that, the pain was too intense. She had to back up and deal with getting the slime off her.

Obviously injured, Dietmar slithered backwards into another workroom, while shooting another volley of his caustic slime covering the floor where he had been and where we'd have to enter to get at him again. As Diana and Carla finished cleaning her off, I finally reached a point where I could see into the original room, which I recognized as his workshop. The odor of the slime covering the floor and walls was sickening. Drago was confused, unable to find a way to get at this damned dragon.

I looked around the room, admiring how well stocked his lab was. Then, I spotted the sack of lime and smiled. A simple Push spell spilled the sack's contents onto the floor. Instant reaction. Fizzing, the lime began neutralizing his slime, just enough that Drago could move out into the room, allowing me to follow him.

We four knew Dietmar was a mage and thus knowing an untold number of spells, many likely to be far more powerful than those we knew. Worse, if he felt threatened and if he was in his true form, he could always Shadow Walk away, and we'd have no way to follow him, much as Adler, the Black, had done previously. We acted.

Trusting our shoes to take a few minutes before they were dissolved—there wasn't time to spread the lime across the whole floor—we four moved into the room, where we had a straight shot at Dietmar, who was guzzling some healing potions, the very same kind he'd pumped into us only days ago. I shot my bolt of lightning at him, vaguely aware the others were doing the same spell.

As I chanted the trigger words, something unexpected happened. I was standing in a void, colorless. Dietmar was ahead of me, all coiled up. Our eyes met. *Damn you for what you've done!* I tried to make my colorless body say that. Although no sounds came out, I found myself standing in the middle of the workroom in the puddle of slime, as my bolt of lightning struck Dietmar. Within seconds of mine, three others also struck his body. Because of the dragon's size, the beast was impossible to miss. His body jerked violently, rose from the floor, and fell back, only to spasm once again. Then, Dietmar exhaled, slumping to the stone floor, lifeless.

"Kill them. Kill them all!" I heard Count Earl screaming from above us. As fast as I could, which was pathetically slowly, I turned and headed up the stairs, leaving the others to finish the job.

Meanwhile at the door to the Throne Room, Lexi decided they should enter. Hiding in the hallway wasn't a good option. "I got this," Ben said, when Molly complained that she was completely helpless. He leaned over, bit down on the iron bar, and pulled backwards, pulling the door open. Tiffany quickly pushed her body into the door, forcing it wide open, and the others filed in, raising a clamor.

"Is that the Count and Countess?" Lexi asked Molly. They were. The eight apprentices fired off their Sleep spells one after the other. Molly watched a dozen courtiers, noble men, and women slump to the ground, some snoring loudly. However, Count Earl and Countess Kayliegh sat on their thrones still awake, and both yelled for their guards. Behind them, Lexi heard some futile attempts to open the main doors we'd entered, but which were now barred. She presumed correctly that there were other ways into the Throne Room.

"Okay, spread out. Expect more guards to come running," Lexi ordered.

"I could kill you," screamed Molly, frustrated she was so helpless and couldn't use her knife on the Count or Countess.

Soon, more guards came running into the Throne Room from the opposite side. Again, the apprentices fired off their Sleep spells. One by one, the guards succumbed, slumping onto the ground, which infuriated Count Earl, who continued to yell for help. Finally, he decided he would have to take action himself. He got up and descended to the floor, picking up a sword from a sleeping guard. With menace in his eyes, he moved toward the line of eight gorgeous women.

First, he threatened Tiffany. She glared at him. "You'd strike me with a sword? Me, with no arms and can barely walk in this getup?"

He paused, thinking better of it. Instead, he gave her a shove. With her legs hobbled and in these heels, Tiffany couldn't avoid falling over backwards. I saw her falling as I entered. I've never been as fast as I was then, casting a Gentle Fall on Tiffany. However, I was surprised. Even while falling, she managed to cast Trip on the Count, who stumbled, dropping the sword in the process. Several more Trip spells followed, keeping him occupied, and I moved on into the Throne Room. She called out, "Wicked!"

Countess Kayleigh shrieked, "Kill them. Kill them all!" As a helpless noblewoman, yelling was about all she could actually do. Still, it infuriated Molly, who moved over to her, as she sat regally on her throne. Molly shoved into her from behind, a move calculated to have the effect it did. The Countess fell forward off her throne. Only by frantically getting to her feet and wobbling wildly did she manage not to fall down. Molly's smile told me all.

By now, more guards entered, running towards the Count, who had retrieved the sword and gotten control of his feet. "Kill them all," he yelled to his men, who raced across the spacious room towards us.

Again, I didn't doubt the apprentices. Lexi gave the command. Another eight Sleep spells fired. If one didn't affect a guard, seven more might. Again, all his guards

118

dropped to the floor. Now, I had to act. He was dangerously close to Lexi. One swing and she'd be history. I focused and acted. Magical energies flashed around Count Earl. His sword clanked onto the floor. He screamed unintelligibly. I had morphed him into a copy of the pony-man that Lyle had purchased for Molly! The Count was now blind, tongueless, and armless. He wore the usual leather harness and loincloth. A bridle was about his head, its iron bit in his mouth. His feet were encased in those heavy, horseshoe-clad boots.

"Wicked!" Tiffany's voice echoed across the room.

Countess Kayleigh shrieked and yelled for more guards, while trying to kick those closest to her awake. I had had enough. I focused and cast again. Suddenly, her high-pitched shrieks joined his, as she was morphed into a pony-man too. Three more guards entered, as another "Wicked" echoed. Poor Tiffany still hadn't found a way to get back onto her feet, but she was enjoying the action.

Smiling, I took charge. "Guards, will you please remove these ridiculous pony-men from the Count's Throne Room. They simply don't belong in here. Take them to the Auction Block. We think the Count and Countess have fled via their secret passage to safety. All is okay in here now. The others are just asleep. They'll be fine when they awake."

The guards looked around and didn't see their Count or Countess, but they did see two pony-men, who obviously didn't belong in the Throne Room, filled with very beautiful noblewomen and sleeping guards. Hastily, they took the reins and pulled the blind pair along. The two tried to speak, tried to protest, but to no avail. The guards led them out of the room.

Once we were alone again, I cast Levitate on Tiffany, helping her get back on her feet. I was rewarded with another enthusiastic, "Wicked! So how long will they be pony-men?"

"Yes, best punishment," Molly added.

"Well, I used a Morph Other spell. They'll stay that way until someone else successfully casts a Dispel Magic on them or until I cancel the spell, which I've no intention of doing."

"Good. They need to experience what they've done to others," Molly declared, using an unusually long sentence. "Now what? The dragon? Edgar?"

"Come on—all of you. Let's see what's going on down below. I think we killed the dragon, but Carla got slimed pretty badly. I hope she's all right." We ten glided slowly across the Throne Room, ten elegantly dressed noblewomen. As we descended the stairs, I was prepared to cast Gentle Fall, should one or more of us make a misstep, but to our credit, we went down slowly and carefully.

"God, it stinks!" Lexi exclaimed, turning up her nose.

"Green's caustic slime, mixed with lime and water," I pointed out.

We followed the hushed voices of Diana, Drago, and Carla, moving past the carcass of the Green dragon, and into another workroom, the very one where the dragon had removed our arms. We found Edgar at last, well the other three had. Dietmar was in the process of making him into another pony-man, but had only gotten his arms removed when we attacked him. Carla was pouring another healing potion down his throat, as we ten glided into the room.

"Oh God, no! Edgar," exclaimed Molly, nearly falling as she tried to move to his side too quickly. They had him sitting up on the narrow bench, his arms lying in a heap to one side.

"We got to him before Dietmar could cut out his tongue or blind him, so that's something," Diana explained to a nearly frantic Molly.

Lexi spoke up, "Don't worry, Edgar, Molly. Give yourself time to adapt. We do nearly everything using our feet and toes; we have different ways of doing thing. We'll show you later. Mostly, you need to ask 'how do I do this?' That's the key. Edgar, Felix here turned both the Count and Countess into pony-men, and the guards have taken them to the Auction Center."

Edgar attempted to smile. "Vile beast is dead. Serves them right. I could kill them, but now I'm as helpless as a noblewoman."

"But look at me," wailed Carla, who had scrounged around for a mirror. "Look at my face and neck! It's horrid." No one said anything. What could we say? She looked horrible. I hoped the healing potions she drunk would help some, but I didn't expect that would be the case. It hadn't with Diana and the Black dragon's acid burns.

Meanwhile, Drago searched the dragon's chambers, confiscating whatever he thought valuable. Diana wisely gathered up nearly two dozen healing potions, stowing them carefully in a leather carrying case, but she was terribly slow, having to cast a variety of spells to do such a simple task. Eve saw what she was trying to do and said, "Like this, Diana." She moved over to the shelf with the bottles, bent over, picking up the next one with her mouth. After walking over to the leather case, she bent over, stowing the precious bottle safely in the bag. "Don't need magic to do this. You just need more practice, Diana. Let us help."

A half hour later, we headed home, pausing at the barred door, allowing Drago to undo the sliding bar, and holding it open for the rest of us. Molly and Edgar walked side by side all the way back. While I would have liked to cut her out of her noblewoman's outfit, I hadn't the means or other clothing for her. That would have to wait a little longer. That Edgar was alive would be enough, at least I hoped so.

We'd not gone halfway back when Lyle and Jodi spotted us. They'd brought his wagon and were searching for us. Molly, Diana, and I had failed to show up for lunch, and suppertime had come. Worried, they'd come in search of us.

From the wagon bed, Jodi exclaimed, "There you are, Molly! You gave us quite a fright! At least you're practicing your walking. Who are these other beautiful

Vic Broquard

noblewomen? I've not seen them around town before. And is that Edgar?"

"We got revenge," Molly barked. "Mage Dietmar is dead, and the Count and Countess are pony-men now. These are Felix and Diana's apprentice mages. We've rescued Edgar, but the dragon already removed his arms. So there! So much for me being noble." She'd said more than she'd desired, but she felt she had to say this much, if only to convince her sister she was done with all this nonsense.

For once, Jodi merely gasped, unable to respond coherently. Lyle did, rather surprising me with his keen insight. "Well, if this is true, then it's long overdue! That Mage Dietmar is actually dead?"

Drago replied succinctly, "Quite. But the foul beast harmed my sister."

"And Count Earl is a pony-man?"

"Felix's doing. Not mine. I'd have ripped his body apart."

"Well, well, Jodi, this is indeed interesting. We'll need new rulers soon, before others in the Beckworth clan can seize the throne. Say, it's past suppertime. How about I treat everyone to a meal at Southby's? It's the finest restaurant in Beckworth."

"Who's going to feed us?" I asked.

"Oh, that's not a problem at Southby's. Drago, you lift everyone into the wagon. What an interesting turn of events this day has brought." While Drago complied, Lyle continued, "I'm on the City Council, you know. I bet you didn't know the Emperor himself has ordered all the ruling Counts and Countesss to follow his new guidelines. Of course, Count Earl refused to go along with the Emperor's orders. Some of us expected severe repercussions, but as yet nothing has come of it."

A few minutes later, we were ushered into the finest inn I'd ever seen. No one paid any attention to how grubby several were; rather all eyes tended to focus on us ten noblewomen, in their eyes, that is. Purposely, Lyle sat between Edgar and Molly, making Jodi sit on the other

122

side of Molly's assistant. The establishment had a number of servant girls who quietly slipped into every other chair, so they could feed the many noblewomen. Diana and Carla sat at the far end of the table, while I sat beside Drago and my two apprentices. Lexi and Tiffany truly enjoyed in this entire experience, bubbling all evening. Drago and I were more or less solemn, while I was frustrated in that I couldn't hear what Lyle was saying to Edgar and Molly, nor could I hear Diana and Carla.

Edgar wanted to be left alone in his misery, to cry, to do anything but be here in the restaurant, but he had no choice. Much later, I learned what they talked about.

Lyle explained, "Edgar, Molly, we've now got a power vacuum in Beckworth."

"Another Beckworth will proclaim himself Count," Molly griped.

"Not so fast, Molly. Yes, under normal times, that's quite true. These aren't normal times. In fact, highly unnormal. You see, the Emperor has issued new orders for all his subordinates, including all Counts and Countesss in the world," Lyle explained. "Lord knows why he's done this, only that he has. His orders state since the Countess must always be a noblewoman, she doesn't need her arms. They and all noblewomen are to have them removed at their earliest convenience." I heard Molly gasp, but had no idea why she did so.

"Yes, but for all other noblewomen, Molly, this is almost a trivial request, assuming a painless way can be found to carry it out. I'm told the Emperor has his doctors working on that one. More importantly, the Emperor has ordered all Counts and all noblemen also to have their arms removed. It is a status thing, according to the Emperor. Noblemen have no need of arms; they use their finances and minds to run their companies. Thus, they too should be highly visible by the common person. He also states in so doing, more poor young men will be given steady employment as their assistants, and that can only benefit our world."

He continued, "What I'm getting at is this. Should

another of the Beckworth clan desire to ascend to the throne, the Emperor insists his arms be removed, per his orders. I'm sure that will dissuade them all. So we need some man who doesn't have them and who we think can do a much better job of running our town and lands. Edgar, I've been watching you for the last five years. You've always had the best interests of Beckworth in mind. You're a fighter."

"Not anymore," he whined, fighting from breaking down yet again.

"Edgar, I'm offering you the throne. You can be our next Count. You'll have the entire City Council's backing. We need an honest ruler this time. Much is at stake. Plus, I want Molly to be your Countess. The rulers don't have to be married. That's in the rule book. So Molly, Edgar, will you two accept the throne of Beckworth? I need your answer tonight. We'll have to take swift action, before any in the Beckworth clan figures out what's going on."

"But I don't want to be a noblewoman. I never did!" Molly pleaded. She looked at Edgar, whose valiant attempts to control his wild emotions slowly began to fail. "Okay, for Edgar's sake, I'll do it. Look at what he's sacrificed for all of us, but I'm not having my arms cut off. No way."

"Good. I'll start making the arrangements. I've a long night ahead of me. With luck, you two will be on the throne tomorrow. Meanwhile, let's get you home, cleaned up, and find some elegant suits for Edgar here. Also, Molly, Jodi wants you to get new gowns too, only now they'll have to be even fancier. A Royal Dressmaker works out of the Manor House. She'll take good care of you."

Back in the wagon an hour later and as we pulled out onto the nearly deserted streets of Beckworth, Lyle announced, "I've some news for everyone. Edgar has agreed to become our next Count, and Molly has agreed to be his Countess. I hope to have them sitting on the thrones sometime tomorrow. I'll drop you off at our place, then I've got to visit many others yet tonight. I guess, Felix, you and your group can walk the rest of the way?"

"Sure. Congratulations, Edgar. You'll make a fine Count. Molly, you'll be a great Countess. Work for changes in the way things are around here," I winked at Molly, hoping she'd get my hint. Now that Lyle mentioned it, I realized I had created a power vacuum. Someone would have to take the throne. Well, if Lyle could make this happen, I thought it would do wonders for Edgar, considering how he must feel about now. I was ambivalent about Molly. I knew how much she hated being made into a helpless noblewoman, but as Countess, perhaps she could become an instigator for positive change.

# Chapter 11—Parting of Ways

"We best not press the Handled button yet," Drago declared when we all entered the Box that night. "We might have more to do here. I'm taking a bath. Have to wash the filth off me. See you in the morning, Felix." He ducked into his quarters.

Carla and Diana headed into hers, so Lexi, Tiffany, and I headed for ours, but then I stopped. "Sorry gang. I forgot." Hastily, I Morphed myself into a version of me when I had arms. As quickly as I could, I helped each one out of the noblewoman outfit, much to their relief. Then, canceling my spell, I followed Lexi and Tiffany into our room.

"Bath time for everyone," Lexi proclaimed. "Don't worry so, Felix. We'll help you remember how to do things with your toes. You mostly need practice." I chuckled. I'd need a lot more than that.

As we three soaked, Tiffany surprised me. "Felix, I can't help but see parallels to the Unarmed Escorts we were a part of and the noblewomen here on this world. You know they even trained us to be able to cross our legs behind our heads to help encourage men to pay for sexual favors, but here they've taken it even farther. So what's the connection between our worlds? We have space travel and are highly advanced, but this is a primitive world. No offense, Felix."

I chuckled. "Don't know the connection, but I find the parallels striking, now that you mention it. Perhaps, the dragons are bringing ideas across the worlds."

"Well, the scarring on your shoulders isn't too bad," Lexi pointed out. I couldn't see too well, not without looking into a mirror. "I wonder how badly Carla was wounded."

In the other room, Carla helped Diana out of her restrictive outfit, and the two headed for their bath. "Just look at my face and neck," Carla complained, looking into the mirror.

"It's bad, no denying that. Try an Alter Self spell and see if you can hide it as I'm able to do with my scarred shoulders," Diana suggested.

Minutes later, two frustrated women continued to bathe and talk. The Gold dragon complained, "If I look this bad in my dragon form, I'm doomed, Diana. No one will ever want to mate with me. I'll be the Ugly Outcast for as long as I live, which should be at least five hundred of your years. This whole Box thing isn't turning out the way I had hoped or expected. I don't want to be so disfigured for the rest of my life, Diana."

"And I don't want to be so helpless either. I know the apprentices have adapted remarkably well—no, incredibly well, but I'm terrified, Carla."

"I hear you. There has to be far safer ways to get magic items and learn spells."

"Quite true," Diana admitted. "We were doing all right with Mage Locklard. I know. It was terribly slow, and I don't know how many power spells he actually knows. Still, this sucks. Probably the fellows will press the 'Handled' button soon, and we'll get more spell pages to study, but I can't even pick them up, not easily. I've no idea how Felix and I got our arms back the last time. It's not likely to happen again. So yes, Carla, this sucks big time. Hell, we can't even go home if we want to. We're on some other world."

"I can get us home. Shadow Walk. I'm going to morph to my true form. The mirror is too small, so I need your honest opinion on how I look. Don't hold back, Diana, please." She moved back and changed, her golden body very nearly filling the room. Diana squeezed around her, slowly examining her from all sides. "Well?"

"Pretty awful, Carla, no doubt about that. The left side of your face and places along your neck are really scarred, like a bad burn that didn't heal right. See if you can wiggle your head close to that mirror. That's the worst spot."

"Damn. Damn. Damn. It's as bad as I feared. Diana,

I'm scarred for life now, doomed to be the ugly Gold dragon that nobody wants. I'll scare kids with this face." She morphed back into her human form. Both women rested their heads on each other's shoulders and cried for a time.

Eventually, Diana admitted, "Yes, I love magic, but I also wanted one day to meet Mr. Right-for-me, get married, and have children and a nice home, putting magic to use for my family. Now like this, I'm doomed to be more or less helpless, even if I can somehow figure out how they do things. No one is going to want me, not when they can have a whole woman instead."

"We're both doomed, Diana. That's obvious. This Box thing is the reason. If we'd just stayed with Mage Locklard, we'd be whole still. None of this craziness would have happened to us. Even Molly is getting screwed, isn't she?"

"What do you mean?"

"Well, she loathes being a noblewoman, but she's now going to be the new Countess and will have to remain a noblewoman. When I first met her, I would have wagered she'd join up with us in the Box here."

"Oh, right. Yes, you're dead on. She loathes it, and yet for Edgar's sake, she's enduring it. What we women do for our men." Both chuckled. Then, Diana asked, "Carla, can your Shadow Walk thing take others with you? Back home, I mean?"

"Sure, but Diana, you don't have arms to hang on."

"Shit."

"Let me think on it some."

The two finished up and Diana then joined her two other companions in her room, namely Ben and Carli. As they brushed out each other's hair, Ben commented, "Well, Diana, the scaring around your shoulders isn't as bad as I thought it might be."

"It's bad enough, Ben!"

"True, but you are still one gorgeous young woman, Diana, but Carli and I've been thinking. I know we both love to be learning these spells, but with this Box thing—

it's incredibly dangerous. We could easily get killed, couldn't we?"

"Duh, now you are talking. Right. Far too dangerous for my liking. I don't want to be like this. No offense you two, but I don't want to be like this. I feel so helpless, so ugly, so well, I don't know what all."

"I wish we could go somewhere that's safe to learn magic."

"Well, there is always Mage Locklard, our original teacher, but our world is a primitive one, compared to your world, Ben."

"That doesn't matter so much to me, if I could be with you, Diana. Would you even consider marrying me? Carli and I would like to marry you. Then, the three of us would always be together and able to help the other out as we're doing now. In spite of all the images in our minds, some things are either impossible for us to do or so damned difficult it's hardly worth the trouble."

Diana smiled. "Are you proposing, Ben?"

"I guess I am. Diana, Carli, will you both marry me? I have some funds, but you know that. Somehow, we'll find a way to support our family. I was thinking if we can learn enough magic spells from your Mage Locklard, we could run a small business, working spells for others." Ben looked hopeful for a moment; then he frowned, adding, "But be honest about this. Each of you is incredibly beautiful. You should be able to have your pick of handsome men, not a freak like me."

Carli said, "Oh don't be so hard on yourself, Ben. Yes, I'll gladly marry you. Why did it take you this long to propose?"

"I will too," Diana added, "on one condition: that we return to my world where we can learn magic spells from Mage Locklard in total safety, compared to this Box thing. I don't want to marry you only to have you slimed to death tomorrow or fried or dissolved in a Black's acid, like I nearly was."

The three leaned into each other, sharing passionate kisses before Ben grasped her full meaning. "Wait, how

129

can we return to your world?"

"I might have a way. If we can, then we can marry. Honestly Ben, if I marry you now, it might have been me that was slimed by the Green dragon. Maybe it will be me next time. This Box is having us tackle foes far beyond our ability to deal with them safely."

"I agree. I can't imagine fighting a dragon," Ben declared.

***

We'd just finished breakfast with Diana and me awkwardly trying to use our feet and toes to feed ourselves, when someone knocked on the Box door. Drago let Molly in, and she made her slow, careful way through the living room to our dining room. She'd walked all the way here from Jodi's home just to talk with us. Drago did point out she was accompanied by a half dozen castle guards who stayed outside the Box.

"Hi. I had to come. Say goodbye. I was going to go away with you. I owe you so much. Can't thank you enough. I hate being a noblewoman. Can't leave Edgar. He's been with me all these years. He has to lead now. Have to help him. He's lost so very much, as you all have too. I so wanted to go away with you, to fight for you. Now, I mustn't. Wouldn't be right to Edgar."

I spoke up, "Molly, we know. You're right. Edgar truly needs you now. Besides, as Countess, you can work for real change in the ways of noblewomen."

She flashed a smile that told all. "It's official. Never knew Lyle was powerful. Crowning will be tomorrow. Please come. Please. You should be honored. It was you who freed us all."

"Sure thing, Countess Molly. We'll be there. What time?" We chatted a bit before she had to leave and join Edgar in the Throne Room.

After she left, Carla declared, "Okay. After we get back from her ceremony, I'm leaving for home, for Byron Falls."

"And I'm going with her," Diana added. "Plus, Ben, Carli, and I are getting married. This whole Box thing is

130

way too dangerous for us. We'll take our time and learn what we can from Mage Locklard."

After that bombshell—I admit I never suspected a thing—Drago brought out the sacks he'd confiscated from Mage Dietmar's chambers. He felt obligated to divide the "loot," especially since we couldn't convince them to stay. Each of us received a large pile of gemstones.

Later when I got Diana alone, I said, "Look, you stay in mom and dad's home. That way you'll have a place to raise a family. One day, I'll be back, but Drago and I have to see this through. There are wrongs to be righted and we can do it."

"I figured we'd stay there. Thanks. One word to the wise. You should propose to Lexi and Tiffany. They are nuts about you, unless you want a whole woman."

I flushed. "They are?" Sheepishly, I agreed to ask them.

A half hour later, Lexi squealed and Tiffany exclaimed, "Wicked."

"Come on. Let's tell the others. Maybe we six can get married here before they leave," I suggested. Love. Who can predict it? Certainly not me, but in the short time I'd known these two women, they'd captured my heart and soul.

\*\*\*

My apprentices made the decision for us. Tiffany spoke for the eight, "Look, this is their coronation, their special day. We should honor them by appearing as they expect noblewomen should look. So do your morph thing and get us all into those outfits. Then, Carla can get you into yours. And stop complaining, big boy," she teased me.

I was pooped by the time I got nine of them into their outfits, but Carla then hastily fixed me up as well. Once more, we ten found ourselves hobbled up, barely able to put one foot in front of the other, but we "glided" along the main streets heading for the castle. Hours later as we approached the outer wall, I was pleased to see someone had taken the skeletons down, and I hoped they had a respectful burial, much as we'd done for Molly's father.

We arrived in time, barely. Squeezing into the packed Throne Room, we saw hundreds of well-dressed men and noblewomen, but few of their servants were present. Edgar looked ill at ease, still highly uncomfortable with his physical limitations, but he wore a nice looking suit, whose arms had been removed and sewn shut, emphasizing his distinct lack of arms.

Molly wore a bright red gown and looked equally ill at ease. I knew how much she hated wearing a noblewoman's outfit. I rather wished I could peer into the future and see what changes she'd eventually bring to this world's noblewoman's attire. It had to be better than the current state.

The ceremony was brief, filled with musical fanfares and City Council members singing the praises of Count Edgar and Countess Molly. A lengthy reception followed, and everyone present eventually was able to meet the pair personally. Of course, many stopped to chat with us ten. We soon learned word had spread about their Emperor asking both noblemen and women to have their arms removed at their convenience. Naturally, Diana and I appeared to these people as some who had already done as their Emperor had requested. Thus, we fielded many questions.

Eve, Kelly, Angela, and Vanna relished this attention. Soon the four saw their experience in the Unarmed Escort was invaluable here. Their ability to be independent became the topic of many conversations, mostly from the noblemen, who would theoretically bear the brunt of these orders. The noblewomen were used to having no use of their arms and hands and thus weren't much interested in what the four had to say.

As the afternoon ended, the four found themselves surrounded by two dozen noblemen and Count Edgar. I was too far away to hear them, but on our long walk back to the Box, Eve told us about it.

She explained as we walked slowly and carefully along the street, "The noblemen have asked us to stay here and assist them, once they obey the Emperor. They had hoped the Emperor's orders would be forgotten in time, since Count Earl totally ignored those orders. Now, they aren't so sure they can. Certainly, Edgar needs our help. They're offering us everything imaginable if we stick around and teach them how we do everything. Tomorrow, we're supposed to meet with them and Edgar, but wearing our usual dresses and shoes. They want to see how we do everything, particularly eating. For once, Felix, what we actually know and can do is vital and necessary for these men. So we might just stay here a while."

"Hey, that's great, but don't forget, there's no easy way for you to return to your home world," I felt obligated to point out.

Eve giggled. "We know, silly boy."

We were all exhausted by the time we finally returned to the Box. However, to our surprise, a Holy Man was there waiting for us. Lyle had sent him to officiate at the weddings. Thus, without much fanfare, Diana, Ben, and Carli were married. Then, Lexi, Tiffany, and I were married. That done, everyone cheered and shared our unique hugs. Surprising us all, Vanna whipped up a wedding cake. Everyone partied, but not until I Morphed into my armed self and got nine of us out of the restrictive apparel.

The next day and wearing their usual, comfortable clothing, Vanna, Angela, Kelly, and Eve headed off to teach Edgar and show the assembled noblemen what was actually possible.

Meanwhile, the other four began packing. I sighed. Diana and I hadn't been apart since we could walk. Now we were married, but more to the point, she and they were about to leave us, and head back to our home in Byron Falls.

"I don't suppose I can talk you out of this," I hinted, hoping against hope.

"Look. Do you see new arms here?" she barked. "Well, I don't either. This Box thing is nice in that via it, we're righting wrongs, so don't get me wrong about that. Yes, it's valuable, but it's putting us beginners up against deadly dragons. We've lost our arms twice now, Felix, and we've only been two places. Look what's happened to Carla. She's disfigured for life. You and I—we could be killed. Those dragons have been playing with us. We should both be dead and you know it. I'm getting out while I can. We'll just have to have patience with Mage Locklard, if he'll even have us half-humans now."

"You're not half-human," I protested.

"Humans have arms. We don't," she slammed me back. I knew her suppressed grief was talking and didn't react. Hell, I had my own suppressed grief there too, just under the surface.

"You be careful, Diana. I love you, you know. I promise you I won't stop until I find a way to get our arms back. There must be magical ways."

"Don't go getting yourself killed, Felix. Love you too." We pressed our bodies into each other and were silent for a time.

Looking back, around this point in time I began feeling funny sensations in my body. After we pulled away, we set to work preparing the four for the Shadow Walk. Drago tied a rope around Carla's large chest, securing four secondary lines to it. He tied her accumulated gems to one line. Then, Diana, Ben, and Carli were secured to the other three lines, with their possessions shrunken and stowed on their bodies. This way, if they slipped off her back, having lost their leg grips, the ropes would keep them tethered to her as she moved through the Shadows.

Here was magic I'd never seen. None of us humans had, and we paid very close attention to the details. In the end, like any new spell, we had no idea how it worked. It just did. We watched as the scarred ninety-foot long Gold dragon spread her wings and leaped into the sky. She flew a short distance and then simply vanished from sight.

"Wicked! I want to learn to do that!" Tiffany declared.

Drago commented, "Well, they should be arriving home right now. I guess it's down to just the four of us, but don't ask me to be your hands. You could have gone back with her, you know."

"Drago, we're here for the long haul. I promised everyone I won't quit until I find the means somehow to restore our arms and Carla's beauty." The dragon smiled.

Later, the other four young women returned, announcing they were going to stay here in Beckworth, assisting the noblemen and Count Edgar with how to do things for themselves. Again, we gave them big hugs and watched as several men carried their things to waiting carriages. After they left, Lexi and Tiffany decided to work together to cook for us three, while Drago decided to lay in some antelope for himself and not bother eating human food.

*** 

Adler left the Emperor's private chambers. The Black dragon was more than a little annoyed. News from Beckworth had just reached him. While both he and the Emperor were pleased that Count Earl Beckworth and his wife, the Countess, had been mysteriously dethroned and that they didn't need to proceed with the planned assassination, Adler wasn't pleased when he heard the descriptions of those who had been behind the coup. He cast several spells and became even more annoyed. The same pair of Gold dragons and their human sidekicks, who had somehow found this world, had intervened yet again. Even more shocking, Adler recognized eight of the Unarmed Escorts. Evidently, they'd joined the original four meddlers.

While the Emperor waited to hear just whom the City Council would install on their throne, Adler paced his private office. *If only you could Wish a person to death. Well, I can't. Worse, I can't touch the damned Gold dragons. That's suicide. I'll need to lay a clever trap for them, where the odds are heavily stacked in my favor. From the memories I viewed of my contacts at the castle, those annoying unarmed women prevented the guards from helping Dietmar. Plus, Dietmar's body showed no signs of the Gold dragons physically ripping him apart. So it had to be those mages and their spells. Felix and*

*Diana. Curse their infernal meddling.*

He paced his office once more. Often a bright idea would appear, if only he walked around his office sufficient times. *Somehow, I need to find out how they discovered this world and what was going on in Beckworth. More importantly, I need to keep them from further interfering. There'll be Hell to pay if they find out about the Emperor and his plans. At least, old Dietmar managed to get their arms removed again. That's something. Hum, while I've no idea how they got them back after I had them deadened, the key detail is they haven't gotten them back after Dietmar slimed them off their bodies. Maybe his slime is what's preventing such magic. From all reports, they are certainly hobbled up as Rainbow's End noblewomen.*

*Ah ha! That's the answer. Keep them hobbled up. Then, I only have two dragons to handle. Too bad I can't just Wish them to death, so I'll just have to get more inventive. Let's see what old Adler can devise to make their lives so miserable they'll quit and go home. That's what I need—have them just go home.*

For a time, he reflected upon all he knew about humans and their anatomy, along with what the Emperor was ordering for all noblewomen and now noblemen. *That's it! They can't avoid this double whammy. I could just blind them or remove their tongues, as the Count did with his pony-men, something the Emperor is considering doing here too. But such things could be countered with spells. Blindness can be dispelled. No, these two changes should do it.* He brought up two images on his computer monitor, a device he'd brought here when he fled Halcion. He tiled them side by side.

Key to his work was having and holding the proper goal firmly in mind as he cast the extremely intricate spell, a top power spell, and one that few humans ever used, but was made to order for someone such as him. With the desired results visible, he chanted for nearly a minute, and then barked, "I Wish. . ."

As always, enormous magical energies flashed.

Adler knew his spell would be successful. "Now to send out some spies to see just how effective this will prove to be. If it's superb, I may well recommend it to the Emperor. Old Earl did have a good idea with his pony-men, I'll give him that much, if little else." He rose and sent for messengers.

That handled, he sat back. *Well, with any luck at all, they'll leave this world soon. If not, they should be begging to return to their home world, for all the good that will do them.* Adler laughed sarcastically.

***

We truly enjoyed our first night as a married trio, though I had the more difficult part, physically that is. More than once, I silently cursed my lack of arms and hands. These two beautiful women deserved more than I was giving them, but they seemed quite contented. However, as we rose and began to get dressed, I knew something was wrong with my body. The same things were also wrong with Lexi and Tiffany's bodies.

Tiffany vocalized it first. "Say, my boobs are much larger, aren't they? Yours are too, or my eyes are deceiving me."

"Right. That's it. They seem heavier or something," I added.

"Well, my feet are all crooked. I guess it wasn't such a good idea to wear their heels," Lexi commented, looking herself over in the mirror close to our bed.

"Wicked! Look at this. They *are* bigger," Tiffany exclaimed. The blouse she'd worn yesterday simply didn't fit her much larger bosom. "Are you messing with us, Felix?"

"Hardly. They were big enough already. My feet are bent. How is this possible?" I countered.

We three compared our vitally needed feet. Definitely, something wasn't right with them. Our moccasins no longer fit our feet. Rather, our feet no longer lay flat on the ground. Still, we managed to get dressed and fix something to eat.

That done, Drago pressed the "Handled" button, while we three held our breaths. I sure hoped the Box

137

didn't want us somehow to alter the way noblewomen were living, let alone find a "cure" for all of the pony-men, who numbered well over a thousand now. Relief. We four saw the bar slide over, locking us inside the Box, followed by a slight vibration as the Box "moved."

"Wicked. Now we can get more spells to learn. Come on. Let's see what we can learn this time," Tiffany suggested full of youthful excitement. Okay, I was excited too, wondering what new spells we'd get to learn. While I doubted there would be one to regrow arms, perhaps we'd get some that might be more effective against dragons, since we seemed to stumble into their plots.

Eagerly, she and Lexi latched onto their new book pages, tucking them between their head and shoulder while carrying them to the table where they'd left their spell books. I had little choice except to emulate their methods, since Drago merely grunted and took his with him. Once I reached the table and dropped my new pages down, I couldn't resist looking at what the Box was attempting to have them learn. They had forty spells, equally divided between Grade 1 and 2, literally about half of the spells from each of those grades. The girls were quite pleased, so I sat down and used my toes to flip through those in my pages.

"Wow! Remove a Curse," I blurted out. "Maybe we three have been cursed or something. Now that would explain it."

"Wicked. Hurry up, learn it, and cast it on us. I swear my knockers are getting heavier than they were when we got up," Tiffany declared. "Oh, look at this—a Magical Missile that always hits! Wicked! I have to learn that one first!"

"I don't know, Tiffany. This Sticky Webs looks good too," Lexi said. "We could have used it to hold off more guards in that battle."

Me, I smiled, recalling the enthusiasm I had when Diana and I first began to learn those two spells. I wished she hadn't gone, but I understood why she did.

We missed the fact we "landed" just a few hours

138

after departing Beckworth, because the four of us spent the day learning how to cast some of these new spells. Yes, I picked up Remove a Curse first, and I cast it a dozen times on myself and then on both Lexi and Tiffany. Nothing happened, nothing at all. At least, I was able to rule out us being cursed. However, by suppertime, I knew we were going to be in big trouble and soon.

The elation of learning new spells faded after our painful attempt to make ourselves supper. We could barely stand. Something was happening to our feet, specifically at the heel, where an unnatural bend continued to grow. Normally a heel touches the floor along with most of the foot, save the arch. Our feet didn't. At the toe side of the heel, ours bent sharply at a ninety-degree angle, forcing the rest of the foot straight downward. The only parts of our feet that we could get flat on the floor were our toes, making standing or walking difficult at best.

Tiffany did find something practical about our twisted feet. "Wicked, Felix. Now we can reach things easier since they are a bit longer, relatively speaking." I had to admit she had a point, for we now had perhaps a four-inch longer reach with our toes. We just couldn't stand or walk much.

While our feet caused us difficulties making supper, our breasts were also aching as they continued to enlarge. As we readied for bed, we gasped at the size of each other's bosoms. Our breasts now protruded some sixteen inches outward, giant melons as Tiffany began calling them. True, they remained perfectly formed as fitting the beauty queens Lexi and Tiffany were, but each was larger than our heads.

"At least they aren't sagging and drooping," Lexi declared with a sigh. "I don't think I could handle them if they did."

"But I can't see my feet over them," I complained bitterly. Well, if I peered at my sides, I could barely see them.

"Well, we must be cursed somehow," Tiffany declared. "What other explanation could there be?"

"Can't be a Curse spell," I answered thoughtfully. "A Curse spell simply can't cause such a huge physical change in our bodies."

Lexi added, "It's almost as if someone out there wants us really hobbled up so we can't do much of anything at all with our magic spells. Don't you think? See if you can Morph yourself back with arms, Felix."

I thought she might be right. Focusing, I cast my usual Morph Me spell, holding onto a memory of myself when I had arms. My stomach tightened into a knot. Nothing happened! "Come on, Felix. Do it," Lexi urged me.

"I tried. Something is horribly wrong," I said. I focused and cast it repeatedly. After ten tries, I felt very sick. My nerves were shot, as I realized I had no quick fix to bypass having to go through life with my body as it was.

"Well, now that *is* interesting, I think. Felix, see if you can Morph me," Lexi continued her analysis of the situation.

I cast my usual Morph Other spell, which should have turned Lexi into a copy of me with arms. I intended to spook her a bit, but I was the one who was spooked. Nothing happened! After trying to morph Lexi and Tiffany a dozen times, I knew something was horribly wrong. Perhaps, I was somehow botching the Grade 4 spells.

With difficulty, I got up and found my spell books. I re-read the Morph Me spell details. Even though I was satisfied I hadn't missed any detail of its casting, I tried it again. Then, I called for Drago. (Okay, I admit I was in a panic.) The three of us could barely walk or stand, and our massive bosoms were constantly in the way of everything.

"Wow. What's going on with you three? Do humans have such large mammary glands? What's with your feet?" Drago asked. We three weren't shy about appearing naked before him, partly because we were spooked and needed his help and partly because he wasn't human.

"Drago, something has been changing our bodies, feet and breasts," I replied.

"And your hair, Felix. It touched your shoulders this morning, but now it's down below your waist."

I hadn't noticed this detail. "Look, Drago, something is horribly wrong. My Morph Me spell isn't working. I can't Morph Others either."

"Oh don't be silly, Felix. Let me try. I finally have those two spells working. I was hung up on my dragon form for ages it seems. Okay, here goes." He focused, chanted, and barked with full intention, "Morph Felix into Lexi." Magical energies flashed as before, but absolutely nothing happened to my body.

"Well, that's funny. That's not happened before," Drago mused. "Let me try it another way." He attempted to Morph Lexi into me and then Tiffany into me, but nothing happened, although magical energies flashed, indicating the changes should have happened.

"Well, isn't this keenly interesting," Drago commented from a purely educational point of view. We were a bit freaked out—okay, I was terrified, but he was merely amused. "Something is blocking magical spells from working on you three. Let's see how far it goes."

"What do you mean? Are you saying that other spells might not work either?" I asked. He nodded. "Okay, Alter Self, Shorten Hair," I commanded, using a Grade 1 spell on myself. Again, nothing happened. Annoyed, I cast it on Drago, intending to lengthen the hair on his morphed human form. Once again, for an instant, I seemed to be somewhere else, a place void of all features, though one might say the world was greyish. Drago was there in dragon form facing me, an amused look on his face. We smiled and magical energies flashed. I was back in the real world. We saw his hair lengthen a few inches, before he cast Alter Self on himself, shortening it once again.

"So, spells with change my physical form are failing," I mulled this over. "We should try others spells that potentially could change my appearance and theirs too," I suggested, nodding to Lexi and Tiffany.

"Wicked. We're on it," Tiffany declared, as she cast the new spell she'd learned this morning, Alter Self. For ten minutes, various spells that should have altered our appearance in some way failed to work on us three.

"So what does this mean?" Lexi finally asked.

I grimaced and replied, "I believe we three have been hit with a magical spell that has done two things. First, it's altered our bodies."

"For the worst," Tiffany interjected.

"For the worst. Second, it's blocking all magical spells that would allow us to alter our physical bodies."

"What kind of spell does all that?" asked Lexi, ever the inquisitive one who just had to have an answer.

"Now that, dear Lexi, is the key question," I replied with a smile. The terror knot in my stomach had finally begun to lessen a bit. "I wish we had access to a magic spell library so we could research this, but we don't."

Drago said dryly, "I think someone has used a Wish spell on you or perhaps a Restricted Lesser Wish spell. That would account for the observed phenomenon."

I didn't like being a "phenomenon," but I had the sickening feeling Drago might just be correct. "Who?" I blurted out.

Two sets of shoulders shrugged, and Drago shook his head. "Well, someone out there is after us, and we darn well have to find out who and fast."

"Hey, did you all notice we've landed already?" Drago changed the topic. We hadn't. "Yep, landed sometime before lunch even. I don't think we could have traveled to another world in so short a time. My speculation is that we're on the same world, this Rainbow's End. However, I'm not going to stick my head outside until I get all these new spells down pat. You with me, Felix?"

"Agreed, especially since Carla and Diana aren't with us. We best play it safer."

Just then, a bit of magical paper scrolled past my eyes, a Message spell from Eve. "Gang, Eve just send me a Message. She and the others are having the same troubles as we are, giant breasts and messed up feet."

"Ah ha," Drago broke in. "That means we're on the same world. Message spells don't work if the parties are on different worlds."

I sent her back a longer Message, outlining what

happened to us and that we were somewhere else on this world. I sensed she was relieved to hear we were somewhat close to them.

Drago's next statement summed it up, "Look, Felix. Tomorrow, I'll see what I can do to get you three shoes and clothes. I simply can't deal with whatever we're supposed to be handling all by myself. So I'll have to get you three able to help out somehow."

The next day was interesting—I'll give it that. Drago left as we were getting up. By the time we managed to get something to eat and slightly dressed, he returned with a shoe maker named Able, who brought a bag of samples with him. "Ah, you are the new noblewomen, yes? The ones our Emperor wishes?"

"No. We're not from this world. We've been cursed," I replied. "We need some shoes we can easily slip on and off. We use our feet as you use your hands, but we have to be able to walk." Thus ensued an hour of trying this and that. Considering no one had feet quite like ours, Able seemed remarkable confident something could be invented.

Eventually, he took a regular slip-on leather shoe and used only its toe area, as only those few inches of our feet were on the ground. The body of the shoe rose vertical from there. We opted for the heel to be made as part of the body; it touched the backside of the toes. In this way, we couldn't accidentally break the heel. Our feet's contact with the ground now had barely a fifth of the surface area they used to have, leaving us with a severe traction difficulty. We'd not be able to push or pull much at all without our feet slipping on the cobblestones. If it snowed, I doubted we could even stand, let alone walk.

Around noon and while trying to deal with making lunch, I suddenly broke into one of those loud, silly laughs. When Lexi and Tiffany finally calmed me down, I explained.

"Duh. Some mages we are. We've got the perfect spell to help us with all these things."

"What?" asked Lexi, a baffled look on her face.

"Invisible Servant. It's a Grade 1 spell. You both know it too."

"Wicked! You're right. Bigger duh!" Tiff exclaimed.

After that, we three began making good use of that spell. Now we could dress, cook, and feed ourselves, among other things. We just had to concentrate on making the actions desired as simple as possible for the spell.

Able returned the following day with two pairs for each of us and was royally paid for his invention. In the meantime, the three of us got creative with our useful spells, such as Mend and Alter, to modify our dresses and tops to fit our gigantic bosoms. Thus, the third day after landing, we finally were properly dressed and had shoes that fit. However, we three discovered we had to learn how to walk all over again. We could only take the tiniest of steps, perhaps three or four inches at most, and those were precariously taken. Oh how arms would have helped! In fact, we walked slower than the noblewomen did.

Drago teased us, saying we looked like Emperor penguins when we walked. He'd seen them in his travels and via a spell, showed us those memories. Normally, I would have laughed while watching them, but this was altogether far too serious for joviality. We were definitely hobbled up, barely able to take a three or four inch step. Worse, we couldn't see over our bosoms to see where we were going, making walking doubly treacherous for us. We quickly found any stairs or steps were immensely challenging, and we considered hiring servant girls to lift us up such obstacles as they did for the noblewomen.

Lexi resolved the situation for us. "Look guys, we can barely walk and stairs are out. We can't see over these knockers. Since we're still on this world and since we know from Lyle that they want us to be noblewomen, why don't we hire some servant girls and 'be' noblewomen. We still have all the fancy outfits."

Poor Drago. We sent him off to hire us three servant girls. He returned rather quickly with three sisters, Victoria, Ella, and Holly, eighteen, sixteen, and fifteen respectively. All three were blondes with braided long hair that just touched the back of their knees. They wore very well-made dresses. These weren't noblewomen's gowns, but did have a flare below their waists. Victoria's face had a sort of ornery, pixy look, quite cute, and with light blue eyes.

Giggling, the trio introduced themselves. Quickly, Victoria, the eldest, became their spokesperson. "We live next door to your new house here. It just appeared in the empty lot. Mr. Drago told us it was a magical appearance. Anyway, mom and dad's shop is next door. Banner's Fashions. They make a lot of noblewomen's gowns and noblemen's suits. I know they're excited to have three noblewomen living next door. Mom wanted me to invite you to supper, if you want to."

"Sure Victoria, we'd love to meet them. Besides, we might like to purchase some new gowns," Lexi replied before I could.

The girls giggled and got us properly dressed in our old noblewoman's outfits, but not until all three really giggled over the fact that I was really a male. Each had to see that for themselves. Well, since one would have to help me with bathroom duties and dressing, they might as well see what they were agreeing to handle. Yes, I really had to swallow my pride and embarrassment. The trio agreed to spend their days with us, helping as needed, ending the day by getting us tucked into bed properly. In return, each would receive the equivalent of twenty gold a week, a sum they considered rather lavish. Victoria also agreed to help us with meals, though we soon began to take our meals at the local inn, one block away.

# Chapter 12—Becoming Comfortable

With our new spells learned and with our personal servants who insisted they walk behind us, we three headed out to have our first look at the world around us. Drago was off looking for his own food, but he was already quite familiar with our surroundings. Our Box was now a white clapboard home nestled beside Banner's Fashions on High Street at its corner with Main Street. Via Victoria, we learned we were in the large city of Imperial. On down High Street across Main Street was Peter's Inn, where we began taking our meals.

As we walked slowly and carefully along, Victoria pointed out, "Look there. You can see the top of the Imperial Palace. That's where our Emperor and Empress live and rule our world. Did you know it's called Rainbow's End?" she asked gaily.

Lexi replied, "Yes. Just last week we were at Beckworth and saw the colorful hills from its western edge, or so we were told. Magnificent colors."

The girls giggled. Victoria continued, "We've only seen pictures of them, but everyone just loves strong, solid colors, particularly in dresses. Now in the lower part of the city, some of the homes are adobe. They import the colored clays from those hills. Up here in the high part, they use wood for our homes."

"And paints," added Holly.

"Whoa. Got you!" Victoria exclaimed. A gust of wind blew straight at us, catching in the voluminous folds of our dresses. All three of us staggered on our toes and lost our balance. We would have fallen, except the girls reacted swiftly to catch us.

"Thanks. You're earning your pay," I teased her.

"Of course," she teased me back. I began to like Victoria. She was sharp.

As we strolled the blocks around the Box, we noticed a number of details. She was right. We were in a wealthier section of the city. Her population estimate suggested a hundred thousand people lived here. Most homes were wooden structures, painted gay rainbow colors. In Beckworth, a tradesman's work area and storefront was part of their home. Here, businesses were housed in separate buildings, for the most part. Banner's Fashions occupied one entire building, while the Banner family residence was in another nearby home and painted bright red.

Men wore either working class clothing or nice looking business suits, while the women we saw wore day dresses or the billowing gowns of noblewomen. Diana and I would certainly look out of place here if we wore our usual leathers. For once, I was glad to be somewhat inconspicuous. We quickly noticed we were just another trio of noblewomen out for a walk, though a few stared at my empty shoulders, and more than once stared at our enormous bosoms.

We took lunch at Peter's Inn, an upscale establishment. Their main doors were wide, allowing noblewomen easier access, which we definitely appreciated. With such tiny soles on the ground, we couldn't easily push our billowing dresses through tight areas. Our feet kept slipping. Not enough friction, Lexi claimed.

We were a bit worried about dining out. Unless we made use of our spells, we were dependent upon these girls to handle our needs and to deal with paying for our meal. I did insist they eat with us, much to their pleasure. "We don't get to eat out all that often," Victoria explained. "This is our first time helping noblewomen dine. I do hope we don't embarrass you."

"Oh we'll get along just fine," Lexi replied diplomatically.

We had finished dining and had just left the inn, when a handsome young man wearing a bright red soldier's uniform walked up to us. His buttons were golden, while his belts were black. One held a cutlass and the other a small, square black leather bag. He took off his black tri-cornered hat, as he stepped up to us, his polished black knee-high boots reflecting the sunlight. Holly and Ella giggled, but Victoria flushed.

"Ladies, noblewomen, good day. Might I have a word with Miss Victoria?" the young man asked. He could be maybe eighteen at most, but he was very polite and charming. He had the poise of an officer.

"Of course," Lexi replied.

As much as possible, I allowed my wives to do most of the talking. I found it less embarrassing, since my voice didn't match my appearance.

"Miss Victoria, will you come to the Royal Ball on Friday night with me?"

She flushed again, before replying. "Sure Ron. Only I'm their servant now, so I will come if they don't need me."

"Royal Ball?" Tiffany queried, adding, "Wicked. Can we come? Or is it a private ball, invite only?"

"Captain Ron Boston, My Lady. It's the Emperor's Royal Ball, but no invitation is needed. Just be there when they open the doors at six. If you come later, there might not be any room inside. Some dance outside if they can't get in. Miss Victoria, you have them there by six, all right?"

"Sure Ron. Thanks."

"Well, got to run. Pleasure meeting all of you wonderful noblewomen. Hope to see you at the ball." He bowed, replaced his hat, pivoted, and walked smartly down the street. I noticed several other men in red milling around, holding onto several brown horses. He joined them.

"That's Victoria's boyfriend," giggled Holly.

"Hush!" Victoria barked.

We spent the afternoon in Banner's Fashions. Harold and Sofia Banner were in their late thirties. Both were fit and trim, but smelled of fabrics. She wore a beautiful deep blue gown that Tiffany fell in love with as soon as she saw it. Both their parents were blonde, and Sofia's hair was as long as Lexi's. She kept it braided so her hair didn't interfere with her work. Harold cut a dashing figure and wore a fine brown suit.

After introductions, Sofia said, "We're so pleased you noblewomen have hired our charming daughters as your personal servants, even if it's temporary. It's wonderful experience for the girls."

"And we certainly need their assistance. They've been simply marvelous today," Lexi replied diplomatically.

Harold commented, "Well, you are extremely beautiful young noblewomen. Victoria says you are visitors to our world?"

"Well, yes we are. Mages in training, actually, just visiting. We spent some time on the western edge of those incredible Rainbow Hills of yours."

"That's what Victoria said," he replied. "We'd be honored if you would dine with us this evening. I'd like to discuss a number of things with you. Say five o'clock? Now then, we'd love to outfit you women in some of our fabulous noblewomen's gowns."

"And Mr. Banner, we'd love to purchase a number of gowns!"

"Wicked!" Tiffany exclaimed.

Lexi ignored her and continued, "But we want only the finest of your gowns. Actually, we've been invited to attend the Royal Ball on Friday. A Captain Ron Boston invited us."

Victoria flushed, while her sisters giggled. Sofia smiled, "Yes, her boyfriend. He has his commission, full captain in the Royal Guards, which makes him a nobleman now. The Emperor and Empress always insist Harold and I go, so you can come with us. And you're right. You'll want special outfits for the ball. Everyone who is anyone will be there. He holds them twice a month."

"Perfect. What colors would you recommend?" Lexi asked.

Sofia lowered her voice and leaned towards us. "Excuse me, but Victoria suggested that she's a male?"

At last, I spoke. "Yes, I am. Before we came to your world, I fell victim to some bad magic, and I've yet to find anyway to undo it. These are my wives."

Her eyes rolled, and I suspected she didn't believe me, even though my voice was a tenor. "Harold, will you look after Felix here?"

"Yes, of course, dear. Magic. Can't stand the stuff myself. No good ever comes from magical spells. Always has a down side. Guess you've discovered that. You must be embarrassed all the time," Harold chatted as we walked to his desk.

"You have no idea," I grinned.

"Have a seat. I'll summon one of my seamstresses. She'll take your measurements. Mind you, we'll need some time to alter bodices to fit you and your wives incredible endowments." He talked on, but I sensed his mind wasn't on his business, but I had no idea on what. At least it wasn't on me, beyond seeing I was being properly serviced as a noblewoman of great financial means.

As five o'clock approached, I had uncovered another key fact. Harold and Sofia had begun their business some twenty years ago, doing all the tailoring and dressmaking themselves. They'd built up a reputation for creating only the finest of apparel. Now, their business was booming. Neither did any of the actual work; their dozen employees did that. They were simply managers and quality control experts, ensuring their workers met their standards for excellence. They were quite wealthy. In fact, they had their own servants, a maid who kept house for them and a chef who prepared their meals.

We dined on pheasant and wild rice, with a curry pudding for desert. We three did appreciate their strong black tea, though Lexi and Tiffany really wanted coffee, but that wasn't found on this world.

As we sat around sipping the tea, Harold began, "You've probably heard of the new edicts our Emperor has issued."

"Not specifically," Lexi said diplomatically. "Could you be more specific?"

"Yes, of course. He's ordered all current and future noblewomen to have their arms removed, since a noblewoman never uses them in the first place. In a way, we concur, since there's no way to hide that awful looking bulge in their upper backs. As you've seen, your body look stunningly shapely—no unsightly back bulge. I think most noblewomen want to comply, at least those we've talked to say they've no reason not to have it done. Most are worried it will be terribly painful. Therefore, the Emperor has his doctors working on that aspect before it is widely implemented. I take it you somehow endured the pain?"

"A Green dragon used his caustic slime along with a Black dragon's acid to remove my arms," I spoke up. "They used a Paralyze spell on me so I couldn't scream or move while he did it to me. And yes, the pain was enormous. I do hope they don't start in until they can make it painless."

"Indeed. We see eye to eye on this aspect."

Sofia spoke up, "But Harold, we should tell them everything." She turned to us across the table. "We've received formal notification we and our family are officially appointed to be nobles. Our business is so successful and we've accumulated so much money that we're more than qualified to become nobles here in Imperial. If truth be told, we should have accepted the noble status years ago."

Harold cleared his throat. "Of course, dear, but if we do, our daughters and our son would also become nobles. Victoria is a little old to begin training as a noblewoman. I'm told they usually start them out when they're ten years old. Might we inquire about how long you've been noblewomen and how difficult it has been for you to adapt? You see, that's my biggest concern—for Sofia and the girls."

This was just what I didn't want to discuss. From my viewpoint, I couldn't see why anyone anywhere would want to spend their life as a helpless noblewoman of this world, constantly attended by a servant. Molly and I saw eye to eye on this, although I truly hoped she'd made the right decision to remain a noblewoman at Edgar's side. However, when in Byron Falls, do as locals do. On this world, we had already seen the elevated, honored status noblewomen had. I couldn't just dismiss this out of hand.

Perhaps the only answer was that people should have a choice in the matter. Before I could say anything, Victoria spoke up.

"We do *so* want to become nobles. That would put our whole family into the highest status, and I'd be free to marry Ron. As a Captain in the Royal Guards, he is a nobleman and thus is expected to only marry a noblewoman. So dad, you just *have* to accept. Besides, it'll help Holly and Ella marry good noblemen too."

"This is a cultural issue," Tiffany spoke before I could or even Lexi. "You see, on our original world, the elite do wear elegant, fancy clothing—top of the line as we say, but we don't believe in hobbling or inhibiting a person so much that they have to have a personal servant or helper to do everything for them. We also believe each person has a right to choose what they wear and how they look. We were kidnaped from our homes and, against our wills, had our bodies modified more or less as they are now. That was more than five years ago now. Yes, we adapted. Had no choice but to adapt, and until we came here and got dolled up in these noblewoman's outfits, we all lived quite independently on our own. We just have different ways of doing things. We use our feet like you use your hands. However, wearing these clothes, we can't do any of that and must have others help us. Your girls are very good at it. So I think each woman should have the choice to become a noblewoman or not. She shouldn't be forced into it." I knew she was thinking of Molly. This was a side of Tiffany I'd not seen before. What a perfect answer to a very dicey question.

"And you, Felix? This happened to you five years ago?" Harold asked.

"Er no. It happened just a few weeks ago. Ran into a very bad magic user who did this to me. Tiffany's right. I'll just add one additional thing. Since every noblewoman we've met so far has had her personal assistant with her to help her with things, I can say it wasn't all that difficult for me to adjust to being one of them, so to speak."

Victoria asked, "So it wasn't too hard to learn how

to be a noblewoman?"

"With proper servants, Victoria, no, not too hard. I was miserable for a time and my feet throbbed, and I was annoyed most of the time, but that's to be expected, since I didn't want to be a noblewoman."

"So it wouldn't be so bad if you had wanted to be a noblewoman?" Victoria insisted on getting me to say it before her parents.

"With proper servants, no, it wouldn't, but if this new ruling from your Emperor holds and the noblewomen lose their arms, there's no going back, Victoria. Make darn sure this is something you really want, for you'll be stuck with it for the rest of your life."

Sofia smiled. "That, Felix, is an excellent point, one that I've been trying to make ever since we were notified we should become nobles."

"Yes, of course," Harold broke in, now turning the conversation to what mattered even more to him. "You've also heard the Emperor has ordered all noblemen to also have their arms removed and to always wear similar boots as our noblewomen."

"No, I'd not heard that, just the bit about losing their arms. So he wants you to also wear those boots?" I replied first.

"Precisely. His argument is since we're noblemen and accompanying our noblewomen, we should walk at their speed. If the boots are good enough for women, they should be good enough for men. With such boots prominently on display, the Emperor claims anyone could tell instantly we're noblemen, just as they can tell instantly a noblewoman by her billowing gown. He claims a lack of arms isn't always visible and that a nobleman should never be mistaken by anyone. All the noblemen who trade with our store are in agreement with that. It's a major social blunder for them not to be recognized as a nobleman. The Emperor claims noblemen don't need arms and hands— that we use our minds and voices, instructing our employees. Well, he has a point there. For about the last five years now, Sofia and I seldom actually work on suits and dresses. We have trained our employees very well, and they do fabulous work. I find it hard to argue against the Emperor's order in this matter."

"As long as you have proper servants," I broke in, not knowing when he would finish up. "However, if you don't wear those boots and wear some you can slip off, then you can learn to do most everything with your feet and toes, becoming independent again."

"I didn't know that. Really? So the key is servants and no boots, if possible. Interesting," Harold said, his voice trailing off as he pondered my reply.

"Still, I don't like it, being so helpless," Sofia added. "Yet, our business could double if we were nobles. Moreover, there are our children to think of. If they were nobles, they would have far more opportunities in our society—meet the right people, have the right doors opened for them."

"Can I ask a question?" I jumped in again. She nodded. "How long has this world had noblewomen bound or dressed as they are today? We're not from here and are curious about it. Is this a recent phenomenon?"

"Lordy, no one knows that. It was present when my grandmother was alive. She helped make noblewomen's gowns and binding corsets," Sofia answered.

Harold added, "As far as I know, it's been a staple for noblewomen to be bound for at least the last two centuries. Could be longer, but there are no records. Well, it's getting late. We best let our daughters get you prepared for bed. I don't want them out too late, if you don't mind."

"Of course. Thank you so much for a lovely dinner and evening," Lexi replied, and we rose carefully, letting our helpers assist us navigating the room and doors.

Shortly, we arrived in our room in the Box. The girls were efficient. Within minutes, they had us undressed except for the corsets. They kindly brushed our hair for us. Then, without warning, they arranged Lexi and Tiffany on my bed and tied their legs at their ankles behind their heads, all proper like. Well, we couldn't fault them for following the rules of their tradition. What to do with me became their problem at once.

Victoria frowned. "Felix, you are supposed to be bound up like they are, but you are the man. I don't think there are any rules for this. I guess we should bind you too." Before I could protest, they whipped my legs up and behind my head, tying my ankles securely. I stifled a yowl of pain, as they quickly draped our hair over our fronts. "Good night. We'll be by in the morning. Thanks for everything."

After we heard the door close, I said, "Crap that hurt! Damn. I'm not that flexible." Rolling my head to one side, I was able to kiss Tiffany. Then, I rolled it to the other side and struggled to reach Lexi, giving her a kiss. "How are we supposed to sleep like this? What if we need something? We're all immobile and helpless."

Tiffany giggled. "Sleep!" I was out in an instant.

"Oh my legs are mush," I complained in the morning as Victoria untied them and gently moved them back down because they refused to work for me. After a bit of a massage, I could move them. Rapidly, they got us dressed and accompanied us over to Peter's Inn for breakfast. After that, we continued our tour of their city, at least the areas within walking distance. By evening, the first of our new gowns was ready for a fitting. After that, we accepted their supper invitation; both Harold and Sofia wanted to continue our discussion. There had been some developments.

Harold explained, "We received a message this afternoon. Apparently, the Emperor's doctors have worked out a painless way to handle all aspects of his proposed changes. We've been given until Saturday to get it done."

"Dad, I've got to see Captain Ron right away," Victoria exclaimed, suddenly worried. I sensed she believed they would have had more time for decisions.

Harold chuckled. He was rather conservative by nature, so I wondered what his laugh meant. "Honey, I knew you would. I've already sent him an invitation to pay us a visit tonight. We have to make this decision, and I'd prefer it if we did it tonight and be done with it, one way or the other. Of course, going against the Emperor's orders could well spell major trouble for us, so we can't take this lightly. Since you two want to marry, Captain Ron should be a part of any decision we make."

Light conversation followed until the arrival of the handsome young captain. From their eyes and smiles, I could tell the two were smitten with each other, just as I was with Lexi and Tiffany. I felt privileged to be allowed to listen in on just how this family made such an important decision.

"Look, as a Captain in the Royal Guards, I'm expected to become a nobleman. They've shown me how I'll still be able to ride my horse. They've rigged up a way for me to control the horse's reins with my feet. It's rather clever, but I'll need a completely new set of uniforms. The new ones will have no trace of arms holes and sleeves. The quartermaster said they look neat and trim."

"When do you get it done?" asked Victoria. "I do so want to be with you."

"Saturday morning. I'm scheduled to be there around ten. A private will become my constant aide, Victoria. Then, we can get married. I checked. If you have it done with me, we can be married right then and help each other recover and all that."

"Where will we live? Servants?" Victoria asked.

"They give all noblemen in the guards our own home, not too far from the palace. It's within walking distance from here. I'll have a private as my aide, but we'll need to hire a servant for you, Victoria. So what are your plans, Mr. Banner?" Cleverly, he tossed it back to Harold.

"That's one reason we're meeting tonight. Have you heard what they are planning to do with those that don't volunteer?"

Captain Ron frowned. "Don't know sir, but it can't be good. The General is planning something, but he's not yet announced anything to us. Oh, one other thing, Miss Victoria, once I do this, becoming a nobleman, I get a promotion to major! With that salary, we'll be on Easy Street."

Nothing about being the way we were was easy, but I didn't stand a chance at convincing them otherwise. I wisely kept quiet, but looked for an opening in which I could interject a more realistic viewpoint. It never occurred. Soon, we headed home to the Box and quickly found ourselves tucked in for the night.

By Friday, we paid for both our three girl's services and for three new outfits for each of us; one was done in a slippery fabric they called satin. Lexi's was bright red contrasting with her golden hair. Tiffany's ball gown was a bright green, while mine was Cobalt blue.

As our three helpers dressed us, Tiffany's comment took me by surprise. "I wonder why the women on this world don't wear much jewelry. On our world, Felix, we'd wear a golden necklace with perhaps a gemstone in it and certainly some earrings to match."

"We were too poor to afford such things back in Byron Falls," I responded, "but maybe Diana and the others can now. You two look so sexy I can hardly stand it. Wow!"

"Hey, you look stunning yourself," Lexi replied with a big grin. "I wonder what we'll uncover at the Royal Ball."

"I wonder how they dance on this world," Tiffany interrupted us. "We haven't any idea how they dance. We're going to look like bumpkins tonight."

Victoria giggled. "Don't worry. We planned on giving you some lessons this morning, once we get you dressed in these new gowns and we get back from breakfast."

Around five, Harold had us over to his home for a quick, light supper. Then, he helped us all into his large carriage, lifting us three up, for there wasn't any way for us in our new gowns to climb the steps. Captain Ron was already there and met the carriage, offering Victoria his hand, as she stepped down, likewise, her sisters, while Howard lifted us out and down. Then, with his arms around Sofia, he led us all up the stone walkway into the huge palace.

The Imperial Palace was simply enormous,

occupying several city blocks. Though not taller than two stories in most places, many interconnected buildings sprawled across the grounds. The Ball Room was a single story building with giant columns supporting the entrance portico. A circular stairs just inside led to an observation deck on the roof, where one could take a romantic aside from the ball proper. Inside, the floor was polished marble, with a raised musician's platform against the opposite wall. On either side of them, refreshments tables beckoned. A dozen black-clad servants dashed about setting various dishes on the tables. To the right was a raised platform with two velvet covered, red chairs, on which the Emperor and Empress often sat while not dancing.

Although we were early, compliments of Harold, the place was teaming with couples. A quick glance suggested at least three-quarters of the women were noblewomen and whose gowns looked much like ours. Even though Captain Ron kept his arm around Victoria, as did Harold with Sofia, I sensed these normal women felt slightly out of place or perhaps nervous because they looked different.

As if reading my mind, Tiffany whispered, "Peer pressure at work here."

I gave her a big smile, noticing at the same time we still had our three helpers, though Victoria was torn between being with Ron and being at my side. I vowed to need her as little as possible this evening.

I knew dancing was going to be problematical. From our practice sessions, we saw that standing on our toes, we could only stump like penguins, hardly graceful dancing, as Tiffany complained. Still, the noblewomen danced by taking their tiny steps following rigid patterns. This we could do, as long as we could remember their complex movements. Victoria said we should just follow the others, but Lexi wasn't so sure that

we could do so with only a few hours practice. In contrast, I wanted to meet with many nobles who were here. Somehow, I needed to find the situation the Box wanted us to "handle." Thus far, we had no clue. Neither did Drago, who spend days traveling around Imperial trying to figure it out.

Earlier this morning after the girls left to get themselves ready for the ball, Drago and we three met to discuss that issue. He explained, "As far as I can tell, Felix, businesses are doing quite well. There doesn't appear to be any kidnaping going on, not as we faced in Byron Falls. There are a few other dragons around, Blacks and Reds mainly, but I believe I saw a Brown and Blue. I didn't bother with the swamps though. Whatever we're to handle, I don't think it involves commerce. Have you had any luck figuring it out?"

"Not really. I can't see how we can change the way they are treating their noblewomen, nor do I think we should meddle in their long-standing traditions or customs. Now this new business about modifying their noblemen—that sure sounds fishy. Maybe we're to do something about that, but honestly, we'd have to change the Emperor's mind and then all the bureaucracy on down. Honestly, it's a stupid move to do this to all their current noblemen and those they're promoting to noblemen."

"You humans do have mysterious ways," Drago mused. "I've heard a lot of talk about this new proclamation of the Emperor, and not all of it is favorable, mind you. Maybe we're supposed to do something about that. I sure wish the Box would give us clues to what it wants us to handle."

We'd left it at that, making plans for our attendance at the Royal Ball. Drago decided to infiltrate the ball by going invisible and seeing what he could "sniff out." A royal fanfare announced the opening of the ball.

The Emperor and Empress entered first, moving both slowly and carefully as all noblewomen did, giving the appearance of gliding effortlessly across the marble dance floor. We knew it was anything but effortless, that she was taking numerous tiny three or four inch steps, the maximum amount she could without losing her balance. However, what shocked me was the Emperor. He too had no arms and wore boots similar to all the noblewomen, except his boots were highly polished and reflected the overhead light coming from hundreds of lanterns. Both wore bright green, though his suit was form-fitting; his jacket and shirt had no trace of sleeves, as if he never had them. She had long, dark brown hair, but definitely wasn't a beauty queen, which rather surprised me, since she was the Empress of this world.

General John Waterson who commanded the Royal Guards strode in next, accompanied by his noblewoman wife, Martha. There wasn't any mistaking his position. He wore a similar bright red uniform with black trim as did Captain Ron. Here was a no nonsense man who found walking at his wife's pace most annoying. For an instant, I felt sympathy for her; I knew she was moving her feet as fast as she could safely manage, which yielded the usual slow, gliding look displayed by all noblewomen.

Dozens of other important men and women followed them, too many for me to observe. When I turned my attention back to the Emperor, he'd already been lifted up onto his temporary throne. "Welcome everyone to our Royal Ball. In case you haven't heard the news, my physicians have invented a painless way to remove noble men and women's arms. I can personally attest to the procedure being painless, as you can plainly see. So now my plan to have our nobles be highly recognized is going forward. Yes, tomorrow, it begins. There'll also be many new wealthy men and women who have accepted my offer for them to upgrade their societal status to nobles. With this Grand Plan, we're ushering in a whole new and magnificent era for our wonderful world of Rainbow's End. Least you still have doubts, tonight, I'm told we're honored to have three visitors who embody the new Imperial customs I'm implementing. Let us give a warm welcome to Felix Pelingham and his wives, Lexi and Tiffany. Personally, I do believe they have taken fashion to a completely new level, but in all fairness, you can't miss them. Felix, Lexi, Tiffany, where are you? Ah, there they are," he nodded towards us.

I was shocked, not expecting anything like this.

How did he know about us? I hate being the center of attention. Hundreds of eyes stared at us. I knew they would be doing so all night long. Could Harold have said something? I doubted that, because when I glanced at him, he seemed as surprised as the rest of us. The Emperor continued, giving me little time to react. "Please, take time tonight to dance a round with our esteemed guests. Now, let the Royal Ball begin." The musicians began to play, making chatting more difficult.

Ron immediately put an arm around Victoria, whisking her off for this first dance. At least the music was slow and stately, and I found I rather liked listening to it. Pipe and drum was about the only music back in Byron Falls.

To my surprise, General John came up to me, slipped his strong arm around my waist, forcing me to dance with him. "I want a word with you, but my God, are you really a man?"

"Yes, lost an unfortunate magical battle. So I make do as best I can."

"I see. Your voice sounds male. You seem to have adapted nicely to being a nobleman of the Emperor's new vintage. I just wanted to make sure you don't cast any harmful spells at our Emperor or Empress. I take their safety seriously."

"I've no reason to wish ill on either, General John, but should I? Have a reason to dislike them and wish them harm?" I felt annoyed and turned it around on him. Besides, I was having a terrible time keeping up with his dance steps. They were too large for our tiny range of motion, but at least he wouldn't let me fall over, which I very nearly did twice.

"Are you really a man?" "How come you have two wives?" Do all men on your world have such giant breasts?" "Don't you miss your arms?" "Did it hurt having them removed?" On it went, question after question, as various men insisted on dancing with me. In fact, not until late in the evening was I finally able to dance with Lexi and Tiffany, who were besieged with questions. By the time we

161

joined up, our feet were killing us, and we just wanted the dance to end.

I think he planned it this way—to meet up with us when we were aching and tired. We'd barely joined each other when the Emperor came up to us. "Please, come with me and chat a while. You must be exhausted. I'm Emperor Karl Bertrand, by the way."

Wild emotions. That's the only way I can describe my senses at that very moment. The Emperor was barely two feet from me. He wasn't human. He was a Black dragon! His eyes gave him away to me, cold and inhuman, though his face had a blackish hue to it, even in the orange light from the soot-covered lanterns high above us. I sensed rising panic from Lexi and Tiffany as well. I swallowed hard. "I'm Felix, but you know that."

"Yes, of course. But which is which?" he asked nodding to the women.

Nodding towards Lexi, I replied, "This is Lexi, and she's Tiffany. We're pleased to meet you, Emperor." *What is going on here? Do these people know they have a dragon as Emperor?*

"So very pleased to meet you both. I must say your figures are incredibly impressive indeed. If I could, I'd legislate them for all our noblewomen. Nature certainly has shone upon you both."

"Well, they're far too large for us," Lexi replied diplomatically. "But thanks for the compliments. You cut a striking figure yourself, Your Majesty. Is that how we're to greet you?"

"Oh that's fine. You can even call me Karl. We're having a tea and snack after the ball is finished, which should be very soon now. Please, I'd love to have you stick around and dine with me. We could chat some. I seldom get an opportunity to chat with aliens from another world. Please do me the honor of sticking around for a while."

*What's with this dragon? He sounds polite enough, though covert. I don't trust him, but do we dare refuse him?* As if sensing my unspoken thoughts, he said, "Don't worry. I've already cleared it with your hosts and servants, the wonderful Banner family. Oh yes, I'm to deliver a message from young Victoria. She has asked you three to be present in the morning when she and her family take the big step and become nobles. Honestly, that family should have become nobles years ago. I think they've been too tied up in their business to think much about it. Do you know their company, Banner's Fashions, makes the very best suits and ball gowns in all of Imperial?"

"Yes, we're wearing their gowns now. Just where are we to meet them? Of course, I'd not think of missing their great day. This is a defining moment in their lives, and we're honored they want us to share it with them, but I've no idea where this is being done." I stalled as much as I could.

"The Royal Hospital here in this very complex—it's where all the immediate conversions are taking place, beginning tomorrow. Once others see how convenient and painless the process now is, I'll license the process out for other doctors to perform. I do so want everything to go extremely well for everyone, especially all the new nobles. Please, I know the Banner daughters have been your servants. What with tomorrow being their big day, I'd be honored if you and your wives would spend the night here in the Royal Palace. My staff will handle your needs. This way, you'll be here to greet the Banners when they arrive for their appointment. You may sit with them throughout and give them moral support, which I'm sure they greatly desire."

He continued, as though just recalling another message. "One more thing, Victoria and soon-to-be Major Ron Boston are being married later tomorrow afternoon, once their recovery is complete and he receives his promotion. Ron has requested you three attend their wedding ceremony. Again, it'll be held here within the Royal Palace at the Royal Guards' Hall. I took the liberty of telling Major Ron you wouldn't miss it. So really, Felix, spending the night here is the wisest choice, unless you don't want to be bothered by the Banners and the wedding."

I wanted to say no to this proposition, but he was being civil, totally polite, and thoughtful. Reluctantly, I agreed, but sent a Message to Drago, saying we were staying the night here as the Emperor's guest. I also told him the man was a Black dragon.

After the last dance, the Emperor called out, "The next Royal Ball will be in two weeks. I hope to see you all then. Besides, we should have a goodly number of new nobles attending. Good night and thank you for coming."

I couldn't help wonder what was going on with this Black Dragon. His parting words were what I might have expected from a friendly ruler. His servants escorted us to a private room just off this giant room. A table of food lined the back wall, while a beautiful walnut table and matching chairs adorned the middle of the room. After they got us seated, the Emperor and Empress entered, sitting down across from us, nodding to us. Then, the servants set about feeding us. I admit the food was good, but then it should have been. This was the world's top ruler.

He did chat with us, but asked merely the same type of questions others had bombarded us with all night. In contrast though, the Empress said little. She seemed dull and not quite all there, but she was human. Just when I was beginning to wonder why he wanted us here with him, he rose and bid us good night. After they left, the servants asked us follow them. At least they were used to our slow, careful walk, but by now, our feet and legs were protesting—aching to be precise. We walked what seemed to be endless corridors before they carried us down several flights of stairs, ending in a series of guest bedrooms.

What I found curious were the beds, which were the usual narrow variety, suitable for noblewomen. The head of each bed was tilted up at about a thirty-degree angle and covered with many soft pillows, necessary for proper sexual relations with one's noblewoman wife. The room had three beds, so I expected they had anticipated we would be staying, long before we even arrived at the ball. These servants were models of efficiency. Within minutes, they had us undressed, chamber potted, and our hair brushed. Quickly, they had us sitting on the bed and then lying back. Before I could say anything, we had our legs tucked up under our heads, tied together at our ankles.

I panicked. I was now helpless. If the dragon wanted to eliminate us, now was a perfect opportunity. Watching the three servants departing, I nearly panicked, unable to move at all. Lexi whispered, "Felix, what do we do if they come to attack us or something? I know we can cast our Fly spell and our Magical Missile spell, but we're almost totally helpless."

Damn. My wives are good! "Brilliant, Lexi. I was so worried that I forgot we have spells. We're not completely helpless, are we?"

Tiffany giggled. "Hardly, but we'll have to rely on our spells, I'm afraid. Say, that dragon didn't seem to be evil or anything. Downright pleasant, for a dragon, I suppose. And what's a dragon doing being their Emperor?"

I had no idea, and we chatted briefly before I had her cast her Sleep spell on me. My legs were throbbing, and I'd never sleep a wink without her spell. I awoke slightly afraid I'd slept through something terrible, but our servants were there handling our morning needs, quietly and efficiently.

After being fed breakfast, we were led to a waiting room. A man wearing a white uniform met us and explained, "Ah, the Pelinghams. Yes, the Banner family and Ron are being handled now. After the operations are finished, they'll be dressed in their new apparel and brought here to this private waiting room. I'm told once everyone is finished, there's to be a wedding ceremony, before you head for your homes. Since it'll likely be early afternoon before everyone is done, someone will assist you with lunch, which will be brought in here for you. So sit back and relax. Your loved ones are safe. This is a painless process. Once they're brought here, you may go ahead and help them practice walking and other things. That's the purpose of the long hallway to your right. As you know, practice makes perfect."

With that, he turned and left. I suspected he had memorized much of his speech. He probably had to repeat most of it many times.

Before long, another young soldier joined us. He wore a bright red uniform with black trim. "Is this the waiting room for Ron Boston and the Banners?" he asked.

"Yes. You must be Major Ron's personal assistant," I made polite conversation with him.

"Yes, but he won't be officially Major Ron until the ceremony that'll take place as soon as he comes in here. I'm to lead him to the General and then to the Royal Chapel. I suppose I'll see you at the wedding too." We chatted, passing the time.

Before long, Ron came walking into the room. An orderly had a steadying arm around him. He wore his old uniform, which was disheveled and in need of a washing, but his boots had been replaced with the new style. The heels were just as high as they were for noblewomen, but their style looked a bit more masculine. They were highly polished, and the toes reflected the dim lantern light here in the waiting room. The boots were tied together at his ankles, just as they had been on our training boots back in Beckworth, forcing him to take no more than a three-inch step, one boot in front of the other. From experience, we knew taking a larger step was tantamount to stumbling and falling.

Ron's complexion was very pale. "Hi. Glad you three are here. I'm scared! This is not quite what I expected. I can barely walk, and I feel so helpless!"

"Practice walking, Ron, and you'll soon get the hang of it. We're glad you want us at your wedding later today," I said as encouragingly as I could. I felt this whole business was completely insane. For a moment, I wondered how it could have gone on for two centuries with their noblewomen.

His private assistant spoke up, "Sir, I'm to lead you to the ceremony room. General John Waterson is officiating at your promotion, but I've heard he's already had this done to himself. Don't worry. I've got you." His arm around Ron's waist held Ron securely, as they continued the slow walk down the hall.

We didn't have to wait long before they brought Victoria out to us, along with her new servant girl. She wore her new billowing, wedding gown, white of course. She looked terrified. "I'm really, really scared, Lexi. I'm so helpless now. We can barely walk in these heels, and I have to walk well when I marry Ron later this afternoon. I don't think I can do this."

"Your gown looks fabulous on you, Victoria, just perfect. Look, the bare shoulders proudly displays you're a noblewoman," Lexi replied diplomatically, knowing what Victoria wanted to hear. "We were terrified at first too, Victoria, but with practice, you'll soon feel better. Come on. Let's walk the long hall as the man suggested. Tiffany, you keep an eye out for the others." Victoria took a deep breath and relaxed slightly.

I added, "We saw Ron just a few minutes ago. He's excited about the wedding, but first he's getting his promotion, and then he gets his new uniform, but I'll give you a clue, he was just as scared as you are. He can barely walk. His fancy boots are tied together as yours are. That's done so you can't possibly take too big a step and fall down. It's also designed to help you get used to taking small steps, so you look as if you're gliding across the floor."

Lexi encouraged her, "Come on, Victoria. Let's walk and practice it. By the time for the wedding, I bet you'll look as if you're gliding."

Within a few minutes, they brought Sofia out. She was just as terrified as the others were. "Maybe we've made a horrid mistake," she whispered. Tiffany jumped in with soothing words and got her and her new servant girl walking the hallway following Lexi and Victoria. Before long, I got to handle Harold, who now wore his new suit that had no arm holes or sleeves, one he'd designed himself, giving him a trim, elegant appearance.

He was terrified too. "Why did I ever consider doing this? Felix, I'm so helpless now. We can barely walk." I let him vent, as I got him and his new servant lad walking the hallway.

After he calmed down some, he insisted we spend our days with him and his family, helping them adjust to this new situation. I agreed. How could I not? Then, I tried something different. "Harold, do you realize your Emperor Karl is actually a dragon, a Black dragon to be precise?"

"What? A dragon? Have you been smoking the weed? There's no such thing as a dragon. They're mythical creatures. Well, that's not entirely true. I've heard tales of large, snake-like creatures inhabiting Brackenmoor Swamp far to the west. Perhaps, that's where you're getting your strange ideas from. Do you really think I'll be able function at all like this? I had no idea it was going to be this horrible."

"Look, Harold. You've lived your whole life having arms and wearing comfortable, practical shoes. Suddenly, both are gone. It's damned scary. It is for us too, but like anything else, practice will make you much more comfortable about it. Come on. We're supposed to get you walking before lunch."

After Ella and Holly were brought into the waiting room, the servants brought in lunch. Then, we headed to the wedding, but not before we received five more pleads for us to come and help the family adapt, which we promised to do.

Like bobbing penguins, we entered the Royal Chapel and took our seats up front. In the rear, Victoria stood nervously waiting. Then, with a short fanfare, Major Ron and his servant stepped up to the altar, entering from a side door. He looked resplendent in his new uniform, made without a hint of armholes or sleeves, as though the body never had such appendages. He looked trim and handsome, but very nervous, if not downright scared. Like us, he wobbled trying to stand still in one place.

Then, even more nervously, Victoria began her walk down the main aisle. Although her frequent wobbles to get her balance back kept us all worried, she did appear to glide down the aisle for Ron. Soon, the two stood side by side, and a minister moved before them, conducting the brief ceremony. "You may kiss your bride. I give you Mr. and Mrs. Ron Boston." None of us could clap, so we cheered instead.

That done, we were ushered out to waiting carriages, where the servants dealt with lifting each of us up and into them. A half hour later, they repeated the process, lifting us down, and we followed the Banners into their home. Ron and Victoria brought up the rear.

***

For us, the two weeks passed rapidly. Each day brought new challenges to the forefront for the members of this family. We did our best to provide guidance and suggestions. However, I'd be remiss if I didn't mention how Ron now managed to ride his horse so he could lead his regiment into battle. The reins were pulled back along the side of the horse and slipped through two O-rings, attached to the front of his saddle. From there, the reins continued on back and were tied to his stirrups. By moving one foot back and the other forward, he could turn the horse's head either direction. Pulling back on both feet reined in the horse. His real problem was in staying on the horse using only his legs, that and mounting and dismounting.

As the two-week mark approached along with the next coming Royal Ball, Harold and Sofia both commented to us nearly the same thing. "I had no idea just how awful life was for the noblewomen. They always looked so elegant, gliding across the streets—I had no idea how awful it is for them." While I wanted to point out if they wore sensible shoes and clothes, they'd not have too many problems getting by on their own, I wisely decided to keep quiet.

By the time of the Royal Ball, they were walking far better. Much of their initial fright had subsided, but they were still very nervous about appearing in public at the ball, and again, our presence was a calming godsend for them, including Ron.

# Chapter 13—The Hammer

"Well, yes, Emperor Karl, I would love to see just how your doctors can remove a person's arms without any pain at all," I agreed.

We were at the Royal Ball, accompanying Ron and the Banners, all of whom were quite nervous about leaving their servants behind and trusting to the Emperor's staff. We had no choice, not if we wanted to go to the ball. At first, the sheer number of armless men and women here floored me. Last time, I was about the only one, ignoring the bound noblewomen, but two weeks later, I counted barely ten with arms out of the thousand in attendance. The blue uniformed servants of the Emperor mingled, helping here and there as needed. Thus, it wasn't surprising that I chatted with the Emperor about how they could have done all this in just two weeks. He grinned and asked if I'd like to stay the night and see how it was done in the morning. Hence, my answer.

"This is almost impossible," Ron declared, greatly annoyed with his and Victoria's pathetic attempt to dance. "We had a ball last time, but now it's all we can do to keep from falling over. Hell, no one is moving much at all."

Victoria did her best to keep her eyes dry, her illusions of noblewomen shattered beyond repair.

Lexi, who was nearby, replied diplomatically, "Easy does it. Small steps and as gracefully as you can manage. I know, Ron. It really shows with your boots, while Victoria's feet are hidden beneath her gown, but you do look quite handsome and dashing." That last brought a slight smile to Victoria's stoical face.

So the night went. Several other new noblemen and women, who knew the Banners had us staying with them these past two weeks, asked us if we could spend some time with them as well. Considering there must be five hundred of these families or more, I couldn't see how we could, but at least I agreed to see what we could do. I didn't say I doubted we could do much at all. Nor did I say we three thought they were incredibly foolish for going along with the Emperor's orders.

Once more, we were quite happy when the ball ended. Our feet were aching. Thus, we eagerly followed the Emperor's servants, who led us down the long halls to the bedroom we'd stayed in last time. To be honest, I didn't suspect a thing. Rather, I looked forward to learning how they could do these operations painlessly and so darn fast. As before, they quickly undressed us, got our legs up and behind our heads, crossed at the ankles, and tied with a soft cloth band. Grimacing, I ask Tiffany to "Sleep" me. After a giggle, she did so.

I know. I should have been screaming, panicking, protesting, yelling, and crying over my physical situation. If left alone, I know I would have broken down completely and become a basket case. Wisely, I kept many others around me and forced myself to do what I could to help others over their panic and fears. And yes, I deeply regret bringing my sister into this, for her mutilation threatened to burn my soul to ashes. I dared not think about the situation; hence, I desperately needed Tiffany's Sleep spell so I wouldn't lay there thinking about all that had happened to my sister and me.

"Wake up!" the deep voice of Emperor Karl Bertrand, the Black dragon, hollered. He stood at the entrance to our guest bedroom. We were far below ground and thus only lanterns provided the illumination. He wore a fine grey suit, whose jacket had no trace of sleeves. His highly polished, knee-high, black boots, with a towering wedge heel, were similar to all those worn by the new noblemen and noblewomen. Thus, as I opened my eyes and saw him standing there, from the wobbling of his torso, I could see he also had some difficulty keeping his balance while standing still. In that instant, I wondered if his dragon form mimicked his human form or if his human form was just for "show."

"We're awake," Lexi declared. "Please, you should send in the servants to attend to our needs and get us properly dressed. It's not polite to see us naked like this, Your Majesty."

Emperor Karl laughed. "I promised you could see just how the operations are done. In fact, I'm doing that one better, you meddling fools. Adler has told me all about you. I'm a man of my word. We're off to the operations room, where you can experience firsthand just how painless the process actually is. I'm having those greyish, dead arms of your wives removed, as well as everyone's legs. You'll soon see limb removal is a painless process. Then, I'll keep you three in my guest bedroom to 'service' other guests who visit from time to time. With only a head and torso remaining, why, you'll cause Adler and me no further troubles. Servants, roll their beds down the hall to the Operations Center."

Three male servants entered. Only now did I notice our narrow, tilted beds had rollers on them. As I started to protest, the three pushed our beds on out of the guest bedroom into the hallway.

I screeched, "You can't do that to us!" The girls merely screamed.

"Of course I can do this. I'm the Emperor, and I can do any damn thing I want to do, especially with meddlers. Adler and I don't want you interfering any further in our operations here on Rainbow's End. So relax. Soon, you'll be just a head and torso, but still quite pretty, mind you!" Emperor Karl roared with laughter, so much so he almost fell down. One of the servants caught him at the last moment, steadying the laughing monarch.

As they pushed our beds single-file down the long hallway with mine in the lead, I had to do something and fast, but with our legs still tied behind our heads, we three were nearly immobile. Because of the incredibly slow pace of Emperor Karl, I had time to think, but Tiffany took action. I heard her voice bark, "Fly!" Lexi's spell detonated mere seconds after Tiffany's did. Suddenly, my beautiful wives with their legs still tied behind their heads came flying past my bed, their hair flowing behind them. I cast my Fly spell and followed them on down the long, underground hallway. Tiffany definitely can think in a crisis!

Our speed was that of a runner, but I knew the duration of their spells was limited to perhaps six to ten minutes; then, they'd have to land and recast it. However, we faced several serious problems, as we fled from the Emperor and his proposed mutilations. First, we were deep underground in some kind of labyrinth of halls barely eight feet wide. Second, none of us knew where anything was located. That is, we were flying blindly down one hallway with no idea where we were going or where an exit to the world was located. Third, Emperor Karl also cast his Fly spell and came after us, leaving his human servants behind, who were unable to run fast enough to catch up with us. Fourth, he was a dragon. At any moment, he could revert to his dragon form and fire off his breath weapon, drenching us in his caustic acid, which would end our flight and lives. Alternatively, he could cast spells at us, such as a Ball of Fire or perhaps an Electrical Bolt, assuming he knew these spells.

As we approached a T in the hall, I heard him cast a Ball of Fire. Without thinking, I veered sharply left, bouncing off the wall as I changed direction.

"Ouch. Oh crap!" Lexi yelled, because she saw the ball of red flames sweeping down the hall behind us.

"Wicked! Cool move, Felix," Tiffany cried, following us down the side hall, racing ahead of the flames. Her exclamation came as the flames ceased expanding, having reached its maximum coverage.

Ahead, I saw another junction and chose to veer to the right this time, figuring it would be harder for the dragon to get a bead on us for another spell. As we turned, I heard Tiffany bark, "Web the Hallway."

Glancing behind me, I saw the hallway completely covered with sticky webs. Any human running into them was sure to become trapped in them. Lexi then cast her Web spell as well. I didn't cast mine. Why? The dragon probably weighted a thousand pounds. While the sticky webs would easily entrap and hold a human, they'd be mere gossamers to a dragon, especially flying as fast as he was going—a small factor of momentum. Tiffany's "Crap," told me I was right. Still, I reminded myself to praise her for her brilliant idea later on.

Right, left, straight—I kept varying our path as intersections and T's appeared. It must have worked because Emperor Karl didn't try to cast another Ball of Fire at us.

Tiffany's voice barked, "Untie legs. Hey, it worked."

I glanced behind and saw her legs now dangling above the floor. She was free, but without our special boots, we weren't walking anywhere. Flying was still our sole option. Lexi quickly cast her Untie spell, as did I. Finally, our legs were free, for what that was worth, not much at the moment.

Eventually, I was bound to run into either a dead end or some other room, perhaps one that exited the Imperial Palace, assuming I got lucky. Luck wasn't with us. Ahead, the hallway ended and there weren't any side passages or even a room, just a dead end. We three sat gently down; the girls had to land because their Fly spell reached its maximum duration. Quickly, both recast theirs while I thought fast.

Either this truly was a dead end, unfinished construction, or there was some form of secret door. Praying we weren't trapped, I barked with complete conviction, "Open All Doors!" Magical energies flashed. To everyone's amazement, a stone door ahead of us rotated open, revealing another lantern-lit hallway. Zoom. We shot down it, and soon flew out into some kind of large living quarters, which I estimated was perhaps forty feet square. Another hallway left the room opposite this entrance and we headed for it.

Behind us, the Black dragon landed and morphed into his dragon form. "Faster!" I yelled, fearing the worst—being drenched in his caustic acid.

I heard Tiffany yell, "Wicked!" That was followed by her laughter.

Incongruous. My mind reeled. We were about to be

drenched in acid and she was laughing. I turned to face the painful death and broke into a laugh myself. Karl's dragon form also had no front legs. Thus, he had no way to walk! He rather pushed himself along with his hind legs, trying to get his neck up into a position from which he could blast us with his cone of acid. He looked ridiculous. Our laughter only frustrated him further. We shot on out of the room and into the hallway.

Twice more, I cast my Open All Doors spell, which opened both normal doors, locked doors, and secret doors. I had to, since without arms, valuable time would be wasted trying to open them with our warped feet. Looking back, I should have realized we were going deeper underground, not upwards towards ground level and perhaps an escape.

Another secret chamber appeared, filled with weapons and bits of armor. A third chamber, also hidden, held stacks of silver and gold coins, along with gemstones. Once more, luck was on our side. Having morphed back into his human form, Emperor Karl cast a Bolt of Electricity at us. Unlike the Ball of Fire, this spell's range is quite long, similar to a lightning bolt. He chose to fire it at us as we passed through the hidden armory. Sparks flew wildly about, as the horde of metal weapons and armor absorbed the electrical charge instead of our bodies.

At this point, I knew either of his power attacking spells would likely kill us if we were directly hit with them. Karl was a very old dragon, which meant his spells and acid breath were particularly lethal. If I didn't do something quickly, sooner or later we'd run out of tunnels, and black doom would arrive. This time, I didn't have Drago around to help me.

How do you slay a dragon? Drago once told me weapons wouldn't even scratch his hide. Rather, only a magically enchanted weapon could harm a dragon. I didn't have such a weapon or hands to wield it.

Ahead, my last Open All Doors spell forced a secret door to open. This time, the door was a large section of the stone wall, and it rose upwards, revealing yet another secret chamber, this one quite spacious. Worse, I saw no exit doors and cast the spell once more, hoping against hope it would reveal some secret way out of this room. No luck.

"Euu! What's that smell?" Tiffany cried out, as she flew into the room and landed.

Talk about luck running out—we'd flown into the dragon's lair! We were trapped—end of the line. I thought faster than I had ever done before. How do you kill a dragon? How do you stop a dragon that must weigh a thousand pounds? It hit me: momentum. I'd seen a Byron Falls lad put a small stone in his sling. He swung it around his head very fast and let the stone fly. The boy was a good shot, and his stone brought down the pheasant. Momentum was the answer.

"Lexi, Tiffany, cast your Levitate spell on that open stone door. I'm going to close it and then help you hold it up," I barked.

They did so. Once I was sure their spells activated, I cast the reverse of my Open All Doors spell, followed at once with my own Levitate spell. We three were barely able to generate enough force to hold the incredibly heavy stone secret door up. Straining their wills to the maximum, both women saw what I intended to do, flashing me a smile. There was no time to exchange words, for Emperor Karl came flying towards us, an evil grin on his face. He knew he had us trapped, trapped in his own secret lair!

"Rats in a maze. You're mine now. Time to get those legs of yours removed," he threatened and began laughing as he flew through the opened secret door.

Timing was everything. "Now!" I yelled, canceling my Levitate spell. A fraction of a second later, Tiffany and Lexi canceled theirs. Gravity pulled the heavy stone door rapidly down. I'd timed it perfectly. As it struck the dragon, his body reverted to his true form, that of a Black dragon. The sound of shattering bones echoed, as the door closed tightly squashing his neck. Emperor Karl died instantly, a section of his very long neck shattered and squashed.

"Is—is he dead?" Lexi asked, still shaken up.

With my Fly spell cancelled, I tiptoed over to his giant head and poked it. "Yes, he's quite dead. We're safe at last."

"Wicked! But where are we? This smell is awful," Tiffany declared, turning up her nose.

"Drago once told me most dragons make themselves a lair, usually underground. They hide all their magical things, gold, gems, and stuff in their lairs. Look there. That's a dragon bed, if I ever saw one." The chamber was about forty feet by eighty, with two supporting columns in the middle. A pile of straw and cloth covered the back half of the room, obviously a bed for a dragon. The section of the room we were in held tables, chairs, couches, desks, and chests.

"Well, we should search this room," Lexi declared with a sharp nod of her head. "He tried to kill us, so I want compensation for that. Right Tiff?"

"Wicked. Right, Lexi. Compensation."

I chuckled. "Okay, but I wish we had our clothes and boots. This stone floor is darn cold. I'll send Drago a Message. Let's see what we can find that might be valuable."

Lexi added, "And figure some way out of here. I think we broke that door, and besides, his body completely blocks the hallway. Warm. That's better. Tiff, cast Warm spells."

Overhead, three lantern groups provided illumination, but the room was chilly. Frequently, "Warm" echoed while we began searching the room. I hoped Drago would soon find us, bringing us our clothes. Heck, he'd also have to pull the dragon's body away, since it blocked our only way out of his lair.

"Plenty of gems. Bet some are valuable," Lexi declared, enthused.

"Wicked, Lexi. Look at this pile of gold coins I'm making. We're rich."

"Good going you girls. I'm having a bitch of a time gathering up anything," I complained. "I found us three rings, a wand, and a rod—all radiating magic of some kind. I'll identify them later. Warm," I grumbled, as I used my toes to push the wand over towards our communal pile of treasure.

Fortuitous. That's the only satisfactory explanation for what I then discovered. I'd use the Open All Doors spell just outside this chamber. The spell does just that, including secret doors and compartments, as long as they are within the range of the spell. I found a small box that had been hidden in a secret compartment of a small writing desk. I used Levitate and Push spells to get it out of its location and onto the floor. I sat down beside it and read the attached card: Karl, Open and use only after our mission is done. Adler.

While I had no idea what their mission was, I speculated it had something to do with making all the wealthier men and women of Rainbow's End unarmed. Using my toes and a good deal of struggling, I managed to open the small box. Inside, I saw an unadorned golden ring. Curious, I cast my Identification spell and gasped. Now, so much began to make sense.

Karl must have voluntarily had his own arms or front legs removed as part of the dragons' plans. When the mission was finished, this ring would restore what he'd lost. It had the incredible ability to regenerate lost body appendages! For my friends and me, this was the find of our lives; its value exceeded all the gems and gold my wives were amassing in the center of the room. I was speechless for several minutes.

Swallowing, I finally said, "Tiffany. Come here. Lexi, you too. Look what I've found." I explained the ring. With much toe fumbling, I managed to get the ring onto Tiffany's little toe.

As I did so, Lexi commented, "How interesting. Tiff, the ring expanded to fit your toe. Now that's really keen."

Once the ring was securely on her toe, magical energies flashed. None of us anticipated or expected what happened in that almost blinding flash of energies. Tiffany's dead arms, grey and almost skin and bone, hung uselessly at her sides. After blinking from the bright illumination, her arms were normal! She had muscles and strength in them. Her horribly distorted feet returned to a usual human foot, and her giant breasts returned to their rather large, but normal size.

"My arms! Wicked! Look at them; they work! What happened? Felix, you have to put it on Lexi's toe now. This is a miracle. No!" she gasped, suddenly realizing much of her body had been restored, undoing the many awful things that had happened to her body. "My face. Lexi, am I homely again? Has it undone that too?" Worry lined her face.

I chucked. "No Tiff. You're still a beauty queen. Your arms, feet, and breasts are fixed up. And look. The ring has already slipped off her toe."

Sure enough, it lay on the stone floor by her foot, indicative of the ring having finished its work on her. I sat down to put the ring on Lexi's little toe, but Tiffany squatted down and did it for me. "Wicked. I can do things so much easier now. Let me, Felix. There, Lexi. Oh my!"

Magical energies again flashed nearly blinding us. When we could see again, Lexi's feet, arms, and breasts were recovered, just as Tiffany's were. Lexi squeaked, "Oh my! Wait, how's my face, Tiff? Is it really ugly now?"

"No, Lexi. It's just the way it was before you put the ring on," Tiffany gushed. "Look, it's fallen off your toe. Okay, Felix. On your toe it goes!"

Magical energies again flashed, but nowhere near as brilliantly as it had before. "Crap," I barked annoyed. I still had no arms.

"Hey, your knockers are gone; that's positive," Lexi optimistically declared.

"And your feet are fixed up," Tiffany added. "No, wait! Wicked. Look Lexi. He's got ghost arms now!"

Sure enough, thin, transparent arms dangled at my sides. The ring was working, but the magic regrowth would take time. Later, we learned it took an entire week to do so. However, Tiffany asked, "Felix, why didn't your arms come back real fast like ours did? Your feet and breasts did."

179

"Right. Why is it taking so long?" Lexi asked. "You'd think it would take time to regrow our dead arms. I mean they really did look like dead arms, and yet," she waved her arms about, "they're just like I remember they were before I was abducted years ago. So why should ours be instantaneous and yours take so long?"

Seeing my somber face, Tiffany interjected, "Don't worry. We'll take care of you now."

I thought before I spoke aloud. "Well, this is a Regeneration Ring. It is supposed to regenerate lost appendages. My arms were removed, so it has to rebuild them. Your arms were still there. No, wait. Your arms were dead arms. It should also take time to fully restore them too."

Lexi interrupted, "But it didn't. So why?"

Tiffany theorized, "What if our dear arms, our monster bosoms, and our mutilated feet were actually the result of some spell? Maybe the ring just cancelled or undid what the spell did."

"Tiff, this is what I so love about you!" I said, a giant grin replacing my frowns. "You're on to something. I bet anything you both were the recipients of a Restricted Wish spell. All three of us also were hit with another one that messed up our feet and turned our bosoms into monsters."

Lexi bit her lip and said, "But I thought you said casting wish spells caused the caster to age prematurely, a year older, if I remember what you said. That's a lot of wishes and whoever did it must be many years older now."

"And that's what I so love about you, Lexi. You're spot on too. Yes, whoever cast it on us and on all the Unarmed Escorts company has aged many, many years. No human in their right mind would do such a thing."

Tiffany asked, "True, so who? Oh, a dragon. Drago said they live very long lives compared to us."

Lexi added, "Adler. I bet he's behind it."

I must have looked extremely pleased. My wives were brilliant and quick. I said, "Yes, it must be Adler. I can see why he was making all the unarmed women and men. His real purpose was to market them to aliens from other worlds. For each one taken off your world, he sent along another dragon. Dragons have a powerful innate ability to Shadow Walk between worlds, but they have to be familiar with the destination world. He sent his dragons along with the aliens who purchased unarmed escorts so his dragon friends would be able to fly between more unknown worlds. Fifty years of aging isn't much when your lifetime exceeds ten times that amount."

"Wicked. But we should take the ring to the others. You know to Vanna, Angela, Kelly, and Eve. Then, we should take it back to your sister, Carli, Ben, and Carla too. It must work on dragons or Adler wouldn't have left it for Karl."

Lexi frowned. "Hold on a second. We've just killed Emperor Karl, disrupting the dragon's plans. When Adler finds out, what's to keep him from using his spells to kill us or maim us again? God, he could turn us into only a head and torso, couldn't he?"

She was fast on the take. "You're right, Lexi. I know, when we're out in public, I can cast my Morph Other spell, making you two and me look like we used to look. Maybe then Adler won't get wise to what we've just done."

Lexi countered, "But that spell wasn't working before. Are you sure it'll work now?"

"Morph Lexi into Lexi of yesterday," I barked with full intention. Unlike before, magical energies flashed, and Lexi once more looked like she had, dead arms and all. I quickly cancelled my spell, a smug grin on my face. I added, "So Adler must have added a clause in his wish so my morph spells would fail. That's one sharp dragon."

"Okay, let Tiff and me finish the searching. It's darn hard for you to do it with just your feet. You think about how we're going to get out of here and how we're going to carry all the stuff with us."

I smiled.

*** 

Drago wasn't idle, but he wasn't very productive. He first tried to find out the total number of dragons around the vicinity of Imperial, at least within a hundred miles.

After counting ten, he realized he could well be counting the same ones multiple times. He then took to spying on those he found in the large city.

After two weeks of clandestine activities, he learned just how the doctors were performing the surgical amputations without any pain—by the use of Blue dragon spit, which was a paralytic agent. It numbed the nerve endings. By coating the arm side of the shoulder socket, all nerves in the upper arm ceased sensing pain, allowing the doctors to do their work rapidly. In addition, Drago learned five dragons, supervised by Mage Alberto, were working full-time making healing potions, which were subsequently given to these patients.

Thus, Drago paid a visit to the mage, striking up a friendship. "Well yes," Mage Alberto opened up to him, "I find what these Black dragons are doing to be most annoying. Look, just between us, Mage Drago, our noblewoman binding tradition goes back four hundred thirty-five years, first mentioned in an ancient text. It probably even dates before writing began, but cutting off the arms of noblemen and women is, is, is, well I don't know, evil or something. It sure isn't a good thing. Frankly, I don't see any point to it."

While adjusting the heat on a brewing kettle of potions, he went on. "I mean, our noblewomen have a choice. If they choose, they can have their arms free from the binding. Of course, then most won't recognize them as noblewomen. Still, they have a choice, at least until their arms atrophy. This new policy of having them painlessly amputated removes all power of choice from both men and women. It's not right, but then I'm not Emperor Karl."

Drago probed, "But you do know Emperor Karl is a Black dragon, don't you?"

"Well, yes."

"So why would your people ever have a dragon as your emperor?"

"Well, he is armless and helpless, just as the others are. Besides, who could possibly argue with a dragon? Here on Rainbow's End, they're at the top of the food chain. Hardly anything will harm them—only certain spells and magically enchanted weapons. Until this latest edict, Emperor Karl's been an okay ruler. Besides, he and his Black dragon friends have kept the warlike barbarians of the Eastern Plains from bothering us. They used to raid villages on the edge of our kingdom, but not since the dragons came here some fifty years ago. So that's a positive development."

"I see, but if all the army leaders are promoted to noblemen and have their arms removed and feet hobbled, how will they be able to defend the kingdom if these barbarians decide to attack again?"

Mage Alberto shrugged his shoulders. "Damned if I know, but then I'm not paid to know that, only oversee the making of hundreds of healing potions for the doctors."

"You do know Black dragons loathe and hate humans, don't you?" Drago pressed his last remaining card.

"Well, so far, we've not seen any evil or hatred. Rather the opposite I would say."

Hearing that, Drago shrugged. Sensing Mage Alberto was a lost cause, he departed, but something he'd said bothered him. Until now, none of us had ever heard of the wild barbarians that sometimes attacked outlying villages. Drago reasoned if all the army leaders were promoted to nobleman status and had their arms removed, the timing would then be perfect for a new barbarian attack. Major Ron was quite dependent upon his assistant and certainly could no longer fight a battle.

Thus, Drago took flight, scouring the edges of the hill country, looking for these invaders. He returned the night of the Royal Ball, but didn't get the chance to relay to me what he'd learned. Later, he explained he'd found the barbarian encampments, but they were only a hundred miles from the outer villages of the rainbow colored hills. At the dance, Drago merely observed, shocked to see so many unarmed men and women. In just two weeks, an incredible number of people had been treated. His thought was merely *foolish humans.*

Early the next morning, I sent him a frantic Message, telling him Emperor Karl was about to have our legs removed and that we were fleeing from him by flying down the hallways. I think that really annoyed Drago, because he charged into the Imperial Palace complex, ignoring guards' orders to halt. He became an unstoppable force, as he charged onto the dance floor, found the stairs that led down to the guest bedrooms, and headed down to find us. After all, a human can't possibly stop a thousand pound dragon.

He quickly became lost in the vast tunnel complex below the buildings. Eventually, he came upon the frustrated servants, still pushing along the three narrow beds on rollers. "That way. They went that way," one explained as Drago smashed into the bed he was pushing. Drago merely glared and continued running.

An hour after we'd managed to drop the stone door onto the neck of Emperor Karl, Drago finally found us. "Hey, you in there Felix?" he bellowed. The Black dragon's corpse completely blocked the entrance and tunnel as well.

"Yes, help Drago, please. We can't get out and need clothes. Warm!" I yelled back.

I heard a heavy, deep grunting sound before the crushed head of Karl along with the stone door were pulled out of the entrance. We saw Drago in his dragon form heaving and pulling the corpse down the hallway, eventually blocking another junction, one we hadn't followed. That done, Drago morphed into his human form and joined us.

"Hum, you three look different."

"Magic ring, Drago. This is Karl's lair. We found Adler's gift or present or reward to Karl—a Regeneration Ring. Come on in and look at Lexi and Tiffany. It's a miracle. Glad you found us."

While Drago examined our naked forms, I explained what we'd discovered and learned. He then commented, "Well, I think you might be right. Perhaps Adler was casting Restricted Wishes to deform your bodies. We should take the ring to Carla and Diana. Maybe it will repair the acid damage to their bodies. I miss my sister."

"Yes, but first we need to get my arms back and then undo the other four who are still in Beckworth. Can you lend us a hand with this treasure? Part of it is yours. We'll divide it up later."

Just then, the three servants arrived, still pushing the three beds before them. Hastily, we confiscated three sheets, wrapping them around us. I ordered them to lead us back to the guest bedroom and our original clothes, which now wouldn't fit well at all.

Two hours later, we finally entered the Box. Over breakfast, we exchanged stories. After Drago explained his findings to us, we saw how they could have churned out over a thousand amputations in just those initial two weeks. They had quite an operation, but we still had no idea why Emperor Karl and Adler wanted the noblemen and women's arms removed.

# Chapter 14—Repercussions

"Well, yes, Emperor Karl is dead. Verified it personally, the old fool," Adler bellowed to a group of ten Black and three Red dragons.

"What about the Plan?" asked Bernhard, the Black.

"Yes, what about the Plan?" put in Arsenio, the Red, suddenly nervous. This death wasn't according to the plan.

"We move the timetable up. That's all," Adler growled. "Look, the humans will dicker around for weeks trying to get a new emperor. Meanwhile, we'll launch the final phase of our plan a bit early. That's all. I've just come from the Royal Hospital. The tally is a little over one thousand here in Imperial alone, ignoring the other towns. That'll give us plenty of humans."

He continued, "Bernhard, you see we have the dragon carts and those who will pull them ready to go. Arsenio, you round up all the spell casters. You know the spell we need cast in the hundreds. I'll pay a visit to the barbarians and get them moving. We'll set Execution Day to be three days from now. Bernhard, Arsenio, can you have them ready by then?"

Bernhard breathed a sigh of relief. "Yes, boss. Not a problem. Even five hundred of them should be sufficient for our needs, but will it actually work? Will the humans go along with it?"

Arsenio chuckled, "Of course, Bernhard. Wait until you see how they think after we're done with them. This will be utterly simple. Of course, if the barbarians come, that'll only make it that much easier. You'll see. Just have the cages ready in time."

"Hey, don't worry about that. We've got dozens made. They're in the forests of Dietmar right now," Bernhard boasted.

"But will they actually work?" Arsenio asked. This was the key question he'd been asking for some months, but the Blacks had only suggested it would. Well, even if it failed, the Reds involved hadn't much to lose, for their role was minimal in Adler's grand plan. Still, if it worked, then all Reds would benefit as well, something he wasn't about to dismiss out of hand. He just didn't want to have hundreds of screaming humans on his hands if it didn't work. He didn't have the patience that Adler had and knew he'd just roast them if they began screaming.

***

The day after we'd killed Emperor Karl, we dropped by Banner's Fashions. We three needed new outfits. I wanted a suit so that I could finally look like a man, ending my continuous nightmare. Although we'd used our Alter spells to adjust the women's gowns, neither wanted to be bound as a noblewoman. Thus, they needed new dresses and gowns as well. Besides, we also wanted to check up on Harold and Sofia Banner and their three girls, Victoria, Ella, and Holly. However, Victoria and Ron Boston had temporarily moved to the army barracks housing.

The sixteen and fifteen year old girls were bubbling with excitement. At the Royal Ball, each had five young men courting their favor. That their two youngest daughters now had many young noblemen after them pleased both Harold and Sofia, who were still struggling mightily to adapt to their entirely new lifestyle, dependent upon their servants for nearly everything.

"At least we don't have to worry about suitors for Ella and Holly," Harold explained to me as we took tea. "But what's happened to you three?"

I had morphed us all into our previous looking bodies, much to our chagrin, but we dared not appear in public completely cured. I had explained to Tiffany before we left to visit the Banner family, "Look. We've only this one ring. It's taking days to regenerate my missing arms. Let's say that it takes a whole week to do it. If we're to use it to regenerate everyone who has had their arms removed, why, we'll be at it for a thousand weeks here in Imperial alone, to say nothing of all those in Beckworth, our friends there, and those pony-men. It's an undoable action, but I promise you we'll use it on our friends back there and somehow on my sister and the others back in Byron Falls."

"When we're done with it," Lexi began, a serious look on her face, "couldn't we leave it with someone here and let them heal everyone else? Let them deal with the many years needed to fully restore everyone's arms."

I sighed. Lexi had a heart of gold, and I'd like nothing more than to do just that. However. "Lexi, we could do that, but we're still fighting dragons and Adler too. Any moment, Adler could get mad at us and wish our arms gone again, maybe even our legs too. If we're going to continue in the Box, for our own safety, we best hang onto this ring. Perhaps after we're done with the Box, we can return here and give it to the people."

Tiffany spoke up. "He's a valid point, Lexi. We're whole for the first time in five or more years. I want to stay whole if I can. Besides, these people chose of their own free will to have their arms removed. It was their choice to make. Who is to say they want us to regenerate their arms?"

Lexi nodded. "Point taken. They did choose to have it done. It's their cultural traditions. However, maybe something could be done for all those in Beckworth who were victims of the Green dragon, like Count Edgar."

Over tea with the Banners, we explained what had happened to us, that we'd killed their Emperor Karl and why. I was curious about how they would take this news. Would they be horrified we'd killed him? In a way, I was testing the waters.

Harold sighed deeply. "Well, that's a good thing. We won't be getting new orders for strange things to be done to our bodies. Our lives have become awful, but then you three know all about that. I say good riddance."

"But dear," Sofia spoke up, "it's also opened many doors for Ella and Holly. For the first time, they have a half dozen young men interested in courting them. This isn't all bad. Our daughters will marry noblemen and have a better life. Besides dear, when was the last time you actually sewed a suit or I sewed a gown? It's as Lexi says, we just need lots of practice and patience. We're nobles now, looked up to by everyone. That's something positive."

He grumbled and then said, "Mark my words, nothing good will come from it."

Just as we were finishing our tea, several young noblemen and their servants came by to visit Ella and Holly, who were extremely pleased by the visit. Quietly, we took our leave. Back in our Box, I cancelled the morph spells.

Lexi commented, "So they are adapting as well as can be expected. We shouldn't leave here until Felix's arms are fully restored. Then, we should briefly visit Vanna and the others. Perhaps Edgar will want his arm regenerated too. After that, does anyone know how we can get the ring to the last four back on your world of Byron Falls?"

"I'll have Drago make the trip using his Shadow Walk. Meanwhile, we have several days. Why don't you girls take my spell book and see if you can learn to cast some more spells? We don't dare close the door and press the Handled button yet. We've got to use this ring on the others first."

Drago entered and caught my last words. He commented, "True, and we should keep watch on the barbarians. I don't trust these Black dragons at all."

The morning of the fourth day after we'd slain their emperor, Victoria knocked frantically on our Box door—actually, her servant girl did the knocking. Hastily, I morphed us back and bade her come inside.

Victoria's face was streaked with wetness. Her face, flushed. She looked frantic and begged, "Please. Can you do something? Major Ron—he's been ordered into battle. It's the barbarians from the eastern plains again. He'll be killed. I just know it. He can't fight, not now, not like he is. Oh why did we ever want to be nobles?"

"Slow down, Victoria. Tell me what's happening," I said, carefully sitting down on one of the living room couches.

She collapsed onto the couch beside me, quite out of breath. From her awkward motions, I concluded that her feet were throbbing and that she must have walked her from her new quarters with the Royal Guards. As she began, that was confirmed.

Early this morning, General John Waterson of the Royal Guards received word the barbarians were invading the Rainbow Hills from the east, attacking the towns and villages there. He ordered Major Ron and the First Regiment to take up a defensive position just outside Pegsworth, a town fifty miles to the east. He'd ordered the other two regiments to protect two nearby towns.

"But he can't fight, not really," Victoria wailed. "He has no arms to hold a sword. He'll be killed, I just know it. Please, can you help him? Please," she begged.

I looked at Drago. He grinned. I knew he was dying to get out of the Box. His deep voice replied, "Miss Victoria, I will fly there now and see what I can do."

"Oh thank you, Drago, thank you, thank you," she effused.

As Drago left, I asked, "So are you staying up at your new home?"

"No, Ron suggested I return home. I—I—I think he thought he wouldn't be coming back and wanted me to be safe." Victoria broke down again, sobbing, while her servant girl silently dabbed her cheeks.

We three walked her home, though it was just next door. Once she was safely inside, we cast our Fly spells and flew far above the city, hoping we could get some kind of distant view. No luck, but we did get a good view of the city. With little else that we could do, we returned to the Box. After I cancelled the Morph spells, the girls resumed studying the spells in my book, while I examined my not quite so ghostly regrowing arms.

Around four, frantic knocking again startled us. I quickly recast the Morph spells and we opened the door. There stood all three sisters with faces white as sheets. In fact, they were trembling and nearly fell while trying to "dash" inside the Box.

"The dragons—they're taking us away!" Victoria burst out before reaching the couch. She moved too fast, stumbled, and fell onto the couch. Her servant girl hastily helped her back up.

"Slow down. What's going on?" I asked, growing concerned.

"They're going house to house. That's what Betsy says. She's a servant to Michelle and friends with Sally here. The dragons are taking noblewomen away and some noblemen too," Victoria explained, terrified.

"Why?" I asked.

Her servant girl, Sally, answered. "My friend says the dragons are saying the barbarians are coming and they are going to protect the nobles, but that can't be right. Victoria's Major Ron and the other solders are out there protecting us. Anyway, it's awful! I walked Miss Veronica to where the dragon told her to go and it was scary."

"Tell me more, Sally."

"Well, sir, at the edge of Imperial, there are a dozen giant Black and Red dragons. The Black ones had a sort of wagon tied to them, but it looks more like a cage than a wagon. One told me that was so the nobles don't accidentally fall out while they are being transported to safety. I suppose that's the reason, since Miss Ella certainly can't hold on. None of them can hold on. Anyway, they put my Miss Michelle into one wagon, along with twenty-five others and told me to go home. I stayed to make sure Miss Michelle would be all right and if she needed any help getting into the wagon cage. That's when I heard the Red dragon cast some kind of spell over her. All I caught was one word, and I don't know what it may mean."

"What was the word?"

"Moron or something like that. Perhaps the dragon was referring to someone else. Anyway, after that Miss Michelle—she seemed very confused. The last I saw of her, she was being lifted into the nearly full wagon cage. I tried to ask them where they were taking her and why they didn't need us servants to go along, but one told me to go home. So I did, but I stopped to tell Sally about it."

Holly interrupted, "As we came over here, they were coming to our house. We don't want to go anywhere, not until Major Ron comes back. We don't trust these dragons.

Can you help us? Mom and dad could be in danger."

Lexi asked me, "What does this mean? What are the dragons doing?"

"I've some ideas, none good. Moron and Michelle's subsequent behavior might mean they cast Moronic Mind on them." Memories of my own experience under that spell came to mind, and I shivered.

"Why? What's it do?" she asked, her voice filled with concern.

"It makes the person's IQ that of a moron. They can barely think. I had it done to me once. It makes the person highly suggestible. They'll do anything you ask of them. I can't imagine any reason why they would be using that spell on them, especially since it cannot be dispelled. It takes a special potion to undo the effects of that spell. It's a quite nasty spell."

I reached a decision. No way was I going to expose Lexi or Tiffany to such a spell. "Lexi, Tiffany, I'm charging you to stay here in the Box and protect Victoria, Ella, and Holly. I'll go see what I can find out. I'll use my Invisibility spell so I'll be in no danger. Send me a Message if anything happens here, but I don't think anyone can actually break into the Box on their own. We have to let them in."

"You be extremely careful," Tiffany declared.

I kissed them both and took my leave. Fortunately, no one asked why our servant girls weren't here or why I was going off without mine. Once outside the Box, I cast Invisibility and then cancelled my Morph spell. Hastily, I walked over to the Banner home. The front door was ajar; only one hinge remained attacked. Obviously, someone had broken into the home. I slipped inside and saw Harold and Sofia's servants moaning and holding their heads. They'd been knocked unconscious. I surmised they had tried to protest going off with the dragons. Silently, I backed out of the home and cast Fly, zooming up high and eastward, since this edge was the closest to me.

After ten minutes of flying and searching, I found the dragon staging area. Twenty Black dragons were attached to strange looking wagons. I swore they looked like prison wagons than anything else. Many were nearly full with noblemen, noblewomen, and armless children. I noticed none was much older than their mid-thirties and none younger than around twelve. Zooming in, I spotted Harold and Sofia sitting in one of the caged wagons. Both looked quite content, a pleased look on their faces.

As another frantic woman was brought up to the wagon, I overheard the Red dragon casting its spell: Moronic Mind. The Red then explained, "You want to be safe from the evil barbarians. We are going to take you somewhere safe. You do want to be safe, don't you?"

"Oh yes. Safe. Yes, yes. I want safe. I can't get in," the woman said worriedly.

"Let me help you."

"Oh, thank you. Thank you. Be safe. So kind. Want be safe."

The Red lifted her into the wagon, and this time, the dragon locked the cage, signaling the Black dragon. As I watched, the Black began pulling the wagon along the ground, heading eastward. Then, the dragon began to gain altitude. As I watched, the dragon and its precious wagon and cargo vanished from sight. I swallowed and blinked. I'd seen the same thing happening when Carla had Shadow Walked back to Byron Falls with my sister and the others strapped to her back. I had no doubt the Black dragon was taking these helpless men, women, and children to some other world!

I had no idea what world or the remotest idea why they might want these people. My stomach knotted. I felt truly helpless. There wasn't any way I could have prevented the dragon's departure. Nearly two dozen dragons arrived here at that moment, and one was sufficient to slay me had I tried to interfere. Sadly, I flew home to the Box, wondering what I could possibly say to the three girls. Their parents were gone, likely never to be seen on this world again.

Landing by the Box, I decided to tell them the truth, insisting they stay with us for the time being, certainly until Major Ron's fate was known. I had a very sick feeling in my stomach, as I recast my Morph spell and entered the Box.

Meanwhile, Drago flew eastward, but wisely decided to do so invisibly. An hour later, he finally found the First Cavalry Regiment, disembarking just east of Pegsworth, a small town of around three thousand souls. Drago hovered overhead and found Major Ron, who was issuing orders to his troops, positioning them in the best defensive positions on the rolling bright blue hillside. He then flew higher and further east, looking for the barbarians.

He found the band of barbarians on foot, racing towards this small town, waving spears and swords, while carrying shields. Drago estimated they'd reach Major Ron's forces in about two hours. The horses had allowed Major Ron to get here in time to set up a defense before the barbarians arrived. However, Drago could see that Ron's forces were outnumbered two to one.

Later when Ron relayed what had happened to Victoria, he wailed, "Helpless humiliation. That's what it felt like. I couldn't do anything to fight back. They swarmed us and simply laughed at me. One gave me a slight shove and I fell over and couldn't even get up again. I felt as if I was nothing more than some tiny baby. I'd be dead if it wasn't for Drago here."

From his height, Drago watched the barbarians swam up to and over the hastily erected defenses of the cavalry. As the front wave fought the defenders, Drago repositioned himself and swooped down, breathing out a cone of deadly flames, searing the barbarians in the rear, ensuring there wouldn't be a second wave of them smashing into the remnants of the cavalrymen. He banked and turned around, and then made a second pass over the barbarians. It took four passes to eliminate those who weren't engaging the defenders.

"I found Major Ron on the ground, struggling to get up. I landed nearby and attacked any who came close to him. Maybe ten minutes after it started, the battle was over. All the barbarians were killed, but the First Regiment was gone. Only Major Ron survived. I brought him back to safety. I don't recommend men without arms and hands fight in sword battles. So what's been happening here in Imperial?"

While Victoria and Ron pressed their bodies into each other, the best they could do for a hug, I outlined the treachery of the Black and Red dragons. I was surprised with Drago's comment.

"I'll bet anything," he declared in his deep voice, "they are being sold to aliens so the dragons can become familiar with more new worlds."

His brash comment caused the three girls to sob once more, but I suspected Drago was right. In a way, the Unarmed Escorts of Halcion-3 and the noblemen and women of Rainbow's End had to be closely related.

"Kids, you four are all staying here in our place until it's safe. Come on. Let's get going on making supper, shall we?"

We spent a nervous few days inside the Box, before I deemed it safe for the three and Ron to venture forth. Drago, of course, gathered information daily. By the eighth day since the death of Emperor Karl, the ring fell off my toe. My arms were back, as good as they had been. Okay, I wasn't a muscular fellow before and certainly wasn't now, but it felt wonderful to have them back, though by now I realized with all the alternative ways we'd seen, I could have survived well without them, had I continued to practice, been patient, or used my servant spell.

Drago and Mage Alberto took temporary charge of Imperial. Together, they observed the battlefields, pronouncing the barbarian invasion ended. The Royal Guards no longer existed. Ron was the only survivor. Half of the younger noblemen of Imperial were gone, but nearly all of the noblewomen under forty were also missing. Thus, the noble houses had to respond to the losses quickly.

I acted swiftly. I knew Major Ron would never be a soldier again. Helpless humiliation had defeated him. Hence, with Harold and Sofia gone, I helped get Victoria and Ron installed as the new heads of Banner's Fashions.

Thus, Ron would continue to be a nobleman. When Ella and Holly came of age, they could join the family business if they desired.

With those four stabilized, we wanted to get the Regeneration Ring to Vanna, Angela, Kelly, and Eve, and to check on Molly and Edgar. I'd no idea whether the new Count and Countess would desire to make use of the ring or not, but I owed it to the other four women we'd brought from Halcion-3.

Our first problem was getting there. If only one of us could use the Teleport spell, but alas, we hadn't reached that level of magic mastery yet. Hence, after going invisible, we three climbed on to Drago's back, and he flew us the several hundred miles across the Rainbow Hills to the western edge where lay the city of Beckworth, adjacent to Brackenmoor Swamp.

I was surprised when we entered the castle Throne Room. Changes had been made already, though I didn't necessarily like them. Count Edgar and Countess Molly were very pleased to see us again. Both insisted on dismissing all other official business, spending hours chatting with us. What shocked me was that Molly had gone ahead and had her arms removed, once the painless method arrived here.

Molly explained, "Look, Vanna, Angela, Kelly, and Eve also had their dead arms removed. They're holding classes for us unarmed men and women. We spend four hours each day working with them, practicing everything. They run three such classes each day, and there's a waiting list to get into one of them. I became convinced that we could do most anything using our feet, toes, and brains. That's why I went ahead and did it."

Count Edgar smiled and added, "Plus, we've been making many other changes in the way things are done around here. I believe we're going to be known as the first benevolent monarchs of Beckworth. More importantly, Molly and I are married now and we're starting our family!" I've never seen a man as pleased looking as Edgar was. Molly merely flushed, as a broad smile illuminated her face.

Later over dinner, we joined Vanna, Angela, Kelly, and Eve. All four looked incredibly happy and insisted on us telling them all about what had been happening in Imperial. News of the Emperor's death had reached them. While Lexi and Tiffany retold our story, I slipped the ring onto each woman's toe. After the initial flash of magic, which restored their feet and bosoms, I took the ring off. True, had they still had their "dead arms," those would have been instantly restored. However, none of the four desired to have theirs regrown.

Angela explained why. "Look Felix, here we four are treated as noblewomen, almost as a Countess. We've offers of more dates with noblemen than we've time for. In fact, we're each going steady with our new boyfriends. In short, we've found a very rewarding life here in Beckworth. Our skills are vitally needed, and we're appreciated and respected. We couldn't ask for more. Now that Molly's married and even expecting, we're even more excited about staying here."

She went on, "We, Molly, and Edgar also agree with you. You can't use the ring on all the many victims of that Green dragon, the pony-men. There are just too many of them. You've said it took a week for you to get your arms regrown. With all the victims here in Beckworth alone, it would take over a thousand weeks to get to everyone. That's twenty years. No, it's best to leave well enough along for now. Most victims and their loved ones wouldn't have the patience to wait that long to be cured. They'd all be fighting any way they could to get to use the ring next. That's chaos. No, what's done is done."

The next day, we decided to let Drago Shadow Walk the ring to Byron Falls, while we stayed here and visited our friends. He'd be gone at least a week, perhaps a few days more. At least here we didn't have to be morphed into our unarmed state, but we defied their noblewoman tradition and dressed as "common folk." Had we returned to the Box, we'd have had to maintain that illusion, one that I now wanted no further part of. I'd been sufficiently humiliated because of it.

Why did we stay behind? Simple. If I returned home, I might not have the desire to come back. In addition, the Box might believe we'd abandoned it and thus go in search of new mages to use it. I hoped our being here in Beckworth would be close enough for the Box. It was. Eight days later, Drago returned with the ring, and shortly after that, we landed beside the waiting Box.

"It worked," he explained. "My sister's face and neck are healed up so well that you can't even see a scar. Oh, and Diana's face is perfect and her arms are back. Ben's elated to appear as a man again. All send their love. I tried to talk them into coming back with us, but the four are adamant on staying. Mage Locklard is teaching them, so that's something. Should we shut the door and press Handled?"

Was it greed, enthusiasm, or intense curiosity we saw in Drago's eyes? I nodded and he pressed the Handled button. We watched as the bar slid over, locking us inside the Box. This time, we all felt a slight vibration as the Box began to move. Hastily, we four raced to the wall to obtain our new pages of spells. I hoped we'd find the Teleport spell among our new ones. No such luck.

The girls were elated, for Ball of Fire and Bolt of Electricity were among their new pages, along with Dispel Magic. Drago and I had a number of Grade 3 and 4 spells. In fact, now we had all known Grade 3 spells in our books. I was particularly pleased to be learning the Immunity Spell, one that made me immune to all Grade 3 and lower spells, as long as this spell was in effect.

Looking over the new spells, I let out a squeal of joy. There was the Mystical Door spell, one which allowed me to create a door and step through it, arriving many hundreds of yards away, such as in a different room. Further, the Skin of Stone spell was on the list. While this spell lasted, any blow couldn't harmed me. I'd be impervious to sword cuts. I also could place this spell on others, namely Lexi and Tiffany, providing them with serious protection. Yes, I was one very happy man, as I dove into the learning of my new spells.

However, I'd be remiss if I didn't tell you one other detail. Suddenly, Tiffany's new spell activated. A giant ball of fire shot out into the long spell casting room, followed by, "Wicked!" My wives were becoming quite formidable in their own right, but I also knew we'd need a couple of weeks to master all of these new spells. It turned out to be three weeks.

# Chapter 15—A Sinister Plot

Drago growled and belched. "This is a horrid world! Would you believe that I had to resort to eating a cow? Of all the nasty things to eat. Not an antelope to be found on this world. Oh, they call it Dickersen-3; sun's rather orangish. It's another one of them alien spaceship-type worlds, all concrete and steel. Hardly any open land. I had to fly five hundred miles to find a stupid cow. And the stench of this world is hideous." He belched again. "Now I'll probably have indigestion all week."

We'd landed a week ago. As usual, Drago had taken off to satisfy his hunger. This time, he was back when we were finally ready to stick our heads out into this new world. Lexi and Tiffany needed more time to learn their new spells, since most were much more difficult that those they had already learned. Since we had been on this world sufficiently long, the Box had already fabricated a wide selection of apparel. Men wore business suits while the women often wore white blouses with grey or black skirts, accompanied by low heels whose color matched their skirts.

As we soon learned, the Box chose to land us in the capital city of St. Leeds, a sprawling city of fifty-story tall skyscrapers, whose walls appeared to be made of glass—a concept I still can't grasp. The Box somehow inserted itself into the side of one of these structures, though our door opened on the side street. Main and 42$^{nd}$ Ave was our location. The sign over our door read St. Agnus Detective Agency. Tiffany did pay a visit to the women's fashion store occupying the first floor of the skyscraper. She suggested the Box magically enhanced space, for she couldn't detect the space the Box was taking from the corner of this store. I decided against visiting this particular store. I've had more than enough embarrassment already.

With our spells mastered, we four dressed up in the

200

appropriate apparel for this world and stepped outside to see our surroundings. The air held a foul odor, one of oil, tar, and other indefinable smells, just as Drago declared.

"Wicked! Modern world for sure," Tiff said enthusiastically. "Ah ha. Yes, there goes a spaceship taking off, but the spaceport must be miles away from here. I wonder what bad things are going on here? Oh look, Lexi. We're beside Mc Bride's Fashions. Golly, those gowns in the windows look very expensive. Felix, before we leave, I want to visit this store."

"I agree, Tiff. I think you'd look smashing in that red one there," Lexi effused.

"No dragons here," Drago said gruffly. "At least I've not seen any for five hundred miles. Heck, barely a cow on this world. It all seems so peaceful. I think the Box really screwed up this time. You humans can't get into any really serious trouble, not like us dragons."

I chuckled. True, dragons had been our nemesis since we began our journey with the Box. "Maybe they aren't openly flying about."

"We have to eat," he countered. "Come on. Let's walk around. You'll see. Nothing going on at all."

We ambled along the sidewalks. Yes, Tiff explained to Drago and me that these were sidewalks constructed for pedestrians, keeping us out of the roadways. Motorized vehicles zoomed along at what I considered breakneck speeds, forty miles per hour. Tiff only laughed at me. The sidewalks were packed with others, all dressed similarly to ourselves, but they seemed not to notice us or anyone else. Lexi suggested they might be walking to work. I was suddenly homesick for Rainbow's End or even Byron Falls. I knew I'd never fit into a world such as this one, though my wives certainly did.

We walked around most of the day. While I saw many strange things (cars, trucks, busses, trains, buildings, hospital, and emergency vehicles), my wives saw them as normal and explained their use and function to Drago and me. I appreciated Byron Falls and Rainbow's End much more after our first day walking the streets of

St. Leeds. However, we saw nothing that needed our attention. The only aspect that stuck with me was building heights. We were in the heart of the city and all buildings that we saw on our walk were at least fifty stories tall—all but one, whose sign read Alcyon Galactic Electronics. This building appeared very glossy and new, compared to the rather dirty appearing skyscrapers, and was a single story affair with windows only at the front entrance. It occupied an entire city block, very unusual compared to all the other skyscrapers.

"With so many people," Tiff explained, "they have to build upwards. There's not enough horizontal space for such a vast population. I'd guess St. Leeds is home to many millions of people."

Sorry, I can't imagine such a large number, though I can deal with thousands, more or less. I guess for that reason alone, Alcyon stuck in my mind. We went to bed without the slightest clue why we were in this place.

We'd just finished breakfast the next morning when someone knocked on our door. I opened it; my wives were right behind me. Drago was still in his room, bored out of his mind. We saw a middle-aged woman wearing a white blouse and black skirt standing there. She had a roundish face and short brown hair. She held a thin stick in one hand, but I noticed her eyes. They had no pupils and irises. She was blind and not by a magical spell.

Her mellow voice asked, "Excuse me. Is this the detective agency?"

"Yes, yes it is. Please come in."

I admit I felt extremely awkward around her. I've never met a blind person before. Thankfully, Lexi took charge. "Hello. Welcome to our agency. I'm Lexi. Here, I have your arm. Let's get comfortable on our couch. With me are Tiffany, Felix, and Drago."

Her hand around the woman's left elbow, Lexi led her to one of the couches. Before she had her sit down, she introduced us one by one. The woman insisted on shaking our hands.

"I'm Mrs. Anna Beck. My husband is Abe Beck. He's

an accountant at Mercantile Exchange, that's five blocks on down Main, one block past the new Alcyon building."

"So what can we do for you?" I asked, as I sat across from her, allowing Tiff and Lexi to sit on either side of Anna.

"Would you like some tea first?" Lexi countered me, diplomatically.

"No thank you, Lexi. I've come to hire you."

"Well then, Mrs. Beck, tell us what we can do for you."

"You can find out what happened to my husband, Abe. You see, he's vanished."

Look, we had no idea what we were supposed to "handle" on this world. So far, we'd seen nothing out of the ordinary, so to speak. A missing man hardly warranted our "skills," but right now, it would give us something to do to fight the boredom until we were able to uncover just what we were supposed to "handle."

"Do you have a picture of Abe?" Lexi asked.

Anna took a few moments to retrieve a photo of Abe from her purse. While she couldn't see the photo, she'd been carrying it around to show first to the police and now to us.

"He looks handsome," Lexi said diplomatically. "Let's start at the beginning. Where do you live? What happened and when?"

"We have a suite in this building, No. 4103. That's on the forty-first floor. As I said, he works at the Mercantile Exchange. He's been there for ten years now. He walks to work every day. He claims it's good exercise. Anyway, for the last year and a half, strange things have been happening here in St. Leeds and other places around our world. Abe left for work eight days ago. He never arrived or so his boss at the exchange claims. How can anyone get lost walking six blocks? I reported it to the police, but they've done nothing about it. I know something terrible has happened to him. I can feel it, but I don't know what. I just think it must have something to do with that new alien company, Alcyon. They tore down a perfectly good skyscraper and built that new, modern building, one that is a terrible waste of city space. It's only one story tall. Can you believe that? Building codes demand all new buildings be at least fifty stories tall."

She continued, "Since the police have done nothing, I took matters into my own hands. Several times, I've walked his usual route to the exchange. I'm afraid Abe has been around me too long. Everything is fixed so I don't have trouble getting things done. So he always followed the same route to work, and I sometimes walked with him."

"Anyway, I asked others along the way if they saw Abe the day he went missing. It was a long shot, I know, but it paid off. So far, I've found four people who reported seeing Abe being forced into the Alcyon building. No one has seen him come back out. I told this to the police, but they said it means nothing. He might have just stopped by to say hello to someone on his way to work. Since they ignore this, I went there and asked some woman at their reception desk, showing her my photo of Abe. She claims she's never seen the man. Four strangers can't all be lying about seeing Abe going in there. So when someone told me about your new office, I decided it was time to hire detectives. I don't know what your fees are, but I'll try to find a way to pay it. Just find my Abe, please."

"We will," Lexi promised.

Drago asked, "What does this Alcyon company do or make?"

"Well, that's just the thing. I don't know. I can't see, so even though I was inside, I couldn't tell what they do. They're an alien company, but from what I've heard on the news, they wield some form of power, but then our world seems to be doing many strange things this past year."

"What kind of strange things?" I asked, wondering if Adler was somehow involved here too.

"Well, President Dick Chesterton has been acting in unusual ways. You see, he was elected on a platform sponsoring education and occupational training for everyone. He got worldwide subsidies passed through the Imperial Senate, which did lower the cost for those furthering their education. However, six months ago, he suddenly raised everyone's taxes and cancelled the subsidization of higher education, just the opposite stand."

She went on, "Then, there is Senator Holly Ann Mobley. For years, she has lobbied for more lands to be set aside for parks. Then nine months ago, she pressed a new bill through the Imperial Senate, drastically reducing the acreage of our world parks, which allowed many mining companies to open up those lands for their operations. In fact, the very block on which the new Alcyon building stands used to be Central Park, but Senator Mobley introduced a bill that sold it to the aliens, who quickly built their new building."

None of this sounded like dragon involvement. However, I decided we needed to see these aliens for ourselves. We couldn't ask Anna if their skin had a blackish or reddish hue to it or if their eyes looked strange and inhuman.

Hence, I asked, "Where can we meet these aliens?"

"They have a weird accent. There's only a few of them. Ambassador Alejo de la Vegas is their planetary representative, and Amidio da Casa is the president of Alcyon. Those two are often in the news or are seen around here. If there are others, they certainly keep to themselves. And that too is strange. I know Dickersen-3 trades with six other worlds. Here in St. Leeds, you'll find many thousands of folks from those worlds, maybe even millions, if you look all over our world. Yet, there are only a handful of those other aliens, and all you ever see is Ambassador de la Vegas or President da Casa."

"Where can we meet and see the ambassador?" I asked, hoping she might know.

"Supposedly, he has an office somewhere in the skyscraper just across Main from their company building."

"Okay, then we should pay this ambassador a visit first. We will keep you informed of our progress."

She thanked us and Lexi helped her outside and into the main lobby of the building. From there, she could find her way to the elevators and her suite. We discussed what we could actually do to find this Abe Beck. All agreed we should pay a visit to Ambassador de la Vegas, if only to prove to ourselves he was a dragon.

Drago stated, "Look, if she's right and the last place Abe was seen was his being forced into this Alcyon building, then we should go there and search the place."

Tiff countered, "Slow down a minute, Drago. This is a modern world. It's likely they have all manner of electronic surveillance to prevent that, such as motion sensors, ID cards to open doors, monitoring cameras. Plus, they're very likely to have heavily armed security guards to stop us—maybe even blasters."

Lexi smiled, "Tiff's right. Boys, this is an advanced world, bearing no resemblance to your world, which will seem quite primitive compared to this one. Let Tiff and me take point on this situation. First, let's check out the ambassador. Then, I think it prudent to pay a visit to the wife of one of these men who, according to Anna, are now acting weirdly."

"I can see why we visit the ambassador," I replied, "and I'm more than willing to let you two take charge. I'm not comfortable about anything in this world, but why do we want to see that wife?"

"Anna suggested he had a sudden complete change in behavior. His wife would know the precise details. How better to get the low-down, eh?" Lexi and Tiffany chuckled, and we four headed out of the Box.

Even though Drago and I wore a suit mirroring the other men we occasionally passed on the sidewalks, we both felt as if we were a fish walking instead of swimming in the river. Did they even have rivers on this world? The wisdom of having the girls along with us in the Box struck me hard. It was brilliant, but then I wondered if the Box might have had a hand in drawing these women and Ben to us. Jerking my head, I shrugged such thoughts off; the Box wasn't alive.

Ambassador de la Casa had oily black hair and a prominent moustache to match his beady black eyes. He was a bit shorter than me, but more importantly, he wasn't a dragon. He did have a strange accent, but later Tiffany claimed she might know what his native language was. However, I had an instant dislike and distrust of this man. Covertness dripped off this man. One ought not turn their back on him.

"Ah, other aliens I see. Welcome to my humble office on this world. How may the ambassador of Eros-4 be of service to you?"

Lexi spoke for us, having introduced us. "Well, being strangers to this world and having just arrived, we couldn't help noticing your Alcyon company building looks so different from all the other skyscrapers here. Our curiosity is aroused. Just what does your company produce? Are your products for sale here in St. Leeds? If so, could you direct us to such stores? I'm afraid we're something of country bumpkins when it comes to this electronics stuff, but we are always interested in taking back new ideas to our world."

"I see. And what is your world?"

"Halcion-3. Can't you tell from our accent?"

Alejo smiled. "Ah yes. I recognize it now. Forgive me. I should have recognized your accent at once. A world much like this one, I believe, modern, and yet just beginning to venture into the vastness of our galaxy."

"Precisely. Perhaps we could take back some electronic gadgets to show our world." I was amazed at how fast Lexi was manipulating this man.

"Well, I'm afraid we don't make smaller-sized gadgets, as you say. Ours are planetary in scope, such a defense shields. Our products are so large that they have to be assembled on their destination sites. However, I can give you some brochures to take with you."

We walked out of the skyscraper barely ten minutes after we entered. Lexi carried a handful of glossy brochures, while I carried far too many questions. She commented, "After talking to him, I feel as if I desperately need a long, hot bath! He's creepy."

Four hours later and after a ride in one of their yellowish vehicles that Tiffany called a taxi, we sipped tea with Mrs. Lana Chesterton, the wife of this country's leader. Again, the girls introduced us and did all the talking. Considering how it went, I was very glad they did.

After the formalities, Lexi hinted, "So we met a blind woman, Mrs. Anna Beck. She told us that President Chesterton has perhaps not been himself recently."

Relief swept across the middle-aged woman's face. "Yes, oh yes. No one's listened to me or even taken me seriously. Dick isn't himself. That's the best way I can describe it."

"Oh please, tell us all about it. Maybe we can be of some small assistance."

"Of course. They say it's good to talk to others about your troubles. Yes. Well, it began about two months ago. One morning when he woke up, he seemed very confused and disoriented. It was as if he was a different person after that morning. I tried to get him to seek medical help, but he claimed he wasn't mentally or physically ill, but he must be, because he acts totally different from the Dick I married."

"You see, he was a staunch conservationist, but now he's pushing and backing all manner of measures designed to exploit our natural resources, at least what remains of them. He got a bill passed that gave these Eros-4 aliens the rights to build another twenty-five of their strange, secretive electronics factories. Honestly, for the past two centuries, no one has been allowed to construct a new building that wasn't at least fifty stories tall, but theirs is a single story building, a complete waste of valuable space. Everyone says so."

"And then there are all these little things. At first, he didn't know our three children or even their names. He forgot the names of his parents, and didn't know my mother passed away last year. He took a taxi to work for the first week, before I reminded him we have our own electric car, but I had to show him where he kept his keys to it. That first morning, I swear he didn't even know where the bathroom was located. And he normally pays almost no attention to me, as if we were strangers."

"Every once in a while, I see the old Dick. He gives me a loving kiss, but tears trickle down his cheeks when he does. It's as if he's has a mental illness, the kind where he thinks he's two people."

"Then, there are the voices in his head. Ten times now, I've overheard him arguing with no one, begging the voices in his head not to do something. I couldn't tell what, but Dick sure didn't want to do what the voice was asking. I'm terrified he's suffering from a very bad case of schizophrenia. I can see no other explanation. However, every time I mention anything about Dick, I'm told to shut up and stop interfering with our president or they'll throw me into jail."

"Five weeks ago, I told his parents about his strange behavior. The next thing I knew, both were arrested and thrown into jail. They told me I was warned to keep quiet and this was the consequence. At least, they let them out three weeks ago. Now I suppose they'll be arresting you."

Lexi replied, "I can't imagine why they'd do that. We've not done anything wrong, nor have you. Thank you for telling us about President Chesterton. If we discover anything that might help, we'll let you know."

We shook hands and left her suite on the top floor. Drago and I found the elevator ride up a bit disorienting, but the ride down was scary. I kept feeling as if I was falling. When the doors opened on the ground floor, we four were taken by complete surprise. There stood a dozen men in blue uniforms, their hands holding small metal objects, which were pointed at us.

One man spoke, "You four are under arrest for subversion. You will come with us or we won't hesitate to execute you where you stand."

I doubted their weapon things would harm Drago, but we'd not come prepared for a battle. If I had had time to cast my new spells on us three humans, then I would have been confident their weapon things wouldn't have harmed us either. In such a case, I'd have resisted. As it was, I didn't want to risk anything bad happening to the girls.

"I'm sorry. We're not from this world. We didn't know taking privately to people was a crime," I replied.

"This way," he barked, ignoring my comments. His dozen men marched us out of the building, while many others stopped to stare at us. We were ushered into a dark metal vehicle Lexi called a truck. Ten minutes later, we were marched into prison cells, locked into two cages. Drago and I were in one, while the girls were in the other.

Tiffany commented, "They must have had her home bugged."

"Huh?"

"Tiny electronic microphones that transmit whatever is said in her home to these people. They are spying on Lana and the president."

"What a strange world," I replied. "I like Byron Falls much better." We four chuckled.

A few minutes later, another official looking man stepped up to our cells, a clipboard in hand. He didn't even ask our names, rather just rattled off some charges indicating we were being subversive to the country. Then, he left us alone.

"Well, this is stupid. We're not going to find out what happened to Abe sitting in this smelly hole," I declared. "Time to depart."

"How?" asked Tiff.

"Like this," I replied. I focused and opened a Mystical Door in my cell, stepped through it, arriving in the girls' cell. Drago laughed. I opened another one and stepped out onto the street. The girls followed me. Still roaring with laughter, Drago pushed up hard against the stone wall; the rock shattered, and he walked out, dusting his suit off.

Tiff commented, "Now that's what I call a jail break, Drago."

We three roared with laughter and looked for a taxi vehicle. Ten minutes later, we returned to the Box. Time for lunch and plan making.

"Look, we don't have any direct evidence these aliens are behind the strange behavior of President

Chesterton and the others. Nothing ties that into the missing Abe Beck," I said.

Tiffany replied, "Not exactly. While we certainly don't know much at all about what's been happening on this world, can it be a coincidence that the troubles with the key leaders began not long after the ambassador arrived on this world? What this has to do with the missing accountant is unknown, I'll admit that. So it's my opinion we should break into this Alcyon building and see what's going on inside. Could be nothing but a small manufacturing operation. In which case, we leave. Felix can get us in, bypassing all their security by using his Mystical Door."

We discussed the situation further, but Tiffany's idea became our plan of action. Hoping to draw less attention, we decided to pay them a visit this afternoon.

# Chapter 16—Foiled

Invisible, we four held hands just outside the Alcyon building's main entrance. Here, I could see inside through the only windows in the whole building. A lone secretary sat at a desk—the receptionist, Tiff suggested. I cast my Mystical Door, centering the exit beyond the woman's desk and as close to the locked doors as possible. This first action was simple. I could see where I wanted the door to open to, but I was going to have to guess where to have the next one open up behind the locked double doors.

"Wow," whispered Tiffany. "Those doors are not only locked, but they've got a keypad too. You have to know the code to enter. Plus, that's a biometric sensor above it. So even knowing the code isn't enough to get passed the doors. Probably only a handful of people can open that door. Talk about security, this is total overkill."

I focused and cast my first spell, opening the door and stepping out, pulling the others along with me. With all of us invisible, coordinated actions are difficult. We were three feet from the large but locked metal doors. As quietly as I could, I spoke the command words. Magical energies flashed and my second Mystical Door appeared. We four stepped through, arriving three feet behind the doors. Yes, I knew the receptionist was likely to have heard my whispered voice and seen the energy flash, but she wouldn't have seen us and maybe ignored the event.

We stood and stared. For Drago and me, this was truly difficult, since we had never seen anything like this before. The girls, however, had. We were in a hallway, six feet wide. Another set of these biometrically locked doors was straight ahead of us, opposite the doors we'd just bypassed. The hall led off to the left and right, but both ended at elevator doors.

Tiffany pointed out, "Look. There are motion sensors on the floor, those there, and there are video cameras mounted up high. We're likely detected already.

What now?"

"Ahead first," I decided, not having enjoyed the previous elevator ride. I cast the spell once more and we stepped beyond this set of doors.

"What?" I whispered.

The room was huge, probably occupying a city block, less the outer walls. Inside, giant machinery hummed with electricity. The numerous giant monitor screens were plainly visible, displaying all manner of sights, from someone walking on a street to what must be people holding meetings. Two men were sitting at some console, occasionally speaking into a microphone, but we couldn't hear what was being said. However, some red lights began flashing. Both men glanced around, but didn't see us. We were still invisible.

My spell was still active, so I pulled everyone back into the hallway. I'd no idea what we'd just seen, but it looked highly suspicious. "Let's try the elevators. The only way is down." Several chuckled; this was a one-story building.

The elevator doors opened. I rather expected they'd be locked too. The panel had only two buttons, unlike what we'd seen in the skyscraper's elevator. I pressed the one with the Down arrow. Again, Drago and I felt very queasy, as though we were falling, and I was prepared to cast a Gentle Fall if needed. The doors opened and we stepped out to a light-bluish illuminated, spacious, but freaky room.

Occupying the central section of the building and behind a thick glass outer wall were twenty-five strange chambers, apparently filled with a fluid, water I guessed. The bluish light came from long fixtures above each chamber. All manner of wire and tubes entered each of the chambers, dropping down from the ceiling. While all this was strange, that's not what so shocked us all.

No, in six of the chambers, we saw four men and two women—rather what was left of their bodies. They were floating, approximately in the middle of the tanks. Their arms and legs were about four inches long, conical in shape. Earphones were attached to their heads. Tubes entered their noses, which were otherwise sealed shut. Another tube went into their mouths, which were also sealed tight. Other tubes came out of their lower orifices. The six just floated in the middle of the tanks, motionless, though one woman's eyes rotated to look for the source of the little noise we made as we gasped at this horrific sight. Worse, we spotted Abe in one of the tanks!

Some giant machine sat on the opposite side of the tanks from where we stood. Other equipment lined the outer walls. We could easily walk all around the central tanks. Still gasping in shock, we began to amble, our minds trying to grasp what could possibly be going on here. Nothing made the remotest sense, not even to Tiffany and Lexi.

Tiffany exclaimed, "They are alive in there!"

"What are they doing to these people?" Lexi asked.

"Well, I still don't see any dragons around here. For once, it isn't us that's behind this," Drago commented, hinting this was worse than what the dragons had been doing.

"Let's walk around as see if we can figure out what's going on," I suggested, "but stay really close in case we need to make a fast getaway. You too, Drago. I think these walls might be too strong for you to smash through. Besides, we're underground."

Slowly, we began walking around the central tanks, our eyes examining wholly unfamiliar equipment and things. I heard a low hissing sound, but much of the machinery was also making distinctive sounds as well. We had gotten halfway around the central chamber when I began to feel dizzy and lightheaded. Then, my legs felt weak. I slumped slowly to the ground, so did the girls. However, we also saw a dozen men wearing strange masks over their faces and holding very large metal objects in their hands, all pointed towards us as they moved slowly our way. I tried to focus to cast a Mystical Door, but the world turned black, as I slipped unconsciousness. At the very last instant, Drago, who could hold his breath a long time, managed to get his Mystical Door cast, and he vanished. Later, I learned he'd managed to get himself up to the hallway outside the control room, where he too fell unconscious, but was still invisible and remained undetected.

Spine-chilling screams roused me, and I reacted by added my own scream to the din. I was lying on a small cushion on a metal cart, my head propped up slightly. My arms and legs looked just like those who were floating in the tanks. Our arms were about four inches long, while our legs were perhaps six inches long. The stumps were conical shaped, tapering down to perhaps an inch or two across at the stump's tip. Tiffany and Lexi lay on similar pillow covered carts beside me, their arms and legs just like mine. The shock wore off, as several men walked up to us.

I recognized Ambassador Alejo de la Vegas, who had a sneering grin on his face. He introduced the other two men. "This is Amidio da Casa, the man who runs this operation, and this is Dr. Basilio Tista, who handles medical needs. Well, you wanted to know what's going on here, and now you're about to find out. It's a real experience, but I'm afraid you won't be writing home about it—no hands. Doctor, please explain what has happened to them."

The doctor was a short man, slightly pudgy, with steely eyes. "That machine behind you, out of which your bodies have just come, is a specially made medical machine. Back on Eros-4, we've invented many marvelous medical healing machines, virtually eliminating the need for hands-on doctoring. Alcyon has modified one of these for the sole purpose of removing a person's arms and legs, but leaving just enough stump on which to attach a prosthesis later on. When you have fulfilled your employment with Alcyon, we'll provide you with proper prostheses for arms and legs. I'm told after six months of physical therapy, you might be able to do some minor things for yourselves, so you won't be completely helpless amputees. However, your memories of what has happened to you while you are here working for us will be wiped from your mind. Instead, you'll be given memories of a terrible accident."

He finished, a pleased look on his face, and Ambassador de la Vegas explained further. "So what are we going to use you for? Simple. Eros-4 is taking over total control of other worlds. We do this without starting galactic wars or invading with armies. Instead, we use the electronic devices our scientists have developed. You've seen the six 'volunteers' we have already working for us. Soon you three will join them in the tanks. Once hooked up, the tank life-support systems will keep your bodies alive for at least fifty years."

"Amidio has picked out the key personnel of this world, the men and women who are in control of vital areas, such as President Dick Chesterton. He has a person picked out for each of you three. Once you are hooked up in the tank, he will focus your monitor on the person whose body you will be taking over. Then, he will activate our Transference Machine, which moves you and your mind into that person. In effect, you will be stealing that person's body for a time. Via the earphones on your body in the tank, he will issue orders for you in your stolen body to follow. Failure to follow them is handled by the simple press of a button on his console, which sends an electrical shock to your brain here, which in turn gives the stolen body a painful migraine until you comply with his orders. If you persist in disobedience, then we'll locate other members of your family and have them join you here in another tank."

"We're just beginning operations here on Dickersen-3. This station will ultimately house twenty-five of you. When we have another twenty of these identical centers established around the world, we will have obtained complete and total control of this world and can make it serve our needs, whatever they may be. We harm no one, but our volunteers, usually around five hundred men and women. See, we have a humane way to conquer other worlds. We'll see the five hundred people are provided with nice prostheses when we finish with them."

"There's no escape possible. You see, often when we've finished with a stolen body, we have them have an accident. Don't worry. If your stolen body dies, you will find yourself automatically back here in your body in the tank. No avoiding that, and don't get any wild ideas that you can steal some other body than the ones we place you into—can't be done. If you try, you'll find you are right back here in your original bodies. You see, you can't escape these bodies. You're locked into them for the duration of your lives, just as everyone is. However, we can control how long you can remain in your stolen bodies. Marvelous technology, don't you agree? Humane way to conquer other worlds, eh?" he insinuated with that covert grin of his.

I needed to stall, knowing we'd be unable to take any actions once they had us hooked up and floating in the tanks. "So tell me, Ambassador, how does this actually work? What do you want of the stolen bodies? I'm afraid I don't see the point. Why not just kill these five hundred people? Why go to all this trouble with us? Won't the local authorities eventually uncover your kidnapping and mutilation of their citizens? Even a blind woman knows something is going on here. Won't the police eventually raid this building?"

This time, Amidio spoke up. "Yes, you raise some interesting questions, Felix. As to how it all works, only our top scientists knows that, something about aesthetics and the yatto-kilohertz vibrations, whatever they are. No, what's more significant is that we simply bring a realtime image of the target person up on the monitor, activate the switches to your body harness, and press the Transfer button. Presto, you and your mind are in that body, totally overpowering and dwarfing the person whose body it is. Admittedly, we have continually to monitor the connection, since sometimes the host person is quite powerful and is able to somewhat push you out of their body. That we don't allow, not until we're through with that person."

"What do we want? Simple. Via you, we have the

key personnel make decisions and pass laws that allow Ambassador de la Vegas here ultimately to run the world as its supreme ruler and lawmaker. If all goes well, as it usually does, ten years from now, our ambassador will be in total control of this world. What he says, goes. After we get what we need out of a stolen person, we then eliminate them. Why? That should be obvious. Once we return you to your body here, the person will have their own volition back and undoubtedly will attempt to void or nullify what he or she's been forced to do. We can't have that, can we? Thus, they meet with a fatal accident. Even if you are still running the stolen body, when it dies, you will immediately find yourself back here in yours. You are ours to use until we've finished with you, at which time we will erase your memories of all this and provide you with proper prostheses. Personally, I don't think you'll be able to do much with them, but it's the best we can provide."

"As far as your comments about the local police force taking action against us, we have that covered. Right now, St. Leeds' police commissioner is under our control. The man you were trying to find, Abe, is controlling his body, making sure the police leave us alone. In fact, we ordered him to have you three arrested. You were asking too many questions. Of course, the police commissioner, as well as we, wants to know how you managed to bust through the walls of one cell and simply vanish from the other. I don't suppose you're willing to tell us that right now. Don't worry. Once we get you hooked up, you'll willingly tell us about it. Massive migraines are quite the persuader."

I replied, "Well, Drago simply walked through the walls. You should have them make sturdier walls in their prisons." Ambassador de la Vegas laughed.

Tiffany spoke up, "But we're helpless like this." She waved her arm and leg stumps slightly. "You've ruined us for life."

Ambassador de la Vegas chuckled again. "Yes, yes, you are helpless. Can't be helped. If we didn't, you could easily get yourselves out of the harness and equipment attached to you while you're in the tank. We can't have that, now can we? But look at it this way, your small sacrifice is saving millions of lives that would be lost had we had to conquer Dickersen-3 with an army. We're sparing your lives as well. Only those few key men and women will actually be killed. You'll be able to live long lives, knowing your sacrifice is a worthy one."

"But what kind of a life can we have like this?" She again waved her stumps about.

"Well, not as active a life as before." And Ambassador de la Vegas laughed heartily.

I'd been stalling, just as Drago asked in the Message that he'd sent me minutes before, just as we woke up. I had no idea where he was at, only that we were to wait until he got to us, if we could. I wasn't about to allow these mad men to hook us up and put us in the tanks.

When we went unconscious, the invisible Drago stepped out of his Mystical Door, arriving in the long hallway on the ground floor. The knockout drug finally affected him, and he dozed off for a time. When he awoke, he found the dozen security guards combing the halls for him. Wisely, he sent a Message to me and then acted. First, he cast a Sticky Webs spell, encasing the twelve men, who struggled futilely to get free, much like a fly in a spider's web. Once he had them all secure, Drago cast his Ball of Fire spell, incinerating the lot. In fact, he cast it three times, making sure all twelve guards were eliminated. He saw no one was in the monitoring room and finally headed down to rescue us. Again, he used a Mystical Door to get down to us, not trusting the elevator. He recast his Invisibility spell so the three men didn't see him as he arrived on our level. From the corner of my eyes, I spotted the flash of magical energies and suspected he'd just arrived via that new spell we'd learned. I gave him another minute to walk over to our vicinity before I took action.

"Sleep!" I barked, followed by "Charm Human." I calculated they'd be least likely to throw off my attempts to charm them if they were asleep. It worked, though they woke up when they hit the floor rather hard. Tiffany then cast her Sleep spell on them, but I had Drago wake the "good" doctor up. I had plans for him.

I spoke firmly. "Good. Dr. Basilio, it's time to unhook the six men from the tanks, give them their promised prostheses, and send them to a rehabilitation center. Plus, you need to give us our prostheses and our clothes."

"Oh yes, yes, I see that is so. Come Mr. Drago. Lend me a hand, please."

Soon, they returned with three wheelchairs, our clothes, and a pile of artificial limbs. After a bit of a struggle, Drago and Dr. Basilio had my arms attached, though the limbs merely hung down at my sides, their silver hooks reflecting light. Dressed, I felt more human again, but almost completely helpless. An hour later, they had Tiffany and Lexi dressed and with their prostheses attached. We three agreed that trying to live with these would be grim indeed.

Thus, while the two headed over to the tanks to free the six others, I concentrated and cast my usual Morph Human. When the magical energies flashed, Tiffany looked like she had this morning, fully clothed.

"Thank you! My God, that was beyond horrible. Looks like we'll need three weeks to regenerate this time," she declared.

I nodded and cast it again on Lexi, and then finally on myself.

Lexi barked, "Damn those men. You can't live like that, at least not well. I've never felt so helpless. I'd have freaked out if I didn't know any magic spells. Thanks dear. I hope we're going to teach these three their lessons."

"Absolutely," I explained, "but only after we get these six victims rescued and off to safety. Come on. Let's check out that medical butchery machine."

Drago lifted the helpless Abe out of the tank, while Dr. Basilio swiftly unhooked him. "Carry him over here to the dryer. I'll get his clothing and his promised prostheses."

The doctor pushed a wheelchair loaded with the

items over to the dryer. Again, Drago watched carefully to see how they were attached to Abe, knowing he'd eventually have to do this by himself. Two mechanical arms ending in silver hooks dangled uselessly from his shoulders. Then, the legs were attached. After that, the two dressed Abe, who could only sit there sobbing.

Dr. Basilio was surprised to see us walking up to the trio. He fumbled, "How? It usually takes six months to regain some limited functionality."

"Magic. Now let's get the others handled."

The better part of an hour passed before we have all six prepared, a local therapy center called, and the six in their wheelchairs waiting on the electric transport to arrive and pick them up. That done, we then had Dr. Basilio show us how to operate his medical butchery machine—twice, once on the sleeping Ambassador Alejo and once on President Amidio. That done, we left them lying on the steel carts, just as they had done us.

"Sleep," Tiffany barked, dropping Dr. Basilio into a sound sleep. Drago caught him so he didn't hit the floor. Quickly, we stripped him and placed him into the machine, arms and legs spread out, eagle fashion. Following the procedure, we closed the door and pressed Activate. Now we waited for the half hour process to complete.

"It's incredible, you know," Lexi commented, "these aliens have perfected a technology that will amputate appendages and heal the body, all in a half hour. Normally, people would need weeks to recover from such surgery, to say nothing of the blood loss during the operation. Amazing technology, but such a waste. The good they could do with such an invention is mind-boggling."

Right on time, the machine released the doctor, and we placed him on the third cart. We wheeled them over to the dressing station, retrieved prostheses, and wheelchairs for the men, but didn't put them on the men just yet. Rather, we waited for them to awaken from the anesthetic of the medical machine.

"We should destroy this facility," Drago proposed. "Soon, those who were being controlled by these men will come here to investigate and very likely try to make use of this terrible machinery. I doubt it would harm a dragon, though."

Tiffany agreed, saying, "Absolutely. Something like this exists only to abuse and harm others. It serves no good purpose, only wicked, evil ones. We need to blow it up somehow."

Although we looked about, we could see no way to accomplish that. Then, the three men awoke, and we had to handle them. After their anticipated initial shocking screams died down, Ambassador de la Vegas laughed. Seconds later, President Amidio and Dr. Basilio also began laughing. This, I could not believe!

Still laughing, Ambassador de la Vegas explained, "We're free at last! We aren't dead, like we were supposed to be. Yahoo. Incredible. Thank you, son, ladies. Thank you."

"Right. Thanks," the other two chimed in.

Gone was the sneering, cold, covert voice of the ambassador, replaced by a normal tone, one that radiated relief and happiness. I simply couldn't grasp the three men's reaction.

Still chuckling, the ambassador explained, "They were controlling us, just like you thought we were controlling the six top men and women on this world. In fact, they've been running our bodies for close to a dozen years. You haven't any idea what it's been like for us. We were paralyzed in our own bodies, watching and listening as someone else operated it, saying and doing things we'd never, ever do. We were always there in the background, completely helpless to run our own bodies."

Tiffany interrupted, "Wicked. So you're saying the man who was being the ambassador isn't you, but someone else, just as Abe was running the St. Leeds' police commissioner?"

"Right. We have been helpless pawns too, but we knew we were going to be killed when they were done using our bodies, just as the police commissioner and the other five would have been eliminated when the Eros-4 people were done using their bodies. We've seen that happen many times during the past twelve years. Can you imagine living as we have been, knowing the only relief will be when they kill our bodies? Suddenly without any warning, you four come along and free us. Like this," he waved his short stumps about, "we're useless to them, and they can't have us harm ourselves as they intended. We're alive and they can't have us kill ourselves, because we can't do much of anything any longer. We're alive! Yahoo."

The ambassador's smile was infectious. We grinned too. The doctor added, "And after we have maybe six months of physical therapy, we might be able to do a few actions for ourselves. If nothing else, we can get automated wheelchairs that we can control with our heads and mouths. I sure as heck didn't want to die. We all have families back on our home world, which isn't Eros-4."

Ambassador de la Vegas added, "He's right, but we should get all the physical therapy we can first before we go home to our wives and families. We need to be as independent as we can be first."

Amidio agreed, "You're right. God, I never thought I'd ever see my wife and boys again. I've missed twelve years of their lives. Say, time's a'wasting. How about getting us fixed up and off to a rehabilitation center now?"

Still smiling, we set about doing just that. However, as we were struggling to get the men into their prostheses, I felt a cold, sneering presence attempting to take over my body. Hastily, I cancelled my Morph spell and those of Tiff and Lexi. Somehow, we three remained upright, silver hooks dangling at our sides, just as they were for the three men. I felt that presence curse and leave me.

Lexi declared, "Wow. Someone was trying to take over my body too. Thanks dear. That did it." Tiff added her me too.

Drago's deep laugh caused us nearly to fall down as we turned to face him. "Whatever they do, they can't take over me." He continued to roar. The three men looked perplexed, but I wasn't about to tell them Drago was a dragon. I doubt they even knew what one was. Still, I knew these Eros-4 people were still trying to regain control of this facility.

After I explained what had happened, Ambassador de la Vegas said, "I figured they would. Look, the only way they can do this is if they can see who is here. If some other normal person comes into this place and they can see them, there's nothing to stop them from taking over that person's body, starting this up all over again."

"So how do we stop them?" I asked.

"Smash all the video cameras around here. Push me along, and I'll show you where they are. Drago can smash them."

A half hour later and with my Morph spells recast, we finished smashing the last of the many spy cameras the Eros-4 people had installed in the facility. We were just in time, too. A van arrived to carry the three men off to their rehabilitation facility. While we were loading them, a hundred soldiers arrived in armored vehicles. They wore heavy body armor and were armed to the teeth. Ignoring us, they charged past us, securing the building. Later, we heard a newscast in which President Dick Chesterton described the insidious plot by Eros-4 to take over Dickersen-3 and that they had now secured the facility.

After the vehicle departed, we four headed home, stopping to visit with Anna. She was elated that we'd found her Abe, but she sobbed when we told her his physical condition. She had us arrange for a vehicle to take her to where he was now staying. Lexi called it a taxi, whatever that is.

We finally returned to the Box late that day. Over a delayed supper, we exchanged our fears. Lexi commented, "Look, we weren't able to destroy those machines. Now they are in the hands of the army of this world. I'll bet anything, their scientists are now studying the machinery. What are the odds they'll begin making use of this as a weapon?"

Tiff replied, "A certainty, Lexi. Their President has subjective knowledge about how it works and how effective it is. You can count on them using it for their own purposes. I'll wager in one year, someone will be using this technology to control this world for their own ends."

"Might not take that long," Lexi lamented.

I spoke up, "What I want to know is what are the ones behind this going to do now? I mean the ones who were running everything from that spaceship. Oh, Tiff, what did the ambassador mean by a geosynchronous orbit?"

"The ship is so far above the surface that it orbits the world in the same amount of time as the ground it's above rotates around once. It makes detection of the spaceship more difficult."

"Okay. So this stuff is very long range then. I'll bet anything they'll try to regain control of their facility. All that equipment and stuff must be expensive."

Tiff countered. "Well yes, probably, but dear, they may well must move on to another world. Look, by now President Dick had probably instigated new procedures designed to counter any one person suddenly espousing new positions, such as allowing the Eros-4 people planet side. So if they tried to take over some others like Abe and force him to slip into President Dick's body again, their new protocols would likely have the President eliminated. What I find curious is there doesn't seem to be any dragons about. I've rather come to expect them to be behind nasty things. No offense, Drago."

He chuckled. "None taken. Blacks, Reds, and Greens loathe humans. Most of the others are more or less neutral towards your species. I think we Golds have the greatest tolerance of you. Personally, I find you three interesting."

I laughed. "I find you quite loveable, Drago, a good friend."

After supper, we turned in. I was exhausted. Then, I realized that was coming from the massive trauma I'd suffered in that medical machine. Lexi and Tiff also realized the same thing. After cancelling their Morph spells, I removed their artificial limbs and tucked each into our bed. Then, I had Drago handle me, laying me down between them, before he headed off to his room.

In the morning, we three experimented a little with the arm and hooks, before giving up on them. I Morphed myself and then inserted our precious ring onto Tiff's right arm stump. We watched as the ring slowly expanded until it slipped on it. None of us, including Drago, expected to see what happened next.

We did expect magical energies to flash; that happened. However, the flash was ten times larger than anticipated. Almost instantly, Tiffany's arms and legs returned to normal, as if she'd not had them amputated by that machine! The ring slipped off her arm, dropping on the floor.

"Wicked! What just happened? I thought it took a week to regenerate lost appendages," she bubbled, testing her arms, hands, and feet.

"I don't understand," I muttered, retrieving the ring and slipping it onto Lexi's arm stump.

This time, we four were prepared for the brilliant display of energies and weren't disappointed. Lexi's missing appendages were almost instantly back to what they'd been before the machine had done its work.

"Okay, let me do you," Lexi ordered.

I cancelled my spell, but only after sitting down on the bed. If I hadn't, I'd have fallen hard. She slipped the ring on my arm stump. Inwardly, I hoped the same thing would happen with me, but I didn't express my worries. Again, we were momentarily blinded by the enormity of the magical energy discharge, but my own arms and legs where back, just as they had been before I entered that building yesterday.

Drago commented, "Get dressed. Then, let's meet. Something isn't right here. This shouldn't have happened this way."

"No kidding, Drago," I piped up, slipping my pants on, while the girls hastily dressed.

We carried the conversation along while dressing. I pointed out, "Look, the reaction to the ring was exactly the same as it was before, when it turned your dead arms back, shrunk our breasts, and repaired our feet."

"Right," Lexi called out. "So can we assume that means their fancy medical machine didn't really cut off our arms and legs? That magic spells were used?"

"That's what I'm thinking," Drago bellowed. "That's the only reasonable explanation. We know it takes a week to regenerate missing arms. My suspicions lead me to postulate it would take two weeks to regenerate both your missing arms and legs. I was so hoping to see if that was the case. So the machine didn't do what that doctor said it did."

I chimed in, "I agree. The machine is a fake. They are using magic somehow and we darn well better figure out how. Also, we should visit Abe and the others and see if the ring will restore their arms and legs."

Tiff pointed out, "With all those soldiers in there, it's going to be hard for us to check that machine out."

"We should take care of Abe first," Lexi pointed out. "The question then is do we restore them for the ambassador and his buddies? I'm inclined not to do that, since the Eros-4 people may well then retake over their bodies."

"Okay. For now, let's not tempt them," I agreed with her.

Two hours later, six men and women were elated with the results. The ring cancelled the magic alterations their bodies were under. On our way back, we passed by Alcyon and saw soldiers were still there in force. Back at our Box, we met to decide how to proceed.

Tiff suggested, "We should go in late at night. The guards will be minimal then, don't you think?"

Drago and I accepted her suggestion, since this world and its people were so foreign to us. After more discussion, we decided we were going to have to dismantle the medical machine to see what was inside it.

Around two in the morning, we four stood invisible at the backside of the Alcyon building. Two soldiers stood guard in the main foyer, but the place seemed otherwise empty. I cast my Mystical Door and stepped through, bringing the others with me. We were in the dimly illuminated, narrow hallway that circumnavigated the main control room with its many giant monitors. Another Mystical Door later and we stood in the outer area of the basement with its many tanks and the machine. Again, only dim night-lights illuminated the giant space. After making sure no one was around, we moved across the space to the giant medical machine.

As we stood there looking at it, Tiff commented, "You know, we put six of us through it yesterday. What I want to know is what did it do with all those arms and legs?"

"I suppose it could use some strong acid or alkaline to dissolve them," Lexi suggested.

After walking around the machine, Tiff pointed out, "Look there. Isn't that some tubes similar to the ones on the people in the tanks?"

"I think so. Are you suggesting there's a person inside?" I asked, finally following her leaps of logic.

"Yep. Has to be a person who can cast powerful spells. So let's see how we can open it up."

I admit I'm completely ignorant of such equipment; nothing remotely like this existed in Byron Falls. After a frustrating few minutes, I simply focused and barked, "Open All Doors." While the doors near the elevator opened up as well as the storehouse doors, more importantly, the machine appeared to break in half. Actually, a cleverly hidden latch had unlocked, and the two halves separated.

"Oh dear God!" exclaimed Lexi.

I simply inhaled sharply, blinking several times to be sure I was seeing what I thought I was seeing. Inside a tiny tank of liquid floated another man, who was hooked up to similar life-preserving lines, just as Abe had been. However, this man's body was nothing more than a head and torso. He appeared quite emaciated as well.

"We'll have you out of there shortly," I managed to say.

Meanwhile, Drago set about unhooking the tubes.

Having done this several times yesterday, he had the man freed in fifteen minutes.

"Okay, let's get him to the Box fast," I ordered. "Don't worry. We'll have you fixed up shortly."

The man was very weak and said little, but allowed us to carry him as we stepped through two Mystical Doors out onto the sidewalk behind the building. As rapidly as we could, we walked the few blocks back to the Box. I carried him; he was incredibly light.

Once home, we poured hot tea into him, covered him with warm blankets, and allowed him to grasp that he was free. Finally, after some chicken soup, he was able to talk to us. His story was grim indeed.

"I'm Archmage Titus Jones. My world is called Rainbow's End. Many years ago, these Eros-4 aliens landed a silver flying ship near our town of Beaker's Point on the southern rim of the Painted Hills. Somehow, these evil men learned I was an Archmage and knew how to cast the Restricted Wish spell. They drugged me and took me onboard their magical silver vessel."

"While I was unconscious, their doctors operated on me, removing my arms and legs from their sockets, just as I am today. When I woke up, they told me that they had also captured my wife and two young sons. They would not be harmed if I did precisely what they told me to do. They drugged me again and I awoke inside that machine of theirs."

"I had no real choice. Often, they showed me images of my family. I used a Restricted Wish to divine what would happen if I disobeyed them. They would simply kidnap them and use them as they have done six local men and women here on this world. I could not let that happen to my family."

Tiffany interrupted him, "So what did they have you doing?"

"Use my Restricted Wish spell. Every time they put another person in the machine, I was to cast it. They showed me images of just what they wanted. Every person was to be mutilated the same way, just as I did to you three. If I varied from the script, if the person came out from their machine different from the specifications, my family would be harmed. At first, I tried to disobey, if only slightly, but the next day, they showed me images my wife with a broken arm. An 'accident,' they claimed. So I've been casting the same spell repeatedly. Worse, I can't use my magic to help them, to get them to safety, unless I'm on the same world as they're on. The Eros-4 people have never taken me back to my home world; they know what I could do there, so they aren't giving me a chance."

"So do you age a year every time you cast it?" she asked.

"Precisely. Magic use has a price. They took me when I was twenty-seven. I should be thirty-seven now, but I'm afraid the body has aged to ninety-eight. Honestly, I kept hoping they'd bring more people to the machine, because my body will die soon. I don't think it can survive another few of those spells."

"But we can use our Regeneration Ring on you—get your arms and legs back," Tiffany suggested, halfheartedly.

She began to see what Titus meant. However, back in Byron Falls, if a man lived to be fifty, he was considered ancient. No one lived past seventy or so. I marveled at their longevity. On her world, people often lived into their nineties.

"I appreciate your freeing me from their torment, Miss Tiffany, but let's not waste that precious magical ring on a dying man. Even if I had them back, I've no way to return to my world. Even if I could find a way back, I'd look like an ancient man. She'll not recognize me, and besides, I hope by now she's found someone else and remarried. If she's found any happiness at all, I'll not disrupt that. My body won't last very long."

"Ninety-eight less thirty-seven," Lexi said, "is sixty-one. So is that how many people you've had to cast your Restricted Wish on, making stumps out of their arms and legs?"

"I've lost count, but that seems right. They've used me to take over two worlds before this one. They suspected

I might just be able to fill their tanks with men and women before what's left of my body dies, but I doubt it. Even with their special system to keep me alive like that, I almost stopped breathing when I was doing the last couple of men."

Lexi went on, "Ambassador de la Vegas said that they usually have around twenty of these centers when they complete taking over a world. So does that mean they have twenty other mages like you imprisoned in their nasty machines?"

"As far as I know, that's correct. I know after they take over total control of a world, they don't need to make more for their tanks. That's when they move the machines and us out of the facilities and on to the next world to be conquered. They pick relatively youthful people to put in their tanks. That way, they can use them and their minds to take over other victim's bodies, when the need arises. They usually exterminate the target people when they're through using them. If they didn't, when they move their people onto others, the target would regain full control of his or her body and spill the beans, as we say. That would cause enormous problems for the Eros-4 people, so they arrange for the death of the hosts, moving their tank people into other host bodies to be controlled. They try to get a good fifty to sixty working years out of each tank person I've made."

Lexi astutely commented, "Probably because there are so few true archmages. I doubt there are any magic users on any modern world."

Titus chuckled. "From the limited travel I've had, I believe you're correct. Even if they regain control of their facility here in St. Leeds, your actions have cost them very dearly, very dearly. I just wish there was some way to free the other nineteen of us. Alas, I have no idea where they are even located. Had they been successful here in St. Leeds and filled up all two dozen tanks, they would have brought in the next one, setting up the next of the needed twenty centers."

She replied, "Indeed. If I knew where they were, I'd

go after them. Rats."

He yawned heavily. "I'm so tired. May I sleep now? I've been doing that an awful lot of the time lately."

Lexi carried him into a spare bedroom and tucked him in, telling him to yell if he needed anything. When she returned to our living room, Drago was talking.

"If these Eros-4 people have a magical ship way up there in the sky and if they have nineteen more of these archmages in the machines, I'll bet anything they will land and try to setup a new Alcyon facility. We best not press the Handled button yet."

Tiffany agreed, adding, "Right, Drago, but they are taking enormous risks trying to capture and imprison an archmage. They are the most powerful magic users anywhere, right?"

Drago nodded. She went on, "I bet it's very dangerous to kidnap an archmage, for humans, that is, but couldn't a dragon capture one? I think what I'm suggesting is maybe the Black and Red dragons are going around capturing archmages who know this particular spell, and trading them to these evil Eros-4 people."

Lexi added, "Tiff, that makes sense, but what could they have that the dragons would want in exchange? Giant gemstones?"

Drago chuckled. "Perhaps. They certainly don't have magic to offer. However, perhaps the dragons see their flying metal ships as being magic items or even their handheld blaster gun things. Certainly, a dragon could well kidnap an archmage, but even so, it would be very dangerous for the dragon. Archmages know some incredibly powerful spells. They'd have to be taken by surprise, as we were in the Alcyon building."

I yawned too. "Gang, I'm tired too. Let's get some sleep. Tomorrow, we best keep a sharp eye out for that Eros-4 ship. Titus may be right; they might try to setup another building and start taking over key people's bodies again."

# Chapter 17—Foiled Again

Onboard the Destroyer, Commander N'Gar fumed, pacing around the CCC, Command and Control Center, threatening to either wear out his shoe leather or cut a grove in the floor. The conquering victor of two previous worlds, N'Gar should have had Dickersen-3 firmly under his control and be launching multiple additional facilities to wrap up the project. What had gone so terribly wrong? That was the question he'd hammered into his subordinates yesterday, and if they didn't come up with the answer soon, he swore he'd put them into the tanks next. Of course, that shook them up, ensuring they'd come up with the explanation or perhaps an explanation.

Facts. N'Gar knew all six key men and women, who had been firmly under control via those in the tanks at the new installation in St. Leeds, were not dead and were no longer under the total control of those in the Alcyon tanks. They should be and must be dead or under control, but they were free from the domination of those in the tanks and taking strong steps to expel everyone from Eros-4. *So much for protocols.* His facial muscles strained taught.

However, it was far worse than a mere failure of those in the tanks to take over and control those six key personnel. Far worse. The three men in charge of the St. Leeds Alcyon factory were gone. *That's not correct. They've been turned into helpless tank people, given their retirement prostheses, and delivered to a physical rehabilitation facility on the edge of St. Leeds. That should never have happened unless I gave such orders, which I damn well didn't.*

He smashed his fist on the metal table as he passed by it on his forty-second trip around his CCC. "How the blazes did we lose the archmage in the medical machine? Answer me that!" His voice was so loud that several nearby junior officers nearly spilled their coffee. The loss of the archmage meant this facility could not become operational until a replacement archmage was installed in the medical machine. That also meant regaining control of the Alcyon building from the government soldiers. Worse, the archmages were critical to the entire operation, but could only cast a limited number of their special spells before they died of old age. The loss of this one, though he was nearing the end of his life span, would cause repercussions further up the chain of command. Back on Eros-4, someone would have to acquire another archmage, often very difficult to manage. Since it happened on his watch, N'Gar knew he'd probably be assigned to find the replacement archmage, perhaps the most dangerous assignment of the entire project.

Around nine in the morning, local time—since the Destroyer was in orbit above St. Leeds, it made sense to keep local time—his four subordinates marched into the CCC. Their faces, pale; their eyes, bloodshot; their stress levels, off the charts. Each hoped what they were about to say would be enough to keep them out of the tanks.

Dr. Jamal offered, "Commander, it's our opinion drastic actions must be taken. Our secretive takeover of this world has been uncovered. Thus, we recommend the extermination of the six key individuals, who now know we're trying to take over their world. We'll send down the Assassination Squad, and then we'll need to. . ."

***

I marveled at Archmage Titus. The sheer number of spells he knew was staggering, and this morning, we four knew we were in the presence of an archmage, even if his body was close to death. At dawn, he was up and at it, having cast a Morph Self spell on his body. Now, he looked young again, but we all knew that was far from the truth. He joined us for breakfast.

"Thank you for freeing me. I have some work to do yet this morning, work that will likely end my days. I've located the Eros-4 flying ship. It's very high up in the sky. I've been using the various Look and Hear Via Another type spells, including Scrying. They aren't taking your

234

interference lightly. In fact, you've caused them considerable difficulties. Had you not disrupted their Aclyon works, they would have easily been able to take over total control of this world. However, now, the key world people know what's going on, that their bodies were taken over by the aliens and forced to do things against their desires and wills. The Eros-4 people are meeting to work out what to do next."

I replied, "I rather expected they would try something. As long as the soldiers control the building, I don't think they can take over any other people's bodies."

"We shall see."

"You look handsome," Tiffany changed the subject.

"Illusion only, my young mage. I've still got a few spells left in me, but not many. After I learn what they are going to do next, I'll take such actions as I can. I've several scores to settle with those on that flying ship of theirs."

An hour later, Titus grimaced, and got our attention. "Okay. They are planning to send an Assassination Squad down here and kill the six people who were being controlled and who now know what the Eros-4 aliens are doing. Then, they will retake control of the Alcyon building, bring down another archmage, kidnap more citizens, and begin again. I can't let that happen. Just remember, you have my sincerest thanks for having freed me from my torment."

I interjected, "Okay, but what are you going to do?"

"Teach them a lesson, just as you did to their ambassador and his underlings. When my body dies, please see that it is cremated somehow. Now, don't disturb me for a time."

He walked back to his room, sat on the edge of his bed, focused, and began lengthy chants. Suddenly, we four began seeing what he was seeing via his See Through Another's Eyes spell. Foreign. I've no other words to describe what I was seeing. Silver metal was everywhere, floor, walls, and ceiling. More importantly, we got a good view of a tall man wearing a blue uniform, likely the commander. He and three others were leaning over a table, drawing up plans.

Without warning, the man slumped to the ground. His pant legs and shirt sleeves folded up; he had four stumps, just as their other victims had. While there wasn't any sound, from his twisted face and open mouth, I suspected he was screaming. Shortly, one of the other three dropped to the metal floor, minus his appendages. The other two followed within a couple of minutes. Suddenly, the viewing spell ended.

"Wicked!" Tiffany exclaimed. "We need to learn how to use spells like that one. It can be very useful."

Lexi interrupted, "We best check on Titus. I've a bad feeling."

Drago got to his room first and stood in the doorway, shaking his head solemnly. As we joined him, I feared the worst. Upon his body's death, his morph spell, along with several others he was just using, ended. What was left of his body lay on the bed. His skin was wrinkled and lined with age.

His deep voice said, "He seems at peace, if I'm interpreting you humans correctly."

I replied, "I think so, Drago. Let's follow his wishes. We can do it in the spell casting room."

An hour later, we cast his ashes on a small lawn, one of the few we could find. As we strolled back to the Box, we discussed our next move.

Drago pointed out, "Look, if we press the Handled button, then I could starve before we land again and I can hunt. So let me take off and grab another one of those awful tasting bovines this world has. When I get back tomorrow, we can press it. I can't see we need to do anything more here."

"I agree with you, Drago," I said. "However, what still bothers me is that electronic device that can force a person and his mind out of his body and into another body, squashing that other person and his mind down. It's body theft, more or less. I wonder if we're meant to destroy the machines that do that."

Lexi spoke up, "Point taken, Felix. If we leave the

machines, I'll bet anything the local scientists will figure out how they work. As soon as they do, you can count on politically motivated people using it, doing just what the Eros-4 group did to the key people here."

"Exchanging one slave master for another," Tiffany added. "We best destroy the machines somehow. Where's a demolitions expert when you need one?"

"What's that?" I asked. Drago nodded too.

"Someone who knows how to blow things up."

We were two blocks from the Alcyon building. Boom! The ground shook. My feet vibrated. Then, the concussion wave slammed into us. I found myself lying on my back looking up at the blue sky, dazed. Turning my head, I saw the others were in similar positions. My head throbbed; it had hit the concrete sidewalk rather hard.

"What was that?" I asked, slowly getting to my feet and testing myself for further damage.

"Huh? Can't hear you," Lexi yelled.

I barely heard her.

"Wicked. Now that's an explosion," Tiffany declared, rubbing the back of her head.

"What?" I asked. "My hearing is messed up."

"Explosion," Tiffany yelled. "You guys okay? I got a bad bump on my head is all."

For a moment, we four padded our bodies this way and that, checking it over for any damage. Other than pains in the backs of our heads, we were otherwise all right. As we continued to walk back towards the Box, we saw a large number of what Lexi called emergency vehicles dashing past us, red lights flashing and sirens wailing.

"Rescue people," Lexi explained for Drago's and my benefit.

A block later, we came upon the block that used to contain the Alcyon building. All around it, numerous rescue vehicles parked in disarray. We saw men dragging other wounded out to these vehicles. However, the center of the one story building with its underground system was now mostly a giant crater. The wounded were the soldiers guarding the facility and who had been knocked out by the blast. Those who were unlucky enough to be inside were completely gone.

As we passed, I commented, "At least those inside didn't have to suffer."

Drago commented, "It seems to me the more civilized and modern a world becomes, the more devastating and deadly it is. There's nothing in Byron Falls that could turn a building into a crater. I hope we're done here. Even Rainbow's End was better than this world."

Lexi jested, "Oh you just don't like this modern world because it has no antelopes." Drago responded with a deep belly laugh.

Later on, once inside the Box, we decided to press the Handled button. As usual, we four held our breaths, hoping the Box accepted the outcome. Four exhales broke the silence, as the bar slid across the door, sealing us inside. We felt the slight vibration and knew the Box was traveling again.

Tiffany exclaimed, "Wicked! We're done here. Let's go get our new spells!"

The girls dashed off to retrieve theirs, while Drago and I brought up the rear. Eagerly, they grabbed their new pages and dashed off to find their spell books, while Drago and I got our new pages.

"Yippee!"

"Wicked!"

The excited girls joined us, holding their books. Tiffany explained, "We are going to learn to Morph Self, just like you are always doing."

Lexi added, "So now we won't be dependent upon you if bad things happen to us."

"Excellent," Drago replied, "and Felix and I are soon to be real mages."

"Huh?" broke in Lexi, curling her forehead. "I thought we all were already mages."

I explained, "True, but among magic users, we sort of have three levels of achievement. The first one happens when you can finally cast Balls of Fire and Bolts of Electricity. The second one happens when you can

Teleport anywhere you want. Mind you, it only works between locations on a world. It's not like Drago's Shadow Walking between worlds."

"So what's the third one?" asked Lexi.

I answered, "When you can cast at least one Grade 9 spell, you're then called an archmage."

"I aim to be Archmage Drago, first in my clan ever to make this level. There are only a couple archmage dragons in all of history, and I intend to be one."

I laughed, "Good goal, Drago, but first we better learn to Teleport. That spell could have been very handy lots of times already."

Thus began a three-week period of intense study, trial, and error. Each of us worked hard from dawn to dusk, though there wasn't any way to tell time inside the Box—we judged time by our stomachs.

"Hello there." My voice startled me, coming from the doorway. "Hello there." My Voice came again. I turned around and saw two bodies that were identical to me standing by the door, giant grins on their faces.

"Wicked, Felix, wicked," one said, and I knew immediately what had happened and who was talking. My gals had learned the Morph Self spell and were proudly proving it to me. I roared with laughter.

"Well done, Tiff, Lexi, well done! But I don't think I can hug myself."

Both giggled and canceled their spells. "See, we can do it now. Isn't this just amazing?" Lexi declared, rightly proud of their accomplishments.

"Absolutely, Lexi, Tiff. We're becoming a powerhouse team, the four of us."

Both giggled and ran off to practice. Drago nodded his appreciation, but complained, "I don't think I'll ever get this Teleport spell to work."

"We just keep at it. Come on. Let's try it again. We're to focus on having our bodies standing on that X and then bark the command words. One more time, Drago. Here goes."

I focused on the X on the floor, imagining I was

standing on it, and spoke "Teleport to the X." After so many failures, magical energies finally flashed. To my utter amazement, I was standing on the X. A few seconds passed before I realized I had actually just successfully Teleported. Then, I cried out in joy. I'd made it. I could proudly call myself a real mage now.

For the next hour, I practiced the spell, successfully each time, which only added to my confidence. Drago, however, continued to have enormous difficulties with the spell. Over supper of the blue goo, he and I discussed his problem.

"I don't get why I can't cast it. I keep saying the words right." His eyes partially closed; his lower lip puffed up and out, creating a frown and sad look on his face.

"Don't give up. Surely, you'll soon get it," Lexi declared optimistically.

Tiffany added, "She's right. We don't give up, not ever."

He cracked a brief smile, before I asked, "Do you suppose the problem involves just how close the Teleport spell is to your native Shadow Walk skill? Are the two getting confused?"

"Well," he drawled, before admitting, "that might be it. I get where I want to go firmly in mind and then sort of walk there. I suppose it must be much like Teleport is supposed to work."

"Okay. Just relax, think of the X, and do it," I ordered.

We sat around our dining room table—we humans sipping our tea. Drago did as I asked. Magical energies flashed and Drago vanished from his chair. We heard a loud bump coming from a distant room. Presently, Drago rejoined us, smiling broadly while rubbing his butt.

"I did it. I did it, but landed on my butt."

We laughed. Tiff exclaimed, "Wicked, Drago. I knew you could do it, only next time land on your feet."

"Good going. See, we don't ever give up," Lexi added.

I merely smiled and shook his hand. In that instant,

we three became good friends with Drago. Until then, he'd been more or less alone, a dragon in the midst of humans, tolerating our presence. Now we felt a strong bond of true friendship. Drago was one of us.

Tiff said, "See, we're the DGU, the Don't Give Up group." I chuckled, but in so many ways, she was spot on.

I hated to admit I couldn't include my sister or Drago's sister Carla in our DGU, because in my mind, they had given up. True, their bodies had taken a severe beating, but then so had ours. Only Drago had thus far been spared significant harm. While thinking of her, I felt pangs in my heart, but I knew why she and Carla had abandoned the Box and the situations it found for us to handle. Don't think less of them. I believe each of us is a unique person, with our own goals and purposes in life. Hers and Carla's are just a little different from those of the DGU.

The next day, things changed. Drago insisted on helping me with my new spells, and then later, he insisted on helping Lexi and Tiffany master some of theirs as well. All the while, Drago chuckled cheerfully. What pleased me were two of the new spells the girls learned: Skin of Stone and Minor Invulnerability to Spells. The first protected their bodies from weapon blows, while the second protected them from spells up to and including balls of fire and electrical bolts. Yes, I rested easier now, knowing they could protect themselves almost as well as I could. Moreover, they could now dish out nearly the same amount of damage as I could. As we felt the Box landing again, I felt enormous pride in my wives.

# Chapter 18—Out of Magic, Out of Gems

"So what are we going to do?" asked Camilo, the young assistant to the town's ruler, his voice trembling, though he twisted his hands together to hide how badly they shook.

Fausto, the Elder, ruled Becktold's Crossing, a desert oasis town of five thousand on the Old Caravan Route, a thousand mile long track through the scorching sands, though he estimated a thousand townsfolk had either died or fled since the arrival of Euric, the Red, an ancient Red dragon, two months ago. He replied with a deep sigh, "Camilo, I'm out of ideas. Euric has taken every magic item anyone in town had. I thought he'd leave us alone after that, but no, he took every precious stone to be found. He's still not departing. Saturday's Donation Time is only a day away. What have we got left he could possibly want?" His body had aged prematurely this past year. Camilo now saw a beaten man, stooped over and in long need of a shave.

May be—may be gold coins," Camilio fumbled his suggestion. With the loss of their precious stones, most of the accumulated wealth of the town was gone. He knew there were very few gold coins in Becktold's Crossing, since most traders preferred gemstones, which were far lighter and smaller.

Heaving another sigh, Fausto replied, "I will take your proposal to Euric, the Red, today. Remember, if I don't return, you're to rule our town in my place."

"P-p-please do come back, sir," Camilo shivered. Just thinking of having to pay a visit to the den of Euric gave him nightmares.

Leaning on his staff, Fausto headed off to make a counter-offer to the dragon. He passed by many red adobe homes. Here, the sands were a vibrant shade of red, and the pale blue waters of their oasis contrasted sharply. Becktold's Crossing cradled against the Red Cliff, a hundred foot tall sandstone monolith, protruding like a giant's finger from the red desert sands. The village ancestors had carved intricate tunnels and chambers in the stone. Today, those chambers provided superb storage spaces for the trade goods of the caravans. However, the largest of these was now the home of Euric, the Red.

Slowly, Fausto, the Elder, walked up to the sandstone wall and the largest dark opening. Reaching it, he sighed and entered. Camilo followed him, but stood quite clear of the opening, hoping and praying Fausto would return. He'd already decided to flee the town if Fausto didn't come out.

The deep voice spoke, "Ah, Fausto. Is it Saturday so soon? Where's my bag of gems?"

The huge Red dragon lay in the center of the reddish chamber, illuminated by a series of Continual Light spells, which the town's mages had cast in there long ago. Surrounding him were numerous magical items that had once belonged to the town's inhabitants or the town. The town's precious Pitcher of Endless Water sat in one corner. It's loss had caused the massive crop failure two months ago, after which so many had fled the dying town. The dragon's bed consisted of hundreds of sparkling gemstones, all colors of the rainbow. Euric rested his head on the red floor, his black eyes staring at the frail human facing him.

"Alas, we have no more gems, just as we have no more magical items. All that we can possibly offer you on Saturday is what few gold coins can be found in town." Fausto stated his final offer.

Even if the dragon accepted the small bag, that would be the end of the town. He knew he'd have to issue the order for everyone to abandon the town, to flee deeper into the desert and beg for sanctuary at other oases, if they would have them. An oasis could only support a finite number of people. Hence, having four thousand men, women, and children fleeing Becktold's Crossing was tantamount to a death sentence, since already a thousand had fled to the surrounding oases, overcrowding them.

"A thousand gold coins will do nicely," Euric bellowed his answer.

"But there are only around a hundred coins in the entire city," Fausto lamented, hoping the dragon would see reason, be reasonable.

"A hundred coins and the prettiest maiden in the town. I'll take the next prettiest maiden the following Saturday, and so on. When they get ugly, I'll simply toast the rest of the town," Euric bellowed, knowing he was shocking the old ruler. He didn't intend to stick around too much longer, unless he removed all the nasty humans who dwelled here. Already he'd seen a fifth of them leave. Perhaps now the rest would follow. He'd found a cozy home and an easy, profitable way to live up to the Black's bargain. *I'm damned clever. It's taken me less than two months to reach what I'm supposed to be doing for Adler, all the while making me wealthier than ever. I'm a genius.*

Fausto bent even lower, adjusted his white linen robe, and walked out of the chamber, his sandals patting the sandstone floor. He knew he couldn't make Saturday's payment. He'd never sacrifice a maiden to this vile dragon. Never. He needed a miracle, and soon.

"You're alive!" Camilo gushed, surprised to see Fausto returning from the dark entrance. "What news? Did the dragon accept our gold?"

Fausto sighed deeply. "Yes and no. He wants the gold, but since it's only a tenth the amount it wants, he's demanding we send along our town's prettiest maiden. And that, my good Camilo, I will not do."

"Then, it's time everyone flees," Camilo pronounced with certainty.

"It would seem so. I'll not sacrifice Gracia to this beast. Besides, he wants more maidens each Saturday until we run out of them. We have one day before everyone must flee. I should make the announcement tonight. Let everyone make their own decisions."

The two padded along the foot-packed streets to

Fausto's home, where they parted company. Just as he was about to head inside, three young maidens came running up to him. Inseparable, Gracia, his eldest daughter, Herminia, and Gabriela were the prettiest eighteen-year-old girls in the town. All three were breathless, having raced to Fausto's home.

Long, black-haired Gracia exclaimed, "Dad, what news? Did the beast accept the coins? It'd be a fool who didn't."

Brown haired Herminia added, "Right. Surely the dragon wants the gold."

Gabriela of the golden locks pointed out, "Everyone's really anxious. You should hold a town meeting soon."

"I will, Gracia, girls," Fausto sighed. "I'm afraid it's time for us to flee. He wants the prettiest maiden in Becktold's Crossing along with our meager gold. And a maiden each Saturday after that. Time to pack up and leave."

"But they'll never be able to flee that fast, dad," Gracia protested.

"What else can we do but flee? I won't sacrifice anyone to this foul, red, inhuman beast, let alone our young, our future generation."

The teens chatted amongst themselves, while Fausto, the Elder, hastily called for a town meeting down by the red sands that sloped into the half-dried up, life-giving oasis. Everyone acutely felt the loss of their magical Pitcher of Endless Water two months ago. The girls listened to Gracia's father explain Euric's ultimatum and his response.

"So I urge you, pack up everything, and leave as soon as possible."

Someone called out, "We can't get out of here that fast."

Another cried, "Where will we go? The other oases are overcrowded. They won't take us in. We've nothing of value to trade. The dragon beast has it all."

So it went. Arguments and protests abounded, but

soon two things became clear to Fausto and everyone else. First, there wasn't enough time for the entire town to flee and yet take enough with them physically to survive the long foot-walk in the desert. Second, Euric, disguised in his human form, appeared, satisfying his own curiosity about how his latest demands were going to be handled. Seeing the town's mass evacuation attempt, which if allowed to happen would booby trap his agreement with Adler, the Black, he returned to his chamber, morphed back to his dragon form, and flew out of the tunnel and over the town.

Anyone attempting to flee met with a roasting flame. Euric didn't actually breathe fire on those fleeing, but focused it just ahead of the people. He didn't have to say a word; everyone got his meaning. Flight from Becktold's Crossing wasn't going to be an option.

Two such cones of fire sent everyone fleeing into their homes. Panic set in. They were trapped. Their crude abode homes wouldn't prevent Euric from getting to them for even a second. Wails and screams echoed around the town. Inside his own home with his daughter, Fausto heard them, and his heart broke even further. He slumped into a chair.

"Dad, the dragon has to sleep sometime. You should tell everyone to flee after dark, late at night."

"There isn't enough time, but you should pack now. I want you to sneak out of town tonight. You're right, as always, Gracia. You so take after your mother." He sighed. Her loss last year still weighed heavily on the town Elder.

"I'm not going without Herminia and Gabriela. I'll go tell them now."

She dashed out of their red adobe home, heading for her friends. Slowly, he got up and left too, this time visiting each family, telling them to flee late at night. Both returned at suppertime.

"Dad, very few are going to be able to flee this quickly. They need more time to sneak out at night." He grunted, already knowing this. "So I've decided I'm going to take the gold bag to Euric. I'll buy you, Herminia,

Gabriela, and everyone else an entire week to flee to safety."

"Honey, you can't do that. I forbid it. The beast will kill you or worse. You pack your things and leave tonight. That's final."

Gracia watched her father's reaction to her proposed sacrifice closely and saw him come more alive than he'd been since her mother died. Nevertheless, her will steeled. *I have to do this. I'm pretty. If I don't buy everyone seven days to flee, they'll all be roasted alive tomorrow. Mom would want me to think of others and not just myself. Probably, the dragon will just eat me quickly—one bite maybe.* She headed to her room, pretending to pack.

As Gracia anticipated, Fausto fell asleep not long after dark. She slipped into his room and picked up the small bag of gold coins. Quietly, she stole out of her home, stepping out onto the chilly night. Stars shone brilliantly, reflecting off the still waters of their oasis. Quietly, she walked along the dark, deserted streets toward the Red Cliff. She paused outside the main entrance that led to Euric's chamber.

*Surely, a week will be enough time for everyone to flee safely. My life for four thousand lives and my two best friends.* She gritted her teeth and walked on into the dark tunnel, feeling her way along until the Continuous Lights of the inner chamber illuminated the red floor and walls of the passage.

"Euric, I'm here with the gold," Gracia called out, her will steeled. She had another plan in the back of her mind. Months ago, several magical blades had been given to the Red dragon. If she could find one and grab it, she'd not go down without a fight. Dragons could be slain—at least they were in the fairy tales she'd heard growing up.

Euric raised his head up and looked at her, his head inches from her face. "You'll do nicely."

"Your gold," she said, glancing around for the magical blades. She saw them resting against a far wall. Slowly, she began backing her way over to them.

Euric smiled, focused, and cast his first spell. He spoke the command words in his own language, but Gracia wouldn't have been able to remember them if he'd spoken them in hers. "Moronic Mind."

Suddenly, Gracia completely forgot what she was trying to do and stopped backing up. She said, "Ooh. You're a very big dragon. You're very red too."

Speaking in her language, he replied, "Yes. And you're a very pretty young woman, but you can be prettier."

"I can?" she asked in awe, wondering how she could be prettier. It seemed desirable to her.

"Yes, the prettier we can make you, why, the better others will want and like you. You do want to be liked by everyone, don't you?"

"Oh, yes, yes. I do so want to be liked. I must be prettier. Can you make me prettier?"

"Yes, I certainly can make you incredibly beautiful. Then, everyone who sees you will just love you. You do want to be incredibly beautiful, don't you?"

"Oh, yes, yes, I do. Please, make me beautiful now."

"All right, but after I do so, we'll need to get you some elegant gowns that will show off your incredible beauty to all whose eyes see you."

Her face slumped. "But we don't have such things in Becktold's Crossing."

"I know that, so I'll have to take you to the big city. There, they'll have only the finest gowns for you to wear. You do want to always look your very best, don't you?"

"Oh, yes, yes, I do. Thank you so much."

"Okay then, let's make you as pretty as possible. First, take off your clothes so I can see what we need to make even prettier."

Hastily, Gracia removed her linen apparel and stood innocently before Euric, who had now morphed into his human form. "Make me even prettier right now."

"All right. Here we go, Gracia." He focused and barked, "Morph," but Gracia didn't understand a word beyond that. She felt energies tingling over her body. Her hair thickened and grew longer. Her bosom tripled in size, becoming melons, and her arms vanished from sight. He chanted and barked, "Make Permanent." Once more, magical energies flashed over her body.

"Ah, Gracia, now you are incredibly prettier than before. Just look at how gorgeous you look."

"But I can't see myself well."

He lifted part of her raven tresses, draping them before her. "Just look at your marvelous hair, so long, so lush, and so thick. And your bosom will get everyone's attention now."

"Oh yes, it is so much longer, but it needs a good brushing. They are awfully heavy though. Do you suppose they need to be this big? I seem to have misplaced my arms. I need them."

"You want everyone to notice you, so yes, they need to be as big as they now are. You don't really need any arms, do you? As a model and noblewoman, why, you will have many servants. Arm so detract from a woman's beauty, don't you think?"

"Oh yes. Arms do so lessen a woman's beauty. I guess I don't need them, not if I have servants. Do I need many of them?"

"Not really. One will do nicely. Now you are truly incredibly beautiful, and everyone will notice and praise your beauty. In fact, your light grey eyes are positively enchanting; your smile, captivating. Since it's late, let's get you to bed. I've a bed ready for you. Tomorrow, we'll get you a servant and elegant gowns to wear so you can display your incredible beauty before everyone. A great mage will come and take you to the Big City and get everything for you."

Gracia yawned. "That's wonderful. It is late. I'm tired. I should sleep."

After assisting her with a Sleep spell, Euric chuckled and sent a Message to Adler, stating that he had one for him. He tossed the small bag of gold coins onto his nest and lay down to doze too, extremely pleased with his spell casting.

Why? This was the first time in Euric's long life that he'd ever been able to make use of his Make Permanent spell. Like nearly all dragons, spell learning was a chaotic or random hit and miss affair. He'd been incredibly lucky to learn the powerful Make Permanent spell, which was needed to create magical items, the least of which were magically enchanted blades. He'd been unfortunate enough to have failed to learn all the spells needed to create the magic items in the first place, before they were made permanent with this spell. Thus, Euric had been frustrated by this spell for hundreds of years. Now, however, Adler, the Black, had given him an interesting new use for his spell. In his defense, he had no idea why Adler wanted the young women appearing this way.

Early the next morning, Fausto, the Elder, cried. He'd found his daughter's brief letter saying what she was doing for the town. As he read it for the sixth time, Gabriela knocked on his door, furiously.

"Sir, come quick. A new adobe home has just appeared near the water's edge! It wasn't there yesterday. It just arrived and no one built it, not like the adobe maker does. You must come and see it. It must be magical, don't you think? Where's Gracia? She should see it too."

Herminia added, "If it's magical, do you think the dragon would take it and leave the town alone? Maybe the dragon can carry the house away. Dragons are strong, aren't they?"

Fausto, the Elder, straightened up slightly. *Could this be my miracle?* "Where is it? Show me, please."

"Bring Gracia," Gabriela requested. Alas, Fausto told them what she'd done. Three somber people walked across the town to this new building. Sure enough, a red abode building now sat barely fifty feet from the water's edge. It certainly wasn't there yesterday; that much Fausto knew. Several dozen men, women, and children already stood nearby, whispering about this strange sight, while waiting for their Elder to address this new situation. Fausto, the Elder, had several choices facing him.

He knew some magic spells, but he wasn't a

proficient mage. He could try to get the dragon to release his daughter and take this magic adobe building, because he'd quickly cast his magic detection spell and found the building was radiating magical energies. Yet, the home must belong to whoever was inside. Probably, they wouldn't abide his trading their home for his daughter. On the other hand, maybe they had magical items he could trade or gemstones. Or maybe they'd want nothing to do with this town and its desperate plight. Dear Gracia had given them seven more days to flee. Thus, he decided to speak truthfully to whomever was inside.

Inside the Box, we waited patiently, knowing the Box would soon produce a local wardrobe for us, which, according to Lexi, would also give us a clue to what kind of place we'd landed. I was relieved to find light linen shirts and pants appearing on the rack beside the door.

While we changed and Drago merely morphed into his human form, which now wore similar clothing, he promised, "This time, I'll hold off finding my dinner until we know more about what we're facing. All right?"

"Perfect. Thanks," I agreed.

"Just remember, I'm starving," he grumbled.

This time when we finally opened the door and stepped out into the world, I felt relieved. It was my kind of world, not one of those "modern" ones to which my wives were accustomed. We saw red, literally red and in all directions, though the sky and the oasis blue provided sharp contrasts. A swarm of men, women, and children stood at a safe distance from the Box. Everyone wore white linen. Arid air, date trees, and distant sand dunes told me we were in a desert region. Red adobe buildings surrounded the pool, whose banks had recently dried up. In the distance, the Red Cliff rose, as if a giant hand thrust it up in disgust with the land.

As always, the Box allowed us to understand the local language, though from the smirks on many faces, I knew we must have a terrible accent. "Hello," I said for starters. "I. Mage Felix. These are Mage Lexi, Mage Tiffany, and Mage Drago. Where are we?"

A bent man leaning on a staff took a step forward. "I'm Fausto, the Elder, leader of our town. This is Becktold's Crossing. Have you come to help us in our hour of desperate need?"

Refreshing. For the first time, someone simply came out with it as soon as we arrived. We didn't have to go hunting around for something amiss. "Pray, what is going on here? How can we help?"

"We have a Red dragon problem. If you will come with me, I'll make us some tea and explain."

A bit later over tea, Fausto launched into the details. His bent and sad demeanor hinted at the stress the man was under, borne out by his story.

"Euric, the Red dragon, first appeared over Becktold's Crossing about two months ago. His fiery breath destroyed one home, killing three. Yes, that got our attention. At first, he demanded magical items. If we failed to deliver them, he'd destroy us all. We're on a major caravan route across the desert. Trade goods are stored in the caverns carved from the red sandstone of the Red Cliff. Euric took up residence in the largest of these caverns, awaiting delivery of our precious items."

"Our ancestors provided the town with a Pitcher of Endless Water, which we used to support our town and grow crops. You can see our withered fields. The water level has dropped dangerously low, and at least a thousand have fled our town."

He continued, explaining that after all magical items had been given to the beast, the dragon then demanded gemstones. Finally, he outlined his most recent visit and Euric's response. "I swore I'd not give him any of our people, especially young maidens. But my own daughter, bless her, took the small bag of gold and donated herself in order to buy time for the rest of us to flee during the night while the beast sleeps. I found her note when I awoke this morning. I've not heard her screams, so she may yet be alive, but I'm not counting on that."

"Mages, is there anything you can do to help us? Alas, we have nothing to offer you. The dragon has taken it all." His voice reflected his abject apathy.

We said consoling words, promising to discuss our options and let him know. Drago said, "Okay. You think about it for a while. I simply must eat. I'll be back as soon as I can find an antelope. In the meantime, I'll reconnoiter the desert around here. Just don't go after that dragon by yourselves. If he's right and Euric is an ancient dragon, then he will be a most formidable opponent, even for me."

We agreed and Drago slipped invisible before morphing into his dragon form and taking flight. For a minute, I wondered where he could find an antelope in the middle of a vast desert. Then, the girls were on me.

"Felix, we have to rescue Gracia," Lexi declared, her hands on her hips. "So how do we do it? And what's a dragon's age got to do with anything?"

"Yes, you'd think an ancient one would be feeble and easy to kill, just like an elderly human," Tiffany added.

For once, I had the answer. Drago had painstakingly explained it to Diana and me shortly after we first met in Mage Locklard's class. "Baby dragons are relatively weak. While they have their breath weapon, it is only hot enough to start a small fire. As the dragon ages, the potency of their breath grows ever stronger, reaching its peak power in their old age. So if you have a young Red dragon, a middle aged one, and an ancient one, the ancient dragon's fire will be the hottest by far, causing the most damage as well. The only saving grace, if one exists, is that when they get really old, they tend to sleep for longer periods of time."

Tiffany replied, "So how do we counter his fiery breath? I bet he also knows a lot of nasty spells too."

"Drago told me that with most dragons, magical spells are mostly random, hit or miss, quite unlike us and even Drago, now that he's studying with us. So yes, Tiff, he probably knows some nasty spells that could wipe us out. I sincerely hope we don't have to fight him."

Lexi declared, "We need a plan."

"He likes magic items," Tiff put in. "Perhaps, we can use that to reach him. Look, we have that nearly useless rod that absorbs strong winds and the wand that shoots dig spells. Maybe we can offer to trade them for Gracia."

"I like that. Maybe toss in that ring that stores three spells," Lexi added.

I agreed with them and dug out the objects. "Look, we could at least pay this Euric a visit and make the offer. We'll not fight or argue with him, just suggest a trade. Drago can't fault us for doing that much while he's off feeding."

"Wicked. Let's do it. We should put all the protection spells on us as we can," Tiffany advised.

Five minutes later, we had them cast upon our bodies. Temporarily, physical blows couldn't harm our bodies. Any lower level spells Euric might cast upon us also wouldn't affect us. I promised to keep my Force Wall spell at the ready, in case he shot his fiery breath at us. Satisfied we were as defensive as possible, we left the Box, nodding to the many townsfolk on the red sandstone streets. Conclusion: a number of families were preparing to depart during the night; loaded push carts stood as silent sentinels outside some homes. I didn't think they'd have much chance of survival walking across the burning desert on foot. This steeled my own determination to put this one to rights.

Ahead, we saw the hundred foot tall cliff and its many openings. Following what Fausto had told us, we made for the largest of these and soon entered the significantly cooler tunnel. Until that moment, I'd not realized just how hot it was outside. That water was the most precious thing became acutely real to me. I had a notion to see if Euric would swap that Pitcher for our items, but a glance at Tiff convinced me otherwise.

The chamber was huge, but only barely large enough to hold this ancient dragon, whose size was many feet larger than Drago's! We saw a number of magic items lining one far wall. A pitcher was one of them. For a moment, I toyed with the notion to go invisible and snatch that pitcher for the town, but the rising of the Red dragon's head convinced me otherwise. He was huge and quite intelligent.

"Euric, we are mages, who've just arrived here. We'd like to trade you some of our magic items for the Elder's daughter, Gracia. I'm called Felix."

His deep voice replied, "Let me see your magic items."

We obliged, but I let him cast his own identification spells on them, though if he goofed, I was prepared to tell him their properties.

"Well, I will accept these three as next week's payment. Just leave them there."

"Sorry, but we want Gracia back," I countered.

"Not going to happen."

"Why not? Have you eaten her already?" Lexi snapped.

Euric laughed, shaking the floor slightly. "Hardly. Humans taste so bad that I'd not eat one even if I were starving. No, she's not here any longer. She's become quite beautiful and is off acquiring elegant gowns to wear. She is a noblewoman now. So be off with you; just leave them over there with the rest of my magic collection."

We didn't leave them, but walked out instead. Just to be safe, I cast my Force Wall, placing it in the tunnel between him and us. If he shot a cone of flames at us, it would bounce off that wall, giving us time to run like mad. He did nothing, thankfully.

Unknown to us, after we left the chamber, Adler, the Black, stepped out of a side tunnel. "Damn! It's those meddling mages again. How did they find this place? Well, no matter. I'll be taking Gracia with me now. Euric, keep up the good work. She's perfect. *And I didn't have to age a year in her making. Rather wish I knew that spell of his.*

He added, "If you can kill those three, so much the better."

"What's in it for me?"

"Name your price, Euric, and I'll see you get it." *The hell I will, but I might if he actually does kill them and if he doesn't ask for much.*

"I'll see what I can do. I should have another

maiden for you each week. That'll be fifty-some in one year. What are you going to do with so many of them? You can't eat them. They taste as bad as skunks smell."

"Trade items. Other humans want them. I'll take as many as you can get me. You'll find the bag I left you filled with rubies and emeralds, payment for this first one. Later, Euric."

With that, he stepped back into the tunnel. He was in his human form, thus not startling Gracia, who stood waiting patiently for him to take her to get her new clothes. He put an arm around her and was about to bark a single command, "Teleport," when Euric called out.

Fausto, the Elder, should have realized Gracia, Herminia, and Gabriela were very best friends for life, BFFL as they called themselves. When we didn't return with Gracia, Herminia and Gabriela realized what Gracia had done for them, sacrificed herself for the BFFL.

"No way," Herminia declared. "She can't do this without us. We should have gone with her."

"You're right. Whatever is happening to her, we should be a part of it. We three together forever—that's what we swore to, isn't it?"

"Right. Together forever. She's not going to get away with this. It should have been all three of us, together, facing that dragon."

"Right. Come on. Maybe it isn't too late. They didn't come back with her, so she must still be in the storage chamber," Gabriela declared.

The two walked as inconspicuously as possible through the town and up to the Red Cliff and the large entrance leading to the huge chamber confiscated by the dragon. Holding hands and without a word, the two teens marched purposely into the tunnel.

As they approached the chamber, Herminia called out, "Oh Euric, we're here—Gracia's girlfriends. We demand to see her and be with her."

"Right," Gabriela added, "We're inseparable. You can't have her without having us too. Where she goes, we go, and that's final." She stomped her sandal on the floor; a patting sound echoed off the walls.

Still in his human form, Euric stepped out of the side tunnel where Adler stood with Gracia. "I've seen you two. You're always with Gracia."

"Observant," declared Herminia. "We are BFFL. Where she goes, we go, and that's final." She purposely repeated Gabriela's words, hoping to add more emphasis to them, convincing him they meant it.

Euric sent a hasty Message to Adler, who replied affirmatively. Leaving Gracia standing somewhat impatiently waiting to be taken shopping, Adler moved down the tunnel so he could watch Euric and the two teens. An idea formed while Euric cast his spells, beginning with his sharp barking, "Moronic Mind." The other spells followed in rapid succession, along with his "you can be prettier" speech. He said much the same things to these two as he'd said to Gracia the previous evening. With the two "prepared," he led them to Adler and Gracia.

"Oh! Herminia, Gabriela, you both look absolutely beautiful!" Gracia exclaimed. "I'm so glad you could come with me too. We're going to get elegant gowns soon and servants too. I think we're now some kind of queens."

"Yes, beauty queens," Gabriela replied, a puzzled look on her face. "I wonder where the Kingdom of Beauty lies. Is it far from here?"

"I surely don't know," Gracia answered, looking around for Adler, intending to ask him. He seemed to know everything.

Adler commented, "Euric, that was magnificent. I have a much better offer for you." He outlined what he had in mind, careful to point out he would provide Euric with double the number of magical items the Red dragon currently had if Euric would come with him and the teens now.

"And leave all these fine things?"

"Yes. I'll see they are replaced twofold."

"And the gems?"

"Those too. We must hurry."

"And I don't get to kill those three mages?"
"At least not right away."

# Chapter 19—Red Removal

"So how are we going to find Gracia?" Tiffany demanded to know the moment we three entered the Box. "We can't just leave her in the hands of the dragons."

"I don't know, Tiff. First, we have to get rid of Euric, which is going to be a major problem. We can't fight him in that chamber. It's too small. Drago couldn't morph into his dragon form to fight him—no more room. We're going to have to get him to come out here, but then we'll risk all manner of collateral damage to the town and its people. You're right, Lexi. We are going to need a plan, a good one."

"How do you kill a dragon?" Lexi asked.

"Drago said it usually took magical blades, though enough powerful spells could also work, except they have a resistance to magic spells," I replied. "We best wait for Drago to return."

An hour later, someone pounded on our door. Upon opening it, I saw an extremely pale-faced Fausto. "Sir, Herminia and Gabriela ran off and joined Gracia in the dragon's den. I just heard from their parents. I should have known those two would follow my Gracia. They've been an inseparable trio since they could walk. Please, can you retrieve them before anything bad happens to them? Gracia's sacrifice has given the rest of the town a week to flee. Please, can you help?"

"Of course. Everyone, check your defensive spells," I ordered.

We spent a couple minutes renewing some and then raced off to the tunnel entrance. Fausto came with us. In part, he felt it was his responsibility that the two teens had done this foolish thing. To be honest, I had no plan in mind, other than to beg for the release of them. We dashed into the tunnel, slowing as we approached the permanently lighted chamber. Gemstones glistened in the light, but no one was here.

"Strange. Euric, where are you?" I called out.

After calling for him a few minutes, I had a sickening feeling in my stomach. "Okay, spread out. Search everywhere. Fausto, where do all these tunnels lead?"

"To smaller storage areas. Herminia, Gabriela, where are you two?"

An hour later, we met in the large chamber, having searched the entire complex. We found no trace of the three teens or the dragon. They'd vanished. However, Drago joined us as we wrapped up the search.

His deep voice suggested, "Look, it's not like a dragon to abandon his treasure pile like this. Even when we fly off to feed, we leave the place under many protection spells. From what you've said, Euric has none in place. This is most peculiar. It's likely he took the three teens somewhere, but to leave his treasures wholly unguarded is very un-dragon-like, very."

"Well, I think we should confiscate everything, returning them to their rightful owners," I suggested. "If he comes back, we'll deal with him. Okay, Fausto, let's get that pitcher of yours working again. Maybe the crops can be saved."

"Thank you," Fausto, the Elder, replied, relieved. "The oasis water level is dangerously low. The pitcher's magic kept it high enough to support everyone. This is our Rod of Cultivation, which we use to help everyone with their fields."

One by one, he identified many of the items along the far wall. Every one of them was designed to assist the survival of the town and its people in some manner. Then, it hit me. Magic wasn't for just some personal power play. Rather its true purpose was to be put to use helping others survive better, to assist people to flourish and prosper. The few enchanted blades would help protect the town and its caravans. The gauntlets of strength were used by workers who moved the heavier loads of supplies into and out of the chambers.

"This is our Wand of Drying. We use it to help dry out adobe bricks and to help preserve foods. I recharge it once a year," Fausto explained.

"Wicked!" exclaimed Tiffany. "This is what magic should be all about—really helping others. Until now, Felix, we've only seen it as helping ourselves stay alive and fight back, but its true purpose is quite different, isn't it?"

I could only nod my head. This was quite a revelation to me. Until this moment, I'd always thought of magic as being highly personal in nature, something to assist in my offence and defense, that is, my own survival and that of my family and even friends—I now considered Drago to be my friend.

We spent an hour collecting up the gemstones and moving them and the items from the cavern to Fausto's home. He admitted it would take him several days to return everything to its rightful owner, though some had already fled Becktold's Crossing. That done, we four met in the Box to try to figure out our next move.

"First, we cast an Alarm spell on the entrance, in case Euric comes back during the night," I proposed.

"And be ready to fly into action if it goes off. I'll be in my dragon form so I can battle him directly, though he could well be much larger than I am."

"We'll use spells on him, Drago. Electrical discharges and magical missiles might work well on him, right?"

"Anything but fire-based spells. He's immune to them, but remember, he'll have a good deal of resistance to magic spells. You might have to cast it several times before it gets through his resistance. And don't hit me," Drago teased us.

Lexi then asked, "But what do we do if Euric doesn't come back? How do we find the girls? We have to find them."

"I know. I'll ask Fausto to Message his daughter. If the spell works, then we know she's still on this world," I answered, thinking aloud.

"But what do we do if she isn't?" my golden haired wife persisted.

Silence. None of us had any answer or idea for this

one. Worse, I felt this was the most likely scenario, that Euric had fled this world taking the teens with him. This thought brought back the awful memories of losing Harold and Sofia Banner of Banner's Fashions, who were taken off their world of Rainbow's End by the dragons. We failed to save them. Were we about to fail to save these three teens as well?

\*\*\*

"We should think this through, Euric," Adler began. He had teleported the teens to Glaston City, the largest city on Rainbow's End, located on a different continent from the Rainbow Hills and Imperial, the emperor's city, and positioned at the end or the beginning of the thousand-mile desert caravan route, depending on which way you wished to go, east or west. The red dragon came with him, eager to acquire vastly more magical items and gems.

"Magic items and gems first. Then, we talk," Euric insisted.

"Very well. Second room on your right. Help yourself. When you're through, we need to discuss keeping you alive."

"What'd ya mean by that? If you haven't noticed, I'm six hundred six years old."

"Go look at the stuff, Euric."

A while later, Euric returned, a very pleased look on his human form's face. "You weren't lying, Adler. What I had accumulated is paltry compared to this. So now, I'm listening. You have my attention. That's an enormous treasure you're giving me."

"Actually, Euric, I've probably saved your red hide. Those four have been most troublesome, even following me from world to world. Let me tell you what I know about them. One is even a Gold dragon."

Euric gasped. Adler outlined what he knew about us, beginning with our appearance and disruption of their enterprise of Unarmed Escorts. Euric pulled on his chin as he listened to the details.

"So you see, Euric, I've probably saved your life. I'm quite certain those meddlers would have attacked you, while they tried to rescue those three teens."

"I should go back and turn them into cinders—melt the skin off their bones!" Euric barked.

"If you were just any other Red, why, I'd let you go do just that, but you're not. You have a spell casting gift that no one else has, one that we truly need. Here's what I have in mind."

He talked for some time, and Euric's grin slowly increased, until he laughed heartily. The Red then said, "Adler, you have some mighty fine connections. Let's do it!"

Adler failed to tell the Red that he suspected he finally had found the world he was searching for all these years. Even if he had said so, Euric wouldn't have known why he was looking for this particular modern world.

***

"Incredible! My Message spell worked!" exclaimed an excited Fausto. "They are somewhere on our world. Yet, how can we possibly find them?"

"We have to get clever," I suggested. "Do you know the See Through Another's Eyes spell?"

"No. I never got the hang of that one."

Lexi cautioned, "Usually, you have to know the person whose eyes you want to use. We don't know Gracia, Herminia, or Gabriela."

"But we have to try," Tiffany pleaded.

Lexi suggested, "Felix, let's all try to cast it on Gracia's eyes. There are four of us. Surely, one of us might be successful. You can also cast your Vision spell on Fausto, so he can see what we're seeing and help us identify where they are located."

*Damn, she's good!* "Excellent ideas. Let's do it," I said, much impressed with Lexi's ability to think on the spot. Each of us focused and cast our spell, barking the command words, "See Through Gracia's Eyes." I then added my Vision spell, which allowed Fausto to see what we four were seeing.

Probability. That's what Lexi gambled upon. My spell activated, but I saw nothing. I had no connection to

Gracia. Neither did Drago, who let out a deep grunt of disappointment. However, Lexi and Tiffany's spells worked. Both suddenly saw what Gracia was seeing at this moment. Via my Vision spell, Fausto and I saw it too.

Two and three story, wooden buildings lined both sides of a wide, cobblestone street, filled with men driving wagons, some loaded with goods, and pedestrians wearing a variety of apparel, suggestive of what we'd seen in Imperial and made by Banner Fashions. Then, I saw a line of camels tied in a line moving past Gracia. They were loaded with non-descript bundles. As Gracia's head turned slightly, we glimpsed a tall man with reddish skin.

Fausto exclaimed, "That's him, Euric! I know that city. It's Glaston City, the desert caravan trailhead on the far side of our desert. It's about a thousand miles from here." His sudden outburst broke our concentration, and the spells terminated abruptly. With magical spells, focus is critical.

Drago's deep voice broke the stillness, "I think we have enough to Teleport us there, Felix. What do you think? We've not tried it in the real world yet."

"I think you're right, but let's target ten feet above the cobblestones. We can all Gentle Fall down."

Tiffany asked, "Why do you want to arrive up in the air?"

Drago answered, "When using the Teleport spell, sometimes there is a bit of an error. If we arrive somewhat low, our feet or worse our whole bodies would materialize underground. Nasty. So we error by aiming a bit high."

"Wicked! That's a scary spell." Drago nodded.

Lexi declared, "Let's check our defensive spells first. I think my Skin of Stone is wearing off."

Hastily, we four recast them, including our new Protection from Grade Three Spells, though I rather wished there was a spell that provided protection from a dragon's breath weapon. Alas, no such spells existed, and besides, there were too many different forms their breath weapons took.

Satisfied we were as protected as we could be, I took

hold of Lexi and Tiffany's hands. "Teleport time. I'll bring them, Drago. Remember, focus and then be prepared to change into your dragon form if Euric does so. Girls, duck and run if the Red dragon breathes out a cone of fire."

Drago and I focused and chanted. Of all the spells we currently knew, the casting of this one, Teleport, was one of the swiftest, but it required intense concentration and a total certainty it would work. Tiffany later told me she saw a bead of sweat trickle down my right temple as I cast the spell. She discounted my argument we were in a desert.

A second separated our arrivals, but it took longer than that for us to grasp the situation as we arrived. We did arrive above ground, forcing us to cast Gentle Fall quickly. As I floated down, the three teens looked gorgeous, much as the many women in the Unarmed Escort service did. In fact, the three could well have been there. Images of Lexi, Tiffany, and the many other unarmed women appeared in my mind. I had to blink. The three wore brightly colored, satin gowns with matching tall heels. Large smiles lined their faces, and their eyes were bright. Although they didn't speak, from their silly facial looks and the absent-look in their eyes, I knew they were under a magical spell, one I'd been under too. Moronic Mind.

As my feet touched the ground, Euric morphed into his huge Red dragon form, but I rather expected that. What I didn't expect were the two alien men wearing drab grey, synthetic uniforms and leaning out of the window above us. Each dropped a cylinder that exploded when it hit the cobblestones, releasing a whitish gas. I landed on my feet, coughing from the fumes. My legs felt weak. My eyes burned, and I shut them, in spite of my fear that Euric would spew his roasting flames on us all. Miraculously, I felt peaceful. All was black, and I was unconscious, knocked out by this alien gas. I was unaware of my body falling onto the cobblestones, along with Tiffany, Lexi, and the teens. Drago was unaffected by the alien's knock-out gas.

Instead, he landed and morphed into his Gold dragon form, comparing his size to that of Euric's, who stood ten feet taller and weighed nearly fifty percent more than Drago. As the two dragons faced each other, Euric realized his fiery hot breath would do nothing to the Gold dragon, which was immune to it, while Drago's electrical bolts would harm the Red. However, just as Drago saw us fall unconscious, he also saw six other Black dragons swooping down from above our position.

Outnumbered and with the three of us no longer functioning, self-preservation kicked in. Without hesitation, Drago took flight, Shadow Walking back to the Box at Becktold's Crossing. He knew he couldn't focus well enough to hazard another Teleport spell. I later learned Adler had the six Black dragons invisible and hovering above the ambush location. They became visible when the Gold dragon appeared and recast their Invisibility the moment Drago vanished, while Euric morphed back into his human form. All this happened within seconds, so the locals on the street blinked but didn't believe what they'd seen, other than the six bodies lying on the cobblestone street.

Our snatch and grab rescue of the three teens failed completely. Adler had precisely anticipated our actions. I have to admit his countermove was brilliantly executed, though I'd not counted on their being aliens or space-faring men on this world. Unconscious, I wasn't aware of the many spells being cast upon the girls and me. If I had been, I probably would have panicked utterly.

# Chapter 20—The Butterfly Effect

"Ah, here they are at long, Dario," a familiar voice woke me up. My mind wasn't working quite right, as I struggled to make sense. I was alive. I hadn't been slain. That voice—so familiar. Finally, my synapses fired—Adler! I opened my eyes. Confusion swept over me like a tsunami! I had no idea where I was at; my body wasn't mine, but Gracia's; and I heard a voice in my head.

"Your name is Gracia now. You're a beauty queen, a princess. Smile and flirt with your new master, who is going to be introduced to you now. You'll follow my orders. Failure to do so will result in this." Suddenly, I sensed a whitish energy flooding my mind, along with an intense pain. Fortunately, it ceased almost as quickly as it had come, just before I would have cried out in pain.

I was sitting on a fancy sofa in a modern office suite. Sterile white walls with many glass panes allowed me to glimpse a world of steel and concrete skyscrapers along with many of those silver flying ships darting about. The biting odor of new, grey carpeting assaulted my nostrils. I recognized the other two teens sitting beside me on the sofa, Herminia and Gabriela.

We looked similar, armless and with giant melons for bosoms. Our hair was thick, slightly wavy, and reached our knees. We were dressed in satin gowns that ended at our knees, while our legs were covered by some kind of black, thin stockings. Our tall heels matched our dresses, bright red in my case contrasting with my raven hair. Theirs were blue and green, respectively.

This wasn't my body, but I could feel with it, smell with it, and see with it. In fact, there wasn't any way I could tell that it wasn't my body, except it was female for sure. No! Wait, that's not true. Faintly, I sensed someone else was here in the body with me. She was in a panic, but helpless to express her terror or even her thoughts. I strained and thought I sensed she was trying hard to be a

267

gorgeous princess, a beauty queen. Besides feeling confused, I also felt very stupid or dumb. I had the gnawing notion I was under the influence of the Moronic Mind spell again and wondered how I could possibly figure out if I was.

Adler brought us three into the present. "Princesses, please stand up and meet your new owner, your master, your benefactor, Mr. Dario del Cruz. He's a very important and wealthy man, who runs one of the largest corporations here on Salazar-3, Galactic Electronics. By the way, you are in Moro City, this world's capital city."

That voice in my head ordered me, "Gracia, stand up and smile at Dario!"

I lunged to my feet, wobbling in the unfamiliar tall heels, trying to get my balance. I found myself babbling, "Oh Dario. I am so pleased finally to meet you. I do hope you like us. We're beauty queens, princesses really."

Herminia and Gabriela made similar comments, but then Gabriela added, "Wicked. I do hope you'll take us to all the fancy places and buy us princess gowns. Adler promised us you would."

In the back of my mind, something Gabriela said had to be important, but what? We three looked at our benefactor. Dario del Cruz was likely in his middle sixties. He had grey hair now, but his facial features hinted that once he'd been quite handsome. He still was immaculately well dressed. His grey suit probably cost more credits than most workers earned in a year. Somehow, I reached that conclusion, recalling how expensive the suits made by Banner Fashions were.

He was tall and slightly overweight. Dario came up to me, his eyes moving upwards from my legs to my eyes, though he paused long on my gigantic bosom. He then hugged me. "Gracia, you three are perfection indeed. Adler wasn't lying. Don't worry. I'll provide you princesses, you beauty queens, with the finest gowns money can buy. We'll attend all the finest events, balls, parties, and symphonies."

For a dark corner of my mind, I heard Gracia's

thoughts, "Oh goodie! I just have to be a beautiful princess." Worse, I found myself saying that!

That strange voice in my head said, "Give him a kiss, since you can't hug him back." I felt repulsed. He was a man, but that white, blinding pain in my head turned on until I responded with a kiss, at which point the pain vanished as suddenly as it came.

He went down the line, hugging Herminia and then Gabriela in turn. He handed Adler a large sack and then said, "Princesses, if you will follow me, I'll take you to my lavish home. Then, we'll get you each many new gowns and heels, fitting for the beauty queens, the princesses that you are."

I found myself saying, "Oh goodie." I suspected that came from Gracia herself, as it wasn't my thought, at least I didn't think so.

Walking was treacherous in these heels, but Dario kept an arm around my waist as well as Herminia's. Gabriela seemed to manage the heels quite well, as did Herminia. Before long, Dario realized I needed support more than the other two did. Thankfully, he provided it.

"Oh! This is a mansion," exclaimed Herminia. We'd just entered a walled compound an entire city block around. Around us, skyscrapers loomed, grey fingers threatening to touch the sky.

"Wicked!" Gabriela added enthusiastically.

I had no words to describe what I was seeing, though I felt Gracia's wonderment in some tiny portion of my mind. The del Cruz estate was a mansion, single storied, with a formal gardens, a grassy lawn, and a blue and gold swimming pool. His was the only grass to be seen in this part of Moro City. Everything about his place spoke of opulence, elegance, and a refined palette for only the finer things in life. Three-dimensional, realistic looking paintings hung on the hallway walls.

"This is your servant, Adoncia," he introduced us to the sixty-year-old matron woman. Even she wore a satin gown, but hers was black. Her greying hair was tied up in a severe bun. Adoncia was barely five-five, but pudgy.

"My Mr. Dario! You've certainly outdone yourself this time. I swear each of these young women is a beauty queen! How ever did you find them? Princesses, I'm Adoncia, your servant and Mr. Dario's housekeeper and cook."

Dario chuckled. "Adoncia, why don't you show them their rooms and then take them shopping? Tonight, I'll take them to Ruffio's." Turning to us, he added, "That's the finest restaurant in the city."

Adoncia chuckled. "And the most expensive too. Princesses, this way please."

During the rest of the day and evening, I focused on trying to figure out what had happened to me and to my wives. While he said we were on some world called Salazar-3, that meant nothing to me. Worse, I had the strange feeling that because of this, I was lost, though I swear my mental processes were barely working. Yet constantly, I sensed the awe and pride springing up from some dark corner of my mind, from Gracia. I allowed her to enjoy the experiences—at least for now, as I tried to work out what happened and what was going on.

All that evening, I had only one fear, terror perhaps, and that was that Dario would desire to make love to me. I found that notion revolting. Fortunately, he merely gave us princesses a good night kiss, allowing Adoncia to tuck us into the same very wide bed.

As we lay there, I whispered, "Tiffany? Is that you?"

"Yes. Oh no!"

My mind was flooded with that whitish energy. Pain turned on, and the mysterious voice in my head said, "Do not use those names any longer. You are Gracia. She is Gabriela. The other is Herminia. Use those names or else."

I didn't want to know what the "else" might be, so I shut up. I think Tiffany must have experienced something similar, for she too became quiet.

During the week, I tried to work out what had happened to us. My mind didn't seem to work very well. It seemed pathetically slow to reach conclusions. Meanwhile, Dario did show us off to the city. He took us to so many different places, that at last, I became continually confused. Nothing made any real sense any longer. It seemed all we were supposed to do was parade around at his side, looking like fabulously gorgeous women, which our bodies were. Later, we three concluded most of my confusion stemmed from being on a "modern" world. Lexi and Tiffany had grown up on such a world and everything seemed ordinary to them, if quite elegant and regal.

Fortunately, the voice in my mind was quiet during this time, and I remained headache-free. However, at night when we were in our bed, Gabriela or Tiffany explained much to us.

"Did you see the way others are looking at Dario and us? Well, if looks could kill, we'd be dead. Certainly, Dario would. I'm beginning to see what's going on here. We should start watching the newscasts."

"Why? What's going on?" Herminia asked, though I was somewhat certain Lexi was talking.

"I think this world is unstable or something. Look, these corporation leaders control everything on Salazar-3. Everyone works for them, and they are the government. I've heard even the army detests these rich people. That's what I heard anyway. We should find out what the political situation is here, since we live here."

That was easy enough to do. Adoncia was very pleased to have us sit and watch the newscasts during the afternoon hours, while she cleaned or prepared meals. Tiffany monitored the news, pointing out the key points to me, though I think Herminia or Lexi saw them for herself.

Ten days after we arrived on this world, it happened. We were dining at Ruffio's, where Dario proudly had us on display. Hundreds of other wealthy patrons continually glanced our way, and several came up to fawn over us, asking Dario how they could "acquire" similar princesses. Quite why anyone would want us eluded me at the moment.

Midway through the meal, four hooded men burst into the room. Each held what Tiffany explained was a machine gun. From my point of view, the devices made a lot of noise and smoke, but then I saw Dario fall out of his chair, bleeding from several "holes" in his body. As soon as he crashed onto the floor, the men fled the scene, leaving hundreds screaming and trying to flee in panic. However, I found this a critical moment, for it felt as if I should be able to attack these men, to stop them with missiles or electrical bolts or even to tie them up in sticky webs until others captured them. Duh, I finally realized I used to be able to cast magical spells! Oh, do I hate that Moronic Mind spell!

A kind couple took us home, where Adoncia looked after us. After that, Tiffany insisted we watch the news all the time. Without Dario to take us to all those fancy places, we had little other choice. Adoncia wasn't about to parade us around the city.

We watched as one man explained, "Dario del Cruz was gunned down while dining at Ruffio's this evening. His three princesses, those incredibly beautiful women of his, were with him, but were unharmed."

A commentator added, "This isn't unexpected. Not really. Look, these corporate bigwigs run everything on Salazar-3. Everyone is their pawns. Now he shows up with three of the most gorgeous women this world has ever seen hanging onto his arm. It's not right. Why should he alone possess such beauty, such princesses? Hell, I bet many of us would dearly love to have our own princesses."

The original man took over. "Based on this, we conducted a poll of our viewers. Ninety-five percent agree. The average person should be able to have their own princess. This shouldn't be the sole province of the ultra-wealthy, the corporate leaders."

A caller phoned in a question. "These ultra-rich men have their own security guards. What I'd like to know is what happened to Dario's security personnel."

Later, someone explained, "Dario's security personnel were and are careful to protect the three princesses, but they refused to defend Dario, claiming he got what he deserved. This has raised the ire of many other corporate leaders." He continued discussing this treasonous act for some time.

The next day, another corporate leader was assassinated, though he didn't have any "princesses" in his possession. The following day, the list of assassinations took an hour to relate! Armed squads roamed the streets of Moro City, determined to eliminate all corporate leaders everywhere! Each time, they left demands that anyone who wanted their own princesses should be allowed to have them.

Late that night, Tiffany explained, "Look, this world was a powder keg waiting for a spark. The corporate leaders must have abused their positions and power over the average man and woman for centuries. Anyway, we were like the butterfly whose flapping wings eventually caused a tornado. It's chaos theory in action. Our coming here as Dario's princesses was the butterfly. Obviously, we've done nothing wrong and neither did Dario. Yet, from this initial condition, we're the spark that set off all this chaos. Look, the assassinations began with just one, Dario, but they increased exponentially, not linearly, which is the trademark of a chaos system."

I looked at her rather stupidly, and not because of the nasty spell. I had no idea what she was talking about.

She saw that and explained. "The butterfly effect is the extreme sensitivity of a chaotic system to tiny changes in initial conditions. Dario acquiring the three princesses was that tiny change, which then rapidly caused the political situation here on Salazar-3 to spin out of control. Look, nearly everything in the universe is potentially a chaos system, from fluctuations in wildlife populations, to arrhythmic heartbeats, to turbulent motions in the seas, air, and clouds, to weather predictions, and to non-linear oscillations in electronic circuits, just scratching the surface. However, don't worry; eventually, the chaotic political mess here will finally reach its strange attractor—its long-term natural behavior—and stabilize."

Me? I still had no idea what she was saying, only that she was intense about it. Tiffany stopped and a strange look appeared on her face. "Oh my! I can think clearly again. Wonderful. Wicked. Now I should be able to cast magic spells again. How about you guys?" She immediately cast a Clean spell, vanishing a tiny bit of dirt on the rug beneath our feet.

"My mind has been getting clearer each day, Tiff," Lexi replied. "Magic. Yes, we used to be able to cast spells. I wonder if I still can. Let's see. Light," she commanded and a bright light appeared positioned on her head.

"How did you do that?" I asked. In the back of my mind, I thought I ought to know how to do that too. Right now, it eluded me.

The next day, the news program interviewed a man whose skin had a blackish hue to it. As the camera focused in on him, I exclaimed, "Adler! That's Adler, the Black dragon."

The newscaster explained, "With the announcement today that the Army will be providing security, others are stepping forward with valuable plans for our future, now that we're rid of those evil corporate leaders. Adler is just one of them. Adler," he motioned for the man to speak.

Adler wore an expensive suit and looked very dignified on camera. "Ladies, gentlemen everywhere. I'm here today to tell you that no longer are these gorgeous princesses the province of the ultra-wealthy. On the contrary. Anyone who wishes their own beauty queen, their own princess, can have one. Of course, the princesses will need a personal servant and elegant apparel. I've worked with other companies and can assure you that such apparel will soon be widely available and quite inexpensive. Temp Workers has stepped up to provide training and employment opportunities for those who wish to enter the career field of princess personal assistant. Finally, Galactic Electronics, once the main culprit of our world, has stepped up to the plate. They will be providing all the new princesses, the new beauty queens, that so many of us want and desire. I'm told any woman can become a princess by undergoing their patented conversion process. To prove the efficacy of their process, here are the first three new princesses. Compare how they look to the original three princesses that the late Dario del Cruz had." Images of six fabulously looking young women appeared on the giant monitor.

"Wicked. They look similar to us," Tiffany declared. "Wait, how did they make those women? Can we find out?"

Before anyone could answer, Adler continued. "Ladies of Salazar-3, any one of you can become a princess. GE's patented process will make even the homeliest, ugliest woman into a gorgeous beauty queen. If you are interested in this new, very exciting, and rewarding position, contact GE. Their number is at the bottom of your screen. Thank you. May all of you who want your own princess have one."

"Well, I'm not a thing!" Lexi protested.

"Still, I can see why many women might want to become princesses. We do attract everyone's attention," Tiffany said. "It feels good to be wanted."

"Well, I want my own body back," Lexi declared. "Anyone know what happened to us? All I remember is arriving and smelling some choking gas. This is Herminia's body, but I think she's still here somewhere."

"Me too. I think Gabriela's in here too. I kind of sense her wishes now and then."

I was about to say something when I heard that voice in my head again. Actually, it was rather faint this time, and I heard two voices, an unfamiliar one was added.

"Well, Salazar-3 didn't go as planned," the new voice said.

"It's a disaster," the familiar voice suggested.

"Just when we had all the key personnel being run by our monitors. I just don't understand what happened here. The whole damn world just went bonkers."

"I can't see why they would want any of those armless princesses, pretty or not. So what are your orders now? Do we try to take over those who step up to be the new leaders?"

"No, my boss said to abandon Salazar-3. So we pack up and evacuate."

"What about those in the tanks?"

"We honor our commitments. Each will be given their new prostheses and taken to a rehab center. Let's get them done and out of here by the end of the week. I want to depart before gunmen come after us."

"Okay, boss. But what about Adler's three special ones?"

"Handle them the same way. They'll be his problem. Pull them out of their host bodies. Hell, I can't see why he wanted them in those bodies anyway."

"On it. Are we heading home next?"

"Yes. We'll need new orders and supplies at the very least. Come on. I'll lend you a hand with them. We've got five hundred to supply and move to rehab centers around this world."

The voices in my head ceased, and I relayed what I'd heard to the others. In doing so, suddenly the fog in my mind vanished. I could think clearly once more.

I exclaimed, "I know what happened to us. Oh God!" I suddenly realized what our bodies must now look like—those poor men and women whom we rescued from the tanks.

"So we were put in the tanks like the others and then sent into these three teen's bodies?" asked Lexi, finally grasping the situation.

"I'll bet anything that's what they did with us. Only now, we're on an unknown planet and will be virtually helpless when they take us out of these bodies here and we go back into ours when they take them out of the tanks," I lamented, finally able to think rather clearly. Somehow, that terrible spell was wearing off me too.

"Crap!" Tiffany declared. "Maybe I won't leave this one so easily. No," she paused, "that wouldn't be fair to Gabriela. Felix, somehow we should find a way to protect them and keep them with us, wherever we are."

"How are we going to get home to the Box?" Lexi asked.

I slumped into the sofa. I had no answers yet. Sighing, I said, "Maybe our spell casting skills will come back to us, and we can morph ourselves into useful bodies.

I don't know how we can whip up a potion to cure the teens and their Moronic Minds. If we don't do that, they'll resist everything except being princesses."

Adoncia was feeding us our morning breakfast when it happened. One second, I was accepting a bite from her spoon and the next instant, I was gasping for breath. Water or some liquid dripped from what remained of my body. A man was holding me up, finishing unhooking wires from me. My arms were about five inches long, conical stumps, and my legs were barely six inches long, also conical. From the corner of my eyes, I saw Lexi and Tiffany in tanks next to mine.

The man spoke softly. "Don't worry. We're living up to our promises. After I get you and the other two dried off and slip on some clothes, we'll take you to Acers Rehabilitation Center, where they will fit you with prosthetic arms and legs and then work with you for six months. In time, you may regain some independence, but you are alive and that's important."

He sat me on a chair and another man put a T-shirt on me and briefs. I watched as Tiffany was extracted and finally Lexi. Both women shrieked when they saw the condition of their actual bodies. Their shock gave way to grief and sobs, however. I was merely numb.

An hour later, we were deposited at Acers Rehab, where friendly staff wheeled us into their facility. Without further ado, a doctor chatted with us, while fastening a pair of hooks onto our arm stumps and legs onto what was left of our legs. That done, he addressed us together. "It won't be easy. There are not enough of your arms or legs left to regain much control, but with a lot of patience and practice, you may be able to feed yourselves with your hooks and you may be able to move about over short distances. To be honest, you'll probably spend the rest of your lives in an assisted living center when you leave here. Right now, we'll provide six months of intensive training, teaching you how to manipulate your hooks and legs. We'll be very pleased if you regain enough control to at least handle your meals and perhaps walk to and from your room to the dining hall. Now then, let's get started."

That turned out to be a joke, only none of us laughed. Pathetic. That was Tiffany's response. After much exertion, she managed to get one hook raised and opened. Seeing her disappointment, I whispered, "Wait until tonight and they take these things off us. We'll see if we can't use our Morph spells and get out of here."

That brought a flash of a smile to both their faces. However, our hopes vanished a minute later. Adler walked into our room!

"Well, well, we meet again. I see you three are having a difficult time getting around, since those from Eros-4 have chosen to abandon Salazar-3. I've come by to make you an offer. Princesses are in demand on this world. Don't ask me why. I've never understood you humans. Nevertheless, you'll come with me now. Don't try anything or I'll use other methods on you. You look helpless, though cute with those tiny appendages."

I debated whether I could attack and defeat a dragon while my body was in its current physical state. Since I couldn't move without using magical spells, I decided not to try it. A quick glance at the girls told me I made the correct decision. Adler had us quickly wheeled out of the rehab center and deposited in one of the silver flying vehicles. Minutes later, we were carried inside the GE corporate headquarters building. As we entered, I noticed a large number of holes in many lower floor's glass panes.

We were taken to some kind of executive waiting room, or so Lexi claimed. Adler left us there, while he went to find Euric. I whispered, "Look, if they try to cast Moronic Mind on us, fight it off, but pretend that it worked." Two pale faces nodded, just as the Red dragon entered.

"You three again. Argh. I see why Adler thinks you are a pain. Why he doesn't just let me incinerate your bodies is beyond me. Oh well. He pays very well. Here we go." He focused and began a series of three Moronic Mind spells. Alert and expecting the spell was all that it took for me to throw off the spell. Yet, I pretended being very stupid, hoping the girls would be able to throw it off as well. They were, much to my relief.

He then cast the Morph Other spell on me, turning me into something of a Gracia lookalike, a gorgeous young woman, with long, rich hair, no arms, but with an enormous bosom. I pretended to be very pleased with my new princess form, and Euric moved on to do Lexi and then Tiffany. While he was tied up with the girls, I finally figured out exactly what was going on and the how of it. This was magical misuse in my book.

Euric merely morphed our bodies into these ideal "princess" forms. That meant, if we could dispel the magic, we'd likely find our own bodies whole once more. However, Euric and Adler found a clever way around the finite duration and/or potential dispelling of the morph spell: the Make Permanent spell, used to finalize a newly made magical item, such as an enchanted weapon. Thus, our Dispel Magic spells would have no effect on the new body forms. With the Moronic Mind spell in effect, we'd not be able to cast any spells, theoretically limiting us to being mere "princesses." That was their plan and obvious modus operandi. Thus, I knew we could cure the three teens, if we could rescue them. The Regeneration Ring would undo these spells on our bodies. Thus, hope flooded my mind, as I suspect it also did with the girls, who probably had also worked all this out as well.

After Euric departed, three matronly women then entered and dressed us up in elegant gowns. We looked very similar to Gracia, Herminia, and Gabriela. Thankfully, Tiffany and Lexi chatted away about how wonderful we looked, how perfect our bodies now were, and how terrific it was to be princesses. Personally, I felt more embarrassed than I ever thought possible. It was one thing to be forced into Gracia's body by that alien technology, because I knew it wasn't me, but this time, it was me.

After we were dressed, another dragon we'd not seen before escorted us over to join the three teens. "You will be staying here with these princesses. Adoncia will look after your needs. If you are lucky, one day someone will want you to be their princess." With that, he left and we joined the three teens, who were sitting on the sofa, waiting patiently for Adoncia.

"Oh, more wonderful princesses," Gracia exclaimed, a big grin on her angelic face. "You three look perfect too. We're going out tomorrow. Adoncia is taking us to see a play. I'm not sure what that is, but we're sure to be seen by everyone, so we must look our very best."

Lexi and Tiffany chatted with the teens, before Adoncia got us ready for bed. Thankfully, she put us newcomers in the spare bedroom. After she left and turned out the lights, we chatted.

Tiffany giggled and said, "Well, Felix, you're now a woman too. You know, Lexi and I could take turns and Morph into men for you." I flushed. "But what I want to know is what happens if we did that and got you pregnant? Can your morphed body get pregnant? If it does, what happens if you Morph back into your male form? What happens to the baby? Does it die or something?"

Now I laughed. "Tiff, I don't recall reading anything about that in the spell documentation. I've no idea, but is it likely to happen?"

Both giggled. Leave it to curious Tiffany. She focused and morphed into a handsome man, modeled on her notions of the most attractive man she'd ever seen. In relatively short order, I became "educated" and the guinea pig test subject. She just had to know the answers.

Later on and back in her normal form, Tiffany whispered, "This is more like it, Felix. Now we aren't helpless any longer. We can make excellent use of our feet."

Lexi added, "We should start making escape plans too and practicing our spells when no one is looking."

As we slipped into sleep, I still felt mostly helpless, but then I'd not spent five years as an Unarmed Escort. I knew I couldn't use the Invisible Servant spell in public. Thus, as I drifted off to sleep, many of those movies of unarmed women doing many things slipped into my mind once more.

# Chapter 21—Drago's Rescue

With so many Black dragons swooping down from their previously invisible positions in the sky and with the six knocked out by the alien gas, Drago had only seconds to get out of the way. While he could dodge one Black dragon's cone of spewing acid, he couldn't dodge this many at one time. Further, he hadn't used his new Teleport spell much and wasn't confident at executing it under fire, so he chose to Shadow Walk, stepping out into the shadows between worlds.

There, he cast Invisibility and stepped back to observe what they would do to his three companions. *They'll probably be killed, but we'll see.* He hovered and then landed nearby so he could overhear Adler's orders.

"Bring all six of them with us. We're heading to Moro City on Salazar-3."

"You don't want them dead?" asked Euric.

"Of course not. They are more useful alive. Besides, I've got the perfect torture designed for these three constant meddlers. Too bad we couldn't just get rid of that meddling Gold dragon though."

"I don't understand what those nutty Golds see in humans? Why even bother with them? Tiny lifetimes, tiny brains, tiny everything. What good are they?"

"Oh don't be silly, Euric. Humans do invent many marvelous things, including magical items. Probably that's because they have such short lifetimes; they have to be frantically inventing things. We're about to make very good use of some human inventions on Salazar-3. Hobart, get the carrier ready."

Another Black dragon hooked another one of the special wagon carts to a third, while Adler and Euric carefully deposited the six unconscious humans into the cart. Drago knew what would happen next. They'd Shadow Walk off to another world. If so, he'd most likely lose them forever. Hence, Drago acted. Still invisible, he moved in

282

behind the wicker cart, latching onto its backside with his mouth. As the other dragons began walking and then stepping into the Shadows, Drago followed along behind, carefully matching their pace.

Soon, they stepped out onto a grassy open area in the middle of tall skyscrapers. Drago had no idea where he was, but continued to trail Adler and the six humans. Soon, he watched them split up. His three friends were carried inside a single story building, but he correctly guessed what was going on inside. It was another of those Eros-4 control buildings. Drago sighed, suspecting the worst for his three companions. Surveying the only entrance, he spotted six black dragons, far too many for him to ignore and charge in, rescuing us. *I have to bide my time. Patience, Drago, patience.*

Later on, he attempted to See Through My Eyes, but saw nothing. Conclusion: I must still be unconscious. He tried again early that evening and got a very confused look. Eventually, he discovered he was looking out of Gracia's eyes, not mine. Stymied, he canceled that spell, recasting it to see from Lexi's eyes. Again, Drago was surprised to see the other two teens and not us. Drago was consistent. He tried it a third time, looking from Tiffany's eyes. At last, he tentatively concluded that our three bodies must be mutilated and being kept alive in one of those awful tanks, while we were being forced to occupy the three young teenaged bodies. Testing his theory, he sent me a Message spell, while watching Gracia via Gabriela's or Tiffany's eyes. While I didn't see anything, he saw the scrolling message appear before my eyes. Drago was convinced, but knew he had a far worse problem.

He couldn't rescue us, because we were not in our bodies, but in these teenaged bodies. We'd have to be returned to our likely mutilated bodies first. If that wasn't enough, he also calculated that we were under the Moronic Mind spell as well.

With little he could do for us, he headed off to study the city and find something to eat. Eventually, he gave up trying to find an antelope, settling for a cow. Hunger satiated, he settled down to watch what the human man Dario did with us, such as taking us out on the town. By tagging along behind us while invisible, he observed our behavior, concluding we were under the moron spell.

Then came the assassinations. At first, Drago believed this was his chance to rescue us, since the security guards fled the mansion estate and Dario was dead. However, because we were still not in our own bodies, he decided against acting rashly. He had no idea how to get us back into our rightful bodies.

Daily, the number of such attacks escalated, until by the tenth day, Drago decided a war was going on, for so many were being killed. He, however, didn't have to worry about taking a stray bullet. Several times, a bullet did strike him. Since they weren't enchanted, magical bullets, the slugs merely bounced off him. However, they did hurt slightly, annoying him.

Finally, the attacks ended. What amazed Drago were the actions Adler then took. Somehow, that Black dragon had gotten himself into a position of power over the humans of Salazar-3, particularly in Moro City, and was espousing the rights of everyone to have their own "princess." Even more surprising, he saw many men begging to have their own princesses, with Adler working to provide them. *Gosh, I hope they don't split the three up, giving them away to other men. If they try that, I'll have to act fast.*

Fortunately, that didn't happen. The three teens stayed in the fancy mansion, watched over by the older woman. Each morning, Drago cast his See Through My Eyes, checking up on me and us. One day, he was taken by surprise. No longer did he see the teens, but he saw us being removed from the tanks! Worse, we looked like the others we'd rescued from the tanks on the other world. Still, Drago didn't despair, since the Regeneration Ring would restore our missing limbs.

Cautiously, he followed the men who took us to the rehab center. Just as he was about to barge in there and pull us out, Adler and his crew arrived. Once more, he went invisible and followed them. He was quite surprised to discover Adler restored our legs and placed us with the three teens in the mansion. Since we could now walk, he began making preparations to rescue the six of us.

Drago knew I wouldn't consider leaving the three teens behind, not after going to all this trouble to return them to their oasis home and parents. However, the magic ring was back in the Box on another world. *I'll Shadow Walk them back to the Box, but how will all six of them be able to hang on to me? They can't, not without arms. I need a plan.*

Several days passed while Drago scouted around, looking for ideas. The only workable way was to use the same wicker cart or wagon the dragons used to bring us here in the first place. After some scouting, Drago found it stored outside of the sprawling city, hidden among a line of trees. Of course, from having watched the dragons bringing us to this world, he knew he needed help. Someone would have to harness him into the contraption. Once he was in harness, he couldn't do much else but Shadow Walk. *Can Felix still use the Morph spell? If not, I can try it, but will they be idiots, unable to deal with the harness?* Drago had many unanswered questions. Plus, they had to be answered before he could begin the rescue operation.

Finally, he decided to see what our situation was like. He sent me a Message: Felix, can you cast spells? Can you Morph Self into a form that has arms? I need someone to harness me up to the Black dragons' wicker cart or wagon, the one that they used to bring you six here. Message me back, if you can.

I spent my days trying to figure out a way to get us all back to Rainbow's End and the desert oasis, while the girls worked with the teens, keeping the princesses contented. Daily, this became more and more of a problem, since now Adoncia hardly ever took all six of us out of the mansion. I suspected she was afraid of being assassinated herself. Of course, the three teens couldn't grasp why they couldn't just go off on their own or why

Adoncia was so hesitant to take them anywhere. Their drastically reduced mental capacities made reasoning with them extremely challenging. Thus, having spent days trying to figure out how and without any luck, I was about to give in and discuss the issue with Adler. Perhaps, the dragon would see reason or something.

So it was at this low point, I received Drago's Message. I responded quickly! Drago! Great to hear from you and that you are okay. Yes, the Moronic Mind spell has worn off us three. All three of us can Morph as needed, but the three teens are still under the spell. We can harness you up. How soon can we get out of here?

We exchanged more messages and decided to leave as soon as possible. He sent me: Okay. I'll come by around eight tomorrow morning. I can teleport us to where they are hiding the cart thing. Shouldn't take very long.

Crap. I sent back: I've been a bit nauseous these past mornings. How about doing it right after lunch? Adoncia will leave us all sitting in the livingroom, while she busies herself with housekeeping duties. We can simply walk out then.

We agreed and I broke the news to Lexi and Tiffany. "So he's been watching over us. Wicked. Say, why don't we just go right after Adoncia feeds us our breakfast, say around eight?"

"Cause I keep getting nauseous these past few mornings. I need to be able to focus. Lord knows how many spells we're going to need to fire off, especially if Adler spots us fleeing here."

Tiffany began laughing, joined by Lexi. My face felt hot. "What? What's so funny?"

She said, "I bet you are pregnant. Morning sickness." Both girls giggled again. I think my face must have turned fiery red, for it sure felt hot. I also felt very nervous. What was happening to me?

Shortly after lunch, Adoncia left us sitting before the entertainment center, while she headed off to vacuum the mansion. Quickly, we three cast Morph Self spells. I was careful to morph myself into a version that still looked like my female form, only it had arms. Tiffany and Lexi now looked normal. We didn't do this on the teens because they'd lose their "princess" or beauty queen look and would protest loudly. Lexi met Drago at the front door, signaling all was ready.

"Gracia, Herminia, Gabriela, let's go out for a walk, shall we?" I suggested. "We princesses should be seen, don't you think?"

"Oh yes, yes. Let's do go out. Adoncia just isn't. Not anymore. Come on. Off we go."

Tiffany and I led the teens through the mansion to the doors, where Lexi and Drago waited. Once we were all outside, Drago latched onto three of us at one time, before focusing and casting his Teleport. A minute later, he reappeared and took the remaining three with him. We found ourselves on a grassy patch, part of a farmer's field I suspected.

"Well, this isn't any good. Where are all the people? I can't stand up very well. Take us to the symphony or diner," Gracia protested.

"She's right. This isn't any good," Gabriela added.

I tuned out the teens confused chatter, focusing on figuring out how to hook Drago, now in his Gold dragon form, to the cart or wagon contraption. At last, we three succeeded and merely lifted the three protesting teens into the cart, and then joining them. Drago needed no encouragement. He began walking and the world around us thinned until we only saw a vast grey nothingness. I felt even sicker to my stomach.

"Wicked. How cool is this?" Tiff exclaimed, very excited with the experience.

"We should observe all we can," Lexi advised.

The teens merely looked blank, and I tried to keep my lunch down. Then, the world that we were more familiar with appeared, thin at first, but growing more solid every second, until at last, I could smell or feel the desert heat, trees, and sand particles in the air. Once we landed, the teens complained they couldn't walk in the sand in their heels. Lexi cleverly told them no princess could and that they were supposed to go barefoot in the sand. The trio accepted this, but I knew we needed to brew up the antidote potion as soon as possible.

Fausto, the Elder, and the other parents were grateful for the safe return of their daughters, but were scared of their precarious mental states and their lack of arms. Lexi took charge, explaining, "They've been the victim of some very nasty magical spells. We will be undoing the spells, returning them to their normal selves as soon as we can. Until we do, you'll have to handle their needs. If you have trouble, just explain to her that she's a princess and this is what princesses are supposed to do. She'll buy that argument, most likely." Several men chuckled.

Minutes later, we four entered the Box and slumped into our own sofas. "Thank you Drago!" Lexi said. "You've saved us." He looked pleased. "Now then, do we have any more of that potion to cure the Moronic Mind spell?"

We didn't, but Drago volunteered to Shadow Walk back to Byron Falls and pick up some from my sister or Mage Locklard. Thus, later that night, we coerced the three teens into drinking the potion, in spite of its bad taste. When they later fell asleep, one by one, we slipped the magic ring on their little toes. As expected, magical energies flashed. After blinking from the brightness, we saw their bodies were fully restored. I was totally convinced that Euric and Adler were simply using magical spells to modify human bodies.

Long after dark, we returned to the Box. One by one, I had the girls cancel their Morph spell and then slipped the ring on their little toe. As expected, magical energies flashed, and their bodies were restored with no damage remaining. "Glad we didn't have to wait a week for our arms," Lexi commented, stretching her arms about.

"But what do we do about Felix here?" Tiffany asked.

"Yes, why do you look like the females of your species?" Drago asked.

I let Tiffany explain what had happened to us and to

me, specifically. Meanwhile, I pondered the situation, though I did cancel my Morph spell, becoming unarmed once more, only now I was a pregnant unarmed woman. While Tiff was telling our story, I headed to my room to see just what I really did look like.

Lexi slipped in behind me. "You have to admit, Felix, you do look incredibly sexy, just like we did—beauty queens with giant bosoms. So what's going to happen to our baby if you use the ring? I'm sure it'll restore your arms, but what about the rest of you? And what will happen to the baby if the ring turns you back into a male again?"

"Lord, Lexi, I've no idea what's going to happen, and frankly, I'm a little scared too. I always dreamed of one day being a father, just not that I'd be the mother." I grinned sheepishly and Lexi chuckled. "I don't want to harm our child. Do you suppose we can continue with our work with me like this? At least until the baby comes?"

Her answer was a silent one. She threw her arms around me, pulling me tightly to her, and planted a passionate kiss on my lips. "That tell you how I feel, big boy, er, big girl? I know Tiff wants the child as much as I do. I think it's incredibly brave of you to do this. I'm sure we can manage just fine. Can you remember all those videos we were shown of unarmed women doing all sorts of things? And then there's the servant spell. We'll get by just fine, love. Besides, women have babies all the time. Our lives don't just stop because we get pregnant, thought I suppose we should eat right and all that."

From the doorway, I heard Tiff. "Wicked. You'll keep our baby then. Wonderful, simply wonderful. We'll make it up to you one day too, won't we, Lexi? Once we master all this magic stuff."

Even though I was in my own bed, I slept ill. Something bothered me, something Drago had said, something about Adler's plans. I awoke in a cold sweat, but with the girls on either side of me, and lacking arms, I couldn't get myself up without waking them. Instead, I gazed first at Tiffany and then Lexi, realizing just how blessed, how fortunate, I was to have met and fallen in love with these incredible people, and that they had fallen in love with me. I wasn't even from their own modern world. In many ways, I was an ignorant primitive bumpkin. They knew so much more than I did, especially Tiff.

"What're you looking at," whispered Tiffany in her mellow voice, whose light grey eyes peered into mine.

"Two incredible angels," I whispered back to my raven-haired wife. She pulled me close and we exchanged a passionate kiss.

# Chapter 22—Enlightenment

Over breakfast and after I cast a Morph Me spell on myself to add working arms to the body, I asked Drago to repeat what he'd overhead Adler saying.

"Well," Drago drawled in his deep voice, "he said, 'We're about to make very good use of some human inventions on Salazar-3.' He and six other dragons, some black and some red, began operating out of a building that had a strange sign on it. I don't know what the words mean. Salazar Center for Biogenetic and Eugenics Research. Nor do I know what inventions he plans to use, but he seemed inordinately happy about it. Why?"

"Tiff, what do those words mean, biogenetic and eugenics? Didn't we hear something like that back on Halcion-3 at the Unarmed Escorts?"

"Eugenics is a science that uses controlled breeding to increase the occurrence of desirable heritable characteristics in a population of plants or animals or humans. You know, tinkering with reproduction to get a new version of white roses or yellow roses or bees that are immune to killer mites. I suppose they could try to make humans who had higher intelligence or super-strong or something."

She went on, "Biogenetic means something that is produced or brought about by living organisms, but more recently it means modification of the body's DNA to produce a desirable alteration in the body, such as curing a fatal illness or repairing a structural problem with a heart or other organ. Our scientists are experimenting with modifying a person's DNA to bring about medical cures, but it's still highly experimental."

Lexi spoke up, "So maybe the scientists on Salazar-3 have developed both far beyond what those on Halcion-3 have. I think Felix is right to be worried. We should investigate this further. Look Tiff, those yellow stripped biogenetic cylinders at the doctor's place at Unarmed

Escorts once must have contained some kind of terrible agent, which was invented or made somewhere, even if it wasn't on our world."

"You're right. The men who came in their thick containment suits were very worried, at least until they found they only contained compressed air. We should take this seriously, Felix," Tiff insisted.

I grew even more worried. What did Adler want with such things? Was he looking for a way to destroy all humans in a city or on a whole world? I felt rushes of wild emotions flooding my senses, something that had never happened to me before.

"So what do we do about it?" Drago asked, since I remained uncommonly silent, fighting my wild surge of disparate feelings.

I took a deep breath and exhaled slowly, calming my nerves slightly. "We should go back there and see what we can find out. This could be nothing at all or it could be vitally important. I'm not shutting the Box's door saying Handled until we do."

"Well, Adler was telling people who wanted to become like you six were— princesses he called them—to report to that building, but I don't think he's going to let me in there nosing about."

"Cast See Through My Eyes and Hear Through My Ears, Drago, and then eavesdrop on what we see and hear. We'll pay that facility a visit. If we morph into the princess forms we had at the mansion with the teens, they should let us inside, don't you think?"

Shrugs replied. An hour later, we three sat astride the Gold dragon's back, holding onto ropes encircling his thick torso. Tiffany claimed this was much like riding a horse, but I laughed. This was anything but a horse ride. One by one, we cast our Invisibility spells, and then Drago began walking and his powerful wings opened up in an explosion of golden rays, nearly blinding in the late morning sunlight. We blinked and the space around us dimmed to the dull grey of the Shadows. I heard him cast his own Invisibility spell. Just as I got nervous about all this, sunlight again replaced that depressing shade. Towering skyscrapers lined the horizon, as Drago gently landed at the grassy park within Moro City.

After getting ourselves dismounted and the ropes stuffed into a sack, Drago morphed into his usual human form, remaining invisible. I cancelled my morph spell, appearing as one of these new princesses. I still wore the red satin gown and tall, matching heels I'd worn when we fled the mansion. One by one, the girls morphed into their previous princess forms, elegantly dressed as well.

That done, we headed out onto the sidewalk with Drago following behind us, whispering directions to the Salazar Center for Biogenetic and Eugenics Research. As we slowly walked along, we spotted a number of other young, armless princesses also dolled up and strolling, often chatting with each other. We spotted a large electronic billboard that advertised the many benefits of becoming a princess. In the lower right corner, it showed a map of the location of the very Salazar Center we were heading for. So much had changed on this world since Dario first brought the three unarmed princess teens to this world. Again, I marveled over how much Tiffany knew about such things, convinced I was the luckiest man in the universe to have her and Lexi as my wives.

My reverie ended as we approached the tall skyscraper. A huge sign stood to the right of the small flight of steps leading up to the giant glass doors. It read: Salazar Center for Biogenetic and Eugenics Research. Several normal women glanced at us and smiled, before entering the doors. Magic was at work. As we approached the doors, I panicked slightly, wondering how we could open them. Suddenly, they opened of their own accord.

Tiffany laughed. "Silly. When you step on the mat, it triggers a sensor, which then activated the doors. These are automatic doors. Most modern buildings have them. It's not magic, dear."

My face felt hot. "Oh," I mumbled as we entered. We were in a narrow, glass-lined corridor. Ahead, we saw the hall split. One side was labeled clearly "princesses," while the other side was labeled "normals." The women who entered ahead of us veered off to the right, while we decided to take the left branch for princesses. We passed though some kind of machine, though it in no way blocked our continued passage down the hall. Thus far, we'd walked maybe ten feet. As I passed through the machine, I felt a sting in the left side of my neck, but nothing more.

Just beyond the machine, we saw a large reception desk and an attractive, young princess sitting behind it, a large smile on her face. "Why, hello and welcome to the Salazar Center for Biogenetic and Eugenics Research. How can we help you?"

"Could we have a tour of this facility?" I asked politely.

"Of course. We princesses are supposed to be widely seen out and about on our own. I'll get a tour guide for you. One moment please." She looked stunning in her light blue gown, which matched her eyes. Her long, wavy blonde hair contrasted nicely, as she tossed her head to one side, rose, and teetered off on her heels.

Shortly, she returned with two men, both wearing expensive grey suits. I recognized Adler at once, inhaling sharply. From his smirking grin, I knew he recognized us. The other man was three inches shorter and wore a white apron-like garment over his suit. He had thick glasses perched on his long nose, incongruous with his black moustache.

"Ah, Felix, Tiffany, and Lexi, if I'm not mistaken," Adler said with a slight condescending sneer. "You're a long way from your Unarmed Escorts home."

Lexi giggled. "Yes, we are. We're getting out and about. Princesses must be seen. Mustn't they? Have you seen the three teens that were living with us? We went out, but they didn't come back. Not yet. Anyway."

Adler's taller frame relaxed. Lexi's silly chatter must have convinced him we were still as he'd left us. "Yes, that is good of you. So you're here for a tour?"

"Why yes. Wouldn't that be great? We've heard women come here to be princesses."

"This is Dr. Roland Theobald, the director of this facility. I'll let him show you around. I'll join you later on."

"If you'll follow me, princesses," the doctor said. His voice was thin and squeaky, but his mind was brilliant. As we soon discovered, he wasn't modest.

He purposely kept his pace slow, matching our tiny steps in our heels, which clicked noisily in unison as we marched deeper into the facility.

"This is the most advanced research facility in the universe. Here, we are able genetically to modify human bodies. In this section, staff modifies those who have heart difficulties, such as weak valves. To your right is where we handle those who have contracted fatal diseases. Hence, the quarantine signs."

We took an elevator to the next floor. "Here is where those who wish to become princesses are handled. You see, thanks to Dr. Adler, the political riots are over now. Everyone is able to afford their own princess, but the challenge is meeting the intense demand for young women such as yourselves. Initially, Dr. Adler and his group made the first of the princesses, but as you know, they couldn't possibly keep up with the demand for such fabulous women, though I know he did try."

"He came to me and asked if we had the ability to turn normal people into princesses. Of course, we did, only until now, we'd never considered such an action. It took our geneticists a week to develop the formula. Now, we're turning out a hundred princesses each day, just from this facility alone. The new government pays us 10,000 Kronars per princess made, so our expenses are fully covered, and the cost to the new princess and her owner is nothing at all, a most marvelous arrangement, if I do say so myself. After all, the revolution was about the average man being able to have his own princess, though some women want them as well."

"Anyway, once we got our production lines going, Dr. Adler asked us to perfect a booster shot for all those princesses that his group had made. Each of you was given your booster shot automatically when you entered this building. Marvel of efficiency, if I do say so. Probably felt like a slight sting."

Tiffany ridged slightly. "What does the booster shot do?"

"Oh, you see, our current princess procedure actually alters the person's DNA. Thus, any children they may eventually have will inherit their special characteristics, just as children do—looking so similar to their parents. Anyway, the booster shot is perfectly harmless to you princesses. It merely alters your DNA to match your current princess forms. That way, when you have children, they will inherit your magnificent appearance. Oh, I'm sorry. I forgot you are princesses and probably haven't understood a word of what I was saying." He looked terribly apologetic.

"I followed most of it, I think," Tiffany countered. "I've not forgotten everything I once knew. So our children would tend to have similar large breasts and look gorgeous?"

"Quite right. And be armless too. While not exact copies of you, they would inherit traits from their parents just as children do, except in this case, the princess traits are dominant."

"Wait, what if we have sons?" Tiffany asked.

Dr. Theobald pulled on his chin, deep in thought. "You know, I'm not entirely sure about that answer. I guess we'll know in due time. Now then, let's go up to the next floor, where we have implemented one of our incredible breakthroughs."

We faced an entire wall of transparent containers. Babies or fetuses of various sizes lay floating inside many of them. I was shocked.

"Here, we are growing babies! Actually, there are two kinds of babies. Some are clones of their parent. You see, if you love your body, when it gets old, you can have it cloned here. Your new clone will be identical to you in all ways. Incredible technology, just incredible. The other kind of babies is what we call test tube babies. That is, there are some women who cannot carry nor have a baby or who don't wish to endure a nine month pregnancy. After their egg is fertilized, it's artificially grown in one of these tanks. After nine months, the baby is removed and given to its parents. A marvel of efficiency. We expect this to be a gigantic growth area, particularly with all of the new princesses we're making. Your sponsors probably will insist any princess pregnancies be brought here so their princess isn't bothered with enduing the nine month pregnancy."

"I suspect we'll be doing a booming business with our 'baby factory.' I assure you each gets nothing but the very best care. In fact, our doctors examine each for birth defects, such as heart problems. Any abnormality found is biogenetically remedied while they are in these artificial wombs. Thus, we 'give birth' only to healthy children. Incredible, simply incredible."

Tiffany replied, "Wicked. I agree. Incredible. Are you sharing this invaluable technology with other worlds? It's lifesaving."

"Don't know about that. That was the arena of the corporation leaders—er, used to be. They're all dead now. I suppose someone in our new government will address that in time. Oh, here comes Dr. Adler. I know he wants to talk to you as well."

"Has Dr. Theobald answered your questions?" Dr. Adler asked politely.

"Yes, he has," Tiffany answered for us.

The human excused himself and departed, leaving us with Adler. "Did he explain about his booster shots?"

"Yes, he did. I'm sure we princesses appreciate such kindness."

Adler smiled coyly. "Indeed. Why use magic when there is a natural method of achieving the desired results? Anyway, we still haven't located the three teens that are staying with you. Any idea where they went on their walk?"

"To see downtown," Lexi suggested, before Tiff or I could say anything. Clever.

Adler led us to the elevator and took us up one floor, where massive construction projects were underway. As we walked slowly to one end, he continued.

"Okay. So you meddlers probably want to know what's going on. Since your meddling Gold dragon isn't here, having abandoned you to your princess fates, I can elaborate. You see it all has to do with birthrates. Your species breeds like rabbits or mice. Probably you have to because of your tiny lifetimes. Dragons usually have a child about every ten years. Our females are fertile once every decade or so. Hence, there are always millions of you to one of our kind."

"Years ago, I came across the first of these so-called modern worlds, planets with silver flying ships that traverse the Shadows, albeit drastically slower than our powerful Shadow Walks. I will concede you humans are incredibly inventive. While exploring Halcion-3, I came across those biogenetic, yellow-banded cylinders. I learned that other worlds possessed powerful bio weapons and genetic skills. Some were growing test tube babies. At long last, I had the potential solution I'd sought for two hundred years."

"I needed to travel to many of these 'modern' worlds, looking for one on which they'd perfected cloning and similar things. Lacking the means, I studied the alien humans who took shore leave from their flying ships. That's when I took over that escort service. I quickly found that unarmed, gorgeous escorts were in demand, with not only these sex-starved aliens, but also other wealthy people on their home worlds. Hence, we quickly began selling some to these people."

"Of course, a Black or Red dragon accompanied the unarmed escort, providing for her needs, so to speak. Actually, this mechanism got my personnel to many of these hitherto unknown modern worlds. Once there, they quickly became familiar with the world. That then allowed them to Shadow Walk there at any time. Slowly, we've been expanding the number of known worlds for all Red and Black dragons. I've added twelve such worlds to our repertoire, worlds other dragon-kind knows nothing about."

"Finally, I found this world, Salazar-3. As you have seen, their scientists have perfected everything I could possibly desire. A wealthy man, that Dario fellow, brought the three teens from that desert oasis here, along with my group and me. I can't tell you how excited I've been. My two hundred year search has finally ended. I've found what I've been looking for!"

"A world that wants lots of princesses?" Tiffany cleverly asked.

Adler chuckled, vibrating the floor slightly. "No, silly woman. I was just as surprised as everyone else was when this world went insane and killed off most everyone associated with the corporations and government. At least, I was able to step in and help bring an end to the fighting, promising everyone their own princess. This group here is becoming fabulously wealthy by converting people into princesses. I admit I had to use Euric, the Red dragon, at first, but he couldn't keep up with the demand. I convinced Dr. Theobald there was vast wealth to be made, and his scientists quickly invented the vaccine that turns a normal human into one of you princesses. Those people you saw taking the right branch at the entrance are now on the floor above us, waiting while their bodies rebuild themselves according to their newly altered DNA. In a few days, these new princesses will be delivered to those who so greatly desire them. I admit I never could understand why humans so wanted them, even at the Unarmed Escorts. Yet they did."

"Anyway, I digress. What we're after are these breeding and cloning facilities. Ah, here we are. Look."

We stared at a larger tank. Floating inside it was a tiny Black dragon.

Adler puffed up and said proudly, "My clone son. He's going to be an exact copy of me. Sixty-three days, not nine months. They are building a hundred large tanks, initially. Many more are planned. Once every ten years, donor females will come and have their eggs harvested. They can pick their children's fathers. The fertilized eggs will then be grown in these tanks, just as the human babies are today. Also, anyone who desires it can have clones made here. I'll soon have ten babies who will be identical to me."

"Word has already gone out to other Black, Red, White, and Green dragons. In a few days, many will be arriving to see for themselves and then avail themselves of one of these two services."

I decided to speak up. "What about all the other types of dragons? The Browns, Greys, Blues, Golds?"

Adler laughed. "Those pathetic fools? No way will we be encouraging them to propagate their kind. No, we will limit the number of Greens and Whites too. Honestly, we Blacks are the master race, though the Reds are almost nearly as good as we are. In a half century or so, we Blacks and Reds will have sufficient numbers that we can finally assume our intrinsic role in the universe, the masters of the worlds and all their inhabitants."

"So you see, you have played a small role in helping Black and Red dragons achieve their full potential, master rulers of the universe. Don't worry. We'll still keep brighter humans around to invent more and powerful things for us, of course. However, this is the end of the tour. The many floors above us are their research laboratories. Ah, here comes Aleta, the princess receptionist now. She'll lead you down and out. Thank you all for coming today. It's been a pleasure talking with you. I suppose I should get you each your own sponsor soon, but I'll wait until we find the three missing teens."

The pretty receptionist smiled her silly moronic grin. "Was it fun? Isn't it great how they are raising our babies so we don't have to carry them for nine months? This way, we will always look our best at all times, like the princesses we are. This way." She led us into the elevator, pressing the One button with her nose.

Soon, we were back outside on the sidewalk. Drago moved up close, guiding us along. "It's worse than I ever feared, Felix. Black and Red dragons running the many worlds? Beyond awful."

"Well," Tiffany stated, "at least they're ensuring

healthy babies. You could call what they do for the babies with physical problems a miracle. Many definitely would."

"What do you do for aching feet? My knees are giving out," I complained.

Tiffany laughed. "You're just out of practice, dear. You should wear them far more often. Then, you'll be used to them."

I groaned, but was glad finally to reach the park. Quickly, we morphed ourselves back, while Drago changed into his dragon form. A few minutes later, we arrived back at our Box.

"I've an errand to run. Back shortly," Drago explained, after dropping us off.

Once inside, I cancelled my spell, returning to my newer body form, that of a pregnant princess, and plopped onto a sofa to think. I had far too many worries and so few answers. Now wearing their usual casual clothes, Lexi and Tiffany soon joined me.

Lexi chatted, "You know, Felix, we should consult an archmage about your body problem. There must be some on this world, Rainbow's End, probably not out here in the desert, but somewhere."

"Wicked idea, Lexi. That's what we should do. Come on. Let's ask Fausto, the Elder, if he knows of one." As the two rose to do that, she added, "I wonder what Adler meant with that booster shot. I got one in my neck as I entered the building."

"So did I," Lexi added. "Wonder what it really does. You stay put, Felix. We'll find out. Back in a bit. So Tiff, can you believe all those princesses we saw on the streets of Moro City? I can see why women who are homily or worse would want to become a princess." Her voice trailed off as the door shut, leaving me alone, pondering this mess.

A few minutes later, the pair, still chatting, entered. Lexi explained, "Good news, Felix. There's an archmage just outside Imperial. Archmage Alison Weatherby. So up and at it, Felix. We're heading there now. Got good directions for you to use to Teleport us."

As I readied myself to cast the spell, I insisted they cast Fly on themselves because I intended to arrive very high. I'd never seen this place and was just going on their description of our arrival location. Best to be safe, very safe in this case. I cast the spell with the girls holding onto me. We arrived about two hundred feet above a small village, but there was no mistaking where the archmage lived. A circular stone tower rose five stories above the many colorful adobe homes of the village. After landing, we walked up to the door. A sign verified we had the correct location. Lexi knocked.

A doorwoman answered. "We desperately need to see Archmage Alison, please," Lexi continued to take charge.

She ushered us inside the hallway into a large outer chamber, which held a long couch, table, and a half dozen well-made chairs. Shortly, an older woman, perhaps fifty, walked in. She wore a light blue robe, which matched her piercing eyes. She had a long nose and angular features, with a scar across her forehead. Several reddish burn patches lined the left side of her face. Her light brown hair was barely shoulder length. Bidding us sit on the couch, she took a chair, but stared long at me. Once more, my face felt as if it were on fire.

"My name is Lexi. This is Tiffany. She's Felix, our husband. We're mages in training—well, he can teleport now. We're not that far along. Anyway, we've a very serious problem and need your advice." Thankfully, Lexi outlined what had happened to us, to me, explaining I was now pregnant.

After listening, Archmage Alison asked, "So Felix, when you cancel all your spells, this is the form your body takes?"

"Yes, it is."

"And you say you're confident the sequence of spells the Red dragon used on you was Morph Other followed by Make Permanent?"

"Yes, he used that sequence on many others. Also, he used Moronic Mind first, but we were able to slough that one off this time."

"Okay. Would you mind if I cast some Identification spells on you? None will harm you in any way."

"Please. Do what you can. We need answers. I don't want to harm our baby if I can help it."

For several minutes, I felt magical energies probing my body, rather tickling me. Finally, she smiled.

"Well, you definitely are pregnant. Congratulations on that. Your analysis of your situation is entirely correct. Well done, all three of you. The Make Permanent spell has established a new base for your Morph spells. As you've discovered, when they are cancelled, you appear as you now are. However, you are correct. When you don that Regeneration Ring, it will cancel this sequence of spells, nullifying the Make Permanent, reverting you back to your original body form, the male body, and restoring lost appendages if any are missing. You're correct in your analysis. Doing so now while you are pregnant will cause your unborn to cease to exist, just as the altered body form ceases to exist when you cancel the Morph spell on your body. It's not really killing it, it's just that it ceases to be in existence. So if you are sincere in not wanting to harm your unborn child, then you simply must endure the nine months and child birth. After that, it'll be totally safe to use the ring to regain your original male body form on a permanent basis."

We thanked her, but she wasn't finished. "Say, are you the ones who helped the Banner family in Imperial, Banner Fashions. Their company makes the best clothes in the city."

"Yes, we are, along with our friend, Drago. I'm sorry we weren't able to rescue their parents though. The dragons absconded with them and many others, taking them to other worlds," I replied.

Archmage Alison smiled. "Well, I've good news for you. The Banners thank you for all you've done. I was able to rescue the girls' parents and ten other adults. They had nothing but praise for you. I think the Banners are adapting to their physical handicaps as well as can be expected and far better than most others are. I'm thankful you were able to remove the dragons from those positions of power. Well done."

Coming from an archmage, these words impinged on all three of us. As I teleported us back to the Box in the oasis, Tiffany commented, "Wow. She sure was powerful. One day, Felix, we're going to be that powerful. She was able to get to the Banners when we couldn't. At least, we shared all those alternate ways to do things with them that we knew. I suppose that's what she meant with them adjusting well. Kind of makes you feel really good, doesn't it?"

I chuckled, "It helps me endure nine months of this. We did good, gang, really good. Teleport. . ."

Again, I took my perch on the sofa while the girls headed to the kitchen to whip up something to eat. Just then, Drago returned, but he had others with him when he entered the Box.

"Diana!" I exclaimed, carefully rising from the sofa. Her blue eyes drilled into mine. "I've missed you so, sis! Oh, sorry, this is really me, Felix." The girls came into the room and squealed. "Tell her, Tiff. This is really me. Oh, hi Ben, Carli. Wow. Carla too. Hi everyone!"

Tiff giggled, "Yes, it's him, Diana. You look good yourself. I guess our ring worked its miracles on you both."

"Hi everyone," Diana said. "Drago and Carla wanted to meet and talk about whatever you just discovered, so we tagged along. I've missed you, Felix, and you two as well. Have you been taking good care of my brother?" she teased them.

"You've heard what happened to us and to him, haven't you?" Lexi asked diplomatically.

"Yes," Ben replied, "but honestly, we didn't believe Drago. Are you really a she now and pregnant too? How?"

"Yes, Euric, the Red dragon, cast a Morph spell on me, turning me into this form, one they call a princess. Then, he cast Make Permanent. We just returned from visiting an archmage. She's confirmed what we suspected. This is my new base form. If I use the Regeneration Ring, it will or should undo this, reverting me back to my male body form, but our baby-to-be will no longer exist. So it looks like I'll be like this for a while. We're starting our family, kind of the wrong way around."

"Wow. Congratulations. Say, we're doing it too, starting our family too," Ben declared, looking at Diana and Carli, who flushed slightly.

"So brother, you are carrying their child?" Diana probed. I nodded. "Don't you know you have it backwards? You're supposed to be the father, and we, they, the mothers." The women giggled. "Seriously, Felix, I'm impressed. You are going through with this and not just using the ring right now. Wow. So who's the father or should I ask?"

Both Tiff and Lexi flushed. I spared them. "Sis, we aren't sure, but one of them is the father. We really don't care about that detail. So you are pregnant too? Carli too?"

Diana beamed. Her face had a glow I'd not seen before. "Yes, about a month we think. We have our parents' house all fixed up now. We're doing very well, actually making money and learning magic too. Tell them, Ben."

"She's right. I know we probably don't know all the spells you do, but we're making a living with the ones we do know. For example, I spend part of every day helping around Byron Falls. I cast Dig spells for the farmers, who claim I'm making their job drastically easier. I use Levitate spells to help them clear new fields of rocks, boulders, fallen trees, and such. We've discovered many spells can help others in the town, so much so that they are more than willing to pay us for our services." Ben's face shone with pride.

Carli added, "Plus, now that we three can cast Balls of Fire and Electrical Bolts, the Duke has appointed us and Carla to the Byron Falls Defense League. We're on a retainer of ten gold a week, whether or not we do anything at all. Of course, we'll fight for the town if anything bad comes, but it's not likely. It's Byron Falls, after all. Nothing much happens there."

We chatted more, sharing stories. I was very pleased Diana was doing so well, and again saw that magic was supposed to be used to help others around us. Further, the ring had done its job. Diana and Carla's awful scars were gone. I couldn't tell either had ever been hurt.

In contrast, our mastery of spells was incredibly different. Ben and Carli still had to learn a few more Grade 1 spells to be complete there. They knew about half of the Grade 2 spells, and a smattering of Grade 3 spells, the latter of which got them positions on the Duke's town defensive team. I think all three of them were shocked to see the sheer number of spells we had in our spell books, especially those of Tiff and Lexi. Finally, I truly realized how much we actually had to "pay" for our incredibly rapid advancement in learning the magical arts. It was steep, incredibly steep, if not outright strange in my case.

Time flew by, but Lexi and Tiffany didn't forget supper, and cleverly managed to stretch it out to feed the additional four. After supper, the discussion became far more serious. Drago and Carla led it. She had Drago and me tell her all that we'd heard and seen concerning what Adler, the Black dragon, was doing on this distant world of Salazar-3.

Diana spoke up, "I don't think it's healthy for the babies to be raised in those tanks. Mothers and their babies share a unique and special bond, which being raised in a tank is totally breaking. Felix, don't go getting any ideas of making use of their strange methods."

I flushed. "I've no intention of doing that, sis."

"You're missing what's truly important," Drago broke in.

"Right," Carla added. "I've now got a boyfriend myself. We dragons only breed about every ten years. If we had children as frequently as you humans do, then during my lifetime, I'd have some four hundred babies. We'd soon overwhelm all sources of food, outnumbering you humans everywhere."

"Right," Drago added, "Adler's actions are creating two absolutely huge problems. First, he's going against nature, in that as he said, soon there will be enormous numbers of more dragons. Second, he's grossly upsetting the balance between our kind, denying it to the lesser colors and us Golds. His plan is obvious. Make us all second class dragons, subject to their whims. While you humans don't yet see these as your problems, let me assure you that in time they will be."

"We should tell our parents about this," Carla declared. "Perhaps, they will know what to do about it."

Curious, I asked, "Do dragons ever go to war among themselves? Like the Golds versus the Blacks?"

Carla chuckled. "Of course. Just as you humans do. It also bothers me that these Black and Red dragons have discovered so many more worlds that none of the other dragon types know about. That bodes ill as well." After a pause, she added, "I assume you four will continue to go wherever this Box thing takes you."

Drago shrugged. "I suppose so. It's working well enough for us."

"Then, you should take me to this Salazar-3 place, in case mom and dad want to do something about it."

"I'll take you now, while it's dark. Much safer that way." Drago and Carla rose and left.

I then suggested, "Come on. Let's take an evening stroll around this oasis. It's lots cooler here at night. The smells are intoxicating, too."

Diana slipped an arm around me, and I led her outside, walking along the warm sands surrounding the waters, which had nearly regained their former height now that the Pitcher of Endless Water was back in it, adding its life-giving waters to those of the spring. Behind us, I could hear the four voices of the Unarmed Escort friends chatting softly, sharing their ideas and feelings.

Ben said, "Seriously, you two should get Felix to do his thing. It's great that we're starting our family. Right Carli?"

She giggled. I turned them out, focusing on just feeling the presence of my sister. I hadn't realized how much I missed her since she left.

After a time, she asked, "So are you ever going to return to Byron Falls? You know you should, but you'll not recognize the place." She chuckled. "You see, Ben and Carli are modernizing us. They are working on something called a water tower, claiming it'll bring running water into our homes, along with something called a toilet. Oh, and running hot water—and you don't have to heat it up in a pot. I don't know if they will be successful or not, but they're working hard on those projects too."

"Sure Diana, sure we are. It's just I can't say when. We're learning so much and helping right so many wrongs. I have to tell you about what the archmage told us today. I've never felt as good as when she said what she said about us and what we did for the Banner family."

She laughed. Oh, how I love to hear her laugh. Emotions. I felt rather adrift in a sea of conflicting emotions, before I realized it was probably just the female body and its hormones adjusting to creating a new life.

Later that night, Carla took them home. As we waved goodbye, Drago said, "Now let's close this door and see if we've handled it all. I'm more than ready to learn some new spells."

"Oh, let's!" declared Lexi. Tiff merely nodded.

With a decisive move, Drago slid the bar across the door, locking us inside. The Handled light turned on, and we all felt a slight vibration as the Box departed this oasis and probably this world. Suddenly, all four of us raced to the wall to retrieve our new spell pages! I brought up the rear, knowing it would take me some time to deal with the pages—either that or cast another Morph Me spell, which I didn't feel like doing just now. I rather felt mellow. Seeing just how good Diana was doing impressed me. I wanted that feeling to last a bit longer.

"Wow, look at all these pages, Felix!" Tiffany declared. "Don't worry. I'm grabbing yours for you. Lexi will insert them in your book for you. Wicked! We're going to learn to cast that Mystical Door. Now we're getting somewhere!"

Drago's booming voice called out, "Felix, we've

really got some power spells this time. We're going to be able to Modify the Weather. Oh, and here's the very spell I've longed for: Disintegrate! Wow. With this, I stand a chance of actually killing Adler without getting myself killed in the process. We're entering the big leagues, old boy, er girl. Come one. Are we going to practice some tonight yet?"

I laughed. "Drago, I'm going to get a good night's sleep first. I don't want to botch these spells."

He bellow laughed, but agreed, still drooling over the impressive array of spells we were going to be learning in the coming days. Secretly, I was impressed as I scanned down the list Tiffany had spread out on the table for me to read. Drago and I were up to learning Grade 6 spells! That alone was impressive. The girls were well into Grade 4 spells and were going to add a few Grade 5 spells to their collection.

Naturally, Drago just had to learn the Disintegrate spell first. However, when he discovered that first, he had to get past Adler's resistance to spells, and that second, Adler had a good chance to dodge out of the way of the spell, the dragon's enthusiasm for the spell lessened considerably. Still, if he got past both of those, the spell would drill a three-inch wide hole through the dragon, likely killing him if his head was the target.

What I found more useful was the In Case Of spell. "In case I am badly wounded, Teleport me to the Box" was one of my initial ideas for this spell. Soon, I had numerous others. So did Drago, who spent the day inventing them. "In case Adler paralyzes me, Teleport me to the Box" was one of his attempts.

True, we learned to Modify the Weather, but I wasn't sure this would be useful fighting dragons, which we seemed to be doing with alarming frequency. Yet, we could use this spell to help others, entire towns or villages even, by moving bad weather away or bringing rain to the area.

We picked up the Major Invulnerability spell, one that would protect us from even Grade 4 spells. If we ran into a battle with powerful mages, this one would help protect my girls; hence, I learned it well.

Then, Drago and I learned to See True, a spell that allowed us never to be fooled or misled by any illusion or lie. This, I found a useful spell indeed. However, the last of the Grade 6 spells we were given turned out to be invaluable, though not just yet. It was the Enchant It spell. This was the first spell in a series that a mage could use to create magical items! One acquired a flawless, very well made item, such as a sword or giant gemstone. After casting this spell on it, you then cast the desired spells into the object, capping it off with the Make Permanent, which was a Grade 8 spell. Yes, Drago and I discovered we now were on the path to being able to make magical items, if only we could get to the Grade 8 spell. Okay, I admit it; we both got greedy over this spell and its potential.

After that, we settled down and began picking up the other Grade 5 spells. In my current state, I found two of these spells particularly useful. One was Telekinesis, which I now used to feed myself and do other small, mundane things. The other was Fetch, which allowed me to fetch to me any object not weighing over twenty pounds and not farther than a mile from my position. Now this was a very useful spell. If I forgot something or needed something from the Box, I could cast Fetch and it would appear beside me or in my hands if I'd morphed into a form that had arms.

Finally, I was surprised and shocked to discover there was a spell that allowed me to send a message to another person on another world and to receive their reply! No longer would I be cut off from Diana!

Two months passed by while we dove into all these new spells. However, after the first month, I received another surprise, a good one. Both Lexi and Tiffany were pregnant too. I used my new spell to let Diana know the good news. On her return message, I could sense how pleased she was for us.

However, as we began learning to cast all these spells, both Tiffany and Lexi spent several days in bed, complaining of aches and pains, particularly in their arms. At first, we thought they must have caught a cold, but by the third day, we knew better. Tiff finally grasped what it was and what we could expect.

"Remember that booster shot we all got while entering that research place on Salazar-3? Well, remember what Adler and that doctor said it was about? Their princess procedure actually alters the person's DNA. He said, 'It merely alters your DNA to match your current princess forms. That way, when you have children, they will inherit your magnificent appearance.' I think that the booster shot has altered Lexi and my bodies DNA and that our bodies are now rebuilding themselves following that blueprint, in as much as it is possible to do so with fully grown people."

I wanted to rub my forehead, but just now, my body was in its new base format and didn't have arms. "So what are you saying?" I muttered, confused and wishing I knew more about such things, that I wasn't a primitive man.

"I think our bodies are going to turn into those of princesses, like yours, Felix," Tiffany replied with a sigh.

"Makes sense," Lexi muttered. "Well, Tiff, we can survive okay as princesses. It's not the end of the world. Besides, we have our morph spells at that ready. I just wish it would hurry up. I hate being sick like this, especially with all these new spells to learn."

I swallowed hard. "Maybe the Regeneration Ring will undo it," I suggested.

"No matter what, Felix, dear, we're not using it until after we have our babies," Tiff declared.

After five days, their "colds" vanished, as did their arms, which dropped off as fall leaves did in the fall. Their bosoms expanded to large melons, comparable to mine. Other than that, we detected no other physical changes. Both began making use of Morph Me or Invisible Servant spells, just as I was doing. However, at other times, they again worked on using their feet and toes to do things, just as those mental images we'd been implanted with suggested. Plus, they convinced me to do the same. I went along with this, not to make them feel better about it, but because I began to wonder about myself. Once I had our child, when I slipped the ring on my toe, would anything change at all? Had my DNA also been altered? I put this worry in the back of my mind. Time enough to worry about such things a year from now.

Curiously, the Box chose not to land until we'd learned our new spells. On the very day the girls finished up, we felt the floor jar slightly and knew we'd landed somewhere. Further, we knew once we opened the door that someone out there was desperate for our help. Taking a deep breath, we opened the door to the unknown, more than ready to come to their aid.

# Chapter 23—A Tale of Two "Sisters"

Manda Perez took after her father, whose passion was the gathering of knowledge. She combined that with her mother's love of studying cultural traditions. As a young child, her parents filled her head with all manner of ancient stories, and Manda dreamed of one day discovering the long lost tomb, El Origen de los Dragones by Beltran, the Wise, last seen millennia ago in a land called the Rainbow Hills. Thus, as an adolescent, Manda, the Gold, headed off on her life's quest, to find that ancient volume and learn where dragon kind originated. Manda wasn't interested in magic, nor was she interested in collecting great wealth. For her, wealth consisted of friends and knowledge, particularly historical studies.

So it was that Manda arrived on Rainbow's End some eight years ago, circling high above a small town on the extreme southern edge of the magnificent Rainbow Hills. Instantly, Manda knew why Beltran, the Wise, had brought his precious tomb here. If ever there was a land created by God, it was these vibrantly colored hills, in which bands of every color in a rainbow could be found and then some. Awestruck with the land's inherent beauty, Manda landed at the edge of the town, Villa Lopez, on a grassy knoll, where a young maiden was gathering up scattered wild flowers for a bouquet.

"Wow. You must be a Gold dragon," exclaimed the exited child. "My name is Blanca de Lopez."

Manda saw a young girl with long, wavy, raven hair, enchanting hazel eyes, and an angular face, quite pretty. In turn, Blanca saw a beautiful golden dragon, some eighty feet long with a huge wingspan. As she watched, Manda morphed into her human-like form. After blinking, Blanca saw a young woman apparently not too much older than herself with long, wavy golden locks. Her skin had a yellowish hue to it, but her large black eyes told anyone in the know she was a dragon.

"Pleased to meet you, Miss Blanca de Lopes. I'm Mandy Perez. The countryside here is breathtaking! What is this town called?"

"Villa Lopez. My father is Count Sanches de Lopez. He rules the town and lands around here. Mom is Countess Alita. She's a noblewoman. I'm picking wild flowers for our dinner table. Mom can't pick them because she's a noblewoman. I'm supposed to become a noblewoman when I reach my twelfth birthday, which is in six months. Of course, once I become a noblewoman, I won't be able to pick wild flowers either, but I still can study history and read books. Dad has the largest library of books for hundreds of miles. I don't know if that's true or not, but he has hundreds of them. I've read only a few so far. I'm still learning. Do you like to read?"

Manda smiled. "You bet I do. I also love history too."

"Well, why don't you come home with me? Papa can show you his library. You simply must come."

Chuckling, Manda agreed. "Sure Blanca. If he has that many books, I'd love to read them too." *Maybe the El Origen de los Dragones is in his collection. Good place to start looking.*

Manda found walking into the sprawling town was enchanting. Adobe homes were built from the colorful clays of the hills. A vibrant red home stood next to a bright green home, next to a royal blue home, next to a canary yellow home. She found this aspect breathtaking. A grey stone manor house stood in the center of the town. Here Count Sanches welcomed her and proudly showed her his library, which filled up one entire room. The odors of ancient volumes permeated the air in the room, filling Manda with a reading lust she'd never felt before.

She met Blanca's mother, Countess Alita, and was at first shocked to see she had no arms. That wasn't true. She had arms, but they were tied horizontally across her back and hidden beneath her billowing gown. Manda was also surprised to see how Alita seemed to float or glide effortlessly across the stone floor. Over supper, Manda was

314

introduced to the centuries-old tradition of these noblewomen. At once, she was enthralled and vowed to study this tradition and learn about its origins in the distant past.

Thus began a close friendship between Manda and Blanca, a friendship that only grew tighter when Blanca was first bound months later.

"This is so hard. I keep almost falling," exclaimed Blanca, when she first tried to stand and walk that first day. She wore a billowing red gown, held out by seven petticoats. Manda had helped tie Blanca's special boots on her feet and saw the incredibly tall wedges. Noblewomen stood almost on their toes, but the wedge helped them keep their balance. To keep from tumbling, they were forced to take tiny steps, barely a few inches per stride. Hence, for the first month or so, a chain that didn't permit too large a stride tied Blanca's boots together—hence, the young girl's complaint.

Countess Alita giggled. "I remember saying almost the same thing, Blanca, when I was first bound. All noblewomen say something similar. Don't worry. In no time, you'll become accustomed to it, and we can remove the chain. Honestly, Manda, you are noble, too. You should be bound."

"I best help dear Blanca learn to walk first," Manda deflected Alita's suggestion.

After that, the two were almost inseparable, though Blanca had a young servant girl to assist her and who followed her everywhere, just as Manda did. Both spent hours each day in the library, while Manda read books aloud for the two of them.

Years later, Manda's great patience paid off. She found a passage in an ancient book that told of the coming of a Gold dragon who called himself Beltran. It said he was an ancient dragon, but extremely wise. The book also alluded to the fact that Beltran loved these colored hills.

During the years, occasionally Manda assisted the Count's solders. Villa Lopez was on the main trade route from the Southern Lands on up through the Rainbow Hills to Imperial, their capital city, where their Emperor lived. Bandits sometimes raided the many caravans. When a caravan was robbed, the Count had no choice but to send out a party to try to capture the bandits and more importantly recover the stolen goods. In such matters, Manda proved invaluable. She would fly high in the sky and locate the fleeing bandits. Since ordinary swords and arrows couldn't even penetrate her skin, she helped in the actual fighting as well, sparing many of the Count's soldiers' lives. Thus, Manda was endeared to this ruling family in many ways, not the least her undying search of the history and origins of their noblewoman traditions.

Not everyone was pleased with the Count. His cousin, Eduardo, and Rodrigo Tito coveted his throne. In fact, Eduardo often complained Sanches stole the throne from his father, though no one living knew the truth of the matter. For years, the pair tried numerous methods to wrestle the throne from Sanches, including sponsoring bandit raids. Those always failed because of the intervention of that damnable Gold dragon, Manda. Hence, the pair finally knew that they'd have to remove the Count and the Gold dragon. Thus, they began their plots.

Removal of a human was easy, while a dragon was not. This, they soon discovered. A pair of assassins slipped into the manor complex late one night. Quickly, they slit the throats of the Count and Countess. Emboldened, they slipped into Blanca's room to execute her as well. Like Alita, her legs were pulled up behind her head, crossed behind her neck, and tied with a satin strip. Just as they crept to her narrow bed to slice her throat, Manda stirred. She was sleeping in a nearby bed. Hearing a slight noise, she rose to see what was going on and saw the two men with swords dripping blood hovering over her dear friend.

At once, the two assassins pivoted to face this yellowish-skinned human, swinging their swords at her. To their shock, both blades bounced off her body, though one blade shattered. Neither man survived Manda's return fist blows. She delivered a blow to their heads, crushing their skulls, killing them instantly, but also waking Blanca.

Manda went to her side, untied her legs, and helped her slip into a nightgown. Together, they found the bodies of Blanca's parents and sounded the alarm.

Because the assassins were dead, they couldn't implicate or tell anyone who had hired them, namely Rodrigo and Eduardo. Immediately, Eduardo claimed the throne and was proclaimed Count Eduardo de Lopez. He appointed Rodrigo as his second in command. Unfortunately, they couldn't just toss Blanca out of the manor house. By law, she was entitled to dwell here until she either died or got married. After the assassination, Manda never left Blanca's side, sleeping beside her to guarantee her dear friend's safety. This, the two new rulers found intolerable, but could do nothing about it, save to do what they could to keep Blanca from having any suitors.

By law, however, if Blanca married, then she and her husband would be the rightful Count and Countess, usurping Count Eduardo. He knew this, but couldn't eliminate Blanca, because Manda was always with her. No one had the means to "kill" a dragon. That required enchanted blades and a lengthy fight during which the odds were the blade wielder would be the one who died, not the dragon.

When Blanca turned eighteen, she insisted on sitting on the throne as the Countess. Count Eduardo hadn't married, but that didn't matter. From Blanca and Manda's extensive readings, they could quote the law, and did so to Eduardo and Rodrigo, who had no choice but to capitulate to her demand. Worse, since she was eighteen, she was now legally able to search for her own suitor. Naturally, Count Eduardo did all he could to dissuade any suitor, including having them murdered.

However, he had no idea she and a childhood friend were serious. His name was Martinez. After several suitors were found murdered, even though Blanca hadn't desired them, Martinez and Blanca decided to keep their relationship a secret and that it might be wise for him to leave the town for a while.

Then word came to Villa Lopez that their Emperor

demanded all noblewomen and noble men have their arms removed. Since the Emperor was setting the example for the realm, most found it difficult to resist the Imperial Decree. With the noblewomen, this was a non-issue. Why?

After having their arms bound horizontally across their middle backs for years on end, only undone while bathing, their arms atrophied and joints calcified, almost to the point where the noblewomen couldn't move them on their own. Thus, removal was in many ways a preferable action. Not so for the noblemen, of course.

Since Eduardo had yet to marry, he found this Imperial Decree odious, and refused to have it done. Further, he insisted Blanca not have it done as well, fearing if she did it, then he'd have to do it too. That strategy worked for several weeks, until the arrival of the Emperor's Representatives. One was a doctor and one was a captain of the Royal Guards. With the pair came a dozen soldiers. The two were tasked with seeing the Emperor's Imperial Decree was implemented in Villa Lopez.

Imperial was five weeks travel north and east of the town. Hence, the representatives had no idea the Emperor (the black dragon) had been killed and this Imperial Decree cancelled or rather made voluntary at the person's discretion. They would only find out about this five weeks from their arrival date.

"But this is madness!" screeched Count Eduardo. "I'm not going to have it done."

"But it is completely painless," the doctor protested.

"I don't care. I'll not have it done. Now get out of my court!"

The captain had anticipated such reactions. He and the doctor bowed respectively and backed out of the throne room, ready to go onto their alternative plan. One way or another, the Emperor's decree would be carried out.

Having heard the commotion, Countess Blanca, accompanied by Manda and her young servant girl, Juana, met the two men as they were leaving.

"Excuse me. I'm sorry I move so slowly," she began apologetically, "but are you here to carry out the Imperial

Decree? To remove noblewomen's arms, which we don't need anyway?"

The captain answered, "Why yes, Countess Blanca. That we are. Your Count Eduardo is being a stubborn man. It must be done. Already Count Edgar and Countess Molly of Beckworth, that's adjacent to Brackenmoor Swamp, have had this done."

"I see. Well, I wish it done. Until now, Count Eduardo wouldn't let me have it done, but since you're here, can I get it done without the Count's permission? I'm of age."

While the captain smiled, the doctor answered her, "Of course, Countess. We should see to it now, if you have the time. It won't take long. It's painless. We'll have you back on your feet in hours."

"Oh thank you. Manda must come with me. She's protecting me from the Count, who had my parents killed and stole my throne. Besides, my shoulders ache when they undo my arms at bath times. I can barely move them."

Several hours later, a broad smile illuminated Blanca's face, as she looked down at the nicely healed, but empty, shoulders. It had been painless as promised, but she felt slightly giddy having drunk several healing potions.

As she and Manda walked slowly back to their section of the large manor house, she said, "There Manda. Now there is no going back on our traditions. I'm a noblewoman for all time. Isn't this just perfect? By the way, if we can ever get rid of Eduardo's spies, why don't we continue our historical research? I thought we might be getting close to the origins of noblewomen's traditions."

"Oh lets. We've ignored our history studies for far too long, Countess Blanca. Let's, but shouldn't you visit with Martinez? He wants your hand in marriage, you know. Oops, now you've no hands." Both giggled and secretly sent a message to Martinez.

The next morning, Count Eduardo sipped his morning ale, prior to diving into the breakfast feasts he insisted upon having. Before he finished the pint, he passed out, compliments of the knockout drug the doctor slipped into his ale. They ignored the other unconscious men, including Rodrigo, and dragged the Count off to the doctor's makeshift room. Hours later, they had some of his men carry him to his bed, where he eventually awoke and shrieked loudly. Everyone in the manor house now knew what had happened to him, that he'd become a proper nobleman, as dictated by the Emperor's Imperial Decree.

Four days later, twenty year old, nobleman Martinez de Lopez, heir to his father's Caravan Outfitters business, and his new servant boy waited behind The Blue House, a popular local pub. He'd gotten a secret message to Countess Blanca, telling her when and where to meet, and that he had a big surprise for her.

Already her staff had altered her gowns to remove the bulk in back where her arms used to lay horizontally. Today, she wore a light blue gown, Martinez's favorite color, hoping to please him with her total commitment to their ancient noblewoman tradition.

In turn, he now wore a specially tailored suit, which had no arms or sleeves. Yes, he desperately wanted to please Countess Blanca and knew that if they could marry, he'd be the true Count, and that per the Emperor's decree, he'd have to have it done. Thus, he'd gone ahead and gotten his arms painlessly removed. Now he waited patiently to surprise the love of his life.

A pair of surprised "Oh's!" echoed behind the pub when the two young lovers met and saw the other. Manda smiled, and commented, "Well, now you two are a perfect match for each other." She and the two servants stepped back, allowing the pair to embrace and whisper privately to each other. However, neither had any idea how they were going to eliminate Count Eduardo.

The Count's disposition turned even more sadistic or perhaps psychotic might be a better description. He ordered the doctor to turn Manda Perez into a proper noblewoman. Alas, the doctor did try, having again used his knockout drug on her. However, to his dismay, none of his cutting tools could pierce her skin. In the end, he just gave up on Manda, much to the annoyance of the Count.

The doctor stayed in the manor house for four weeks, performing many other surgeries, though most were on noblewomen. After hearing what happened to the Count, many noblemen left town on "urgent business," returning only after the Emperor's Representatives moved on south to the next major town.

***

Euric, though very pleased with his giant pile of magic items, grew quite bored on Salazar-3, once the biogenetic agents that altered a person's DNA were developed. These reformed human bodies into the familiar princess form Euric had made using his spells. Thus, Adler was relieved when Euric announced he was leaving for his home world.

With bags of magic items tied to his dragon form, Euric Shadow Walked back to Rainbow's End. However, this time, he decided he didn't want to live in a desert. For a time, he flew around the world and quickly became fascinated with the Rainbow Hills. Here, he decided he'd make his new home, but he needed to find a secure cavern in which to store his accumulated wealth. For days, he flew over these painted hills, looking for just a place. Then by total chance, he found a secluded opening in a hillside, far from any human habitation, but somewhat north of Villa Lopez.

Squeezing inside, he discovered the ancient home of another dragon, one who loved books. Euric had nothing but disdain for books and shoved them off into a giant pile in once corner. Then, he undid his many bags of treasure and magical items. Finally satisfied his new home was in order, he took off, visiting the nearest town to get orientated.

Euric knew the Counts were always a good source of income and treasure. Thus, he changed to his human form and paid a visit on Count Eduardo. Yes, he was very surprised to find the man as armless as the many princesses he'd made these past many months.

"I'm here to offer my services for pay, mind you,"

Euric began. "I am called Euric. I'm an ancient Red dragon. None can withstand my blazing hot fires. If you have enemies, I can roast them for you. I take magical items and gems as payment."

"I don't believe you. Anyone can say they're a red dragon, but it's quite another thing actually to be one," he retorted.

Annoyed, Euric morphed into his huge dragon form, shocking everyone in the throne room. After morphing back, he bellowed, "Fool!"

Count Eduardo recovered from his shock and declared, "Euric, I believe we need to talk! Everyone, out. Get out. Leave us be."

Hastily, the other courtesans fled the room, though the noblewomen moved very slowly, compared to the men. Rodrigo was hesitant to leave, but Count Eduardo nodded, their secret sign that the Count was serious. Once they were alone, the Count explained.

"Look. I have a problem in my court. It's that damnable Gold dragon called Manda. She's always with the Countess Blanca, so I can't get to the Countess and kill her. If she marries, her husband could take my throne, and I can't have that, now can I? No, I can't. Over the years, Manda has endeared herself to many in this town. With the Imperial Decree that all noblewomen have their arms removed, I tried to have the doctor do that to her, but the man claimed his knives wouldn't cut her. I should have taken that chance to murder the Countess, but alas, I thought the doctor would succeed."

"You want that nasty Gold dead?" Euric asked, seeing a potentially large profit to be made here.

"Er, for all her damned meddling, that would be too kind. No, I'd like her hobbled up like a true noblewoman."

"Heh, heh, heh, I do believe I might be of service here," Euric bellowed. He made his own suggestion, one that only required his spells. "I believe I can make her into a perfect noblewoman, a princess, and at the same time, prevent her from ever morphing back into her dragon form."

"Perfect! Perfect! Perfect! Make it so, Euric; make it so. What payment do you desire?"

An hour later, Count Eduardo summoned the unsuspecting Manda to the throne room. "Sit. Sit. We've some business to discuss. It seems bandits are attacking a caravan making its way to Villa Lopez. We could use your help once more. Drink up. It's the best ale from my private stock." He took another sip, though his servant boy had to hold the mug to his lips, something that forever would annoy the Count, who felt more like a helpless baby than a man. *Well, soon, this damnable Gold dragon will know how it feels too.* He watched her take a drink as well.

Manda knew he was up to some trickery, but didn't know what. She had stopped bandits many times for the late Count, so it wasn't surprising that Count Eduardo would ask her to do the same thing. Then, she sensed the drug affecting her system. "What have you done to me?" she bellowed.

Count Eduardo sneered and laughed. "Knocking you out, foolish dragon!"

As soon as he said that, he knew he should have kept quiet, at least until the drug took full effect. Manda partially morphed into her Gold dragon form, just enough to release a blast of searing flames from her mouth. She slumped unconscious on the floor. Her partially morphed form slowly reverted back to her human shape.

Unfortunately, for Count Eduardo, Rodrigo, and the servant boy, they found themselves in the direct path of her blast. Rodrigo dove out of the way; the flames roasted his legs, crippling him. In the tall wedge-heeled boots, Count Eduardo could barely move and was roasted alive along with his young servant.

Euric stepped into the room, saw the unconscious Manda, and stepped on Rodrigo's head, putting the man out of his misery. He picked up the large bag of gemstones. "I always deliver what I promise. Too bad the Count isn't alive to see the result." The dragon set to work.

He knew Gold dragons had a high resistance to magic, perhaps even higher than he did. Hence, he cast the

Moronic Mind spell on the unconscious Manda a dozen times, just to make sure at least one time it succeeded. He then cast his usual Morph Other spell, but had to do it ten times before it finally took on the unconscious dragon. He paused, smiling at the perfection of his handiwork, which alas the Count wouldn't be able to appreciate. However, Euric would. He'd not have to kill this dragon. Next, he focused and cast his special spell, the one that had made him fabulously wealthy in his old age. After the eighth casting, he felt it take on her.

Now, she was an idiot in human form, looking just like one of the many gorgeous unarmed princesses with the giant bosom that he'd made. Further, with the IQ of a moron, she'd not be able to cast any spells. More importantly, she'd not be able to morph back into her dragon form. She was doomed to be eternally in this nearly helpless human form for the next five hundred years or so. Bellow laughing, Euric walked out of the throne room, carrying his new bag of treasure.

Seeing him come out, Countess Blanca went inside, though her servant had to open the door for her. "Oh my God! What's happened here? Manda, Manda. Please, see if you can wake her up. Is she alive? The Count. My God. He's dead. What happened here?"

"Countess, she's alive. I don't know. What shall we do?" asked Juana.

"Send word to Martinez. Tell him to come at once. Guards. Guards, come. Carry her to my chambers."

Several guards rushed in, saw the carnage, realized the Countess was now in charge, and struggled to carry the very heavy Manda off. Meanwhile, Juana rushed out to send the homing pigeon with its message to Martinez.

He arrived very worried. Just as slowly, he entered the throne room first. Seeing the dead men, he relaxed and moved carefully in his tall wedge-heeled boots to her chambers, his manservant following him discretely.

"Oh Blanca, what's happened here?" he gushed upon entering her quarters.

Slowly, the pair moved over to each other, sharing

at last a brief kiss. Blanca then told him what she knew, which was very little. An hour later, their servants managed to awaken Manda, who shrieked and then settled down.

"Oh, I'm pretty now. Aren't I? I'm a perfect noblewoman too, just like you, Blanca. How wonderful." She babbled on for a time. "Oh, I need proper dresses, don't I?"

Countess Blanca sent for her dressmakers, who hastily got Manda properly attired, though Blanca insisted they chain her boots together until Manda learned to take the proper tiny steps, especially hard to do since her feet were hidden from view beneath the billowing gown.

By the time they had Manda dressed, Countess Blanca and Martinez knew something was horribly wrong with Manda's mind. She was acting as if she were a small child and had no idea of adult matters.

Thus, Countess Blanca took control. "Martinez, marry me now. That way, you will be the undisputed Count. Together, we will rule Villa Lopez before anyone can challenge us. I'm so glad you went ahead and became a proper nobleman. Now, no one can challenge you or us."

Martinez grinned. "I always dreamed we would marry, so I wanted to be the proper nobleman for you. I'm so honored, Blanca, but I think you're right. We should do this at once, before others get their own ideas. Villa Lopez has had enough of Eduardo's tyranny."

"You should marry," Manda babbled. "But how do you walk? I can't see my feet. Are they tied together? Why? I'm hungry. Who's going to feed me? I think I need help. This is a pretty dress. Do I look pretty too? Blanca is very pretty. Don't you think so, Martinez?" She babbled on.

Blanca quickly took charge. She knew something was profoundly wrong with Manda, but had no idea what. By evening, she'd summoned the town's priest, had him marry them, and hired a new servant girl for Manda. Ria had some experience helping her mother, who was also a noblewoman. She seamlessly slipped into her new role with Manda, greatly lessening the dragon's confusion.

After the three were fed their dinner in the Great Hall, Ria led Manda to her usual room. "But I protect Blanca."

"She has a lot of soldiers doing that now. We need to get you undressed and into bed, like the proper noblewoman you are, Manda."

"Oh. Well okay then. I want to be proper. This is my room. Those dresses won't fit me now."

"We know, Manda. Tomorrow, the dressmakers will prepare more gowns for you."

Once undressed, Ria had her lie down on the narrow bed. Gently, she brushed out Manda's long golden tresses, currently nearly two feet longer than she normally kept them. "Now then, lie back. I'll bind your feet like a proper noblewoman."

It took some effort on the young girl's part to get Manda's legs tucked up under her head, crossed at her ankles. Hastily, she secured her ankles together with a satin ribbon. "There you go, Manda. You look perfect now."

"But I can't move. I'm helpless like this. Are you sure this is right? Oh, I remember. It must be. Blanca always sleeps like this. My legs are throbbing. Is that right? Should they hurt so? I might not be able to sleep. Will you stay with me a while, Ria? I'm so hungry. Why am I so hungry?"

Ria giggled. "But we just had supper, Manda. Go to sleep. It's been a very trying day, I think. You look perfect and very beautiful. One day, I hope to be as beautiful as you are, Manda."

"I am? That's good. I should be beautiful. . ." Her voice trailed off as she fell into a deep sleep, in spite of being hungry and with aching hips.

Countess Blanca and Count Martinez were kept very busy in the ensuing days. Out with the old, corrupt personnel and in with the new was their motto. After nearly a week, Ria finally had to do something about Manda and her incessant complaints about being hungry.

"Countess, it's noblewoman Manda. She's

constantly complaining about being hungry, no matter how much I feed her. I think something must be wrong with her." Ria was only twelve, but she could see that Manda was growing steadily weaker and must be ill.

"Oh my goodness! I just remembered," Countess Blanca exclaimed in a flash of insight. "She's a dragon. She always took off to feed once a week. Manda once joked we could only satisfy her hunger if she ate all our suppers for a week. Come on. Let's tell her she has to change into her dragon form and go feed."

Slowly, Blanca and Martinez walked from their throne room to Manda's private quarters, next to the suite Blanca had used until marrying. While Blanca in her billowing dress was quite used to taking the requisite tiny steps, Martinez was still getting used to being a nobleman. His boots were chained together so that he couldn't overstep and take a nasty tumble. While he never complained openly, Blanca sensed Martinez was hiding that he was positively terrified.

"Hungry. Blanca, hungry," Manda said softly. She was lying on her sofa, right where Ria left her after dressing her.

"Manda, you are supposed to change into your Gold dragon form and fly off to hunt and feed. You have been doing it once a week," Blanca explained.

"Don't know how. Do you know how to change me? Am I really a dragon? I look like a pretty princess. You have princesses here, don't you?"

"Surely you can remember how to change, Manda. You have to."

"Ria changes my dress. Maybe she can change me too."

After more silly exchanges, Blanca gave up. Sadly, she and Martinez walked back to the throne room to continue to deal with the day's business matters. However, she left orders for the staff to prepare more food and for Ria to feed Manda several more times each day.

After three weeks, it was obvious this wasn't working. Manda had become so weak that Ria was unable to get her out of bed. Blanca sobbed and fretted over Manda, fearing she was soon going to lose her childhood friend and "sister."

# Chapter 24—Recoveries

The Box landed, and we were actually ready for it, eagerly anticipating our next challenge. I had my Invisible Servant spell working to perfection, making it appear as though I really did have a personal servant helping me with my needs. Admittedly, I did find using the spell vastly easier than using my feet and toes as fingers and hands as I was supposed to be doing. Besides, I was determined to make this work. I wasn't about to eliminate my son or daughter by using the Regeneration Ring to undo Euric's magical alteration of my body.

As Tiff said, "I was about to have a unique experience that no men ever had." That wasn't what concerned me the most. Rather, I couldn't bring myself to eliminate the new life that we'd created. I consider life precious. Likewise, Tiffany and Lexi now looked like I did and took to using their Invisible Servant spells as well, though we three would cast our Morph Me spells as soon as we needed bodies with arms.

Drago said, "Well, I'm powerfully hungry, gang. I've eaten up all the food I stashed in here, so I'm going to have to go hunting soon. Please don't go getting yourselves in trouble until I get back."

"We'll try to stay out of trouble," I teased, allowing Drago to open the door. All ignored the familiar message that said to press Handled when done.

Stepping outside, I exclaimed, "What? Where are we?"

Glancing around, it seemed we were inside a building of some kind! The walls were stone, but here the floor was hardwood. As I looked around, a sign appeared on the Box, which said Doctors. On the second look, I got oriented a little. We were at one end of a hallway. A servant woman carrying bedding came around the far corner, saw us, shrieked, dropped her load, and fled. A young girl came out of the next room to see what was going on. She saw the sign over the Box and the four of us.

"Are you the doctors? Manda needs help badly. I'm Ria, her servant. She's now a noblewoman too."

Just then, several soldiers came rushing up, swords drawn. "Who are you? Where did you come from?" one called out. "Be careful, Ria. These could be assassins."

"Hello. We just arrived. If someone is ill, we might be able to help them," I spoke up.

"She's a noblewoman, not an assassin. Lower your swords, men. Fetch the Count and Countess. Best let them decide what to do. You stay with Manda, Ria." The leader of the guards lowered his sword, and I relaxed.

Noblewoman? Could we be back on the same world, Rainbow's End? If so, the girls and I would fit right in and help gain instant acceptance of our group. I hazarded a question.

"Excuse me, but are we on the Rainbow's End?"

"You're in the Count and Countess's manor house in Villa Lopez at the southern edge of the Rainbow Hills," the guard answered, eying us closely.

I relaxed, knowing we were already accepted as their society's noblewomen. For once, our body forms opened doors, so to speak. Presently, the rulers appeared. She seemed to glide along the hall, her flared gown floating along. In contrast, he wore a fine suit and the same highly polished boots with very tall wedge heels that Major Ron wore. I concluded he recently had become a nobleman, since a chain held his boots close together so he couldn't take too large a step. Neither had the slightest trace of arms, just as we hadn't. When they saw us, their faces visibly relaxed. Obviously, we were also noblewomen, and thus not a threat.

"Hello. We've just arrived in our magic box behind us. Is someone ill? Perhaps we can help," I offered, breaking the ice. "I'm Felix Pelingham." I decided not to introduce the others just yet, especially Drago, for obvious reasons.

"Mages?" he asked.

"Yes, we're all mages."

"I'm Count Martinez. This is my wife, Countess Blanca de Lopez. Blanca's dearest friend and companion is very ill. Please, could you look at her and see if you can save her life?"

"Manda—she's a Gold dragon, but a vicious Red dragon named Euric came here a few weeks back and turned her into a noblewoman, but she's dying," Blanca said. "Please, you must save her."

From the corner of my eyes, I saw Drago jerk to attention at the mention of a Gold dragon. I couldn't help but smile.

"Sure, let's see her," I suggested.

Slowly, the pair continued to move towards us, but then turned into the room partway down the hall. Quickly, we joined them, moving many times faster than the pair did. Silently, I was thankful I wasn't wearing the boots these rulers were wearing. Drago nearly knocked me over, as he rushed to the bedside of the ill woman. While he examined her, I asked Countess Blanca to tell us what had happened to her and in as much detail as possible.

She told us about the assassination of her parents and that Manda had saved her life, frustrating the usurper of the throne, Count Eduardo. She rapidly explained all that had happened, with particular emphasis on what happened to Manda Perez, the Gold dragon. While she was telling us her tale, we watched as Drago hovered over Manda. She looked incredibly weak, but Euric had made her look as if she was a fabulous looking beauty queen or princess. Okay, I admit it. I found her very attractive too. That speaks to Euric's art, even if it's a despicable use of magic.

"Manda's starving to death," Drago pronounced. "She's definitely under that awful Moronic Mind spell, which is preventing her from being able to morph back into her native form. Even if she could morph back, without her arms or front legs, she couldn't even walk. She'll be as helpless as the emperor was."

"That's what I thought, Drago. So how do we help her?" I asked.

"We've got to get her back into her native form or she's going to die."

"Okay. We still have a couple of the curing potions. I'll fetch them."

Tiff chuckled. "Are you going to float them out here?"

Now it was my turn to chuckle. We both knew I could have retrieved them using my Invisible Servant spell or my new Fetch spell, but that might shock these people. She darted back inside the Box, returning a minute later with our last two potions, holding a bag with them in it between her teeth. As she carried them to Drago, I hoped we'd never need this kind of potion again. That spell was incredibly nasty on the victim.

As we watched him administer the potions, I saw a side of Drago I'd never seen before. He was extremely gentle with her, but efficient, getting both potions into her system. Considering she was only marginally conscious, I was thankful he was doing it. Cradling her head up in one arm, he gentle poured small amounts of the greyish liquid into her mouth, forced open by his thumb.

"Well, I hope two will do the job. If it doesn't, I'll head back to Byron Falls tomorrow. Now we wait. By morning, she should be able to morph back, but we'll see."

"Drago, I don't understand something. If she was starving, why couldn't they just keep pumping food into her?" I envisioned sitting beside her and continuously feeding her nourishing meals.

Drago's deep laugh brought a smile to my face. "Silly human. Her physical size is now that of one of you humans, barely one-fifteenth her normal size. Her stomach is very tiny in this form. There's no way you could get fifteen times the amount of food you normally eat into her or any other human. She's been slowly starving to death. I swear I'm going to kill Euric!"

"I'm with you, Drago. What can we do for her now? Wait until tomorrow?"

"Yes, wait. If she wakes up, see if you can get some meats in her system. Meanwhile, I'm going to fly about and locate some antelope and a good place to take her, like a grassy knoll. I'll have antelope there ready to feed her, once I get her there. She's likely to be too weak to fly there, so I'll carry her. Message me if there's any change in her."

"Will do. Let us know if there's anything else we can do for her."

"Locate where Euric is hiding," he growled and left, a guard showing him the way out of the manor house.

Tiffany suggested, "You know, Lexi, what we need is to puree the food so she can rather drink it and so that it's more digestible. For once, I regret not having our electrical appliances."

"What's a puree?" I asked.

Lexi replied, "I agree, Tiff. Maybe we can find a way to puree it using some of our spells. Come on. Let's find the kitchen around here. Oh, dear, it's a smooth pulp of liquidized food, usually fruits and vegetables, but her idea is to do it to meat, making it easier for her body to rapidly digest it."

I felt useless in the kitchen and accepted Countess Blanca's invitation to join them in their throne room.

"So tell me, what did Euric do to you?" she asked.

With little else to do, I decided to tell her most everything. Besides, we had eliminated the Black dragon posing as their Emperor. Yes, my story was quite lengthy, since much of it happened on this world, first in the western edge of the Rainbow Hills, then in the northern section of Imperial, then on another continent, and now here in the south of the Rainbow Hills.

"What? You mean it was one of those nasty dragons that ordered us noblemen to have our arms removed and to wear these hobbling boots?" exclaimed Martinez.

"To be quite blunt about it, Count, yes. It was all a diabolical plot. Having made all the key officers in the Royal Guards helpless men, the dragons ordered the barbarians of the eastern lands to attack. With the officers completely helpless to fight back, your towns and cities would have soon been overrun. They also took many of the new noblemen and women off world, selling them into sexual slavery. We were able to stop the barbarians and even rescue a few of your nobles. I'm afraid you're stuck being as you are, just as Count Edgar and Countess Molly are over in Beckworth near the start of the swamplands. You two couples have much in common. Perhaps, you could visit them."

"You mean they're completely helpless too?" he asked.

"Yes, but you don't have to be helpless. We can do many things using our feet and toes as our hands. True, I've been cheating a whole lot by using one of my spells, the Invisible Servant. Actually, Tiffany, Lexi, and I can show you both how to do some things. We did that for Count Edgar and Countess Molly. I'll see about arranging a visit as soon as we get Manda saved."

"Oh would you? I can't begin to tell you how terrified I am," he responded. "I'm petrified all the time, every hour, every minute. I so want to be the best for Blanca, but honestly, I can't do much of anything."

"I agree. As long as you both wear those boots, which you can't take off by yourselves, there's darn little you can do. Heck, walking is a big enough challenge." I hoped to set them at ease. It worked.

Count Martinez laughed. "That's an understatement, if I ever heard one. Really, I can see why they have to chain my boots together, forcing me to take small steps. Weeks ago, I had my servant boy not chain them. First thing I did was fall on my face. God, that was so weird. I was flailing my arms to get my balance and nothing happened! Well, that's not true. I got a bloody nose for my trouble."

Blanca giggled. "I keep telling him, we noblewomen have always had this problem. I did too when they first bound my arms and put these wedge boots on me. I was twelve and dependent on Manda for lots of help. After a month, they unchained my boots. Don't worry, dear, you'll soon get used to it and won't have to have them chained. Actually, it's much worse for noblewomen. We can't even see our feet, which often get tangled up in the petticoats."

"I hope so, but what bothers me is I've done all this for you and it's for no good purpose," he lamented. "I can't even help you with your needs."

"Hey, many noblemen have been victimized, just as you have been. What matters now is how you handle it. Flourish and prosper. Don't let your handicaps rule your lives," I replied.

"Say, is it possible for us to learn how to cast that Invisible Servant spell of yours? Blanca, if we could, then we'd not be so darn helpless."

"Well, it is a beginning spell, Grade 1 to be precise. Let me think about that. Not everyone is able to wield magical energies."

"I can't ask for more. Maybe this Count Edgar can give me some additional hints. I would never have had this done to me if I wasn't totally devoted to Blanca."

"I can see that. Now you can even start your own family, just as we are."

Both grinned sheepishly, and I suspected they'd already been working on that one.

The girls returned bringing a pitcher of a brownish looking liquid. Tiffany declared, "We did it. This pitcher holds an entire roast. Now the trick will be to get it into Manda's system. You coming?"

"Okay. Back later on, Count, Countess." Carefully, I rose and followed them, thankful I was wearing my moccasins and not those tall-heeled boots.

As I watched the girls, I marveled at their skill and efficiency. Both had morphed into forms with arms, so while one lifted up Manda's head, the other spoon-fed her the thick puree. By the time we were ready for bed, they had managed to get the entire pitcher into Manda's stomach. By morning, we were convinced this action made all other actions possible, for she'd regained a little strength.

Drago gently lifted Manda up and carried her out of the manor house. We three followed behind them, morphed into forms with arms and ready to help in any way we could. He teleported to a grassy knoll on a yellow

335

hillside. Here, green fought with yellow, though at the top of the knoll, a band of red earth appeared. He had brought two antelope here last night, and he laid her down next to one of the carcasses. We landed beside them and watched.

"Okay, Manda, you simply have to morph into your dragon form. If you don't, you're going to die of starvation," Drago said. "Please, you must try; you must live."

She whispered, "I'm so weak. I don't know if I can do it."

"Sure you can. You're lots stronger than these humans are, and they've done an awful lot of morphing. So I know you can do it."

As we watched, keeping our new fingers crossed, she focused and made the attempt. Drago and I both sensed she simply wasn't going to make it. In desperation, I focused and cast Morph Other, attempting to morph her into a dragon's form. Drago saw what I was doing. He rapidly cast his spell too. Lexi and Tiffany were only seconds behind him. Together, we shot four Morph Other spells on to Manda, adding our energies to hers.

I've never been as thankful for a magical energy flash as I was then. We blinked and Manda's real body lay on her side, nearly eighty feet long. We dove out of the way. Drago exhaled heavily. Then, he lugged one carcass over to her head and mouth. Honestly, Manda's Golden head was as large as my entire body. Impressive. "Come on, Manda. Eat. The worst is over," Drago encouraged her.

Finally, her jaws opened and he pushed the antelope into her mouth. The crunch sound startled us. I admit I've never seen a dragon actually eat before. We three found it more than unsettling. She pulverized the bones as we might chew a steak. I swallowed hard.

A half hour later, the antelope was gone, and Manda was asleep again. Drago took us aside. "Thanks. We've done it. I couldn't have succeeded without your help. I'll stay here and watch over her. It'll be a few days before she's regained her strength."

"Okay, Drago. We'll see what we can do to find the

red dragon's lair. We all have scores to settle with Euric now," I declared. He nodded.

First, we returned to the Manor House in Villa Lopez to relay the good news to the Countess and Count. Yes, Countess Blanca actually began crying, overcome with emotion.

"Thank you. Thank you," she said repeatedly. We hugged her and then headed off to the Box to make some additional preparations.

Lexi asked, "Okay, so how do we find this dragon's lair? It must be underground, right?"

I replied, "I can't imagine any other location. He was in a cavern before, so he's likely found a large cavern around here."

"Got it. So we should begin by asking the locals about caverns somewhere around here. Come on. Let's get going. Oh, wait. Should we appear as their noblewomen or not?"

Sighing, I answered, "I suppose you've a point. They may more readily talk to us if we appear as noblewomen. Only let's not wear their wedge-heeled boots."

A half hour later, we cancelled our Morph spells, having used them to don our noblewomen dresses, complete with layers of petticoats. We stepped out of the Box and into the manor house, and soon hit the streets. While everyone treated us with respect, the only clue we received was one old man's suggestion there might be caves over by Westfold, a tiny village some five miles due west of Villa Lopez.

"Let's rent some horses," Lexi suggested.

"Can't Felix just teleport us there? I really don't want to smell like a horse tonight," Tiffany asked.

"I've a better idea. Let's fly there," I responded. "I've an idea. Since apparently Euric has never been in these parts before, how do you suppose he found his new cavern home?" I didn't wait for either to respond. "He must have been flying about the countryside. So let's see if we can find it just as he found it. Besides, we don't have to stop and change clothes."

"Felix, it's going to look very strange for these locals to see three noblewomen in their billowing dresses flying about the countryside," Lexi pointed out. "We should go invisible too."

She had a point. Soon, three invisible noblewomen flew westward from Villa Lopez. The Rainbow Hills with its rolling grasslands and occasional patches of forests were breathtaking. Layers of reds, greens, blues, yellows, oranges, browns, and even blacks blended, carved over eons by the small creeks. We flew over some crop fields. Again, the color of the dirt was that of the current layer, making every farmstead just as colorful.

As we approached Westfold, we saw how it got its name. A red layer was folded over a brown layer, forming the top of a low hill on which the village stood.

"Wicked! Beautiful," Tiff's voice came from seemingly nowhere. I smiled. After overflying the collection of perhaps fifty homes, we landed on an orange hill with pale green grass. Farther west, the land flattened considerably. To the south, the land leveled off and soft black ground stretched off as far as we could see. Neither direction looked hopeful for underground caverns.

Northward, the hills grew steeper, as the Rainbow Hills officially began. Since the hills proper were actually soft clays of brilliant colors, I didn't expect to find caverns there either. Limestone or soft sandstone bedrock would support cavern complexes, as it had near the desert oasis of Becktold's Crossing. Sadly, we turned around and headed back towards Villa Lopez.

As we approached the town from the west, we zoomed over a rough patch of forest that covered an orange hill and adjacent brown valley. Tiffany's sharp eyes spotted it first.

"Hey," she called out. "What's that black thing down there?"

Whatever it was, it was not easily seen when flying towards Westfold, but flying eastward, there it was, a dark spot below. We descended, landing on the ground among the trees. Here was a cave opening, no doubt about it.

Studying the ground around it, I pointed out the giant claw-foot prints, some leading to the hole, others moving away from it.

"We should leave before we draw his attention," Lexi whispered nervously.

Quietly, we resumed our flight back to town.

"So how do we kill a red dragon?" asked Tiffany.

We had morphed back into our usual forms with arms, changed clothes into our comfortable soft leathers, fixed supper, and were sipping our after-dinner tea. Drago hadn't returned yet, but we did send him a Message letting him know we likely found Euric's lair. Actually, none of us had a good answer, and by mutual agreement, we decided to wait for Drago to return.

That didn't happen for three more days, since he wasn't about to leave Manda's side until she'd recovered her strength. While she wouldn't be full strength for another week or so, she was doing well when the pair returned to Villa Lopez. Arm in arm, the pair entered the Throne Room. Manda wanted to check on Countess Blanca, verifying with her own eyes that she was all right. We three walked in and saw the teary-eyed Blanca and Manda hugging each other.

"I'm so glad you are all right. I was so scared you were dying, Manda, and I was helpless to do anything about it."

"And I'm glad you and Martinez have finally married, becoming the rightful rulers of Villa Lopez. You've met this charming, handsome Gold dragon, Drago Hagan?"

She chuckled. "Yes, I begged him and his companions to save your life. These three, they are noblewomen too, just like me, but from some other place."

"I know, Blanca. They are powerful mages. We're going to need them. We have to kill that red dragon Euric. If we don't, your lands won't be safe. The mages have located his lair. We should make plans to slay him, Blanca. I'll talk with you and Martinez more when we get this dirty job done."

She begged her to be careful, but I sensed Blanca and Martinez didn't expect any of us to be returning from this mission. Drago bowed and led Manda out of the Throne Room and to our Box, chatting softly with her all the way, completely ignoring the three of us, who followed along behind them.

Lexi whispered, "I think Drago has fallen for Manda."

Tiff giggled, "He's in love, isn't he?"

"How can you tell?" I asked, merely wondering why Drago wasn't paying any attention to us. The girls merely giggled.

After Drago finished giving her a guided tour of the Box, the five of us sat on the sofas in the living room area, finally discussing what was critical: how to kill a red dragon.

Drago pointed out, "Look, he's immune to fire based weapons and spells, just as Manda and I are immune to his fiery hot breath flames. He won't be immune to our electrical bolts, though he can dodge them. The trouble is he will have a strong resistance to our magical spells too, though not a much as we Golds have."

Manda interrupted, "Euric had to cast some of his spells on me close to ten times before one of them took. Unfortunately, it was the Moronic Mind spell. You may have to cast your power spells many times on him before one of them affects him. Worse, you three aren't immune to his fiery breath, which probably is hot enough to melt iron."

I countered, "Quite true, Manda, but this is our fight too. My God, what that dragon has done to me and to my wives—well, he has to pay. Don't worry about us. We'll dodge out of the way, if we can. Besides, Manda, five of us to one of him is much better odds, don't you think?"

She nodded, and asked, "So is it true? Are you really a man, but Euric has morphed you into a noblewoman and permanently so?"

"Yes. We have a Regeneration Ring, which we're hoping will undo his nasty magical spells turning me back.

I'm not using it until I've had our child." I didn't mention the "booster shot" that they gave us when we visited them on Salazar-3. Even thinking about that made me sick at my stomach.

Late afternoon, with all the protection spells I could think of cast on us three, we teleported close to the grove of trees that hid the black cavern hole from view. We took cover behind some oak trees, while Drago and I argued over who would cast their Spying Eye spell. He won, barely. With this spell, we brought into existence a movable eye attached on an extensible stalk to the center of our foreheads. We could move the eye nearly a quarter mile from where we stood, while seeing through it, hence the spell's name. Slowly, Drago's extra eye moved off from him, entering the black hole and the dragon's lair. This was a very safe way of seeing inside without triggering the deadly traps the Red dragon was sure to have setup for intruders.

"He's not there," Drago grumbled a half hour later. "It's his lair all right. Tons of magical things are on shelves no less, and he's got a bed of gemstones, but he's not here."

"Probably off eating," Manda suggested. "Why don't we see if we can find him around here? Maybe we can take him out in the open where no one else can get hurt."

With the two dragons circling around high in the sky, we three waited until they spotted him. Minutes later, we got word from Manda, who spotted Euric. We cast our invisibility spells. Holding hands, I teleported us three to Manda's location, on a low yellow hill not far from the main north-south road, and perhaps five miles north of town. She and Drago were also invisible, watching the action down on the road.

This was the first time I had a bird's eye view of a dragon firing off his or her breath weapon. Already the five men in the group were dead, their bodies smoldering cinders. However, Euric shot off another fiery breath of flames as a sort of victory celebration. Intense flames flew from his gaping mouth in a cone spray. I estimated the cone's angle was about thirty degrees at his mouth and shot out close to three hundred feet from him. At the end of the cone, the flame's width was one hundred-fifty feet!

Just then, six antelope crested the hill, saw the dragon, and bolted. Euric must have been hungry, for his giant wings flapped vigorously. He chased after the fleeing deer, snatching one in his powerful claws, puncturing it's body. He flew off, blood dripping onto the ground from his talons.

We cancelled our Invisibility spells and inspected the fires, intending to put them out and see if anything could be salvaged. The metal buckles on the men's suits, horse harnesses, and their swords had melted completely! Even Drago and Manda were impressed with the intensity of Euric's flames.

"Gosh, Drago," Manda exclaimed, "Euric has one hot breath. Look at that sword; at least I think it was a sword." The iron had melted and flowed slightly onto the ground.

There wasn't much to bury, but we put out the fires and did cover what little remained, probably from their horses. Again, we used our Dig spells to good advantage here, all the while chatting about the safest way to eliminate this dragon. Euric had to be slain, of that there was no doubt. He'd harmed us and nearly killed Manda, to say nothing of the countless other humans he'd harmed by turning them into "princesses." No, the real question we discussed was the how.

"Look, if we fight him out here in the open, there's little chance of collateral damage," I pointed out.

Drago countered, "However, if we do so, we run the strong risk of having him Shadow Walk away if he gets badly wounded."

"What if he has one of your In Case Of spells on him?" Lexi inquired. "We might hurt him badly but he then teleports away somewhere."

Tiffany added, "We could try to sneak up on him while he's sleeping. That's assuming we could get by and deactivate all his traps and guard spells."

Drago grumbled, "Ordinarily, I'd just physically

fight and strangle him, after what he's done to Miss Manda, but he's much larger than I am and stronger too."

Tiffany began laughing. "Gang, we should take a hint from Euric himself. Look, he first used some kind of knockout gas on Manda in the Throne Room, before he could harm her. So why don't we return the favor? Knock him out and then exterminate him."

Lexi added, "Brilliant. I know where we can get the gas, Tiff—on our world, Halcion-3. Drago, Shadow Walk us back to our world where you first met us at the Unarmed Escorts. Come on, Tiff. Let's get this nasty worm."

Manda and I headed after Euric, keeping watch over his activities. He'd just eaten, and predictably returned to his cavern home. Quietly, we took up watch, waiting on the others. Drago, Lexi, and Tiffany returned to their home world and came back several hours later.

"Okay, put these masks on like this," Lexi explained.

"I look funny. I sound funny," I complained, my voice muffled through the mask, which made me and the others look like some kind of monster.

She replied, "Don't take them off until I tell you, unless you want to get knocked out too. Here we go." She had what she called a gun that fired the canisters into the cavern, though lobbed might be a better description. When they landed, they exploded, releasing a whitish cloud of gas. She fired off ten shots.

Next, Drago and I slowly crept into the cavern. Both of us cast our Trap Detection spell, a vital necessity in this case. Before we finally arrived beside his unconscious gigantic form, we'd detected and disarmed seven traps, four of which could well have been deadly, including a nasty Exploding Runes set on the last foot of the tunnel that opened up into the vast chamber in which he'd taken up residence.

Obviously, Euric didn't build this underground complex. It was likely quiet ancient. Eight-foot tall oak bookcases lined one wall, now filled with the dragon's magical item collection. He lay sleeping upon his pile of gemstones. The five of us crept up to him and readied our spells.

Drago's idea was that of a coordinated attack. Since Euric had a strong resistance to magical spells, if the five of us hit him nearly simultaneously, perhaps one or more of our spells would affect him. With a sudden downward motion of his hand, Drago gave us the go-ahead.

Lexi and Tiffany each cast large volumes of acid arrows, which not only hit causing damage, the dripping acid caused additional wounds for several more minutes after their attack. I cast my Disintegrate spell at his head, while Manda shot her powerful electrically charged breath on his torso. To my surprise, Drago didn't use his Disintegrate spell, choosing instead to throttle him while casting a spell of some kind.

Each of us suddenly found ourselves on a featureless grey plan facing Euric, who stared back at us, not quite comprehending what was happening to him. Tiffany's arrows struck, causing his body to groan. Alerted to what she was doing, he managed to fight off Lexi's identical spell. Unfortunately, just as my spell detonated, Manda's electrical jolt reached his body, which involuntarily arced high in response to the searing, deadly electrical current flowing through his body. This caused my Disintegrate spell to bore a hole through his jaw and teeth instead of his targeted brain. At this point, Drago physically landed on Euric's body, his front claws throttling the red as his spell detonated.

Just when I thought we might just succeed, Euric frantically Shadow Walked, taking Drago with him.

"What the. . ." I yelled muffled by the gas mask.

"Where?" Tiff added.

"Oh no! Drago," cried Manda.

We four stood there stunned, before Lexi took action. She cast a Wind spell and began dissipating the knockout gas. Tiffany quickly cast hers and together, they aired the cavern, though that took a number of minutes. Just as we finally were able to remove the masks, Drago reappeared, a giant grin on his face.

"What happened?" I cried. "I thought we'd lost you.

Euric?"

"He's in a fine pickle—I think that's your human's phrase. I figured he might try to escape and he did. So I throttled him, forcing him to take me with him into the Shadows. However, my spell worked, since he can't do two things at once. He's gotten a taste of his own medicine. He now has a Moronic Mind."

Manda exclaimed, "Drago, is he still in the Shadows?" Her dragon face looked shocked, if I interpreted her lizard expression correctly.

"You bet he is." Seeing the blank looks on our faces, he added, "Intelligence is what allows one to move through the Shadows. As a moron, Euric is now motionless in the Shadows, doomed to drift endlessly on the tiny eddies. He's in great pain, near death's door as well, so he'll drift on until he finally succumbs to his wounds. No one will ever see that dragon again."

"Well done, Drago!" I declared, patting him on his dragon side.

He and Manda morphed into their human forms, as Lexi and Tiffany cancelled their Wind spells.

"Wicked! Look at all this stuff!"

The bookshelves were filled with objects, swords, daggers, knives, rings, wands, and apparel. Several staves leaned against the elegant shelves. The center floor was filled with hundreds of multi-colored gemstones, rubies, emeralds, diamonds, and others.

"Oh my! Look," Manda called out, pointing to the far corner.

We saw hundreds of leather bound books lying in a jumbled heap where Euric had tossed them from their shelves to make room for his magical items. All manner of furniture was packed into a tunnel that led from this room. I spotted at least a table and chair there, and suspected this once was a fancy underground reading room or library as Tiffany later educated me. As we five stared at this mess, we had no idea that handling this situation would take us months.

# Chapter 25—Discoveries

"We need to identify each of these items and see if we can return them to their rightful owner," Drago explained.

"Right, Drago. That's the only ethical thing to do," Tiffany added. "I suppose we should carry them all back to the Count's manor house, where they can be guarded or even put them in the Box so we can ID them with our spells."

"What I want to know," interrupted Manda, "is what is this place? Who had it? What are all these books? Who owned them? Are they still alive?"

"Well, first we move the magic items to the Box, along with all these gems," Lexi suggested, "and then we can put the books onto the shelves and dig the furniture out of that tunnel. I wonder where it leads."

We spent two days moving Euric's stuff to our Box, filling up one of the spare bedrooms. I knew we needed to identify them and see if we could return them, but jeesh, this was going to take a long time. I had no idea it would take so long.

Another afternoon passed as we retrieved the books and stored them on the shelves.

Suddenly, Manda shrieked. "Oh my God! This is it! I've found it. Drago, this is <u>El Origen de los Dragones</u> by Beltran, the Wise!"

Drago looked confused. "You mean that ancient dragon that supposedly lived over a thousand years ago? Isn't that just a child's story? A fairy tale?"

"No, Drago. It's real. I came here years ago looking for this book. See." She showed him the dragon hide cover. "This is the find of the millennia!"

"What's it about?" I asked.

"Supposedly, Beltran knew about the origins of how dragons came to be," Manda said. "I've got to study this!"

"Hey, here's an interesting title," Tiffany spoke up, storing the volume on the shelf. "<u>On the Noblewoman</u>

<u>Tradition</u>, by Archmage Enrica Gomez. I wonder if it talks about the binding of women in this land."

"Maybe so," Manda replied. "Countess Blanca and I were also searching for books that might explain how their noblewoman tradition began. She'll want to read this too. We both do. What an incredible find this is."

Late afternoon, we finally began retrieving the furniture from the tunnel down which Euric must have stuffed them. Soon, we had a real reading room setup, complete with bright overhead permanent light, a spell we all knew.

Curiosity struck. Here was a tunnel that led eastward, but to where? What other treasures lay down its dark path? I'll admit I simply couldn't resist exploring, even though we were getting hungry. I cast my Light spell, positioning it on top of my head, and led the way. Off we went. Soon, I had to bat spider webs out of the way. Later, I had to duck a swarm of bats that had made this section's roof their home. On we walked. The tunnel was straight as an arrow and level too.

"I think the tunnel was made by a spell and not by hand," Manda suggested. "I've seen some miner's tunnels with Blanca. These walls are perfectly smooth. I think a mage made the tunnel using spells, but where's it going?"

We walked for some time before I reached its end. Before me was a stone wall! Okay, I also saw a lever. Grinning, I pulled it as the others joined me and stared at the wall. A grating sound accompanied the slow moving wall as it pivoted, revealing the Throne Room.

"What?" exclaimed Count Martinez.

"Felix?" asked a surprised Countess Blanca.

"I'll be! Blanca, Martinez, bet you didn't know you have a secret tunnel that leads to that underground book room," I explained, stepping out into the room so the others could join us.

When Manda joined us, she said, "Blanca, we've found it—Beltran's secret tunnel and even a book that might have the origins of your noblewoman tradition in it."

Blanca gushed, "Incredible, Manda. We'll have to

read it tomorrow! Come. We're heading off to supper. Join us. Tell me all about the books. I'll come with you in the morning. I want to see them and read them too. Do you think they'll be safe there? Or should we bring them into the manor house?"

***

Days stretched into weeks and on into months because of two key actions on our part. First, we felt a strong obligation to identify the magical items and attempt to locate their rightful owners. Second, we wanted to study the incredible books this ancient mage had assembled. Also, when Lexi and Tiffany returned to their world to acquire the knockout gas, they also picked up a number of books for me to read so I could learn more about the math, science, engineering of their world.

As time progressed, both Drago and I worried the Box would become impatient for us, perhaps even abandoning us on this world. However, no such thing happened, leading me to conclude it too wanted us to try to return the magic items to their rightful owners.

We began with the easier items, the weapons. Admittedly, I knew almost nothing about them, other than they came in different sizes and shapes. However, we were able to tell the degree of enchantment each weapon had. A few were highly enchanted and thus worth a small fortune. Usually, somewhere on these, the owner's crest or symbol was etched. Count Martinez knew quite a few of these, having studied them as a young boy. Thus, some weapons we were able quickly to return to their owning families. Soon, we found others via Archmage Alison Weatherby, who learned of our discovery and volunteered to assist us with the giant project.

Some of the apparel was fascinating. Gloves of Strength, Shirt and Pants of Warmth, Speed Walking Boots, Boots of Jumping, Boots of Flying—these had tiny wings attached to their heels—Gloves of Grasping, Cloak of Hiding, and Cloak of Warmth were some of these. Our minds soon were flooded with ideas for highly useful magical items. We saw an entirely new aspect of magic

348

we'd not realized existed and vowed to make things like these ourselves.

Archmage Alison shone. We identified the items, and she traveled around the world, searching for their owners or for clues to who might have once possessed such an item. Often, we had to settle for returning something to the owner's children or grandchildren. This was especially the case with the weapons.

In the end, we were unable to locate the rightful owners of more than half the objects. While we decided to each keep a magical dagger and knife, the rest we donated to others, particularly to Count Martinez, Count Edgar, and the new rulers in Imperial, in hopes they could use these to protect their lands from the barbarians or dragons.

We also kept some of the apparel, whose owners we never did locate. Archmage Alison hinted that many of these items might have come from other worlds. By way of proof, she pointed out the different construction methods or cloth fibers. We decided to make a communal pile of these magical items, so each of us could don what we thought most appropriate for what we were doing at the time.

One ring out of the dozens of magical rings was very special, particularly to us. It contained a single spell, a Full Wish. I had a strong feeling one day we would need this Wish. Finding the owner of the rings was far more difficult than the weapons. In the end, we gave many to our friends here in the Rainbow Hills.

The enchanted Needle of Sewing we gave to the Banners, who provided much needed maternity clothes for us. I watched fascinated as the needle rapidly sewed a dress with perfect, tiny, precise stitches. One didn't even have to thread that needle.

"Wicked use of magic," Tiffany declared.

Manda kept the enchanted writing quill, which automatically wrote down what one said or copied the contents of a book.

We destroyed one item in the collection, per

Tiffany's order. "This is a blaster. It's a common gun on our world. It's not magical at all, but it's incredibly deadly. I can see why Euric thought it was magical. We should destroy it. You don't want this to fall into enemy hands."

She demonstrated it by pointing it at the stone wall of the hallway and firing. A two-inch hole appeared in the foot thick stone block. Impressive. We destroyed it.

The value of the gemstones was problematical. Depending upon the world you were from, their value varied greatly. Worse, we found it nearly impossible to figure out who may have once owned a gem. Only for a couple very large ones, that is, famous gems, was Archmage Alison able to locate their owners's children. We gave some of the cache to Count Edgar and to Count Martinez, in hopes the extra funds would help stabilize their lands.

The remainder, we divided five ways, figuring Manda deserved a fair share too. Depending upon the value a world placed on the gems, we each had the equivalent of nearly a hundred thousand gold, but then what was a gold coin worth? I found the gemstone evaluation perplexing, but they were pretty.

In contrast, we were able to return the gold and gem encrusted crowns to their rightful kingdoms, compliments of Archmage Alison. So yes, we endeared ourselves to a great many individuals and groups across the world of Rainbow's End. Our theory was that Adler and his dragons confiscated much of these things from the noblemen and women when they stole the people, taking them off world as slaves.

By the time we finished this mammoth project, none of us was walking properly; rather we were waddling along, in our ninth month. Yes, I was having quite an experience. By mutual agreement, we decided to stay put until after the babies were born. In fact, Countess Blanca was also entering her ninth month, as was Countess Molly.

Further, Drago and Manda mated. Her near death experience triggered her breeding cycle. She either had to mate or had to create an egg inside a shell to be later fertilized and grown. We learned something about their reproduction cycle. Instead of nine months, the usual dragon gestation period was sixty-three days. However, there were two methods of reproduction. The first one emulated the human system, in which she'd carry the fetus until it was born, giving birth similar to humans. The second one emulated lizards and was used when the breeding cycle arrived and her mate wasn't available. In this case, she'd expel a foot in diameter, hard shell egg. Later on, a male would fertilize it. Then when it gestated the sixty-some days, the baby dragon would peck its way out of the shell. Naturally, most dragons preferred the first method, resorting to the hard shell egg only as a last resort. Manda's due date was close to ours.

During these many months, often we teleported Blanca and Martinez over to Edgar and Molly's place, or vice versa, though we also brought our old Unarmed Escort friends with us, namely Eve, Kelly, Angela, and Vanna. These four also helped Blanca and Martinez learn how to do many things using their feet and toes. At last, Martinez was able to write again. He was intensely proud of this achievement, for he could write out his own orders, dispatches, and decrees.

While we were dealing with all the magical items, we also spent time studying the many volumes in old Beltran's library, as we began to call his underground location. While much was arcane lore, some of what we learned might be of interest. Blanca and Manda finally reached one of their learning goals: uncovering the origin of their noblewoman tradition.

The author of the volume claimed to have heard this story from his grandmother when he was a boy. As far back as anyone can remember, noblewomen wore the billowing gowns as a status symbol, telling everyone of their importance as wealthy nobles. Approximately four hundred thirty-five years ago in Imperial, Emperor James and Empress Emma Beckworth were beloved leaders of the Rainbow Hills. She was afflicted by the gods and was born without any arms. Emma was nevertheless very pretty, but she was also highly intelligent, wise, kind, and considerate of everyone. When Emperor James died suddenly in a hunting accident, Empress Emma continued to reign over the land for over thirty years. A youthful woman who acted as her hands when needed always accompanied her. During Empress Emma's long life, she changed servant girls when they grew older. Thus, she provided steady employment for young girls who otherwise might not have had gainful employment.

According to the grandmother, Emma was the most admired woman in the kingdom. Noble women wanted to emulate her and thus began binding themselves and hiring young girls to be their arms. The practice spread rapidly to other towns, and within a few years, the entire Rainbow Hills adopted this as the standard for all noblewomen. What better way to both show your highest respect for Empress Emma and your own noble status?

According to this book, the next Emperor and Empress had a different problem. Empress Amy was a very short woman, while the Emperor was tall. She asked the Royal Cobbler to design her some boots that would make her seem taller. His design was the tall wedge heel, which made her seem six inches taller. Within a few years, this change became standard for all noblewomen.

Some two hundred fifty-six years ago, Emperor Karl Kettlebaum faced a different marital problem with his Empress Frieda. She loathed children, didn't want any of her own, and failed to tell Karl about this before they were married. Later, she often avoided the matrimonial bed, claiming she had a headache among other excuses. According to the book, Emperor Karl finally could take no more of her ranting and had her legs tied up behind her head. It was also reported that Emperor Karl was something of a sadist too, but few dared hint that he was. Shortly after that, he issued an Imperial Decree that all noblewomen were to be bound in this manner each evening, as an invitation to their husbands and to show their willingness to participate fully in their marriage.

The author of the volume also pointed out that even

before that last decree, few, if any, recalled the actual reason for the noblewoman tradition. It had become the totally accepted practice, and financially improved the lives of younger women who weren't nobles, providing them with lucrative employment. Everyone won, or so the book claimed. Curiously, a man wrote it.

Countess Blanca and Manda were keenly interested in this book and its hints of the past. Blanca finally relaxed about her entire situation, for she felt in some small way she was honoring the legendary Empress Emma who had run the kingdom for some thirty years after her husband's death. It was no longer just a status thing with her and to a lesser extent with Count Martinez. She also had a memorial statue of Empress Emma erected just outside the manor house. Countess Blanca also had copies of the book made and sent to Imperial and other towns, along with her suggestion they erect a memorial statue to Emma, too.

Countess Molly and Count Edgar were also very relieved to hear the full story, especially Molly who finally understood the "why" behind the tradition she'd protested against all her life. That she was honoring their legendary Empress Emma changed her attitude about it, at least somewhat.

Years later when we visited the Rainbow Hills to see all of our friends, I learned that every major town had their Emma Memorial. Further, noblewomen everywhere now knew the origins of their tradition and swore to pass that on down to their children. Never again would the reason behind their tradition be lost. Countess Blanca and Manda were pleased with what they'd done for all noblewomen.

On May Day morning, I had severe cramps, but I ignored them for a while, waddling out to help fix breakfast for us. Later on, Tiffany finally asked, "Felix, what's the matter? You're acting like something's wrong or something."

When I mentioned the cramps, she yelled, "Drago, go fetch the midwife. Felix is having our baby! Wicked!"

Late May Day, our daughter May entered the world.

Of course, I thought she was a princess. She had Tiffany's black hair. Though none of us commented upon it, May had no arms. Later, when I pressed her, Tiffany said this was to be expected, since our DNA had been altered by that booster shot. I swore I'd dive into the books they'd brought back from Halcyon-3 and learn about this genetics thing. Oh yes, I named her May because she arrived on May Day, rather pleasing me.

Two weeks later, Lexi gave birth to our second daughter, Ashley, named after Lexi's grandmother. She had Lexi's golden hair and was also unarmed, as was her mother. Tiffany had our son, Adrian, a few days later. He had raven hair, like his mother. He was born unarmed, but by now, we fully expected this would happen.

Three days later, Manda gave birth to Alano, so she and Drago had a son. Both were very pleased. However, the births didn't end there. The last day of May, Countess Blanca gave birth to the future Count Esteban. He had black hair and arms, just as Countess Molly's girl, Melissa, who entered the world on June 3.

Since their children had arms and ours did not, Tiffany felt obligated to explain why. I doubt that they understood about altered DNA, for I sure didn't fully grasp what she was saying. However, they did accept the simple statement that our children took after us; we were currently unarmed.

For a few weeks, life was incredibly hectic. I was learning many things I never expect to have to learn, especially messy diapers. However, on the positive side, when I nursed May, I felt a bond with her that I simply had no words for. Looking back on this period, I think these wild experiences helped make me far wiser person and certainly more understanding of women.

By late June, we more or less had a routine down. It was time to use the Regeneration Ring. While none of us spoke much about it, by now I had doubts that it would do anything for us. I slipped it on Tiffany's little toe. We waited expectantly, but nothing happened, other than the ring slipped off her toe. I repeated the process with Lexi and had the same result.

"Well, that's what I expected," Tiffany declared, "but we should try it on Felix too." She slipped it on my toe with the same result. She stated dryly, "They've altered our DNA, Lexi. On the positive side, we know tons more about how this regeneration magic works. It must be tied to the person's DNA, their building block or body blue print. It restores anything missing from that blue print. Hence, it found us three in perfect health, nothing to restore."

"Well, this isn't good, is it?" Lexi sighed. "We're stuck like this for now. We can continue to get by using our Invisible Servant spells and our Morph spells. However, we're going to have to continue to use this Box so we can learn spells that are even more powerful. Eventually, if we learn the Make Permanent spell, we can then do what Euric originally did to us and make ourselves and children whole again, or perhaps we can learn the Wish type spells. I won't mind aging a year to put all of our bodies and our children right. We've no choice really, except to press that Handled button and keep on with this Box."

"Wicked! I certainly want to keep on with it."

"Okay ladies, I can take a hint. I'll save that ring with a Wish spell for now. Considering how nasty things have been for us, we might need it for other situations. Besides, as soon as I learn those spells, I give you my promise to make our bodies right, as well as our children's too. We best check with Drago and say our goodbyes to all our friends on this world."

Not surprising, Manda and Alano wanted to join us, pleasing Drago, who didn't want to give up his quest to learn all the magic he could. Thus, we finally pressed the Handled button. The bar slid across, locking us inside the Box. We felt a slight vibration under our feet and knew we were on our way to another place where our aid was needed.

Thanks to the midwives, we each had carrying sacks for our babies. Three excited humans carrying their babies rushed to the dispenser, along with Drago, who carried his little Alano perched on his shoulder, watching the goings on, a miniature Gold dragon.

"Wicked! Look at all these new spells," Tiffany declared.

As Drago and I looked over our new pages, he became as excited as Tiff. "Look! We're about to learn the Restricted Wish spell too! We're up to the Grade 7 spells." Most all of our new spells were from Grade 6, however. Still, Drago and I immediately set to work on learning that spell!

In the back of my mind, I had doubts about using it. After all, as Lexi said, we were doing just fine as we were. In fact, we three could now write using our toes. We usually used our Invisible Servant spells to handle many things, especially our babies. In addition, we often used our Morph spells to gain arms when truly needed or desired, but it was done for convenience. That's why I began to have doubts.

Was it wise to use the Restricted Wish simply for our convenience? As Unarmed Escorts, they had learned to live without arms. The psych had filled our minds with countless videos of unarmed women doing everything imaginable, though for me I had no reality on changing a tire or flying one of those flying silver bird things. Hence, as new activities sprang up, we had a vast collection of video memories on which to draw. Thus far, they hadn't failed us. Instead, it was just a darn inconvenience, making life slower and requiring thought and patience on our parts.

Then, there were the spells that we could and often did use. Both handled our need for hands or arms. True, they could be canceled by a Dispel Magic spell. Yet, was that alone sufficient reason to attempt to use this powerful wish spell? Its cost was steep, aging a year per casting. I'd have to cast it six time, aging six years. I had promised to do so, but perhaps the price was too steep just to gain some convenience. Plus, just how badly did I want to get my male body back? Again, convenience. I could do so with a Morph spell, even if it was temporary. What price convenience? That, I couldn't answer.

As we stood there looking over the new spells to learn, the largest blast of magical energies we'd seen enveloped us. Involuntarily, I closed my eyes, so bright were the energies. Tiffany's "Wicked!" brought me alert. "You're back! Wow, I'm back! Wow, so are the babies!"

"Incredible! Wonderful. It's a miracle," Lexi declared.

Me? I just stood there, mouth opened with no sounds coming out. My body was back to what it once had been, a male with arms. It was as if none of these terrible things had ever happened to it. Little May in my carrying sack across my chest had new arms too. I glanced up at Tiffany and Lexi. They had their arms back as well as our babies.

"What just happened?" asked a surprised Manda. "Who cast such a powerful spell?"

Drago added, "More like what kind of spell was that anyway?"

Tiffany stated the obvious. "Must have been some kind of Wish spell, so Drago, did you cast it on us or did you cast it, Felix?"

Drago shrugged his shoulders. "Er, not me. I just looked at the spell. I've not read its details yet. How about you three? One of you cast it?"

"You wish!" Lexi declared.

I knew neither of the girls had cast such a spell, and neither had I. "Perhaps somehow our ring cast it."

Everyone nodded or agreed with me. Quickly, I retrieved the ring from our room. All five of us checked the ring. Yes, it was a magical ring that contained one Wish spell. No, it hadn't yet been used. Yes, it was fully charged.

"Wicked," Tiff declared, having verified it herself. "So who cast that Wish spell? If we didn't and the ring didn't cast it, then who did?"

Drago piped up, "Well, it happened once before—remember? Felix and Diana got their arms back during the night."

"Are you suggesting the Box did it?" Lexi concluded.

The dragon shrugged his shoulders again. "What

else is there? It wasn't us. It wasn't the new magic ring. Maybe the Box wants us to be in the best shape possible in order to handle these situations."

Lexi protested. "But how? It's not alive. It's not a living creature. It's just a magically enchanted box."

Just then, Tiffany began casting Morph spells, appearing as me, as her unarmed self, and finally as she'd been with arms. "Fascinating, Lexi. Do you realize that magic trumps genetics and DNA?"

"Huh?" Lexi mumbled, not grasping Tiff's leap of logic. Me, I stood there clueless, as did Drago and Manda.

"Look, we know the men on Salazar-3 altered our genetic makeup, our DNA, our body's blueprint. How do we know that for certain? Our babies were born like us. Now, we and our babies are normal, but the definitive test will be to get pregnant again. I'm certain those babies would be born perfectly normal too. Conclusion. . ."

"Lexi interrupted her, finishing her thought. "Magic trumps genetics and our DNA. How fascinating!"

"Unless this is all just an illusion," Tiffany added.

I finally had some inkling of what she meant. I felt rather ignorant again. My wives were a constant reminder of just how much I had to learn.

However, at that moment, the Box landed with a slight jar. We looked at each other and laughed. Tiffany declared, "We best hurry up and get these spells learned. Out there, someone really needs our help."
The End.

# A Favor to Other Readers

How about helping other readers? Many readers rely on reviews to make the decision whether to buy a book. You can help them make their decision by leaving your opinions and viewpoint in a short review of the positive things of this book. Writing the review and expressing your opinion only takes a few minutes, and other readers will appreciate your efforts.

Click this link: Dragons, Magic, and Me Volume 1 The Box scroll down to Customer Reviews; click on Write a Review, and enter your review. Thank you.

# Author Information

## Visit My Amazon.com Author Page
Vic Broquard Author Page

## Follow My Blog
Vic Broquard's Blog

## Follow Me on Social Media
Facebook
Google+
LinkedIn
YouTube

# Other Books by Vic Broquard

Planet of the Orange-red Sun Series: (science fiction)
Volume 1 When Kingdoms Fall
Volume 2 Dark Ages
Volume 3 Age of the Towers
Volume 4 Difficillis Exitus
Volume 5 Age of the Lords
Volume 6 The Renegade Tower
Volume 7 Rebellions
Volume 8 The Aliens Return
Volume 9 Power Struggles
Volume 10 Guilds, Genetics, and Gods
Volume 11 Magi, Witches, Swords, and Superstitions
Volume 12 The Voyage of the Eagle's Seed
Volume 13 Eagle's Seed and Origins
Volume 14 Justifications
Volume 15 Responsibilities

The Return of the Wizards: Twelve Companions – The Making of Wizards (fantasy)

Slow Comes the Dark Series: (science fiction)
Volume 1 Creeping Darkness
Volume 2 Serendipity
Volume 3 Darkness Descends
Volume 4 Perversion Incarnate
Volume 5 Extermination Wars

Reclamation Series (science fiction)
Volume 1 For the Want of a Pill
Volume 2 Organ Donors
Volume 3 Total Care

Dragons, Magic, and Me (fantasy)
Volume 1 The Box

www.ingramcontent.com/pod-product-compliance
Lightning Source LLC
Chambersburg PA
CBHW060848250626
47159CB00013B/2452